A whisper of sound came from the tub.

A man's dark head and broad shoulders sliced slowly, cleanly through the surface, causing barely a ripple.

Meg froze and pressed her fist to the base of her trembling ribs.

He'd been in the tub all along, submerged. Had it really been only a minute or two since she'd stumbled into this exclusively male domain?

His eyes were closed. Water streamed across a straight nose, cleanly defined lips, and square jaw. A broad forehead and high cheekbones boasted of aristocratic bloodlines. Swarthy skin and the thin line of a scar across the arch of his left cheekbone branded him a man who flirted with the dangerous side of life.

He was attractive in a brash, piratical fashion she found dark and disturbing.

A shiver raced down Meg's back.

This was a disaster. Jacob Talbert was nothing like the crude sailor she'd imagined, counted on. And as if that wasn't destructive enough to her plans, he opened his eyes and fixed her with a steely gaze.

How could she expect to control this man?

Comments on *The Last Warrior*

"Extraordinary! With *The Last Warrior*, Kristen Kyle uniquely blends cultures and passionate characters to create a powerful tribute to love, honor, and redemption."

—Lorraine Heath, author of *A Rogue in Texas*

"*The Last Warrior* is an original with a refreshing plot. . . . Kristen Kyle has a superior talent that quivers so closely to the edge."

—Harriet Klausner, Painted Rock reviewer

"Thrilling action and sensual romance leap from the page in this well-written story of a code of honor and love that conquers all."

—Kathy Baker, Waldenbooks

Kristen Kyle

THE LAST WARRIOR

BANTAM BOOKS

New York Toronto London
Sydney Auckland

THE LAST WARRIOR

A Bantam Fanfare Book / May 1999

FANFARE and the portrayal of a boxed "ff" are trademarks
of Bantam Books, a division of Random House, Inc.

ISBN 0-553-57963-0

Published simultaneously in the United States and Canada

Bantam Books are published by Bantam Books, a division of Random House,
Inc. Its trademark, consisting of the words "Bantam Books" and the portrayal
of a rooster, is Registered in U.S. Patent and Trademark Office and in other
countries. Marca Registrada. Bantam Books, 1540 Broadway, New York, New
York 10036.

PRINTED IN THE UNITED STATES OF AMERICA

OPM   10   9   8   7   6   5   4   3   2   1

To Jaret, for the solid strength woven beneath your gentle spirit. Always the charmer, never doubt that your greatest gifts lie in your intelligence, spontaneity, sense of humor, and loving nature, not in your hunky good looks (that's just a bonus)!

To Eric, for your incredible powers of observation and the generous sense of giving that emerges when I need it most. Cherish your gifts—it's a rare blessing to have intelligence, athletic prowess, and a snappy sense of humor combined in one fiesty package.

God blessed me with the two most unique, charming, exasperating personalities possible . . . all that, and world-class hugs, too! You lighten my heart. I love you, guys.

Acknowledgments

To Linda Hyatt, my agent, and Roberta Brown, for being my cheering section and giving my confidence that little boost when I need it most.

To Ramona Helble, for her invaluable input on Japanese culture and terminology.

The poems used in this book are translations of ancient Japanese verses. I fell in love with these gems from the past, particularly because they demonstrate the timelessness and universality of joy, grief, loneliness, and passion. Love is God's greatest gift—the same for all men and women, regardless of culture, nationality, or the era in which we are born.

—Kristen Kyle

The poems in this book are excerpted from *From the Country of Eight Islands* by Hiroaki Sato and Burton Watson. Copyright 1981 by Hiroaki Sato and Burton Watson. Used by permission of Doubleday, a division of Random House, Inc.

THE LAST WARRIOR

I go on loving him—
a man awesome as the waves
of the Sea of Ise
that thunder in
upon the shore.

—Lady Kasa (eighth century)

Chapter One

A warrior walks, swishing the dew aside with the ends of his bow.
—YOSA BUSON (1716–1783)

"YOU'RE CERTAIN THIS is where he can be found?"

"I've been followin' Cap'n Talbert, jes' like you asked me to, fer the last three days. He's been comin' to this place every evening at the same time. That's how I knew to send you a message to come."

Meghan McLowry looked up at the Oriental script over the door of the small building. The white lettering glowed with the last rays of the setting sun, bold strokes against the dark, weathered wood. She clutched the hood of her cloak beneath her chin, as much to conceal her face and hair as to protect herself from the brisk wind blowing in from the bay.

"What kind of place is this, Mr. Boone?"

"Don't know, rightly. All I can tell you is the cap'n has a powerful hankerin' fer heathen things from the East. Ain't enough for him that we make port in Malaysia, Japan, the Philippines, the Sandwich Islands, takin' on cargo . . . he heads straight fer this little Japanese corner of San Francisco soon as we drop anchor."

So this was Japanese writing. Meg examined the characters with interest, noting the differences from the Chinese script she'd seen since 1852, when her parents first brought her to this booming city.

"Why does Captain Talbert come here?"

Boone rubbed his short brown beard and took a step forward. He offered snidely, "Maybe it's a whorehouse."

She looked at him sharply. "A bit small and out of the usual style, wouldn't you say?"

Shrugging, he shifted forward again, coming closer in a way that Meg immediately recognized as encroaching. "Like I said, the man has a yen fer the mysteries of the Orient, including them dark-haired, slanty-eyed women. The only thing more important to him is his collection of swords and daggers." His grin showed teeth marred by a career at sea and several bouts with scurvy. "Now me, I prefer my women white, blond, and fully fleshed out."

His hand suddenly appeared at her cheek. Meg caught a glimpse of dirt-stained fingernails just before he caressed a wayward lock of her hair. Damn her unruly curls, forever escaping their bonds.

She refused to flinch or back away, drawing confidence from the cold, familiar companionship of the pistol hidden beneath her cloak. Eighteen years in this city, since the age of nine, had taught her that although the most rough-hewn miner could treat a lady with the same deference afforded the shiny metal of his dreams, there was the occasional scum who considered women easy prey. In this case, however, she didn't need to use the gun for defense.

Two hulking figures, identical in height and breadth of shoulder, stepped from the shadow of the building behind her.

"Don't touch," warned one of the young men in a voice that rumbled from the depths of a barrel chest. They both strode forward on legs like tree trunks, their blond hair and beards glittering in the light of the setting sun.

"Understand?" the other growled, jabbing Boone in the chest. The seaman staggered back, nodding vigorously.

Meg struggled not to laugh at the expression on the man's face. "Meet the Richter twins, Mr. Boone, newly emigrated from Germany. Their mastery of English is minimal, yet effective. I'm not so foolish as to venture into this part of town alone. Now, I believe we have a business transaction to complete."

He straightened and jerked his coat into place, then spat in the dirt at Peter's feet. Quickly, she reached out and touched Peter's thick forearm. His beefy fists unclenched slowly.

"What I can't figure," Boone said sourly, "is why you're interested in the cap'n because he got hisself into trouble on the Barb'ry Coast the night we made port."

"What interests me is the fact he managed to extricate himself from that trouble, and the manner in which he accomplished the feat."

"Eh?"

"The fight, sir." His knitted brow cleared now that she was talking down on his vocabulary level. Meg slipped the pistol into the deep pocket of her gown, then pulled out a small velvet bag, communicating in a language he could understand even better. The distinctive clink of coins caused Boone to lick his lips.

"Gold?" he rasped.

"That was our agreement."

"Let me see."

His hand shot out. Meg caught the dangling bag firmly in her fist, jerking it beyond his grasping fingers.

Boone backed off with a wary glance at the glowering twins.

Annoyed by his transparent greed, she snapped. "Not yet. First, I need to confirm some things. The newspaper article was true, wasn't it? Four men, armed with knives and cudgels, attacked Captain Talbert on the waterfront?"

Boone snorted. "Four men as dumb as miners' mules, you mean."

"You were there? You saw the fight?"

"It were hard to miss, when that first fella' came flying through the window of The Golden Mermaid, where me and my crew mates were liftin' a mug o' ale. He's the one ended up with cuts and a cracked skull. Everyone in the tavern rushed out to watch the fight. Yep, another paid fer his trouble with a broken wrist, the third with cracked ribs," Boone stated, drawing himself up as if he'd played a role in the outcome. "Don't know why Talbert let the last one get away. Guess those boys were new to San Francisco. Didn't know any better, poor dumb bastards."

So Jacob Augustus Talbert did have a reputation. Better and better. Meg could only hope word of that reputation had made its way to Chinatown.

She tugged open the string of the bag and poured the coins onto her palm. Boone's fingers twitched. His Adam's apple jumped as he swallowed.

"One last thing. The newspaper article mentioned that Captain Talbert struck blows with his feet in the fight, as well as his fists. Is this true? I don't want to base my decisions on secondhand information."

"I can give you a guar-un-tee on that one. I watch the cap'n practice them heathen eastern moves on the ship every day. It's like some kinda' religion with him."

Relief washed through Meg, leaving a tingle of anticipation in its wake. She wasn't wasting her time here. "Thank you, Mr. Boone." She replaced the coins and tossed the bag his way.

He caught it deftly. "Jes' one word of advice, missie. Don't let on to the cap'n that you learned about him from that story in the paper."

"Why not?"

"He's real partic'lar about having his privacy cut up," he said ominously. "That's why I ain't stupid enough to return to the *Shinjiro*." With one last glare at the twins, Boone turned and disappeared into the gathering darkness.

Well, that didn't bode well, for Meg was about to cut up Talbert's privacy in a way that went beyond the machinations of a nosy newspaper reporter.

For both our sakes, Captain Talbert, I hope you accept my first offer.

Meg took a deep, fortifying breath and pressed her palm against the rough, weathered wood. She now had the captain on neutral ground, where she needn't suffer the indignity, the disadvantage, of seeking him out on his ship. Time for the next step in her plan.

She pushed open the door.

MEG CAME TO an abrupt halt inside, surprised by the constricted, dimly lit entryway. A partition rose almost to the ceiling, not much more than an arm's length away.

The smell of wet wood permeated the place. How odd. Just as Meg's natural curiosity peaked, a stoop-shouldered Asian man no taller than her chin rushed at her from the shadows. He jabbered indignantly in what she could only assume was Japanese. The shooing motion of his hands was universal—he wanted her to leave.

Now. He ignored the twins. Whatever the nature of this place, women apparently weren't welcome.

Meg stood her ground. Captain Talbert had proven too elusive to allow this opportunity to slip away. When she didn't move, the gray-haired doorkeeper grabbed her upper arm and turned her toward the exit.

"Don't touch!" Phillip Richter snapped. He grabbed the man's collar and lifted him as if he were no bigger than a week old puppy.

"Aiyeee!" the little man cried. The whites of his eyes glowed in the dim light. His legs flailed.

"It's all right, Phillip. Put him down," Meg said wearily. She cherished the twins' loyalty and their protection, but high drama always trailed in their wake. They were just too intimidating . . . to all except a certain breed of men who had brought danger into her family's sheltered world.

As soon as the old man's feet touched the floor, he bolted out the front door.

Meg blinked over his rapid departure. She'd been willing to pay him for entry, generously, but he'd just saved her the trouble. When no one else came forward to challenge their intrusion, she told the brothers, "Stay here. I'll call if I need you."

Now was her chance. She'd charmed miners, saloon owners, politicians, bankers, railroad barons. Surely she could manage one crude captain of a clipper ship . . . no matter how dangerous, or how well deserved his reputation. Ignoring the butterflies of doubt fluttering in her stomach, she walked around the partition.

A strangled yelp—high in pitch yet distinctly male— brought her to a grinding halt.

Meg felt like echoing the sound when she realized what she'd blithely walked into.

A bathhouse! She was going to throttle Boone!

The dismayed cry had come from the only person in the room, a young Asian man, likely in his mid-twenties, standing less than eight feet away.

And he was naked, for heaven's sake, with only a square of white cloth held strategically over his loins!

A huge wooden tub stood off to Meg's right, deep and wide enough to comfortably hold several people. It appeared empty at the moment. A long pipe, angling down from the side wall, extended out over the tub.

A bar of soap dropped from the man's left hand into the bucket at his feet, splashing water onto the plain wood floor. He stared at Meghan, his eyes like black marbles in his pale face. She stared back, equally frozen despite her frantic, jumbled thoughts.

No, this couldn't be Jacob Talbert. Impossible! This man was too small, too slender, too young.

As air dragged into her constricted lungs, she reined in her spiraling dismay. Of course this wasn't the captain of the *Shinjiro*. Although Talbert's origins were a secret known only to himself, the newspaper story clearly indicated he was of European or American descent.

The Japanese man backed away—thank goodness he had the presence of mind not to turn around—still clutching the cloth while he gathered a pile of neatly folded clothes into his other arm. Pausing in a narrow doorway, he bowed.

Meg curtsied automatically. Then he was gone.

She opened her mouth. A little squeak came out. She closed it again with a click of her teeth. Oh, mercy, she'd just curtsied to a man who wore little more than when he'd emerged from his mother's womb!

Meg shoved back her hood, speared her hands into her hair, and pressed cool palms to her flaming cheeks.

The seconds ticked away in hot, humiliating silence, marked off by the steady drip-drip of water from the leaky pipe into the tub. Ten . . . fifteen seconds, though it seemed like a damned eternity. The steam was intolerable. She plucked free the tie at her throat, anxious to escape the choking sensation, then wrenched off the cloak.

Wadding up the fine wool garment, she threw it into a corner. She'd been duped! Boone was walking away with her gold, and she had nothing to show for three days of effort and desperate hope.

A whisper of sound came from the tub.

A man's dark head and broad shoulders sliced slowly, cleanly through the surface, causing barely a ripple. Long, water-slicked hair reflected the flicker of the gas wall sconces, reminding Meg of the sheen of firelight on black satin.

Meg froze and pressed her fist to the base of her trembling ribs. The row of buttons up the front of her blue shirtwaist dug into her knuckles.

He'd been in the tub all along, submerged. Had it really been only a minute or two since she'd stumbled into this exclusively male domain?

His eyes were closed . . . deep-set western eyes. Water streamed across a straight nose, cleanly defined lips, and a square jaw. A broad forehead and high cheekbones boasted of aristocratic bloodlines. The serene expression on his strong face, as he enjoyed the soft caress of the water, declared him a sensual creature who sought out pleasure. Swarthy skin and the thin line of a scar across the arch of his left cheekbone branded him a man who flirted with the dangerous side of life.

A shiver raced down Meg's back. This was what the black sheep of every noble family of Europe throughout the centuries must have, or should have, looked like.

He was attractive, but in a brash, piratical fashion she found dark and disturbing. This man was a creature of the shadows, unlike the blond beauty of the men she typically admired, the handsome, charming sons of San Francisco's most wealthy and influential families.

He certainly fit the reputation.

This was a disaster. Jacob Talbert was nothing like the crude sailor she'd imagined, counted on. As if that weren't destructive enough to her plans, he opened his eyes and fixed her with a steely gaze. His eyes were the clear gray of hammered silver, intelligence swirling in their depths like the perilous tidal undercurrents off the coast. How could she expect to control this man?

Wisdom demanded a quick retreat, but it was already too late. She had set things in motion that would profoundly affect Talbert's business, his life. If she didn't face him now, he would only hunt her down.

And he was her only hope.

"The women's bathhouse is in the building directly behind us."

She tried to ignore the way his deep voice jarred along her nerves like the explosive flight of a flock of doves. "Are you Captain Jacob Talbert?" she demanded, seeking confirmation, although she felt the affirmative answer in her bones.

His expression grew shuttered. "I am."

"Then I'm in the right place, sir. You needn't imply that I'm lost."

"Aren't you a bit late?" He leaned back against the side of the tub and stretched out his arms along the rim. Shoulder and bicep muscles bulged. The edge of the water swayed across his bronzed chest, showing teasing glimpses of flat brown nipples. Tiny, translucent black pearls of water shimmered on his eyelashes and chest hair.

"Late? For . . . for what?" Meg managed to force past

a suddenly dry throat. Had the man no modesty? Then she detected the dance of amusement in his eyes. He was enjoying her discomfiture, nay, deliberately causing it! Anger restored her poise. She countered sarcastically, "What are you waiting for, Captain? Someone to scrub your back?"

"Are you volunteering?"

"Don't be ridiculous!"

He inclined his head toward the abandoned bucket and soap. "Actually, I've already scrubbed my own back. The Japanese custom is to wash before entering the tub."

"Then what, exactly, am I supposedly late for? Surely you didn't know I was coming."

"Why not? No fewer than half a dozen women approached me yesterday, after that damn article in the *Alta California* made me appear like some bloody knight in shining armor."

"What were the women after?" she asked, stunned at the idea of possible competition. "Your protection?"

His brows rose. "Something like that, plus services of a more personal nature."

Heat swept up Meg's neck as his meaning sank in. "They must have been women of . . . of very questionable virtue. I resent your categorizing me—" Her righteous indignation choked off as the sound of feminine giggles drifted over the partition behind the tub. Crossing her arms beneath her breasts, Meg added coldly, "More of your besotted admirers, Captain?"

"No, thank goodness," he muttered, scowling. A wave of his hand drew her attention to the pipe. "Attendants with more hot water. Don't worry, they know better than to intrude on a man in the privacy of his bath."

Before Meg could think of a suitable retort to his latest reprimand, he started to rise.

More skin appeared, striking her speechless. The surface of the water reached the base of his ribs, then his waist, receding as he stretched upward. When his hand reached the spigot, he stopped. Meg felt a contrary, utterly foolish twinge of disappointment.

He opened the spigot. A slender waterfall cascaded into the tub. Fresh steam rose, adding an aura of unreality to an already bizarre situation. Loose tendrils of her hair curled tighter, adding to her irritation.

Cutting off the flow, he sat back, resuming his former position . . . the one that did a disturbingly good job of showing off his muscular arms and chest.

"I never asked for 'besotted admirers,' as you put it. The whole thing has proven a damned nuisance. I'd like to get my hands on that nosy reporter."

"Well, rest assured I'm not one of those women anxious to fling herself on your person. You're safe from my unwanted attentions."

One corner of his mouth kicked up. "So, you don't want anything from me. You just dropped in for a cozy little chat."

"Well, I—" Of course she wanted something from him. A stab of guilt, combined with a sudden fixation on the roguish tilt of his mouth, stole Meg's ability to speak coherently.

"You still haven't told me your name."

"Meghan McLowry," she said automatically. The sound of her own voice resurrected her sense of purpose. The name McLowry was synonymous with wealth and influence in San Francisco society. She lifted her chin and stated clearly, "I wish to hire you as a bodyguard."

His cool gaze wandered slowly down her figure, assessing every inch of her blue gown and what lay beneath. Somehow, the lack of interest in his expression irritated her more than the naked lust she was accustomed to seeing in the men of San Francisco.

"Whose body would I be guarding?" he drawled. "Yours?"

She snapped, "Not me! My father, Douglass McLowry. There have been two attempts on his life in the past three weeks. The attackers were Asian. I believe they were members of a Chinese Tong."

"Why should I be interested?"

"I am willing to pay you a great deal of money."

"I'm not for sale. My ship and cargo are my first priorities, and the *Shinjiro* sets sail in two days."

"I wouldn't count on it, Captain."

His eyes narrowed. "What do you mean?"

"There has been a recent outcry against the opium trade, ever since two young white men were found dead in a Chinatown den. Coincidentally, you frequently sail from China and the Far East. All it takes is a word of warning in the right ear and you will find your ship searched, your cargo confiscated."

She would do anything to ensure his cooperation. He was her best, perhaps only, hope of saving her father.

"You're bluffing." His knuckles whitened on the rim of the tub.

"No, I guarantee you I am not. I've already seen to it personally. Only I can see it undone. The chief of police is one of my father's oldest and dearest friends."

"I don't deal in opium. They wouldn't find anything aboard."

"They wouldn't have to. It's the inconvenience associated with a very lengthy investigation that you might wish to avoid, Captain. A significant delay would result in a comparable loss of profit."

"Is this how you always get what you want, Miss

McLowry?" he asked, leaning forward slightly. "If you can't buy cooperation, you coerce it with threats?" The water swayed, rising higher and higher against the sides of the tub, as if he gathered momentum to launch himself at her throat.

Meg's heart pounded a warning, but that was secondary to her mounting desperation. All her plans were beginning to crumble. Fear of failure added an infuriating tremor to her voice when she insisted, "My father needs someone with your skills. He refuses to acknowledge the danger to himself, even though I know it's real. Whoever is trying to harm him has the mystery of the ancient Chinese arts on their side. I don't understand their world. Our normal security is proving inadequate. I need someone who knows how to walk among them and not be afraid."

He watched her intently for several moments. Meg held her breath.

"Forget it. You've got the wrong man."

He was still saying no, even after she'd pleaded with him. She made a point of never revealing her vulnerability to anyone! Frustration and rage blazed a caustic trail through her bloodstream.

"Apparently so," she snapped. "I was hoping to find a man with compassion and courage."

A muscle ticked under his scar. "Then you should have given more thought to where you looked."

"Damn you!" Giving full rein to her temper, Meg strode forward and turned the spigot on full blast. She then pivoted on her heel, swept up her cloak, and stalked out of the room.

Talbert's shout of outrage—and hopefully pain— thundered behind her. Water sloshed like crashing surf as he leaped out from under the scalding flow from the pipe. She heard the slap of his feet against the wooden floor and tried not to picture what else was bare.

Meg derived a surprising degree of satisfaction from her impulsive act, considering that she'd just ruined her best chance at protecting her father.

Chapter Two

J AKE TALBERT CURLED his toes, grounding himself against the well-sanded deck of his ship while he mentally prepared for the rigorous *kata*. He anticipated the workout, eager to burn away the surfeit of energy skittering across his nerve endings.

That temperamental hoyden had tried to boil him alive!

His hand tightened around the hilt of the Japanese *katana*. The criss-crossed wrapping of silk bands nestled into his palm like an extension of his own skin. His left hand lightly clasped the sword's scabbard, or *saya*, thrust through the sash at his waist, cutting edge upward. The saya's lacquered surface shone as black as the water of the bay. A half-moon cast a silver glow over the other ships in the harbor, a weak attempt to hold back the surrounding night.

Jake stood motionless a moment longer, allowing the late May breeze to soothe the reddened flesh of his bare chest. If only his anger could cool as easily. Two hours after quitting the bathhouse and returning to the *Shinjiro*, every muscle in his body remained tense, as if he had yet to do battle rather than having survived a minor skirmish.

He bit back the swearwords that came so readily to mind after sixteen years sailing with Americans. Despite being raised in the Japanese way of concealing strong emotions, he was experiencing an almost overwhelming urge to shake a spoiled society miss until her teeth rattled.

Meghan McLowry qualified as a menace, her brash behavior an antithesis to the modesty of the Asian women he admired.

No Japanese woman would dare offend a samurai.

Forcing his jaw to relax, Jake adjusted the saya. The angle should be ideal for a smooth, swift draw of the blade as he prepared to practice *iaijutsu*, the samurai art of drawing the katana in a way that cut and killed an enemy in one or two blows.

Jake drew the sword rapidly with an effortless grace born of over two decades of daily practice. Immediately, he brought the tip around in a horizontal cutting motion. The katana then circled and arced over his head—every moment like an extension of his own arm, for he had long since mastered *ken shin ichi nyo*, the philosophy of sword and mind as one.

Grasping the hilt with both hands, he flexed his knees and used his whole body to magnify the power of the downward stroke. Air whooshed through the blood groove carved into the length of steel. The sound confirmed what he already knew by instinct—that the stroke was straight and true, that neither human flesh nor bone could withstand the cutting power of the katana.

He brought the blade, edge upward, across his left forearm. The web formed by his thumb and forefinger around the mouth of the *saya* guided the tip home. Each technique of *iaijutsu* began and ended with the sword sheathed. The katana slid inside with only a whisper of steel against wood.

Again and again, for over an hour, Jake practiced a variety of patterns. He worked with single-minded intensity, seeking the ideal that came only with discipline and repetition, although he could never achieve the true goal of *iaijutsu*: perfection of character.

The muscles of his neck corded with the painful irony of it all. His soul was too flawed. How could he hope to approach that pinnacle? But defeat meant death, either in real combat or in succumbing to the demons of guilt and shame that sought to consume him. *Saigo made eizoku suru*—persist to the end.

Never accepting defeat was key to Bushido, the Way of the Warrior, the heart of samurai beliefs. Once a samurai attained peace and power by transcending his fear of death, he was free to pursue the equally important codes of conduct, among them courage, sincerity, loyalty, self-control, and above all, honor.

Honor.

The black cotton of Jake's baggy trousers, known as *hakama*, brushed the top of his feet as he moved. Lazy waves slapped against the side of the ship. The breeze touched his sweat-dampened skin like the caress of soft, cool hair.

An image of blond, unruly curls flashed into his mind.

Startled, Jake's concentration shattered mid-kata. Before he could grow angry over Meghan McLowry's renewed assault on his thoughts, a sixth sense warned him that someone approached.

He pivoted quickly, sword raised. A familiar figure climbed the stairs to the quarter-deck, moving with the silent tread of an experienced warrior.

Another samurai . . . a truly worthy opponent. Much more worthy than he deserved, Jake thought with a swell of pride for his Japanese friend and a sharp twinge of old sorrow for himself. When they had left Japan sixteen years ago, Komatsu Akira had not been the one under a cloud of dishonor.

Akira's dignified face showed few of the lines one would expect in a man of fifty-six years. The knot high on the back of his head held his long, nearly gray hair firmly in place. His eyes were little more than dark slits between chiseled cheekbones and the thick skin of his Asian eyelids. A regal, uncompromising expression represented generations of men who'd lived by the strict code of Bushido. Humor did find root, however, in the smile of anticipation dancing across his thin lips.

Jake's mouth slanted in an answering grin. He sheathed his sword. It had been over a fortnight since he and Akira had matched skills, thanks to the rigors of their voyage up the Pacific coast from Mexico.

Jake bowed. Akira mirrored the movement.

"Find you what you seek in the kata?" Akira asked as he straightened, speaking in his crisp, careful English.

"I found renewed focus, Akira-san," Jake answered, holding his bow a little longer to show deference to the samurai twenty years his senior, even though Akira scoffed at the notion of being called *sensei*, or teacher. Years ago, he had declared Jake a *meijin*, fellow master of the sword, a samurai whose swordsmanship is so perfected through repetition and painstaking experience that each move takes place without conscious effort.

"We see, yes? Only a monkey tries to catch the moon in a pond."

When Akira chose to speak in obscure proverbs, his motivation was either to teach or to tease. Jake chuckled, recognizing the latter in this case. "You think yourself as elusive as the moon? Shall we see if my blade can find you?"

"I speak of the woman in *sento*."

Jake grimaced. He should have known better than to confide the bathhouse incident to his traveling companion, whose wisdom was as powerful as the waters off the Cape and whose sense of humor just as shifting and treacherous.

"A little hot water make you shout like a man gored by a wild boar."

"A *little* hot water? That woman nearly scalded me to death!"

"You should have warned her your skin is sensitive," Akira commented smoothly. He hooked his thumbs in the sash binding his brown kimono.

"I assume there's a point to all this," Jake grumbled.

"I have never seen you angry at a woman before. Perhaps you wish she assault you in other ways?"

"The McLowry chit is not to my taste."

"Ah, yes." Akira nodded sagely. "You say she is neither meek nor demure, does not walk with mincing steps or lowered eyes as she should. Her hair not the color of midnight, her body fashioned with too many curves. Not a daughter of Nihon."

"Exactly."

"A great pity. The curves would be a nice diversion for you."

Jake smiled wryly. "You must be languishing of boredom, Akira-san, if your only entertainment is to bait me. There's obviously only one way to keep you from talking so much." His hand went to his sword.

Akira, not looking in the least bored, gripped the yellow-and-black hilt of his own katana.

Steel flashed into the moonlight like twin goddesses of shining silver. The clang of blade striking blade shattered the silence of the bay.

Exhilaration poured through Jake as they sparred.

Each slash, each block resembled an exquisite dance, with precise control maintained over every movement. The katana was a serious, refined weapon of war. The slightest miscalculation could cut or even disembowel a friendly opponent. The training from his youth had left enough thin scars across Jake's torso and arms to prove that point.

Then there were the deeper scars, not of the body but of the spirit . . . jagged wounds he lived with every day, every night in the violent shadows of his nightmares. It would have been more merciful if he had been disemboweled sixteen years ago in Japan.

A deep shudder ripped through him, throwing off his rhythm. Jake immediately broke off, stepping back and lowering his sword before the loss of control resulted in injury to his opponent.

Akira froze, then stepped back as well. Shadows of understanding, a hint of sympathy, flickered through his dark eyes. Taking a deep breath, Jake grounded himself in that look. He may be a man without a country, without a home, but he was not completely alone in the world. *Miren o motanai koto* . . . hadn't he heard the advice about not clinging to the past often enough? But, more importantly, he owed the rest of his life, if need be, to repaying a debt that had carried him around the world several times in his quest.

"One would think you the elder, Takeru-san, you tire so quickly," Akira broke the awkward silence, using the name Jake's adoptive Japanese family had bestowed on a shipwrecked ten-year-old boy when they could not pronounce his western name.

Jake's sword flashed up. "Come, let us go again."

"Perhaps you have more stamina than my humble self, but—your focus?" Akira shook his head. "No more tonight."

Disappointment curled through Jake, but Akira was right. He sheathed his sword, then bowed and backed away, demonstrating respect for Akira's age and skill. At the head of the steps, Jake turned and headed down toward his cabin.

The ship was silent, the crew ashore for their last round of mayhem on the Barbary Coast, except for the two men standing guard. He could hear their breathing and the rustle of their clothes, louder than his own movements, feel their sudden alertness as their captain passed by.

He opened the door to his cabin. Passing by the boots he'd left by the entrance earlier, he stepped into his little corner of Japan.

The room gleamed with a soft burgundy hue. The low table for meals, the cabinets containing his treasures, even his desk—the only tall, westernized piece of furniture in the room—were fashioned of polished cherry wood. Rice-paper shutters covered the windows. A *futon* sleeping mat occupied one corner.

Jake held the katana out before him, balanced horizontally on his hands, and performed his *torei* bow to honor this weapon that had saved his life more than once.

Seeking a means to quiet his strange, restless mood, he tilted the katana blade slowly beneath the desk lantern. The steel alone was a work of art forged almost three hundred years ago, but this blade paled in comparison to the five heirloom swords that Jake had sought since leaving Japan—his goal to return them to the Matsuda family home, their rightful place before being stolen in the midst of violence and treachery.

Before the past could release him, he must fulfill the vow he had made as a young man.

Despite the distraction of his moody thoughts, *zanshin*

did not fail him. As a teenager, his training had included being whacked with a bamboo cane by anyone who could sneak up on him, until his instincts were honed to a razor-sharp edge. With a warrior's alertness, he knew the instant Akira stepped silently through the door behind him.

"There is talk in Chinatown of a man who possesses swords with a curved edge," Akira said. "Old blades, Takeru-san."

Jake's head snapped up. "What do they look like?"

"The one who spoke to me had not seen them."

"It could be another false lead," Jake said bitterly, "like the many other dead ends in our search." Pushing away from the desk, he said resolutely, "But I'll go in the morning, after I've seen the last of the cargo loaded. Whether samurai swords or not, if the blades interest me I'll make the man a generous offer. You stay here in case Miss Meddling McLowry decides to follow through on her threat to raid my ship."

And maybe the Chinatown business would provide a reason to delay his voyage a day. His stung pride was already seeking an excuse for one last encounter with Meghan. The lady needed a lesson in humility.

JAKE MANEUVERED HIS way through the bustling streets of Chinatown.

Storefronts displayed brightly colored lanterns and signs, while itinerant merchants plied their trade in depressing little street stands. The spicy scent of incense contrasted with the odors of fish, crabs, and eels in open-air baskets. Men gathered for a bit of gambling over fantan or mah-jongg and joked in rapid-fire Cantonese. Everything imitated the assault on the senses Jake had

experienced in port cities throughout the Orient. . . .
He was very much in his element here.

Following the directions Akira had provided, Jake
rapped the door knocker against the entrance to Chen
Lee's home. The scales of the brass dragon felt cold and
rough beneath his fingertips.

The door opened to reveal a Chinese man wearing a black skullcap. His clothes were plain gray. A
servant.

"Captain Jacob Talbert to see Chen Lee on a matter
of business," Jake announced firmly. As anticipated, the
doorman shook his head and started to swing the heavy
wooden panel shut.

The door came up short against the heel of Jake's palm.

Before the doorman could protest, Jake bowed and
repeated his request in Cantonese.

"How many white men speak the language of your
homeland?" Jake added, his tone more commanding
than coaxing. "Chen Lee will be curious about me. You
would dishonor your master by failing to tell him of my
arrival."

The doorman's lips tightened. Bowing, he backed up,
opening the door wider. Jake passed through, leaving
Chinatown's dingy streets behind as he stepped into a
world of evident prosperity.

"Wait here," the doorman muttered as he disappeared
down an adjacent hallway.

Immediately, Jake sensed the two men standing behind screens at opposite ends of the large entryway.
Guards—the evidence of wealth when poverty lurked
just outside the door—these were pieces in a pattern
he'd seen before. Chen Lee may masquerade as a legiti-
mate businessman, and in some respects perhaps he was,
but Jake would guess the man was very highly placed in

one of the Tongs. Money flowed through here . . . blood money.

The doorman returned. Signaling for Jake to follow, he led him down a long hall, a waist-length pigtail swaying as he moved. They penetrated the inner sanctum of the house, past the opulence of thick red carpets, black lacquered furniture, and gold accents. The dragon motif was everywhere, fierce guardians over an exotic domain.

His guide stopped before a set of double doors. The servant knocked timidly. After a command bade them enter, the servant bowed reverently to his master, then beat a hasty retreat. The man who inspired such fear rose from behind a massive desk.

A sense of recognition swept over Jake. How could that be? He never forgot a face, and Chen Lee's lean, high-boned features were unfamiliar.

Chen's black hair was cut short, in defiance of the edict that each citizen of China wear his hair long in obeisance to their emperor. The long-sleeved tunic and trousers that covered his tall, slender frame were fashioned of black silk, with embroidered gold-and-green dragons cavorting over one shoulder.

"You wished to see me?" Chen said in cultured tones.

This was a man who'd invested an impressive amount of time and effort in distilling his accent and adapting to the ways of the West. Chen Lee apparently enjoyed the power and money to be gained in California. Befitting Chen's position and obvious conceit, two *boo how doy*, or bodyguards, stood watch from either side of the room.

"Yes," Jake confirmed, bowing as he gauged the distance to the guards and the *jujitsu* moves he might use to counter an attack. "I'm a collector of swords. I've heard that you have some old Japanese blades I might be interested in buying."

A muscle twitched alongside Chen's slender nose. Before Jake could read more of his reaction, his host tugged on a tasseled cord behind the desk.

"Swords, you say? An interesting rumor," Chen commented blandly. "Tea, Captain?"

Accustomed to the complexities of eastern manners and the subtleties of negotiation, Jake accepted. Chen apparently wanted to keep him here awhile.

A young Chinese woman, almost too beautiful to be real, emerged through a red curtain. The nearest guard shifted to help her with the heavy tea tray, but a curt shake of her head gave him pause. Jake watched the interchange—and the fact that Chen's back was turned—with interest.

She set the tray on a tea table in one corner of the room and began to pour. Jake recognized her type—one of hundreds of slave girls sold into prostitution by their families in China. This one was breathtaking, yet instead of carnal desire, he felt only compassion.

He followed Chen to the table. Once seated, the girl served them tea.

"This is Yeung Lian. She is a pearl beyond compare, would you not say?" Chen caught her chin on the crook of his finger. She stilled, lifting her head but not her gaze. Although Lian didn't flinch away, her hands trembled. "Her name means—"

"Graceful willow," Jake finished for him. "She's exquisite." *She's also terrified of you.*

"Lian came to us when she was nine. She is seventeen now . . . old, I know, but she is still a virgin, and well trained in how to pleasure a man. I have been saving her for someone special. Someone who can appreciate her."

You mean you don't want such beauty wasted in an ordinary brothel, you bastard, or to see her wither and die young from abuse, disease, or childbirth, Jake thought acidly. He concealed his anger behind a swallow of tea, then said dryly, "You mean someone with money."

"How crude, Captain," Chen admonished, without denial.

"It's in my nature to be blunt."

"Good, then we can understand one another." Chen smiled.

Something cold slithered down Jake's spine. "That remains to be seen."

"I have heard of you, Captain Talbert. I know you own a fleet of ships, fast ships." Grasping Lian by the arm, Chen pulled her closer and placed her pale hand in Jake's sun-darkened one. "The beautiful Lian can be yours."

Outwardly at least, Lian's perfect face remained the picture of serenity. Most men would find her acquiescence a powerful aphrodisiac. . . . Jake felt as if he'd just been doused with a bucket of ice water. She was like a lamb meekly heading for slaughter.

She deserved better than what Chen planned for her life. Jake squeezed her hand before letting it go, hoping to communicate that she could turn to him for help.

"Get to the point, Chen."

"Several weeks ago, a shipment of my goods was lost at sea. I was forced to make special arrangements for another shipment. It has been delayed, or perhaps sunk, as well. I need a captain whose reputation I can count on."

You want me to ship opium and slave girls for you. Meghan McLowry would jump for joy if I were caught, Jake thought cynically while he longed to slam a fist into Chen's nose. "I'd like to help you, but I have all the business I can handle."

"Then you make changes."

"Sorry. I always follow through on my commitments. You would think less of me otherwise."

Chen's palm smoothed down the embroidered dragons on his tunic. "True, but you may find much of that business lost to you in future," he said softly.

"I do not doubt your power or influence in Chinatown," Jake countered, inclining his head in a minimal bow. "Do not make the mistake of underestimating me."

Lian looked up for the first time, her lips parted with surprise and the barest hint of hope, of possibilities. No doubt this was the first time she'd heard someone defy her master.

Jake couldn't help her unless she committed wholeheartedly to the idea of escape. He'd been duped into playing the role of rescuer once before, two years ago, only to have the panicky girl rush back to her master at the first sign of trouble. He knew the obstacles: Chen's reach was all-encompassing in Chinatown, and the world beyond, the white man's domain, was even more frightening.

He held Lian's gaze a moment longer, willing her to find the courage. Instead, she lowered her eyes, the picture of submissive frailty. *No, dammit!* the denial reverberated through Jake's head. *I can't help you unless you trust me.*

She turned and slipped through the curtains. The red silk swayed slightly, as if brushed by a gentle breeze.

Forcing his expression to remain neutral, Jake said, "I am humbled by your offer of the beautiful Lian, Chen, but I must decline. Now, about the swords—"

"If I had such treasures, do you think I would dangle them in front of you as bait to gain your cooperation?"

"If you truly consider them treasures, they would be the last thing you wish to part with."

"True." Chen's mouth twisted bitterly. "I had a set of swords for many years, but I was forced to give them up to . . . meet an obligation. Three weeks they have been gone."

Jake briefly described the five blades he'd searched for nearly half his lifetime. "Did your swords look like any of those, Chen?"

"No, Captain. I am sorry."

Jake probed Chen's expression, searching for signs of deceit, finding nothing definitive in the cold, empty wells of the Chinaman's dark eyes. If Chen was lying, he did it exceedingly well.

Instead of the usual disappointment over another dead end in his quest, Jake felt only relief. Dealing with a man of Chen Lee's ilk would have been like selling a piece of his soul.

"Sung Kwan," Chen snapped, turning to the boo how doy who had sought to help Lian. "Show Captain Talbert to the door." The Tong leader then rose, bowed curtly, and left the room.

Kwan escorted Jake to the door, then surprised him by speaking in English.

"Why you refuse Lian?" he asked earnestly.

"If I want a woman, it will be one who chooses me, not one tied to me by bondage." Acting on a hunch about the man's earlier protectiveness, Jake added quickly, "If you love Lian, why don't you help her escape from this?"

Pain distorted the man's handsome face. "You not know."

The emotion ripping through the Asian's voice twisted something deep inside Jake. To love a woman so much that it tore you up inside to see her unhappy, to have your blood run cold at the idea of her lying with another man . . . a man would have to be insane to seek such agony.

"I know there's no place to hide in Chinatown, that you'd have to leave San Francisco. But I have ships that can take you and Lian anywhere you want to go."

"Chen kill me, then beat Lian and sell her."

"Just think about—" Jake urged, only to have the slamming door cut off his words.

He glared at the brass door knocker. He could not save all the prostitutes in Chinatown.

But he would have rescued this one, and any other slave girl willing to face the risks of freedom. Dammit, why did Lian have to be so docile and accepting?

Like Meghan McLowry, the girl should battle for what she wanted out of life.

The comparison stunned Jake. Meghan was a spoiled, temperamental siren. . . . Yet he could not picture her meekly accepting any injustice. She would fight, tooth and nail, to protect her loved ones as well as her chosen future.

Annoyed by the revelation, he spun sharply on his heel, reminding himself bitterly how Meghan had sought to use that same tenacity against him.

Chapter Three

Although I am sure that he will not be coming, in the evening light when the locusts shrilly call, I go to the door and wait.

—ANONYMOUS

MEG ENTERED THE house after her ride, feeling refreshed. Thankfully, the exercise had boosted some of her flagging spirits after last evening's debacle with Captain Talbert.

It had been a good bluff while it lasted, carefully thought out, plausible because she could have followed through on her threat to have the *Shinjiro* raided. Instead, she'd left the bathhouse and called the whole thing off. What would have been the point? A man colossally arrogant enough to call her bluff, indecent enough to destroy her composure by reclining in a tub like some fallen angel, was surely capable of stubbornly sitting on his cargo until it rotted.

Meg sighed, knowing Talbert was still her best hope, particularly after seeing his quicksilver gaze and athletic build. Her father had been attacked twice at the fringes of the financial district, not too far from the bank, in an area that Douglass was accustomed to walking with impunity. If the twins hadn't been with him the first time, and some policeman hadn't intervened the second—Meg shuddered, though her father insisted the attacks were nothing more than robbery attempts. Since the Chinese were chased off each time—just barely—there was no proof of a murder attempt. Yet Meg's every instinct cried of danger. The attacks were too bold, hardly typical of criminals whose territory seldom extended beyond Chinatown.

She needed a man who understood the Chinese, who could fight them with skill, as well as seek out the source of the threat and stop it.

But if the promise of money didn't tempt Talbert, then what would? Even offering herself would have been doomed to failure, Meg thought sarcastically, given that he favored porcelain dolls of the Orient and their raven's-wing hair.

So much for her improved mood.

The heels of her riding boots rang a staccato beat on the green-and-white-veined marble floor of the foyer. The soaring stucco ceiling and curving staircase welcomed her home. She tugged off her gloves as the butler approached.

"Miss Meghan, Mister McLowry wishes to see you in his study right away."

"Thank you, Robert," she replied. She could easily guess what her esteemed sire wished to know, but he was characteristically late in asking.

She knocked on the study door. Douglass's booming voice granted admittance.

"Hello, Father. You're home early."

He moved from the shelves behind his desk, an open book cradled in his palm. The corners of the desk were stacked high with ledgers and newspapers. Light from the gas wall sconces caught the glitter of gray threaded throughout his dark red hair, thick mustache, and bushy, fashionable side-whiskers that extended halfway down his jaw. His blue eyes watched her steadily.

"Some special business needed my attention, lass," Douglass responded in his Scots burr.

"Of course."

"And how are plans coming for the party tomorrow night?"

"Well enough," Meg answered without enthusiasm.

"Has everyone responded?" Eagerness sharpened his tone. The book snapped shut in his hands.

"All the usual people said they would come, of course, plus a few extras. I still wonder why you added those to the guest list."

"You wouldna want anyone to feel slighted!" Douglass declared, the portrait of the conscientious host.

Meg knew better. The assortment of unknown couples and single men were all potential, lucrative clients for the bank.

"I was hoping you would help with some of the preparations this time," she said. Picking up a marble paperweight from his desk, Meg pretended to concentrate on the cool stone, turning it over and over between her palms. "Will you be at home tomorrow . . . even part of the day?"

He looked startled, then evasive. "You know I'm no' good at such things." He came around the desk and gently took the polished marble from her hands. Perhaps he feared the stone would end up on the lawn, amidst shattered window panes, the fate of a similar paperweight when she was nineteen. But Meg knew she was beyond such displays of frustration and temper. Setting it down, he coaxed, "I'll be there for every minute of the party."

Meg raised pleading eyes. "But it's for my birthday, Father. I thought—"

"Aye!" he interrupted jovially. "My only daughter will be twenty-seven, and still the most bonny lass in all of San Francisco."

Meg knew she was losing ground when he resorted to flattery. This time, she vowed, she wouldn't let him get off so easily. Planting her hands on her hips, she lapsed into the lilting burr that he'd taken such pains to train out of her with years of tutors. "Aye, and 'tis glad I am to hear that you remember. Might I be asking what you got your only daughter for her birthday? And dinna be telling me that you forgot, dear Father."

His face took on nearly the same hue as his hair. "Of course I didna forget. I gave the modiste carte blanche to make all the gowns your heart desires."

"I dinna need any more clothes, Da. My closet is fairly burstin' with damned gowns!"

His fist crashed down on the desk. Meg didn't even flinch. "You best be watching your tongue, lass! A lady doesna talk so. I dinna know what would hurt your sainted mother more, hearing you resort to cursing or imitating my burr again. You're half American, and shouldn't be talking like an immigrant fresh from the Highlands."

The fight went out of Meg at the mention of her mother, leaving her deflated and empty. Softly, she said, "I believe Mother would say that a gift should come from the heart. You've bought me clothes every one of the twelve years since she died. It's not the same thing, Father."

"Ah, Meggie," Douglass groaned. Grasping her upper arms lightly, he pulled her close and kissed her forehead. His mustache and side-whiskers tickled her skin. Then he did something he hadn't done in months: He pulled her into a bear-hug embrace. Thrilled, Meg hugged him back.

"Have mercy, lass. You know I lack the talent or imagination for gift giving."

The better part of Meg's elation died. She would be happy with a little knickknack, something that showed he understood who she was inside, that reflected her love

of beauty and music. Better yet, he could cancel the
party and they could spend tomorrow doing something
together, just the two of them, like having a picnic or
riding along the beach. Even the president of Comstock
National Bank deserved a day of relaxation.

But the opportunity to lavishly entertain his business
acquaintances was just too good to pass up.

She sniffed. "I was just hoping for something different. Silly of me, I suppose."

"Anything, lass, you just name it. I swear. You know I
cannot stand to see you unhappy. Forgive me?"

"Of course." The words slid out automatically.

He set her back, his sad expression transformed by an
engaging grin. The years melted away from his face. His
blue eyes sparkled with enthusiasm. "Come, let me show
you the latest additions to my collection. I think you'll
be pleased."

Despite her inclination to indulge in self-pity, Meg
found herself suddenly intrigued. Sword collecting was
one interest they shared in common. She'd learned
everything from a father eager to pass on his knowledge.
Although she couldn't share his interest in the weapons'
role in war, she did value the clarity of design, the
strength matched by grace, and the care talented smiths
had put into crafting their masterpieces.

Meg followed him to the display room. Passing
through the portal was like stepping back in time, surrounding one with swords and daggers ranging from five
to five hundred years of age. Each blade held a story of
battles, heroism, treachery.

Scottish claymores and dirks formed the bulk of the
collection. The rest consisted of an astonishing variety of
cavalry sabers, scimitars, broadswords, axes, Renaissance
rapiers, and much more.

A mahogany table, meant for examining individual pieces, dominated the center of the room. A lumpy length of black velvet covered most of its surface. With a flourish, Douglass swept away the cloth protecting his latest treasures.

Meg gasped.

Her father's chest swelled, pleased with her reaction . . . although he couldn't possibly know the full import of her suddenly pounding heart.

The five blades were Japanese in origin.

Meg had once seen a painting of a fierce, bloodthirsty samurai warrior severing an enemy's head with his sword, the shorter matching weapon thrust through his belt. Never before had she beheld either type of blade in real life. If she felt this gripping thrill of discovery, this shortness of breath, how much more so a man fascinated with artifacts from the East?

The captain has a yen for the mysteries of the Orient, including those dark-haired, slanty-eyed women. The only thing more important to him is his collection of swords and daggers.

Boone's words came back to her . . . and with them the rebirth of her hope. If the stubborn Captain Talbert could not be influenced by money to help her, or coerced by threats, perhaps he could be lured by his greatest weakness.

Mouth curving with anticipation, Meg moved forward to touch one of the swords. Although their history was synonymous with violence, there was no denying the exquisite craftsmanship of the hilts and scabbards. She'd never seen their equal.

"They're wonderful. Where did you find these, Father?"

Silence greeted her question at first, then Douglass cleared his throat from the opposite side of the table. Glancing up in surprise, Meg discovered him rubbing the knuckles of his right hand against his chest. He only did that when he was nervous or feeling guilty. Meg's brow creased in concern.

"Did I say something wrong?"

"Nay, Meggie. 'Tis just a sad story." Clasping his hands behind his back, he began to pace.

Apprehension flickered through her. Was this something that could spoil her fledgling plan? "Tell me."

"Someone at the bank loaned money to a local fellow in the . . . er, import business. A large shipment he had coming in, three ships' worth, sank in a storm. Three weeks ago the loan came due. The swords were his only collateral. I offered for them, in exchange for covering the loan out of my own pocket." He stopped pacing and ran his fingertips up the length of one scabbard. "I had a specialist clean and oil them, and here they are," he finished reverently.

"Oh," Meg managed sadly. She couldn't accomplish her goals on someone else's misfortune. "Poor man. Maybe you should give him a chance to earn them back."

Douglass looked up abruptly. "Nay!" he burst out.

Meg frowned. "Is there something you're not telling me?"

Clearing his throat again, Douglass said crisply, "The man has accepted his loss, Meggie. It would . . . insult him if I tried to return them."

"Oh, I see," Meg whispered. *It's all right, then. This will work.* Renewed excitement fluttered in her chest. "Father, I've decided on the perfect gift for my birthday."

"There's the spirit, lass!" His sigh of relief was audible. "Now, you tell me what I can get you."

"These swords," she stated firmly.

Douglass's thick ruddy brows drew together in a thunderous frown. "You canna be serious, Meghan."

"I'm perfectly serious. You said so yourself . . . 'Anything, lass, you just name it.' "

"Now, Meggie, surely there must be something else," he coaxed. "Jewelry, perhaps?"

"I have all the jewelry, clothes, and silly feminine gewgaws that I need. Frankly, I'm tired of such things. I want these blades. They are the *only* thing I want for my birthday, Father," she emphasized. An odd choking sound came from his throat. "They will form the perfect start for my own collection."

In his big hands, the velvet cloth slowly turned to a wad of crushed finery.

"You swore, Father," Meghan reminded.

His eyes widened. She had him neatly trapped in the mire of his own promise. "Blessed Saint Ninian!" he suddenly roared. "Where did you learn to manipulate a body like this?"

"From you."

He stared at her for a moment, then shook his head wryly. "Aye, so you did. I suppose it'll be all right, since they'll stay in the family. Very well, they're yours," he grumbled. Fixing her with a parental glare, he warned, "But you must leave them in this room until you marry and move to your own place."

"Don't worry. I promise the swords will stay here until they find a new home."

He nodded, apparently satisfied, not recognizing the deliberately vague nature of her vow. If all went as planned, the swords would soon find a new home in Captain Talbert's collection.

She would deal with her father's inevitable wrath when the time came. The full measure of his anger would be like the sting of blowing sand compared to the agony of his death.

No price was too high for her father's life. His safety depended on her, including protecting Douglass from his own belief that nothing would go wrong in life unless he decreed it. Maybe that's why he'd been so devastated when her mother died, leaving Meg to pick up the pieces of their lives. She couldn't bear the idea of losing another parent.

"You must swear," Meg said earnestly, "not to sell them to anybody, no matter the amount of money offered."

"Aye, they are yours, lass." His gentle smile switched to a scowl. "As long as you swear the same."

"I can guarantee I won't sell the blades." There, that didn't preclude her giving the blades away, with no money changing hands, in exchange for services rendered. She let out a slow breath meant to calm the trembling of her insides.

It didn't work.

"You strike a hard bargain, Meggie." He chuckled. "I taught you well."

Rolling out a deep drawer beneath the table, Douglass pulled out a bottle and two snifters. He poured some brandy into each.

Raising his glass in salute, Douglass's voice rang through the room. "Happy birthday, Meggie."

Meg raised the glass and drank, but her real toast was that Talbert would work a miracle and keep her father alive. Then she excused herself, suddenly anxious to pen a note to the captain, one with just enough information to dangle the lure . . . no more.

He must agree to meet with her.

Chapter Four

Drawn on by moonlight, he passes up the inn where he meant to stay, a traveler in the night walking tomorrow's road.

—KYOGOKU TAMEKANE (1254–1332)

"DIZ IZ DA place?"

Meg wholeheartedly agreed with the note of disapproval in Peter's tone, but she couldn't share his shock. She knew the measure of Captain Talbert's arrogance. As she and her twin escorts stared down the stairs leading to the ramshackle building on Meigg's Wharf, she cursed her naiveté at underestimating his audacity.

The sign over the open doorway proclaimed the saloon as Abe Warner's Cobweb Palace.

Now she understood the prickle of apprehension that had run up her nape when Talbert's response to her note arrived earlier this afternoon. He'd been too agreeable, too courteous, even going so far as to suggest a location.

Years' worth of grime clouded the windows, justifying the dim interior of the building during broad daylight. Rickety-looking, uneven boards covered what might be called a front porch—in someone's distorted fantasies. Broken packing crates stacked against the wall served as perches for—of all the oddities—five wireframe cages containing exotic parrots. The birds' bright plumage formed a startling contrast to the salt-bleached wood of the exterior.

Sounds of drunken merriment rose to a crescendo and spilled out through the open doorway. To Meg's astonishment, that wasn't all that poured outside.

Two long-tailed monkeys scampered through the opening. They continued rapidly up the steps in an impressive display of agility, then stopped abruptly in front of her. Phillip and Peter's mouths dropped open.

One monkey tugged on her skirts in an imperious summons. The second, after grabbing the dangling strings of her reticule, looked up from a bewhiskered brown-and-white face, baring its teeth in a comical expression that was more grin than snarl. Fascinated, Meg spoke soothingly and gently pried its fingers loose from her reticule.

The purpose of the meeting site became obvious: Talbert meant to disconcert and embarrass her again, to scare her off permanently. No doubt he hoped she wouldn't even have the nerve to enter the building.

Far from being disconcerted, Meg was intrigued.

What fascinating oddities awaited her inside? This was a side of San Francisco she hadn't seen in ages—not since her family's first two years in a gold-hungry town where prices were inflated beyond sanity. Creativity in making money had been the watchword of survival, and she'd contributed her own rare talent. The raucous sounds from Abe Warner's were no different from dozens of other saloons and gaming hells where she'd played the piano, its rowdy patrons cut from the same coarse cloth as the gold miners who'd subsided into appreciative silence when her fingers touched the keyboard. Their kind words then— saying her music eased their loneliness, their homesickness, their hunger for beauty—had meant more to her than any amount of praise from her teachers in Boston.

With a wistful smile, Meg accepted the monkeys' invitation. She lifted the hem of her gray walking dress and started down the stairs. The greeting committee darted ahead into the saloon.

"Nein!" exclaimed Peter, finding his voice.

Phillip came after her, lumbering halfway down the steps, his size making the old wood creak ominously. He grasped her upper arm in a light yet insistent grip. *"Fraulein,* no, not diz place. Your papa—" he pleaded, stopping when adequate words failed him.

Meg could easily fill in the gaps. Douglass would be appalled to find his only daughter in the type of place he'd worked so hard to free her from.

Suddenly more determined than ever to satisfy her curiosity, Meg laid her hand over Phillip's broad fingers. "You know this is my last chance to speak with Captain Talbert before his ship sails," she said firmly. "I want you to wait for me outside."

He frowned.

"It will be all right, Phillip. You'll be close by if I need you."

He released her with obvious reluctance. Peter cuffed Phillip on the shoulder, which started an argument in German. Meg, accustomed to their fighting when she made their job difficult, ignored them and slipped inside.

Conversation in the crowded main room ceased when she entered. No doubt the appearance of a lady in Abe Warner's created as many shock waves as an earthquake. Looking around in amazement, Meg wondered how the place survived the tremors that occasionally shook the city.

Bottles of every shape and size littered the shelves behind the long, polished bar, in addition to model ships, brass sextants and compasses. Walrus tusks were scattered everywhere, as if some mythical arctic graveyard had coughed up the ivory as a morbid joke. Some tusks were carved with elaborate scrimshaw designs; others remained smooth and white, awaiting the knife of a lonely, artistic sailor. Dozens of framed pictures covered the walls, perhaps nailed down . . . more likely glued tight by the solid matting of cobwebs.

The Cobweb Palace was appropriately named. The bar, glasses, tables, and floor were scrubbed clean, but high on the walls and ceiling, across the picture frames and knickknacks, the saloon offered a spider's paradise. Cobwebs so old and thick they hung in ragged sheets gave evidence of an astonishing case of deliberate neglect.

Meg wanted to laugh aloud. The place fascinated her like nothing she'd seen before, a true jewel of San Francisco daring and eccentricity.

The growing volume of masculine whispers reminded her that she was the center of attention. It was nothing new, unfortunately, even though she'd dressed in her most subdued gown of gray with black lace trim, her hair tightly controlled under a tilted hat. Growing up amidst the boisterous, lonely, male population of San Francisco had taught her poise and confidence in the company of men. Under her cool, direct gaze, the patrons averted their eyes as she scanned the room for her quarry.

Jacob Talbert sat in a far corner, his back to her. There was no mistaking the long, thick waves of his black hair tied back with a leather string. The breadth of his shoulders threatened to split his tan cotton shirt down the middle.

There was a certain primitive male beauty about him, Meg admitted as her gaze traced his sculpted, muscular back.

He stood, then turned. Heavens, with his hard-edged

good looks, sensual mouth, and large, graceful hands, he looked supremely capable of plundering any woman's virtue.

The glittering anger in his eyes, however, said he'd reserved a different role for Meg—probably as a set of grotesque bleached bones to warn thieves away from his buried treasure. A shiver raced down her spine. The question of whether he'd forgiven her veiled threats from the evening before had been answered.

Pulling out a chair for her, he arched one dark eyebrow in the most blatant challenge she'd ever encountered in a simple facial expression.

With heart pounding, her nerves on edge, Meg stepped up to the proffered seat, her back to him.

Suddenly, a low, rasping voice behind her demanded, *"Give us a kiss!"*

Shock at Talbert's effrontery recoiled through her body. Meg spun around, her palm aiming straight for his cheek.

His head ducked back with phenomenal speed, neatly avoiding the slap. Meg gasped as her momentum, without the expected contact, carried her full circle. Her legs tangled in her petticoats; her balance failed to compensate.

She plopped down into the chair. Enraged, she tried to jump up again. A hand like a steel manacle clamped down on her shoulder, holding her in place.

"A kiss, sweetie!" added the same raspy voice, louder this time . . . a voice that now she realized wasn't even human.

Meg twisted around just as Talbert reached back to pet a green-and-yellow parrot sitting on a tall perch fashioned of driftwood. Too late she realized the bird was the source of the ribald comments. She'd been so focused on Talbert's powerful presence that she hadn't even noticed the parrot in the corner.

A wave of male chuckles swept through the room, but she was too angry to be mortified.

"You could have told me the bird can talk," she hissed as he took the seat opposite.

He smiled.

Meg ground her teeth. The look of sham innocence on his face belonged there about as much as sugar blended with vinegar. He took particular delight in provoking her.

"Many of these parrots imitate human speech," Talbert explained belatedly. "Blackbeard is my favorite. His vocabulary is particularly . . . colorful."

The parrot rocked from one foot to the other. He squawked, a surprisingly powerful, abrasive noise from a bird whose body wasn't any longer than her forearm.

"How charming," Meg said dryly.

"The parrots are part of the appeal of the place."

"Not to mention a unique opportunity to embarrass me." She instantly regretted the peevish remark, no matter how true. There was no mistaking the glint of amusement in Talbert's eyes.

"Don't you approve of my choice of rendezvous, Miss McLowry?"

Meg's fingers crushed the reticule in her lap, curbing the urge to slam his heavy ale mug down on his unprotected fingers. "Oh, no, it's quite ideal . . . perfectly suited to your character." Why did he raise her ire so easily? What hole had opened up and swallowed her celebrated poise?

The corners of his mouth tilted upward.

"Shall we get down to business, Captain?" she ground out, annoyed with herself for noticing the smoothly curved, sinfully masculine lines of his lips.

He leaned back and crossed his arms over his chest.

"First, tell me why I should deal with you at all when you are planning on detaining my ship under the pretense of opium smuggling?"

She blinked. "Oh, that. I called off the raid."

"You make it sound as if you canceled a lady's tea party," he said sourly. "Do you expect me to thank you?"

"For saving you a great deal of time, trouble, and expense? I wouldn't dream of it," she retorted sarcastically.

"Good," he countered, "because I see no sense in thanking you for stopping something you had no business starting in the first place."

The fact he was right made her even angrier. "Whether or not it was my business is inconsequential, Captain. The point is, I had the power to do exactly what I promised." She folded her arms on the table and leaned forward, saying, "It was very tempting."

He likewise crossed his arms and leaned close, bringing their faces within inches of one another. "Then I applaud your generosity and your restraint," he growled.

They glared at each other, both refusing to back down. She noticed the dark line ringing his gray irises. A bit of silver hair mixed in with the black at his temples, making him seem more . . . mortal. Heat built between them like the stifling feel of an approaching storm in late August.

One of the monkeys jumped on the table, shattering the growing tension. Talbert sat back. Meg breathed a sigh of relief, certain a lightning display had just been averted. Her stomach felt queer—light and jittery.

The monkey lunged for Talbert's shirt-front pocket with one slender arm. Talbert deflected its nimble hand, then rapped the table once with his knuckles. Contrite as a wealthy woman's lapdog, the monkey sat on its haunches and held out its hand. Talbert pulled a peanut from his pocket and placed it in the animal's palm. The monkey ripped open the shell with sharp teeth. After the meat disappeared in a few quick bites, the animal thrust out its hand again.

While Talbert produced another nut, Meg stared at the contrast between his large, bronzed hand and the monkey's frail fingers.

The second peanut met the same fate as the first. Cheeks stuffed near to bursting, the monkey opened its mouth and chattered a muffled demand for more.

"Want to feed him?" Talbert thrust a peanut into Meg's open hand without waiting for confirmation.

The monkey turned, grabbed wildly. Meg had the distinct impression that if she didn't feed it fast enough, the aggressive little creature would grope at her bodice in a fruitless search for peanut-rich pockets. The monkey's aura of civilized behavior was fleeting at best . . . not unlike that of the man across the table.

"No! You can be in charge of the local wildlife," she insisted, tossing the nut back at Talbert.

He caught it neatly in midair with one hand. Why did everything have to come so easily to him? It was a miscarriage of justice when a black-hearted rogue embodied all that masculine grace and athletic prowess.

"Aak! Keelhaul the blighter," grated the parrot.

"An excellent notion, Blackbeard," Meg muttered. "Just give the order, sir."

Talbert arched one dark brow in that irritating fashion— the one that made her want to smack him at the same time it sent a shiver down her back.

"I've heard you are an avid collector of swords, Captain."

"Certain types of weapons catch my fancy." He fed the monkey, then shooed it off the table. "I've accumulated a fair collection during my travels."

"Oriental blades in particular, perhaps?"

His eyes narrowed. "Are your blades Oriental? You didn't specify in your note. Don't toy with me, Miss McLowry."

She could never do the swords justice with a mere description. No, he must see them to appreciate them, to be ensnared by their allure until he could not say no to her proposal. "The blades are at my house. They are . . . too valuable to risk bringing to the waterfront," she improvised. "You must come there to see them and make your decision." She told him the address, then held her breath, awaiting his answer with trepidation.

"Describe them—" he began in a hard tone, only to be interrupted by a strident voice.

"Aaak! Hoist her skirts, matie!"

With a gasp, Meg jumped to her feet and glared at the parrot. "Traitor!" She spun back to face Talbert. He was smiling, his white teeth offering a stunning contrast to his sun-bronzed face. Why did he choose to share that beautiful, heart-stopping smile now, when he'd succeeded in humiliating her? Heat flooded her neck and face. "Are you coming or not?" she demanded.

The smile faded. "I think not. I've already been on one wild-goose chase this morning, Miss McLowry. The idea of another holds little appeal."

"Scurvy bastard!" Blackbeard squawked.

Meg braced her palms flat on the table and hissed, "You know, I've just forgiven Blackbeard for all his indelicate remarks. In fact, I might very well offer to buy that bird. He seems an excellent judge of character!"

Wrenching away, torn by conflicting emotions too chaotic to define, Meg searched for the exit. She discovered that vision obscured by tears didn't help the Cobweb Palace look any better.

Jacob Talbert was, by far, the most arrogant, belligerent

man she'd ever met! Worse, he'd said no again. Her last desperate attempt had failed, and Meg wasn't accustomed to desperation, or failure, in any situation. Fear for her father came back with a vengeance, squeezing her heart. The tears thickened, spilling over her lower lids. She brushed them away quickly, hoping Talbert wouldn't notice, but she couldn't stop a tiny sniff.

"Miss McLowry."

Meg froze. "Yes?" she asked stiffly, refusing to turn around.

"I'll meet you at your house in twenty minutes," he said flatly. "Don't keep me waiting."

It took every shred of Meg's self-control to depart with dignity, rather than lift her skirt and run from the saloon with renewed excitement.

"THIS IS MY father's weapons room. He is an avid collector of anything with a blade. Don't you think it prophetic that you and he share the same interest, Captain Talbert?"

Jake bit back a sarcastic comment that he thought it merely an unfortunate coincidence. He just wanted this farce over with as quickly as possible.

He couldn't believe he'd let a few tears get to him. For that matter, he couldn't understand why he'd taken such pleasure in baiting Meghan. The goal of selecting Abe Warner's as a meeting place had been to shock her refined sensibilities, embarrass her, and give her every reason to leave him alone. Except the spoiled society miss had proven braver than anticipated. In fact, all-out war had nearly erupted between them. Dammit, he hadn't felt this alive in years!

The butler—who'd shown him to his room, an appealing place that glowed with oiled wood and light from several small chandeliers—tilted his head to listen to Meghan's whispered instructions. He moved to leave, pulling the double doors shut with a click, but not before shooting Jake a look laced with disapproval and warning.

Jake turned away with a wry twist to his mouth. If only the butler knew the truth—he'd just callously left Jake alone with a woman who demonstrated all the instincts of a shark. She wasn't the one at risk here.

Slowly, Jake navigated the perimeter of the room, amazed that Douglass McLowry kept his collection so private. Jake's travels and contacts had supposedly made him familiar with every collector of repute around the world.

But nothing in the cases resembled the blades he sought. Swallowing the sour taste of disappointment, a sensation he should have grown accustomed to after countless such failures, he turned to Meghan.

She stood in front of a central table, her blue eyes glittering. Her left hand cradled her chin, the forefinger pressing tightly to her lips. Something of her intensity communicated itself to him, whether he welcomed it or not, causing his hands and chest muscles to flex.

Striding forward, Jake relished the opportunity to say he wasn't interested—once and for all, irrevocably, no longer open to negotiation. Her eyes widened at his approach; her hand lowered slowly, dragging her lower lip down.

His gaze riveted on the lush fullness of her mouth and the shine of even, white teeth. Every detail of her face had been deeply etched on his brain since their nose-to-nose encounter at the Cobweb Palace.

Aggravated over something that shouldn't distract him yet did a damnable good job of it anyway, Jake spoke. "I admit I'm impressed with your father's taste. Nevertheless, I don't see anything here valuable enough to add to my own collection."

"The latest acquisitions are mine, not my father's, and they have yet to be put on display."

She stepped aside, simultaneously sweeping away a dark cloth that covered the surface of the table.

The delicate barrier separating the present from Jake's past ripped in two. He struggled to regain the breath knocked from his lungs, to push back the darkness crowding his peripheral vision.

At first he was afraid to move, lest the five blades—the hunt for which had consumed nearly half his life—vanish again like some cruel dream.

Jake's gaze skimmed past the smallest blade, despite the beauty of gold, colored enamels, and small jewels decorating the hilt. Longer than a European-style dagger, yet smaller than the other blades, the *tanto* invoked too many painful memories.

His attention settled on one samurai pair of long and short swords, or *daisho*. He reached for the longer katana, although it seemed wrong somehow to watch a broader, older version of his hand stretch out before him. These swords had been fashioned strictly for war, their deep burgundy color lending a classic dignity. A bold pattern of wisteria vines, fashioned in pure silver, adorned the length of the matching sayas.

When he gripped the silk-wrapped hilt of the katana, everything else in the room receded into misty shadows. How could one describe the utter familiarity of handling a sword that had been an integral part of one's youth for ten years, drawn in practice three hundred times a day?

The blade slid out of the saya, the katana so perfectly fashioned, so sublimely balanced that it felt light and buoyant in his hand. Jake slashed the steel through the air once, twice, in a motion that felt like a natural extension of his arm. Light reflected from the polished surface, flashing across the walls.

Traditional Japanese belief held that the katana was the soul of the samurai. This blade had shared his soul . . . when he'd had a spirit to impart, before heartrending choices and bitter failure had robbed him of his honor sixteen years before.

He resheathed the katana and laid it gently on the table, struggling to control the trembling in his hand, knowing he was no longer worthy of carrying such a noble blade. Deep, slow breaths didn't ease the sudden tightness in his chest.

He turned to the other daisho pair, almost ceremonial in their richness. The subdued brown of the sayas, the coloring of smooth wet sand, was offset by the sparkle of inlaid gold beneath the lacquer. Tracing the katana's saya with his fingertips, Jake admired the superb lacquerwork. Gold badges the size of large coins, embossed with the Matsuda family's chrysanthemum *mon*, as well as thousands of tiny flakes of gold, were forever suspended in clear resin. These swords had been a familiar sight once, thrust through the sash of Matsuda Shinjiro—beloved adoptive cousin who'd been dearer than a brother, namesake for the flagship of Jake's modest fleet.

A sharp pang of loss ripped through him.

With all the vivid clarity of his nightmares Jake pictured the Kyoshu battlefield again, felt the clashing of steel vibrate through his arm, heard the screams of dying men, struggled to maintain his balance in the slick mud. Their small band of samurai had tried to stop the raiding Chinese . . . and lost.

He'd returned to the village afterward, his slow movements caused more by shock and sorrow than the stiffness of mud-caked samurai armor. Flies had buzzed, attracted to his still seeping wounds. His wisteria swords were gone, stolen while he was unconscious, suffering the same fate as the heirloom blades belonging to the headless body draped across the horse behind him. Cradled gently in one arm, carefully washed and wrapped in his *firoshiko*, he'd carried Shinjiro's severed head. Jake's skin had itched where tears carved tracks through the dried blood of his slashed cheek.

Grief had still been a numb unreality when he'd faced his adoptive father, Matsuda Hiroshi. Jake's battered body had protested when he'd dropped to his knees and bowed, asking for the forgiveness he knew he didn't deserve. Hiroshi-sama, face frozen in a disapproving scowl, had listened to the tale of his nephew's death . . . and Jake's shame. Then he'd turned away, forever shunning his adopted *gaijin* son.

"Captain Talbert?"

Meghan's soft voice penetrated with the pure clarity of church bells, wrenching Jake back to reality. He pulled his hand back from the katana, ruthlessly reining in his raging emotions at the same time.

His sixteen-year quest was at an end. It was disconcerting, to say the least, to realize that the force that had driven him across Japan, to the coast of China, and thence to every major port in the world had turned to dust in Meghan McLowry's manipulative little hands. Exultation at reaching his goal should be charging through him. Instead, he felt unaccountably weary, torn by resurrected grief and guilt, wondering what direction his life should take now.

"Don't tell me you're not interested in these blades," Meg whispered. "I'll know it for a bald-faced lie. You look like you've seen a ghost."

Jake winced. He'd allowed her to witness the depths

of his interest. Now she could command an outrageous price and, damnation, he would pay it.

"Very well, Miss McLowry, you have my complete attention," he said, despising the ragged edge to his voice. "How much do you want for all five?"

"I'm afraid you will find these swords far beyond your financial means, sir."

He stiffened. "You underestimate my 'means.' "

"I doubt that, because these particular blades are not for sale. Not at any price."

In that instant, he hated her. He felt raw, his nerve endings exposed. She sought to deny him what he'd sacrificed so much to find.

"Then why the hell did you bring me here?" he said through his teeth.

"These swords cannot be bought, but . . . they can be earned."

"Go on," he said coldly.

She squared her shoulders and said resolutely, "The price for these swords is my father's life, Captain. Nothing less."

Fury drove him forward a step. "That sounds suspiciously like blackmail."

"Call it what you will," she declared unrepentantly, lifting her chin. "My father is in danger. I will do whatever it takes to recruit the necessary people to protect him."

"The swords are rightfully mine. I shouldn't have to bargain for them, dammit!"

"What do you mean, rightfully yours?"

He caught himself before he revealed even a hint of their significance. He would never give her that kind of power over him! "These are Japanese swords, but their greatest value is in their history, not the gold. They were stolen from a powerful family in Japan who has long sought their return as an important symbol of their heritage, their honor. It is an insult for them to be used as a bargaining chip."

She lowered her lashes, concealing her eyes. "I respect that, truly I do, but the swords are mine now to do with as I see fit. You have it within your power to deliver them to that family. Shall we come to an arrangement, Captain, or should I find someone else willing to earn such a prize?"

"And what, exactly, do you expect me to do?"

"Take charge of my father's security," she clarified, meeting his gaze again. "Hire the men you need, but you are personally to see to his safety."

"For how long?"

"Unless you want the assignment to go on indefinitely, I suggest you discover the source of the threat and eliminate it."

"Are you talking murder, Miss McLowry?" Taking a step closer, he snarled, "I'm not a damned *ninja* assassin."

Her lips parted on a sharp intake of breath. "No—no, of course not. But with the Tongs involved, I can't imagine cold-blooded assassination would play any part in it. Prove the men involved in prostitution, collusion, murder, then have them arrested. Have them shanghaied, dammit, and sent back to China."

Jake snorted and shook his head in amazement. "You don't ask much, do you?" He should find Meghan's lack of appropriate feminine deference offensive. So why the hell was his blood pounding, his every sense tingling?

Furious, Jake bore down on her, relishing the fact that he must look as menacing as he felt. Her eyes widened. She backed away until a display case halted her progress.

His palms flattened on the glass on either side of her head, effectively trapping her, their bodies close yet not quite touching. "Very well, Miss McLowry, I agree to your terms. You have your bodyguard. But don't be smug about your little victory, because there's a reason I'm not often welcome in polite society."

She looked him straight in the eye. "Does it have anything to do with being a boor and a bully?"

"At the very least."

"Let me go," she whispered with a slight quaver to her voice.

"When it suits me."

"I don't like being trapped, damn you."

His short burst of bitter laughter cracked through the room like a whip. "Now, isn't that the height of hypocrisy. You don't seem to suffer guilt over trapping me, from practically blackmailing me into putting my business, my life, on hold."

"Why should I feel in the least bit contrite? You'll be well compensated with the swords, sir," she retorted indignantly.

"For paying an idle crew to entertain themselves for days on end? A portion of my cargo is also on commission. Do I just look on helplessly while those owners retrieve their merchandise and approach other captains who can promise on-time delivery? The grievances mount, Miss McLowry."

He dipped his head, brushing the plane of his left cheek parallel to hers with only a whisper of air between their faces. He deliberately sought to intimidate, to shift the balance of power his way. From the way she froze, avoiding any contact, the tactic worked.

Although he intended to immediately pull back, the warmth of her skin held him, the brush of her rapid breathing against his neck anchored him to the spot. His lungs inhaled deeply, taking in her scent. Rather than the cloying floral perfume he expected from a spoiled socialite, she smelled of soap and sunshine and . . . woman.

His manhood stirred. Dammit, she wasn't at all the type of woman he found attractive! His hands curled into fists against the glass.

His voice was low, threatening, when he murmured in her ear, "Maybe I don't regard the compensation as adequate. A bonus arrangement is called for here, something more . . . personal." Although he had no intention of pursuing anything intimate, it didn't hurt to give her something to worry about.

Meghan drew a sharp breath. He expected her to shove him away, to sputter in maidenly outrage. Instead she started laughing, a merry sound that raked velvet claws down his chest and into his groin. At first he thought she had touched him—so tangible, so intimate was the sensation. Yet, at the same time, her humor deeply offended his pride.

He straightened and scowled. What the hell was so amusing about his advances?

"Nice try, Captain," she said cheerfully. "But I know I'm safe from any lustful intent on your part. I have it on very good authority that your interest in women is strictly limited to black-haired beauties of Asian descent. You could hardly be interested in a blue-eyed American with wild hair the color of wheat chaff."

More like the color of sunshine glowing through honey, the unexpected thought intruded as his gaze shifted to her hair. Her mockery infuriated him. With her intriguing combination of beauty, confident poise, and sensual appeal, she must be accustomed to wrapping besotted men around her little finger. How would she react if he threw down a gauntlet of his own?

He stepped back, freeing her. Brusquely, he announced, "My man, Komatsu Akira, and I will be moving into the house tomorrow morning."

"Move in?" she squeaked, an octave higher than normal for her husky voice.

"Surely you can find room for us in this monstrosity of a mansion?"

"There's a small guest house on the property. I intended for you to stay there."

"Not good enough. It's essential I stay in the main house."

"You must be mad! That would create . . . complications."

"Of what sort? Surely a woman willing to blackmail a complete stranger has no qualms about her reputation."

She planted her hands on her hips. "My reputation is spotless, I'll have you know. And we often have guests stay in our home."

"Then I don't see the problem. How do you expect me to guard your father unless I'm near him twenty-four hours a day?"

She opened her mouth, then closed it again.

Masculine satisfaction curled through him. It must be a monumental event when Meghan McLowry was struck speechless.

Jake spun on his heel and headed for the door. "I'll have those swords. Just make sure they go to no one else." Tempted to slam out of the room, Jake stopped himself at the last second, remembering that a samurai didn't lower himself to displays of strong emotion. Jaw clenched, he shut the door quietly behind him.

The click of the latch released the tension holding Meg like a marble statue. Even the elation over her victory, her profound sense of relief over achieving Talbert's cooperation, couldn't override the perverse shaking that suddenly claimed her limbs.

Twenty-four hours a day. Talbert would be in her

home, in and out of every room, a constant looming presence. Even though it was for her father's sake, it meant being around her as well, close at hand with all that dark, potent masculinity, those stormy gray eyes with their haunting secrets.

This wasn't turning out at all as she'd planned.

Chapter Five

When I see how in this life nothing remains constant, I hold my heart apart from the world and spend many days in thought.
—OTOMO NO YAKAMOCHI (EIGHTH CENTURY)

MEG TILTED HER face into the oncoming breeze, invigorated by the crisp dawn air and the surging power of her horse. Resting her weight in the stirrups, she kept her body pliant, merging with the surrounding rhythms of nature: the relaxed cadence of the bay mare's canter, the sway of tall yellowed grasses, the crash of surf in the distance, the soaring dance of a hawk as it mastered the air currents like a symphony conductor.

This morning she needed the stillness and shelter of her favorite refuge . . . to fortify her patience, not to mention her peace of mind, before Jacob Talbert invaded her home.

Meg's bare hands tightened convulsively on the leather, reining in her mount at the top of the next hill. At the sight of the beautiful tableau ahead, she felt the tension of the past several days begin to ease from her shoulders.

The morning fog hadn't quite completed its retreat to the sea. Fingers of white mist still invaded portions of the forest, concealing many of the lesser evergreens, but not the giants whose pointed tops thrust regally above the fog.

Anxious to lose herself in the solitude of the redwoods, Meg urged the mare forward. Within minutes,
she went from feeling tall and significant in the world of
men, to tiny and fragile among the towering trees. There
was no need to imagine fairies and brownies here, she
thought whimsically, for in this realm of ancient giants
she was the tiny golden-haired fairy of children's fables.
It was all a matter of proportion.

After tying the mare to the branch of a fallen tree,
Meg moved deeper into the forest, seeking out her most
treasured spot. She picked her way through emerald
ferns and a thick carpet of brown needles, stepping over
gnarled tree roots that pushed up through the soil. Sunlight filtered through the overhead canopy as the fog
dissipated.

She came to her favorite tree, the largest and—she
could only assume—the oldest here. Without hesitation,
she pressed her cheek to the rust brown bark, undeterred
by the thin, fragile cobwebs that wove over every inch of
rough surface. She spread her arms, embracing a small
part of the giant's impressive girth.

She loved hugging this tree, although she didn't quite
understand why. Doing so touched something deep inside, something simple and instinctive and childlike.

It was as if the wisdom and patience of the ages were
stored within this one redwood. Its silent, unchanging
dignity offered a startling contrast to the antlike frenzy of
men who scrambled about California in a frantic pursuit
of glittering wealth and relief from boredom.

Except for Jacob Talbert. There was nothing frantic
about the man. He pursued what he wanted with all the
patience, concentration, and stealth of a stalking tiger.

Thinking about the captain destroyed the peace of the
moment.

Emitting a low growl of frustration, Meg slumped down with her back against the tree. The memories of last evening haunted her. At least here she could think clearly and work through the disturbing images flooding her mind.

Talbert's face had tightened with pain, rather than greed, when he'd first seen the swords. She'd been startled to learn that he and the blades shared some history, then delighted, because their new significance offered an additional hold over him.

But when his eyes darkened—those stormy gray eyes churning with frightening secrets—something had compelled her to speak, to distract him from apparently painful memories. She'd felt . . . uneasy, somehow, when his eyes no longer focused with the clarity of a warrior's polished steel blade. The strangest urge to touch his arm, to draw him back from the shadows, had come over her. Only the knowledge that the gesture wouldn't be welcome had kept her hands at her sides.

Everything had changed when she laid out the terms for earning the swords. Anger had shuttered his gaze in an instant, shattering her silly notions of a soul in torment, along with any comprehension of why he'd awakened her protective instincts in the first place. And yet . . . she'd tensed with awareness of every movement of his large body, every shift in his moods.

Sighing deeply, Meg bent her knees and propped her chin on her crossed arms. *Admit the truth: You find the captain fascinating.* She could understand why. He was as easy to get along with as a porcupine. Nevertheless, when they clashed she felt . . . alive, invigorated, daring.

Disloyal.

All her attention should be focused on tonight and the opportunity to dance and flirt with Carl again so soon. Basking in the glow of his charm and attention offered her the only remaining opportunity to feel special and cherished on her birthday.

With his blond hair, green eyes, and quick smile, Carl Edwards was the antithesis of Talbert—sunshine versus dark, openness versus secrets and seething passions, security rather than disturbing, barely leashed strength. Blessed with a bright future as her father's protégé at the bank, Carl charmed her friends with his polished wit. He fit perfectly into her world, and he'd made it very clear he envisioned a future at her side.

He hadn't spoken of marriage recently, but then, she'd asked him for time to think. Not sure why she'd put him off twice before, Meg knew only that she felt a stirring of annoyance when he tried to pressure her into saying yes. Soon she would accept, for—as everyone agreed—they were ideally suited, the banker's stylish daughter and the former colonel in the Union calvary.

Meg's chin jerked up. That was exactly her point! Carl knew how to place a woman on a pedestal and treat her like a lady. He would never trap her against a wall and murmur silky threats in a dark, menacing tone.

Checking the watch pinned to her blouse, Meg groaned. It was time to return and face all the work that remained before the party, then play the dual roles of gracious hostess and cheerful birthday girl that everyone expected.

"MISS MEGHAN. CAPTAIN Talbert has arrived."

Meg's hand slipped as she cut through the stem of a rose, narrowly missing slicing her thumb. It was shortly after noon, and the butler had found her arranging flowers in the ballroom.

Her heart beat at an erratic pace. "Thank you, Robert,"

she responded tightly. "Is the captain's companion with him?"

"Yes, Miss."

"Please have someone show them to the rooms I've assigned."

"Very good. May I ask, however, where we should put—that is, what would you like me to do with—I don't quite—bloody hell, Miss Meghan, I don't want to touch the things!"

Meg stared. Robert never swore, nor did his voice normally rise in a harassed tone. His British pride revolved around maintaining his dignity under the most dire of circumstances. "What the devil are you talking about?"

A woman's squeal of horror tore down the hall leading from the main entryway.

Robert rolled his eyes, muttering, "Silly twit. There's no need for the maid to go into hysterics." He turned and strode hastily from the ballroom.

Astonished by the sudden deterioration of her orderly household, Meg dropped the rose and scissors on the table and rushed after her butler.

Discovering the entry foyer crowded with her entire staff of twelve, including a footman helping a still-woozy Millie up from the floor, Meg was struck by the force of Jake Talbert's tall, enigmatic presence, an eye of calm in a tropical storm—a tempest he had created, damn him.

Meg took a deep breath and let it out slowly. "You didn't mention anything about pets, Captain Talbert."

"You didn't ask, Miss McLowry," Talbert countered. He raised his right arm, displaying the largest lizard she'd ever seen, clinging to his biceps.

He was either mad, or utterly diabolical in his attempts to make her pay for blackmailing him—no, wait, that was the ridiculous term he'd applied to their bargain. Had she believed his company invigorating? What nonsense. The man was infuriating!

Robert ordered the servants back to their duties, though he remained in the foyer, apparently awaiting her final verdict concerning the extra "guests."

Meg glanced at the Japanese gentlemen who cradled the second iguana in his folded arms.

"Miss McLowry, may I present my friend, Komatsu Akira."

Although the older man's face was set in stern lines, laughter sparkled in his dark eyes as he bowed. Everyone seemed to be enjoying the joke at her expense.

"Mr. Komatsu," Meg acknowledged, bowing her head in turn.

Turning back to Talbert, she said dryly, "You actually expect me to keep lizards in my house?"

"Naturally. They go where I go." His black brows arched sardonically. "And these aren't ordinary lizards. They are iguanas from the Pacific coast of Mexico."

Talbert smiled—a predatory, too-white tiger smile. Meg suddenly felt trapped in her own home. Her sanity would soon be in shambles, following quickly on the heels of her lacerated temper.

"Captain, I'd like to have a word with you," Meg said coldly. "In private."

She stalked to the study. Turning at her father's desk, Meg leaned back against the solid oak and gripped the edge to keep from pacing.

Talbert entered the room, still carrying the iguana. It now perched across his broad shoulders, its slender tail nearly the length of his right arm. Its claws gripped Talbert's gray shirt, pulling the material tight across his chest.

Meg struggled to draw breath. This scene was worthy of a circus, and she paused to admire the man's chest? What the devil was wrong with her?

"Don't worry, Miss McLowry, the iguanas don't bite . . . unless provoked."

"I'm more worried about you, sir," she said irritably.

"Now that's a different situation altogether." He smiled that smile again, all teeth and no warmth. "I definitely bite at the slightest provocation."

She didn't dare encourage his outrageousness by responding to that taunt. They glared at each other in silence. The same strange heat that had sparked between them at the Cobweb Palace flared to life again. He must have felt it, too—and found it equally disturbing—for his eyes narrowed.

"The butler will have someone show you to your room," she said quickly.

"In the main house?"

"Yes. As much as I wish otherwise, you will be staying here. You made that point very clear, Captain." She drew a deep breath. "Don't be concerned with the preparations under way. We are hosting a large party tonight."

He scowled. "Cancel it."

She laughed, then sobered instantly when the thunderous look on his face registered. "You're serious!" she exclaimed. Her knuckles began to ache, so tightly did she grip the desk. "That's ludicrous. I can't call off an event of this magnitude at this late hour. What of the food, the decorations, the orchestra, not to mention contacting all the guests?"

"These things are more important than your father's safety?"

"Of course not. But this party has been planned for weeks, long before any of these problems cropped up, and," she added tartly, "I promise there's not a single Tong member on the guest list."

He snorted. "What do you really know of the Tong, Miss McLowry?"

Abandoning her grip on the desk, Meg crossed her arms tightly beneath her breasts. "I know there is more than one group, some more powerful than others, constantly battling over territorial rights. They rule Chinatown like medieval despots, terrorizing their own people. Their assassins favor hatchets as weapons. The police turn a blind eye to the killing, until the wars affect the affluent people of San Francisco."

"Which raises an interesting question: Why would any Tong leader want to kill your father?"

"Some imagined slight or insult? Many San Francisco businessmen have dealings with Chinese merchants, including my father. He is a boisterous and blunt man, Captain, who doesn't always approach things diplomatically. He may have inadvertently said the wrong thing to the wrong person."

Talbert's shuttered eyes revealed no reaction. "The Chinese are very sensitive to insult. If the offense is serious enough—from their perspective, which seldom makes sense to a Westerner—then it warrants killing the offender to save face."

"Save face?"

"Reputation, respect from their peers, deference and obedience from those beneath them," he explained brusquely. "Their social structure revolves around it."

"Unfortunately, I don't know the reason, and neither does Father. He maintains that the attacks must have been random, not targeting him personally at all."

"You don't seem to share his opinion, even though every sort of violence is common in this city," Talbert probed.

"There were two separate attacks on the fringes of the financial district," Meg insisted. "How can that be random? Thank goodness Peter and Phillip were with him the first time. In the last attempt, two policemen were injured—" Her voice failed as she thought of the bravery of those men and her father's narrow escape. If the policemen hadn't been walking their beat just around the corner, hadn't heard her father's shout . . . . Meg shuddered. The police chief had declared it a robbery attempt, saying that only greater numbers had chased off the two Chinamen. Douglass had agreed. But if the goal was merely robbery, why had the men carried hatchets?

Talbert took a step forward. In a low, angry voice, he said, "Then you have some understanding, however small, of how dangerous the Tong can be. They'll only become more aggressive. I'm of little use if you don't value my advice. A party provides too perfect an opportunity for a large number of people to get close to your father."

"Actually, I'd like very much to cancel the party, but my father insists on it going ahead as scheduled," Meg declared. Pain shot through her at the reminder that she had this night yet to endure, in stoic good humor, and Talbert was making everything so much worse!

"What other plans do you have in mind to make my job difficult?" he demanded as he advanced slowly.

His challenging attitude finally succeeded in igniting Meg's temper.

"Let's see, my father has his weekly poker game with his friends Thursday night. Tea is scheduled Friday afternoon for members of the Ladies' Benevolent Society. Both are great risks to security, I'm sure. Oh, and lest I forget, there's the wild orgy planned for this weekend." Venting her anger with cutting sarcasm felt so good that she realized her mistake too late: Her determination not to retreat had enabled Talbert to close the gap and trap her against the desk.

His broad shoulders dominated her field of vision. The iguana swiveled its scaly head and stared at her with gold-black eyes—the richness of doubloons and black pearls from a pirate's treasure chest. The reptile and the man made a strange, exotic pair . . . both unpredictable, both predatory.

"I assume your joking about the orgy," he said coldly. "Nevertheless, I admire a woman who practices extreme modesty."

"And I admire a man with scruples, not to mention manners," she retorted breathlessly.

His chin jerked as if she'd struck a blow. "Manners are so much a part of the Japanese culture, so polished, they are practically an art form."

"Then you've obviously been away too long."

Her words penetrated his mask of jaded arrogance. Was that regret she saw in his stormy eyes?

Preferring their antagonism to this unsettling glimpse of dark passions, Meg blurted out, "Do you truly insist on keeping those creatures here?"

Much to her relief, he eased back, giving her breathing space, which she needed if the odd flutter in her chest was any indication.

"It would grieve me to be separated from them."

Meg suppressed an unladylike urge to snort. "And what kind of special accommodations do your iguanas require, Captain?"

"Someplace clean, with plenty of plants, fresh water, and most importantly, lots of sunshine. And it must be enclosed . . . the little buggers are escape artists."

"Of course. What else would they be?" She wouldn't do it; she wouldn't complain that he pursued this only to vex her. They both knew it, but acknowledging it aloud would grant him some kind of perverse victory. "Come along, then. I believe I have the perfect place for them."

Jake couldn't think of a suitable retort. He was too busy watching her expressive mouth. Those smooth pink contours reflected every change in her mood, every emotion.

Akira waited just outside the study. He thrust the second reptile into Jake's arms. The first iguana, resentful of this intrusion on her human perch, intensified her grip on Jake's shirt. Sharp claws pricked deeply into his shoulders. He winced. A slight shrug eased her grip enough to make it bearable.

Meghan kept moving toward a hallway opposite, her shoulders squared in that obstinate fashion that grated on his nerves. He glared after her.

Akira-san chuckled. "The pretty lady not scream, not swoon. Are you disappointed, Takeru-san?"

"That's not why I brought the iguanas," Jake grumbled.

"No?"

"We couldn't very well leave them on the ship, unattended. Daniel should have been here by now to pick them up." Frowning as he settled the second iguana along his left arm, Jake continued, "Something must have gone wrong to delay his journey north from San Diego. You know how he specifically asked me to bring two female iguanas back to add to his menagerie."

"He give you the name of someone to leave them with, if he not come in time. I think you do not trust anyone else to care for them."

"You're suggesting I'm concerned about a pair of reptiles? That's ridiculous. I just honor my commitments." The iguana on his shoulders started to slip. He grasped the base of her tail, shifting her higher until she was secure again.

"Ah . . . then you must bring them to make Miss Meg angry, to show that she not control you. The angry part work very well. What of the other?"

"I'm beginning to think I should have left you on the ship."

"Ah, but now I am pleased you ask me to come. This may offer a new path of—" Akira paused, then with a smile and a bow, he finished, "enlightenment."

Jake glared at him.

Meg turned at the far end of the hall and, setting her hands on her hips, complained, "Are you coming or not, Captain?"

"I'm a bit overburdened here, Miss McLowry. Would you like to carry one?" he called, starting in her direction.

"How generous of you," she answered, too sweetly. "But I wouldn't want to deprive you of the benefits of iguana ownership. I'm sure you brought them because you couldn't bear to be away from them."

"I believe I mentioned that already," he countered.

Rosy color blossomed in her cheeks. Sparks of anger deepened the blue of her eyes. Excitement coiled tightly inside Jake, not unlike the invigoration of battling for control of his ship during a violent storm. Just as he was anticipating one of her clever, sassy rejoinders, she pivoted abruptly and stalked down the adjoining hallway.

The wind dumped out of his sails.

She was just too damned unpredictable. He followed, searching for flaws.

A tight chignon struggled to contain the unruly curls of her hair, which, if set free, would no doubt prove as untamed as the woman. The design of her gown hugged her waist immodestly. Whereas Japanese women walked with mincing, restrained steps, Meghan swayed her hips with bold sensuality. He waited for this sight to cause the same distaste he felt in watching the crass mannerisms of most western women, yet he could only think how Meghan moved with the fluid grace of a deer.

"Here we are: iguana paradise," Meghan declared upon reaching the center of the mansion.

The glass door before them was set in a wall of windows, providing a panoramic view into a large atrium. White gravel crunched beneath Jake's boots as he stepped into the open-air garden. The path, winding between overflowing masses of thick greenery, ended in a large fountain at the far end. Bright sunlight shone through the open roof, reflecting off strategically placed white iron benches.

The place resembled an overgrown jungle, a far cry from the carefully designed, aesthetically pleasing gardens of Japan, but the smell of freshly turned soil tantalized his senses and the music of running water soothed his soul in the same way as those distant refuges. He ached suddenly for signs of home: the sweet smell of cherry blossoms, the exotic scent of incense, the shuddering sigh of wind through the willow trees. That's where he belonged—if he had a place anywhere in this world—once he earned the Matsuda family's forgiveness, once he completed the restoration of his lost honor by returning the swords.

The gritty sound of Meghan's shoes in the gravel wrenched Jake back to the present. The pain of loneliness, of not belonging, lanced through his chest.

Warily, he watched as she stepped in front of him. When she cocked her head to examine the iguana lying along his forearm, Jake's gaze traveled down the saucy angle of her neck and the graceful curve of one shoulder.

"Will he let me pet him?"

The word "pet" jarred through Jake like an unexpected clap of thunder. "It's a she, actually," he muttered, frowning at the reaction. "I really can't say. It took me a good three weeks of constant attention, coaxing, and feeding before I earned their trust. If she doesn't like it, she'll lash out with her tail."

Meg smiled. "I'll take my chances."

Jake couldn't tear his gaze from the dance of emotions across the dusky pink curves of her lips. Damn all women with expressive mouths. And why should he care?

He didn't have time to wonder, for he felt the iguana on his shoulder gather its body for a leap.

He immediately hunkered down on his heels, before the reptile could jump from a height that would cause serious injury.

"What's wrong?" Meg exclaimed.

It leaped from his shoulders, landing in the dirt with a plop, then disappeared into the dense network of green leaves. "Nothing, actually. They apparently like it here." The iguana on his forearm squirmed. When he set her down, she lifted her long body high on four legs and raced down the gravel path, quickly slipping into the vegetation.

Meg gasped. "They're quite fast!"

"Yes, and they'll be the very devil to catch when it's time for them to go," Jake grouched as he straightened.

"An iguana roundup," she said, laughing that musical laugh again . . . the same one that had cut so deeply into his pride yesterday when she scoffed at his threat of seduction. "Is that anything like rounding up cattle?"

She was trying to share a joke with him, but, dammit, he didn't want to feel in charity with her. The iguanas had lightened her mood, earning that breathtaking smile, not him. And he was angry over his forced confinement and her devil's bargain. "I wouldn't know," he snapped, brushing off his shirt with rough sweeps of his hands.

She stiffened. "If you'll excuse me, I must explain to

the staff about keeping away from the atrium. I'll see that the door is kept locked and you are given a key. You, of course, will be responsible for feeding them."

Meg turned away, uneasy with his mercurial moods, not to mention the way her attention fixed on the dark curve of his sensual mouth. Unfortunately, he followed right behind her, stealing the opportunity for her pounding heart to slow. As if that wasn't bad enough, she almost ran headlong into her father in the hallway.

Reluctantly, she performed introductions. "This is the man I was telling you about, Father. Captain Talbert, this is my father, Douglass McLowry."

"Eh? Oh, aye, that bodyguard nonsense." Douglass snorted. "A lot of fuss over nothing, to my way of thinking," her father continued in a helpful manner she could easily have done without. Douglass extended his hand to shake Talbert's. "But as long as it makes my daughter feel more at—" Stopping in midsentence, his eyes widened, and his mustache twitched. "Would that happen to be Jacob Augustus Talbert?"

"Yes, sir."

Douglass pumped the captain's hand with renewed vigor. "Welcome to my home, sir."

"You know him?" Meg burst out, flabbergasted by her father's abrupt change from polite host to enthusiastic businessman.

"I know of him. Why, Captain Talbert here owns five prime clipper ships and side-wheelers . . . a very respectable fleet." Nodding and smiling, Douglass released Talbert's hand and clapped him on the shoulder. "I hear you have access to ports in Japan and other areas of the East that most captains wouldn'a have a prayer of getting into. How do you do it?"

Talbert bowed slightly. "It helps to cultivate friends in

exotic places, sir, not to mention capitalizing on the ability to speak Japanese and Cantonese."

Douglass hooted with laughter. "Aye, I'll bet it does."

Meg's indignation curled like charred paper as heat climbed up her neck. Talbert was the owner of the *Shinjiro,* not just a hired captain? Good gracious, he was wealthy! Not on the scale of the railroad or silver barons who would be in attendance at her party tonight, surely, but her father reserved this particular brand of charm for potential bank customers—men with enough money to make a difference. And she'd offered to hire Talbert, then mocked his ability to afford the swords!

A frown of confusion replaced Douglass's smile. "What I dinna ken, is how you come to be acquainted with my Meggie. And why would you trouble yourself with my family affairs?"

Meg shot Talbert a warning look. He'd left the display room yesterday evening in such an abrupt fashion that she hadn't the opportunity to caution him against mentioning the blades to her father. This bit of information she intended to keep closely guarded—Douglass might, just might, take back his gift if he thought selling Talbert the swords would secure a coveted account for the bank.

"Your daughter and I met through a mutual acquaintance," Talbert answered, "someone with the public waterworks project. She told me of your difficulty with the Tongs. I was more than happy to help."

A choked sound escaped Meg's throat.

Douglass glanced at her. "Are you all right, lass?'

"I was just wondering that myself, Father. I think I feel a case of indigestion coming on." She glowered at Talbert. *Happy to help? Waterworks project?*

"Maybe you should go see Cook about a glass of milk for your stomach," Douglass offered. He turned back to Talbert, cutting off any effort to draw him away from this potentially explosive situation. "I still dinna understand, Captain. Why would you spend your time watching over an ornery old Scotsman like me?"

"Spending several months at sea can grow quite tedious. I've long thought a change of pace for a few weeks would do me good. Your daughter heard of my fascination with the Orient and the martial arts and charmingly asked me to share my expertise."

Smiling, Douglass hooked his thumbs under his lapels and rocked on his heels. "Aye, my Meggie's a clever lass, and that smile of hers has wrapped many a man around her finger."

Meg cringed. Couldn't Douglass hear the captain's sarcasm pulling beneath the surface like a dark undertow? The last thing Talbert needed to hear was her doting father's nonsense about how she habitually wrapped men around her finger. Talbert already considered her a shamefully manipulative—

"Do I have your permission to make some changes around the house for the sake of security, sir?"

"Aye, do as you see fit. Robert will assign some of the staff to help you. And dinna mind the cost. If you feel the change worthwhile, then surely the money will be well spent." Douglass's blue gaze took on a new intensity. "You will be attending our party tonight, will you no'?"

Meg's heart skipped a beat.

Hastily, she pointed out, "It will be difficult for the captain to fit a party into his schedule on such short notice." The first time her father bothered to stir himself for her party preparations, and he chose to call disaster down upon her head!

"I might be able to manage it," Talbert offered.

In a voice as dry as Death Valley, she said, "That would be delightful, but you won't know anyone there. I wouldn't want you to feel left out."

"You can take me under your wing and introduce me around."

"My wings, unfortunately, will be as small as a hummingbird's and moving just as fast tonight. With two hundred guests, I'll have no time to devote to a single one."

"I've fended for myself before. I believe I can manage."

Couldn't the man take a hint? Apparently only blatant rudeness penetrated that thick skull, but she couldn't very well succumb to her boiling temper with her father looking on.

"But I've yet to be invited," Talbert stressed. His eyes glittered with unholy amusement.

Her nails pressed painful half-moons into her palms. Well, why not invite him? She'd love to watch his arrogance wither among her polished friends. Talbert's experience was at sea, not in the ballroom. For once he would feel out of his element, and she would be there to enjoy his discomfiture.

"Consider yourself on the guest list, Captain Talbert."

He bowed slightly. "Since it means so much to you, Miss McLowry, I'll be happy to attend."

Silence reigned as their gazes locked in continuing antagonism. Gradually, Meg became aware of her father's intent watchfulness. She'd completely forgotten his presence!

"Excellent!" Douglass exclaimed, grinning. "I must be getting back to the bank, Meggie. Still much of the day left. I'll be seeing you at dinner, Captain, promptly at six-thirty." He bid them farewell and left.

Meg stifled a groan. Dinner, too? If Talbert did attend, she had no hope of enjoying this night.

Through her teeth, she informed him of the obvious. "You are a complete and utter scoundrel."

"You like me that way."

"On the contrary, I prefer men who are polite, gentle, and infinitely more civilized."

"Then you should be glad I'm not one of them," he countered coldly. "You misunderstood me, Miss McLowry. I meant that your type of gentleman—soft, pampered, socially prominent—would not be up to your task of fighting the Tong. A scoundrel, on the other hand, is just what you need." He took a step closer, looming over her. "Maybe you should keep closer track of your priorities rather than planning frivolous parties."

Releasing all her bottled-up frustration and anger, Meg swung her fist at Talbert's handsome face.

Her knuckles connected painfully with his callused palm. One instant his hand wasn't there, the next it erected an impenetrable shield against her attack. She cried out as his fingers captured and held her fist like a steel claw.

She should have remembered the speed he'd demonstrated at the Cobweb Palace. But he had a knack for shattering her poise.

His rough fingers slid down to clasp her wrist.

"That's not the proper way to make a fist, Miss McLowry."

Meg swallowed nervously. He was too quiet. Did his volume decrease in reverse proportion to his mounting fury? Had she pushed him too far?

He traced the ridges of her white knuckles. "So tight," he said wryly. "You're restricting the blood flow into your hand. Relax just a little."

Somehow, the command from her brain got past the chaos in her body. Renewed blood flow pinkened her knuckles.

Unbending her thumb from the base of her index finger, he moved it around to the front of her folded knuckles. "That's where it belongs. The other way not only weakens the fist, you'd likely break your thumb . . . if you ever connected with anything."

She'd like to connect with his nose right now. That would be a satisfying cure for this odd shortness of breath.

As if hearing her thoughts, Talbert carried her hand in a slow arc toward his face and pressed her clenched fist against his jaw.

"That's how it's done."

His skin was warm, roughened by the perpetual growth of beard that always darkened his jaw. Bronzed fingers engulfed her fist, making it look small and frail in comparison. A riot of sensations raced down Meg's spine. She snatched her hand away.

Rubbing her palm against her skirt, she said acidly, "Thank you for the lesson. I'll try to put it to good use very soon."

Gathering together the tattered edges of her dignity, she hurried down the hallway, intending to bury herself in work so she wouldn't have the time or energy to dwell on that momentary, disturbing urge to unfurl her hand against Talbert's cheek. She had wanted to experience the full measure of his warmth and texture against her palm. He was the most incredibly masculine man she'd ever encountered. But darkness seethed in his soul . . . and she preferred sunshine.

MEG CURBED HER haste, stopping for one last look in the mirror outside the drawing room. She tightened the rosettes holding her hair high on her head and checked the pearls threaded through her cascading curls. The fashionable arrangements of apricot-colored silk ribbon and white lace matched her ball gown. Some detached corner of Meg's mind acknowledged that she looked her best tonight, but she took little pleasure in the fact.

She'd been on pins and needles all afternoon wondering whether Talbert would actually follow through on his promise—or threat, depending on how one looked at it—to attend.

Stepping resolutely away from the mirror, Meg faced the drawing-room door. If she kept glowering at her own reflection it would prove impossible to smooth the rebellious, petulant expression from her mouth.

At least there was one small measure of hope for tonight. Talbert had remained busy until late, interviewing the servants, securing windows on the second floor, and working with the footmen to trim back trees that brushed against the house. There'd been no opportunity for him to prepare for this evening's festivities.

It would be so much better if he didn't come. He could prowl the night outside the house for all she cared. In fact, that's where he best fit in, with his dark coloring, aura of mystery, and tigerlike stealth.

"Is it time for us to go in?"

The rumble of Talbert's voice came from directly behind her.

A cold, sinking sensation overcame Meg. She spun around and froze, astonished.

Captain Talbert modeled the picture of masculine elegance in a black long-tailed coat and trousers, crisp white shirt, and ecru silk neckcloth complete with black pearl stickpin. A leather tie secured his long hair at the nape of his neck. Only his cleanly shaven face defied fashion, spurning the handlebar mustaches and exaggerated side-whiskers worn by nearly every man.

"My apologies, Miss McLowry. I didn't mean to startle you."

His intent gaze brought her back to reality. However

stunning, this did not rank as a complete transformation. He wasn't tamed, merely . . . restrained a bit. Clothes alone did not turn an arrogant sailor into a gentlemen.

"Breathe, Meghan," he said softly.

Inhaling sharply, she realized she'd been holding her breath. She had hired him because he was intelligent and observant, as well as physically perfect—for the task of bodyguard, that is—but she didn't want those keen gray eyes noting her every reaction!

"I haven't given you permission to use my first name," she ground out.

His mouth slanted up at one corner. He didn't appear contrite in the least.

"Don't you think you should patrol around the house tonight?" Meg suggested firmly. "*Outside,* I mean, to make sure no unsavory characters approach."

His smile widened. "I'm a bit overdressed for that, don't you think? Besides, I've arranged for patrols outside, leaving me free to play an important role in the house."

"Surely my father faces no threat with all these people around. You may consider yourself free to continue with your security arrangements instead," she insisted, waving her hand to encompass the entire property. "Put the time to good use, Captain."

"That's exactly what I am doing. This is an ideal opportunity to meet your father's acquaintances, to observe their reactions, overhear conversations, search for subtle hostilities. Danger can come from misplaced trust as easily as from a stranger, Miss McLowry."

And which type of danger do you pose for me, Captain? Mentally sidestepping the unwelcome question, she groused, "Oh, very well. By all means, join us." She reached for the doorknob.

"Your graciousness overwhelms me." He intercepted her hand, capturing and tucking it into the crook of his left arm. "We should present a united, congenial front, or raise a lot of uncomfortable questions. Try not to look like you've swallowed a sea urchin, Meghan."

Chapter Six

Soaked in sluices, fed from valley streams, it yields up silver dew that trickles through the fingers.

—TACHIBANA AKEMI (1812–1868)

MEG ATTEMPTED TO pull her hand back, but Talbert clamped it snugly against his side, trapping it between the hard ridge of his bicep and the solid wall of his chest. Only a major battle could pull her hand loose.

She was angry enough to oblige him, until he proved the strategic brilliance of his devious mind by opening the drawing-room door. How could she struggle to free herself in full view of her father and dinner guests?

Several comments about his lack of fair play sprang to her lips, but just then his warm breath feathered across her cheek, smelling of peppermint. The heat of his body invaded her arm, reminding her forcibly of all that potent masculinity.

"Maybe you can define 'unsavory characters' for me during dinner," he murmured as they stepped into the room.

His taunting comment grounded her quickly. Meg said through her teeth, "No need. You provide the perfect example."

A vibration rippled along his ribs into her arm.

He was laughing.

Feeling Jacob Talbert chuckle, when no one else in

the room could hear him, struck Meg as strangely intimate. She stared stupidly at her fingers curled over the
bulge of his upper arm, as if they belonged to someone
else. Her mind felt numb, detached, but her senses filled
with the texture of fine wool against her palm, the lingering scent of peppermint, and the sounds of her father's approach.

"About time the two of you joined us," Douglass said
jovially. "Come, Captain Talbert, and meet our other
guests."

Her father drew his new bodyguard away. A chill
swept across Meg's skin at the sudden loss of Talbert's
warmth.

Forcing her thoughts into less threatening channels,
Meg scanned the room with the trained eye of a woman
who'd run her father's household since age fifteen. Donald Harcourt, vice president of the bank, stood with his
customary whiskey in one hand, pausing long enough in
his habit of twirling the ends of his handlebar mustache
to shake Talbert's hand. Eugenie Harcourt—dressed in a
violet-and-white confection totally inappropriate for a
woman of her age and weight—exchanged greetings,
then watched the captain speculatively over the rim of
her wineglass. Their daughter, Tiffany, a lovely eighteen-
year-old with titian hair, blushed prettily.

Carl Edwards looked quite the polished gentleman in
a coat and vest of dove gray atop snowy white linen, Meg
noted proudly. He entertained the widow Bartlett and
her twenty-year-old son, Algernon, with some tale, but
paused to look Meg's way and bestow a warm smile.

Flattered by his attention, Meg felt color rising into
her cheeks.

Douglass returned, claiming her attention by taking
her hand. "You look lovely, Meggie. Happy birthday."

"Thank you, Father, but I've asked everyone not to

make a fuss. The invitations requested people to make a charitable donation in lieu of gifts."

"I wish you wouldna do that, Meggie. People like to give you pretty things."

Recalling the expensive, impersonal, and useless gifts she'd received last year, Meg said sadly, "I don't want them to feel obliged." *In many ways, today doesn't even feel like my birthday,* she wanted to add, but knew Douglass wouldn't understand. What a luxury it would be to receive a gift noted for its craftsmanship rather than its price, something made by loving hands rather than the jeweler's art, a token that fit her personality and love of beauty.

A gift from the heart.

That seemed as likely as finding an easy solution to the danger stalking her father . . . and a mercifully quick end to her turbulent association with Captain Talbert, the same man who balanced her reputation in those strong, callused hands. The simple truth would suffice to destroy her good name—she'd walked in on a naked man during his bath, visited a notorious alehouse on Meigg's Wharf, and taken a swing at Talbert's face on two occasions like a rowdy saloon wench. Could she trust him to keep such secrets?

Meg groaned inwardly, recalling iguanas, wild monkeys, parrots who squawked obscenities, and other creative means of retribution he'd employed.

She was doomed.

Carl approached with a glass of wine just as Mrs. Harcourt, one of the most notorious gossips in town, brought her daughter to Captain Talbert's attention. Meg stiffened. The silly woman was simpering, for heaven's sake, as if she considered Talbert a potential son-in-law!

Meg accepted the glass from Carl and took a long, bracing swallow.

Moving closer, Carl took up a position that restricted her view of the room and its occupants. She briefly wondered if he was monopolizing her attention, then dismissed the idea as uncharitable. *Someone,* she thought peevishly as she watched the group gather around Talbert, was making her paranoid about the motivations of every man.

Carl clinked his glass against her own, startling her. She didn't realize her attention had drifted.

"You look quite beautiful tonight," he said earnestly.

She relaxed, basking in the light of his approval. "Thank you."

"So this is the Talbert fellow your father mentioned this afternoon."

"Yes."

"And he's a houseguest? Meghan, are you sure that's wise?" After a backward glance, he lowered his voice and said emphatically, "How can you be sure the man made his money through honest means? He looks more the sort for train robbery. I, for one, wouldn't be surprised to see his face on a wanted poster."

"Don't you think your being a little harsh?"

"Not when your safety is involved."

She smiled gently, touched by his concern. His gaze dropped to her mouth.

A loud gasp and a giggle like tinkling bells came from the other side of the room. Meg leaned to the right, peering over Carl's shoulder.

Talbert stood with hands on hips, holding back the sides of his coat. Mrs. Harcourt fanned herself briskly, Tiffany giggled again, and Douglass slipped his reading glasses out of his breast pocket to look more closely at . . .

what? Some intriguing piece of jewelry? Talbert's black pearl stickpin was rare, but not that fascinating. With the captain standing in profile, Meg couldn't see what had claimed everyone's attention. Mrs. Bartlett and Algie gathered around. Even Donald seemed interested.

"What are they looking at?" Meg muttered.

Carl scowled. "Nothing of significance, I'm certain."

"You must show this to Meghan, Captain," Douglass boomed. "The lass loves all forms of art."

Talbert removed his hands from his hips. The coat fell into place, maintaining the mystery as he moved in her direction.

An odd breathlessness gripped Meg when he stood before her, his enigmatic gaze fixed on her face. Her undisciplined thoughts recalled their first encounter in the bathhouse, filled with the decadent images of sleek muscles and tight skin.

Talbert pulled back the lapels of his coat. His vest boasted the most exquisite, detailed embroidery she'd ever seen. Instantly captivated, she managed to shake off the disturbing images and regain her composure.

On the left, a garden of greenery and rocks surrounded a temple. Within the temple, beneath its curved eaves, stood a tomb—no, Meg realized as she took a step closer—it was a shrine of some sort, with collections of flowers and strange brown sticks around its base. The scene on the right portrayed an Asian couple in a passionate embrace.

This is what had earned giggles from Tiffany and scandalized gasps from Mrs. Harcourt? The man and woman were fully clothed. Meg thought the scene tasteful and full of artistic grace, with the lovers' pale faces, jet black hair, and lovely garments. Although fashioned of silk thread, something about the way the man's hand tenderly cupped the woman's cheek caused tears to swell behind Meg's eyes. Compelled to touch, to fully appreciate, Meg reached out and stroked her fingertips across the soft silk of the couple's faces.

There was nothing soft about the man beneath the vest. Even with a light touch, she detected hard muscle, sinew and a primitive heat.

She swallowed twice before finding her voice. "It's quite beautiful."

"Thank you," he said gruffly.

Dear heavens, she thought frantically, what had possessed her to display such familiarity with the captain? What must the others think? A decent young woman didn't caress a man's chest.

Withdrawing her fingertips from Talbert's vest casually, as if there were no cause for embarrassment, Meg laughed and said lightly, "Embroidery of this quality should be in a museum. Don't you agree, Father?"

"Aye, 'tis very fine." Douglass's brisk, cheerful tone cut through the tense atmosphere. "Maybe I'll ask the captain if he has more such vests . . . a bit larger in size, of course," he added with a chuckle, patting his hands against his barrel chest.

"Oh, yes, quite exquisite," chimed in Mrs. Bartlett, sounding relieved.

"I think so, too," agreed Tiffany, stepping forward. Her mother grasped her by the wrist and pulled her back.

Talbert bowed. "The Japanese woman who embroidered this would be pleased that you place such value on her work."

Donald Harcourt grunted and drained the last of his whiskey. "I think you're all making a lot of fuss over nothing."

Mrs. Bartlett shot him a quelling glance, then asked, "The garments on the figures are particularly lovely, Captain. What are they called?"

"Kimonos."

Meg breathed a sigh of relief. The crisis was past. They had all brushed off the incident as insignificant. If only she could do the same. Was her wretched curiosity to blame? She wasn't sure what disturbed her more . . . the immodesty of finding it so natural to reach out and touch Talbert, or the way his eyes had darkened and stirred when she did.

Algie leaned forward for a closer look at the vest. "I say, what are the brown sticks in that little temple?"

"The building is a shrine," Talbert explained. "The sticks are burning incense."

"Then you must be of the Buddhist persuasion, Captain," Carl cut in dryly, instantly changing the tone of the conversation from inquisitive to challenging. Meg glanced at him in dismay. However religiously tolerant the residents of San Francisco might fancy themselves, feeling against the Chinese ran high and it was no light matter to accuse someone of practicing Buddhism.

Talbert leveled his cool gray gaze on her father's protégé. "The shrine is Shinto, Mr. Edwards, a complex faith that focuses on honoring one's ancestors. I was born into a Protestant family in Europe, then raised in a Japanese village whose people have passed down Christianity to each generation from the time of the Jesuit missionaries. But I respect the culture and other religions of my adopted country."

With the lack of tact inherent in the young, Algie blurted out, "How did you come to be in Japan, Captain?"

At first Meg expected Talbert to sidestep the question with his usual skill. Then his dark gaze shifted her way, capturing her like a fear-frozen mouse in the path of a hunting hawk.

"I was shipwrecked there at the age of ten."

His unemotional answer echoed in her ears even after he turned back to the guests.

"Oh, my, so young!" Algie's mother exclaimed in sympathy. "Didn't you have family to watch over you?"

"I sailed with my father, ma'am, but he died in the shipwreck along with his crew. I was the only one to make it ashore alive."

Mrs. Harcourt shuddered. "How horrid for you! To lose your dear father, then to be trapped alone in that barbaric country!"

Meg winced, recalling his sensitivity to any criticism of Japan. *Manners are so much a part of the Japanese culture, so polished, they are practically an art form.*

"I suppose it's a matter of perspective, ma'am. The Japanese call outsiders *gaijin*, their own term for foreign barbarian."

Mrs. Harcourt laughed and sipped her wine daintily, as if the idea that she could be considered barbaric was ludicrous.

Carl interjected, "And they let you live? I've heard the Japanese practiced a fanatical isolationist policy. The presence of a foreigner on their shores was punishable by death."

"That is true," Talbert admitted. "Before the arrival of Commodore Perry sixteen years ago, and the establishment of a treaty with the Americans, only the Dutch were allowed to trade in Japan."

"Ah . . . then you must be Dutch, Captain," Carl drawled. "Perhaps that is why I can't place your odd accent."

"My accent, or lack of, comes from living in many countries and speaking several languages."

Carl narrowed his eyes.

"But how did you survive if they killed outsiders?" Algie asked eagerly, his eyes alight with fascination.

"Apparently even the Japanese hesitate to kill a ten-year-old boy."

"Still, it must have been very frightening for you," Tiffany commented softly. Her sincere voice provided a refreshing contrast to Carl's challenging tone and the other guests' rather morbid fascination.

Apparently touched by her genuine sympathy, Talbert smiled as he added, "I often wonder how different things might have been if I had come ashore farther north. I was lucky to arrive on the southern island of Kyoshu, where the Christian influence is the strongest. The entire local village took me in, considering me a sign from God because of the cross I wore about my neck."

He touched his neckcloth. Meg's gaze dropped to the lean, tapered fingers of his hand. Did he still have the cross? Did he wear it even now, nestled among the crisp black hairs on his chest? Was it warmed by his skin? She suddenly felt rather warm herself. Dammit, where was Robert to announce dinner?

"How exciting!" exclaimed Mrs. Bartlett. "Why, that's a story you'll be able to tell your own children someday . . . when you return home and settle down, that is. Where is your home, Captain?"

The muscles beneath Talbert's eyes tightened almost imperceptibly.

Robert arrived to announce that dinner was served.

Carl appeared instantly at Meg's side, cutting off her view of Talbert's intriguing reaction. He offered his arm. "May I escort you in to dinner, my dear?"

Meg frowned. "I shouldn't let you, not after the way you've been baiting Captain Talbert," she scolded in hushed tones. "You are forgetting that he is a guest in my home."

"No, that's exactly what bothers me. That fellow is

living under your roof, able to see you every day when I'm not afforded the same privilege."

Meg felt a twinge of guilt at the reminder of how she'd rejected his marriage proposals.

The other guests paired off behind them—except for the captain, whose last-minute addition to the party precluded finding him a dinner partner. Meg rested her fingers on Carl's sleeve. On the way to the dining room, however, she found herself more aware of the lone figure at the rear of the group than the man at her side.

"And, as I told you, I don't trust the man," Carl hissed. "I'm concerned for your safety, Meghan, and it makes me say crazy things."

"That's no excuse for rudeness."

He pulled out her chair when they reached the long, rectangular table. "Then I must admit the truth." Bending over her shoulder as she sat down, he whispered, "I'm quite jealous." His warm breath tickled her neck.

Meg resisted the urge to scratch her ear. "Jealous? Of Captain Talbert?" Candlelight highlighted Carl's blond hair. Meg indulged in a little frisson of pleasure. This incredibly handsome man was jealous? Over her?

"Yes, my dear. I beg you, tell me there's no need."

"Of course not. The very notion is ridiculous. Talbert is merely in charge of my father's security."

"Excellent," he responded, smiling broadly. "That's what I wanted to hear." He briefly squeezed her shoulder before taking his seat opposite.

Carl's hands were strong and cool, smooth, refined. A contrasting image flashed into her mind: a pair of rugged, deeply bronzed hands holding a wild iguana in a way that the creature instinctively felt safe, secure, protected.

Meg looked up suddenly to find Talbert watching her, his gaze dark, shuttered. Her breath caught, fluttering in her chest like a trapped bird. She looked down and smoothed her napkin over the gown.

Questions continued throughout dinner, though Talbert deftly steered the subject away from anything personal, focusing all attention on his travels. Carl, apparently honoring Meghan's request, dedicated himself to charming Mrs. Bartlett and Mrs. Harcourt.

Meg picked irritably at her food, managing to take a bite now and then before the plates were removed for each subsequent course.

Her annoyance was directed at herself. It took others to shine light on the fact that Jacob Talbert had led a fascinating life, though touched by tragedy, and she hadn't even thought to ask.

Then again, she didn't want to know, didn't want to become more aware that he had been a man with a life, obligations, and goals before she knocked him off his chosen path.

He was a man hardened by experience, supremely capable of carrying out the terms of their bargain.

So why couldn't she stop thinking of the ten-year-old boy he'd once been—bereft of his father, cut off from his home, and lost in a strange and violent land?

AFTER DINNER THE number of guests grew significantly, along with the volume of noise. Jake quickly discovered that the party—which he'd demanded Meg cancel—celebrated her birthday, and for some unfathomable reason, that darkened his mood even more than Mrs. Harcourt's bigotry or Carl Edwards's subtle attacks.

What had compelled him to share even a portion of his background? Some wayward desire to startle those pompous dinner guests out of their complacency?

He could only recall the open expression on Meghan's face when she touched his vest. Her intensity, her sincere appreciation of the art, had sliced through some barrier he'd erected long ago.

He watched Meghan from across the ballroom as she made her guests feel welcome. She appeared ethereal in her apricot gown, the coloring complementing her skin like the soft reflection of lamplight on peach marble.

He noted her poise, the friendly smiles, the ladylike reserve. She remained cool and collected, even when San Francisco's elite vied for her attention, young men stuttered and blushed, intimidated by her beauty, or servants whispered to her of minor crises.

Apparently, he was the only one who drove Meghan McLowry to distraction.

Jake smiled grimly.

She held his past, his future, his means of redemption in her graceful hands. He could not forget that, not even for a moment. Having to bargain for the swords qualified as a serious affront to his honor. Nothing was more important to a samurai than duty and honor—he ought to know better than most, for what little he had left was so very precious.

An hour later, once the merriment was well under way, Douglass broke away from the group and headed for a door at the far end of the ballroom. Four men trailed in his wake.

Jake came instantly alert, though he perceived no threat. Four aging gentlemen with expanding paunches and salt-and-pepper whiskers hardly fit the mold of assassin he'd learned to distinguish over the years.

Nevertheless, he followed, slipping through a forest of colorful gowns. A variety of liberally applied perfumes, from florals to musk, clashed in an assault on his senses.

The smell of cigar smoke clung to men's coats, adding an unpleasant tang to the air.

He entered the room where the five men had disappeared, immediately recognizing the sound of a fresh, stiff deck of cards being shuffled. A half-dozen card tables were arranged beneath the chandeliers, all vacant this early in the party, except for the one occupied by Douglass and his cronies. A servant moved about the round table, setting stacks of chips and a clean glass at the elbow of each man. Just before departing, the servant placed a bottle of Scotch whiskey near the host.

Douglass looked up and grinned. "Hello, Captain. We were about to sit down to a friendly hand of poker. I'm no' much for dancing." He rapped the deck on the hardwood table, squaring the corners, then shuffled the cards again. "Would you care to join us?"

"Thank you, but no," Jake responded, frowning. Poker? What about the other guests? Surely Douglass wasn't leaving the responsibilities of hosting the party entirely to Meghan . . . particularly on her birthday?

The Scotsman's ruddy brows rose. "Ah, I see. You've come in here to watch over me. That bodyguard nonsense."

"Something like that," Jake countered ironically. The difference between Meghan's obsession and her father's dismissive attitude was proving an additional challenge. He moved around to stand at the father's shoulder.

Chuckling, Douglass dealt out the cards. "The only danger here is that these lads will fleece me of my money." Ripples of amusement followed the click of chips as the men tossed their ante into the center. "Be off with you, Captain. You're suppose to be enjoying the party."

"I think I should stay."

"Blessed Saint Ninian, you're as stubborn as Meggie! Nay, lad, you'll just make me nervous if you hover over me like a mother hen. I need to concentrate on the game." He hesitated in the act of arranging his cards, leaning close to Jake to whisper hopefully, "Unless those eastern skills of yours help you sense when a man is bluffing?"

They did, but Jake refused to allow Douglass to use him in gaining an unfair advantage. "Sorry, sir, but I left Japan before they got to that part of the training."

"Too bad." Douglass sighed. "You do dance, though?"

"Yes, sir." Music and dancing were two of the few things Jake truly enjoyed about western culture.

"Then go ask Meggie for the next waltz."

Startled by the suggestion, Jake protested, "Miss McLowry will be much in demand tonight. I doubt she'll have the time or the inclination to dance with me." That was phrasing it mildly. Meghan would love to hand him a blistering set-down in front of her friends. He wasn't fool enough to give her the chance.

A smile curved the Scotsman's lips. "You might be surprised, lad." He laid his cards on the table, facedown, and picked up the deck. Looking about expectantly, he drawled, "Well, gentlemen?"

Initial bets joined the chips in the center. One man tucked his chin and grumbled, "Give me three." The other three men followed with requests for one card each.

"Dinna let the evening go by without asking Meggie to dance. 'Tis her birthday, after all," Douglass insisted as he dealt two cards for himself.

Douglass seemed determined to chase him off, and actually, Jake didn't want to miss the opportunity to observe the guests. Yet the idea of leaving Douglass unattended caused him a nagging unease.

Briefly, Jake thought of Akira, then immediately dismissed the idea. He wanted to involve his friend in this business as little as possible. Neither would Akira feel comfortable in the profoundly western atmosphere of the party. Jake had left the old samurai upstairs, enjoying quiet meditation and some of his favorite pursuits.

Jake called over the footman, who was placing cards, chips, and ashtrays on the other tables to prepare for the tobacco-smoking scions of society who would soon gravitate to this room.

"Wilkins," Jake began, recognizing the footman as one of the young men who'd helped trim trees that afternoon, "Will you tell Phillip I need him here, right away?"

"Yes, sir."

Five minutes later, Phillip arrived, taking up a position near the door, alert and watchful from his vantage point.

Jake relaxed, knowing Douglass would be safe. He might as well join the party, though he belonged with these people about as much as a street-toughened mongrel among pampered pedigreed dogs.

Stepping through the door, Jake immediately collided with Algernon Bartlett, who barreled into him while looking back over his shoulder.

Algie grunted as he hit. "I say, now!" he exclaimed, staggering back a step. His young face flushed with embarrassment. "Oh, it's you, Captain Talbert. My apologies. I guess I wasn't watching where I was going."

"That much I noticed," Jake muttered. "Where are you off to in such a hurry?"

"Uh . . . well . . . nowhere in particular," Algie hedged, smoothing back a lock of blond hair that had tumbled over his forehead.

"Then I suppose going through me is as good a way as any to get there," Jake teased.

Algie grinned. "Just need to get away from my mother for a while. Fond of the dear woman, of course, but she has trouble loosening the apron strings. You know how it is." With a sharp tug on his coat, he continued on course, disappearing through an adjacent doorway.

Jake's amusement died like a snuffed candle flame. He stood frozen, alone, the sharp sting of regret lancing through his chest.

No, Algie, I don't know how it is. I don't even remember what my real mother looked like. Maybe you should appreciate what you have.

He did remember images, impressions: the slide of a brush through Sophia Talbert's glossy black hair, the melodious depth of her voice when she sang to him in Italian, the way she would fling herself into his father's arms each time Michael Talbert returned from the sea.

Why couldn't he remember her face, dammit!

He lifted one hand to his neckcloth, pressing the warm metal of the gold, Roman-style cross into his skin, feeling its shape. This was all he had left of his mother. She'd fastened the chain about his neck just before he and his father left on that ill-fated voyage.

After he'd left Japan, efforts to find his widowed mother in Britain had failed. Too much had changed in twenty-six years. Apparently she'd remarried, but the church records had been destroyed in a fire, obliterating any record of her new name and severing his ability to trace her. For all he knew, she could be dead.

There was no sense in looking back.

Shoving aside the sad memories, Jake shifted his attention back to the crowd. Time to mingle and see what he could learn about Douglass's acquaintances.

He noticed that Tiffany slipped away a few minutes later . . . through the same doorway Algie had used. Her oblivious mother stood in animated conversation with a group of women.

Jake sighed with resignation. This promised to be a long, tedious night if a tryst between two young lovers proved the most interesting thing to catch his attention.

"I JUST LOVE Meghan's garden, don't you, Algie?" Tiffany purred. "It's open to the sky and has that beautiful fountain. So romantic."

"That's why I thought of bringing you here, sweetest. It's the perfect private place for a man and woman who feel about each other the way we do." Algernon tried the knob on the glass door. "Damn!"

"Oh, no, it's locked!" she cried, thrusting her lower lip out in that pouty way that drove him to distraction. "I guess we'll just have to go back."

"Wait!" he burst out. "I think my pocket knife has a blade that will fit. It just might—"

"You mean pick the lock? How naughty." She didn't sound particularly scandalized.

He bent over to work on the lock. "I want you all to myself, Tiff. I'm a desperate man."

She giggled. "Hurry, Algie. I hate to miss the party. The McLowrys give the best parties, don't you think?"

"Yes, of course, the very best," he muttered, while trying to give his complete attention to the task at hand. But how could he concentrate when she breathed on the back of his ear? His fingers trembled. The lock gave way with a snick, but he accidentally broke off the slender blade inside. The entire mechanism jammed open, including the latch. Oh, well, he thought with a shrug, pocketing the knife.

Hiding the damage from Tiffany, he guided her inside the atrium. The fountain gurgled at the opposite end of the garden, an ideal backdrop for a romantic tryst. He urged her over to the nearest bench. The dark, mysterious tangle of vegetation crowded the edges of the path. She toppled into his lap with a tiny "Oh" when he tugged on her arm. He stopped her sudden fit of giggles by pulling her mouth down to meet his.

She returned his kiss eagerly, tasting of champagne. Grateful for a low décolletage, he pulled back and hungrily eyed the dark crevice just above a tantalizing edging of lace. Soon she would be begging for him to undo her bodice. He was just burying his face in the rose-scented valley between her breasts when she suddenly tensed.

"What was that?" she whispered.

Algernon sighed. "My nose, darling. I know it's a little—just a very little, mind you—on the large side. I promise to be more careful next time." He dove for her cleavage again.

She grasped his shoulders and shoved back, stopping him just short of his goal. "No, silly. The noise. Didn't you hear it?" she asked.

Stifling a groan of impatience, he murmured, "It's the beat of my heart, dearest, pounding out a rhythm of love and devotion." That sort of declaration gained a melting sigh from her every time. Warming up his lips with kissing motions, he zeroed in on the delectable target that kept eluding him. A petite yet firm hand unexpectedly cupped his chin and shoved upward. Algernon suddenly found himself, muzzled and immobilized, staring up into Tiffany's intense face.

"No, Algie, you idiot, the sound was nothing like that. It—" She broke off with a gasp. "There it is again! Are you deaf? I think it came from right behind the bench."

With his head tilted at an awkward angle and his compressed jaw causing a ringing in his ears, Algernon couldn't hear a thing. His answer came out a garbled "Mmmrph" against the fingers pressed over his lips.

Leaning close, she whispered in a tone of excited horror, "It sounded like some creature lurking through the plants behind you." Suddenly she shrieked, scaring the wits out of him, and leaped off his lap. Backing slowly, she pointed a shaking finger in his general direction and hissed, "Something . . . something is there! I saw that bush move, Algie!"

"Now, love," he soothed, standing and massaging his chin. "It's just your imagination. No need for hysterics."

She paused in her retreat and gaped. "You don't believe me?" she asked, sounding a tad bit indignant.

"Oh, no, not that, it's just—" He ground to a halt, realizing he was floundering.

Her glare barely resembled the sweet, affable Tiffany he knew. "Hmmph! Some knight in shining armor you are!" Twitching her skirt out of the way, she turned and flounced toward the door.

"Of course I'm your brave knight, sweetest," he called after her, giving in to desperation. "Don't go! Just let me find a sword and shield, fair Tiffany, and I'll slay dragons for you!"

Gesturing grandly with his right arm, he spun to face their abandoned seat, only to see something out of a nightmare leap onto the bench. He froze, missing the remainder of his beloved's dramatic departure. The creature's tail, as long as its huge body, snaked against the white metal. Horrible spines lined its scaly back. It opened its mouth and hissed.

At any moment, Algernon expected its fiery breath to light up the night.

Staggering backward in a panic, he tripped and landed hard on his rump. Gravel pressed painfully into his palms, then pelted the vegetation like hailstones when he flipped over and scrambled for the exit.

Panting, he yanked the door shut behind him. As he

leaned against the glass, trying to slow his genuinely pounding heart, Algernon began to feel quite ridiculous. A dragon, indeed! He chuckled raggedly. His imagination, nothing more, a product of too much champagne and Tiffany's silly rantings.

If fact, he thought, brightening, maybe they'd both simply been overcome by passion. Clinging to that hope, he smoothed back his hair and tugged down his vest, then started after her. As an afterthought, he brushed off the seat of his trousers.

The damaged latch failed to hold.

The door slowly drifted open.

Chapter Seven

Submit to you—could that be what you're saying? The way ripples on the water submit to an idling wind?
— Ono no Komachi (ninth century)

"WHAT WAS MEGHAN thinking? I can't comprehend the effect she was trying to achieve with that . . . that oddity!"

At the sound of Mrs. Harcourt's voice, Meg stopped cold in the doorway of the small dining parlor. The room was empty except for two women, Mrs. Charles Crocker and Eugenie Harcourt, both so intent on their discussion they didn't see her standing there.

The food display that had earned Mrs. Harcourt's derision remained out of Meg's line of sight, set back into a shallow alcove. What could possibly be wrong? The chef considered the fruit and vegetable table—whimsically fashioned like a tropical jungle, complete with a colorful mountain and trees fashioned of celery and lettuce—his crowning achievement for the party.

Dismay cut through Meg. Although she could easily dismiss Mrs. Harcourt's criticisms, for the woman typically spoke out of envy, Meg deeply admired Mrs. Crocker. The wife of the chairman of the Central Pacific Railroad was well known for her graciousness and charitable works.

Regarding the display in question with a thoughtful expression, Mrs. Crocker tapped one forefinger against her lower lip. "I find it very original, Eugenie," she countered. "I do believe Meghan has achieved a delightful representation of a prehistoric world. I like the volcano and palm trees, and that centerpiece makes the perfect dinosaur."

Volcano? Dinosaur? Meg stared at the women. How had her delicious tropical paradise turned into a prehistoric landscape?

"Whatever are you talking about?" Mrs. Harcourt retorted.

"Really, Eugenie, don't you read any part of the newspaper other than the fashion and social sections? There have been discoveries in recent years—some, I'm proud to say, first found by surveyors for my husband's railroad—of bones belonging to huge lizards, called dinosaurs, that lived millions of years ago. Why, the creatures were apparently bigger than my private railroad car!"

Meg's heart started racing at the word "lizards." No . . . it couldn't be. . . . Talbert wouldn't stoop that low. Would he?

Eugenie huffed. "Nevertheless, it's enough to put off one's appetite for fruit forever. Why would she put that strawberry in its mouth? It's not a succulent pig, for Pete's sake."

"I'm sure even dinosaurs had to eat," Mrs. Crocker said dryly. "Just be glad it's not a carnivore."

"A what?" asked Mrs. Harcourt.

Mrs. Crocker sighed.

Meg couldn't stand the suspense. Fearing the worst, she moved forward to join the women. The scene on the table came into view.

One of the iguanas lay atop the mountain of fruit, perched on slices of cantaloupe and formerly neat rows of strawberries. The gaslight on the rear wall clearly outlined its spiny silhouette. It must have gorged itself on the meticulously arranged display, for it sat motionless, in no hurry to finish off the strawberry held in its open mouth.

Mrs. Crocker greeted Meg with a warm smile. "Oh, there you are, my dear. We were just admiring your clever centerpiece. Weren't we, Eugenie?"

Mrs. Harcourt lifted her double chin and sniffed. "Well, I will say this, it is certainly . . . inventive."

They didn't know it was alive! Meg's knees wobbled with relief.

Forming her lips into an awkward smile, Meg wondered how one chased a scion of society out of one's dining parlor. A dozen flimsy excuses churned through her mind.

The iguana had no intention of waiting for a brilliant revelation to strike. As Meg stood frozen, the reptile slowly swiveled its head toward Eugenie Harcourt. The poor woman's mouth dropped open. Then, the iguana slowly bit down on the strawberry. Red juices from the crushed fruit dribbled down its jaw, making it look like a predator dining on a bloody carcass.

Meg wanted to cover her eyes, or better yet, her ears, since it didn't take a scientist to figure out what was coming next.

Mrs. Harcourt shrieked—a plaintive, half-choked sound. Her eyes rolled up to the back of her head as she slowly crumpled.

Feeling as if she watched the dramatic display from a distance, Meg was surprised when the plump woman's weight burdened her arms. Only when she sank with the helpless woman to the floor did Meg realize she had rushed forward to break the fall. She kneeled on the carpet, using her lap to cradle Mrs. Harcourt's head.

No one rushed into the room. Thankfully, the music and merriment in the ballroom had prevented anyone from hearing Mrs. Harcourt's scream.

Yet the worst had happened, for the one woman whose good opinion Meg desperately desired had borne witness to it all.

"I'm so sorry," she moaned, looking up at Mrs. Crocker.

Instead of launching into a scold, the railroad baron's wife chuckled and knelt down next to her, carefully arranging the hem of her ivory satin gown. "What is that odd creature?"

"An iguana, from the Pacific coast of Mexico," Meg said dully, able to do little more than repeat Talbert's description.

"And did you have the iguana brought all the way here to be a centerpiece on your table, Meghan?" Mrs. Crocker asked gently.

It took a second for the comment to register, to realize the older woman was teasing. Meg's sudden crack of laughter came out more like a squeak. No wonder the Crockers were known as a fun, energetic couple, beloved by all of San Francisco society. The railroad baron's wife found this amusing rather than scandalous!

"It belongs to Captain Talbert. We were keeping it for him in our garden atrium, which I thought was locked."

"So, in addition to being delightfully attractive, the captain keeps an iguana as a pet. How intriguing."

Meg refrained from pointing out that he was no doubt the troublesome prankster who had loosed the iguana on her party. "Actually, he brought two of—" She stopped with a gasp. "Oh, no! Where is the other one?"

"Two iguanas? I suggest you take care of this one first,

before any other guests decide to visit the fruit table. Then you can hunt down the other."

"Yes, yes, of course. Could you . . . I mean, would you mind—?" Meg pleaded, glancing down at the still insensible Mrs. Harcourt.

"Certainly." They exchanged positions, shifting the woman to Mrs. Crocker's lap.

Feeling too guilty to abandon Mrs. Harcourt just yet, Meg grabbed a linen napkin and began fanning the woman's ashen face.

In a voice vibrating with amusement, Mrs. Crocker pointed out, "Meghan, do stop trying to rouse Eugenie. How can I convince her that she imagined the whole thing if she awakes to find the iguana still here?"

"Oh," Meg exclaimed, abruptly dropping the napkin. "You would do that for me?"

Mrs. Crocker spoke in a secretive tone, "Just between you and me, Eugenie spread some rather ugly gossip about a friend of mine last year. I've never quite forgiven her for that."

Impulsively, Meg laid her palm over the older woman's hand. "You are so kind, Mrs. Crocker. Thank you so much."

"I've always thought you a delightful young woman, quite out of the common way. And I admire the way you help Mary Lambert and her girls."

Meg tensed. "You know about that?"

Smiling, Mrs. Crocker added, "I found out only recently. I have my own charities, and even devoted volunteers tend to talk among themselves. I can see why you keep it secret, however. There are many among us who just wouldn't understand giving aid to Chinese prostitutes."

Meg found herself explaining. "Most of those poor

girls don't have a choice. They are sold into slavery as children, then raised to believe that selling themselves for their masters' gain is the only way to survive. Mary Lambert is the only missionary I know with the courage to offer the girls refuge. The situation is so horrible."

"Yes, quite tragic," Mrs. Crocker agreed, shuddering.

Just then, a servant came into the room with a tray of clean plates. The man stopped abruptly, gaping at the women, then the iguana.

Rising, Meg sighed in relief, "Saul, you picked the perfect moment to come in. As you can see, one of Captain Talbert's pets has escaped. I need you to catch it and take it back to the atrium."

"Me, Miss Meghan? You mean . . . touch it?" Shaking his head, he backed up a few steps. "No, no, I couldn't possibly. Sorry, miss, I've a dread fear of reptiles, and somethin' that big, well—it just ain't natural! What if he bites me?" He sucked in his breath. "Can a body catch rabies from a 'gator?"

Terrific. All she needed now was for Saul to spread panic among the rest of her staff. She snapped in disgust, "It's an iguana, not an alligator, and I believe it's impossible for a reptile to carry rabies." She didn't have time for him to return to the kitchen for help. It was essential she remove the iguana before Mrs. Harcourt awoke or anyone else walked in. "Oh, bother, I'll do it myself. The least you can do is clear the dishes off that small side table and hand me the tablecloth."

Saul obeyed quickly, handing her the white linen.

Meg gingerly lowered the tablecloth over the iguana, fearful it would start struggling in a wild bid for escape. She'd seen the power of those legs in action.

It proved surprisingly docile. She fervently hoped a

full iguana proved to be a happy iguana. Tucking the tablecloth around it securely, she restricted the movements of its legs while taking care not to bind it too tight.

"Throw out the fruit it was sitting on, Saul, and what fell on the floor, then rearrange the display quickly," she ordered. "Bring more fruit from the kitchen to fill in the gaps."

Meg gathered the volatile package into her arms. She murmured low, husky words to the iguana, feeling rather silly but trusting that an oversized lizard could be soothed in the same manner one could calm a skittish horse.

After checking to make sure she wouldn't step on the iguana's tail, which dangled nearly to her hem, Meg rushed from the site of the near disaster. A last glimpse of Mrs. Harcourt struck a discordant note of guilt.

Hurrying down the empty hallway with the awkward bundle, Meg tried to imagine herself carrying a very long lapdog. The comparison struck her as ridiculous.

She smiled.

The muscles beneath her cheekbones trembled.

Meg ground to a halt. Were her cheek muscles so underutilized that they shook with the strain of a little humor? Did she really smile so seldom?

Warily, she inched in front of a gold-framed mirror hanging on the wall. The sophisticated woman staring back with wide blue eyes was one of San Francisco's leading hostesses, a daughter Douglass McLowry could be proud of. She had lived up to—even exceeded—everyone's expectations.

Wasn't that something to smile about? Meg spread her mouth in a broad, experimental grin. The muscles twitched again, a spasmodic reaction beyond her control.

The smile dropped away like a stone. More unsettled than she cared to admit, Meg impulsively stuck out her tongue at her reflection. The gesture felt so natural that, with a shock, she realized she didn't particularly like what she saw . . . or who she'd become.

Meg recalled laughing and smiling a great deal before her mother died. Harsh reality had demanded an instantaneous, seamless transition from mourning fifteen-year-old to capable lady of the house. Without her help, Douglass would have wallowed in his grief. His helplessness in domestic and social matters would have sabotaged a rising career in banking. He'd counted on her, and she'd risen from the ashes of her own grief to meet his needs and hold her family together.

But she'd lost something of herself in the process.

And she wasn't sure how to define it, much less get it back.

Loneliness squeezed her heart. A recurring dream came to mind—a comforting shoulder to lean on, a strength greater than her own. The man she'd created in her fantasies remained misted in shadows, faceless, even though she found complete security in his arms. She attempted, not for the first time, to transpose Carl's face over the image. Something rejected the combination; it didn't feel quite right. And why should it, for the man in her dream was too perfect, too good to be true!

The iguana squirmed. Effectively wrenched from her thoughts, Meg glanced down at the beast. She stroked its chest through the cloth, and it settled quietly in appreciation.

Why did she live to please everyone else when the sacrifice made her miserable?

And why, exactly, was she letting Jacob Talbert get away with this latest prank without paying penance?

A new sense of daring nudged aside the melancholy. An almost forgotten sense of mischief glittered through Meg. Oddly enough, her confrontations with Talbert had been the only times that she'd felt truly alive, exhilarated, and the loneliness had retreated before the sheer force of his vitality.

A footman crossed the hallway, a tray full of champagne glasses balanced high on one hand.

Meg called him over. "Please find Captain Talbert and tell him to meet me in the west parlor in five minutes."

The footman blinked owlishly after tearing his gaze from the iguana. "Er . . . yes, Miss Meghan, right away." He hurried off, the golden champagne swaying perilously close to the rims of the glasses.

"Now I'll have a chance to sit down. You're getting heavy," Meg muttered to the iguana as she started toward the parlor. "Well, my fruit-loving friend, I wonder how your master will react when I return you to him? Since he must have turned you loose in the first place, being confronted with his misdeed ought to put a chink in his armor of arrogance."

The reptile bobbed its head as if in complete accord with her plan.

JAKE SENSED MEGHAN'S gaze boring into him the moment he stepped through the parlor door. A samurai's refined instincts always warned him when danger approached, but with Meghan it took on a unique character of its own—like a jolt of lightning setting fire to his skin.

His heart rate doubled when he recognized the scaly head and tail sticking out of the bundle on her lap.

This could prove very interesting.

Jake's lips indulged in a slow, lazy curl as he closed the door and moved into the room. Sitting on the blue settee, Meghan looked magnificent. The lightning tingle of anticipation skittered along his nerve endings until his whole body felt invigorated, alive in a way he'd never experienced before.

Bless the iguanas. Bringing them from the ship had been a stroke of genius, though he had no idea how this one had escaped from the atrium.

"Captain Talbert," she began with a cool reserve that didn't diminish the spark in her eyes. "I believe your pet got loose."

"So I see," he countered calmly, concealing his admiration for her courage. Most women would faint dead away at the idea of holding an iguana. He felt like applauding her bravado, but he didn't want to do anything that would lessen her anger and the resultant heat between them. He found this Meghan much more intriguing than the ice maiden.

"I knew you would be worried about her, so I thought it best to return her to you right away," Meghan said, too sweetly.

She rose and gently thrust the iguana into his arms, tablecloth and all.

He recognized the cutting wit balanced on the edge of Meghan's voice. In that moment, he didn't care about making her pay a price for manipulating him. He only wanted to move closer, match wits with her, see how she would react if he returned fire with fire.

Jake stilled, stunned by the revelation. With this woman, his sole priority should be a subtle retaliation while gaining possession of the swords.

Securing his hold on the reptile, he said dryly. "Very thoughtful of you, Miss McLowry, to watch out for my pet."

"I wonder how this one could have escaped? As you may recall, Captain, the door to the atrium was locked."

At first he didn't believe his ears, then Jake realized he

should have guessed she would jump to the conclusion
that he'd released the iguana.

His gaze dropped to her parted lips. Desire hit him,
hard, driving all the way to his bones, leaving him shaken.
Unlike the manageable lust of his usual encounters, this
possessed a life of its own, all-consuming.

Dammit, he was behaving no better than an undisciplined youth ruled by his loins. A samurai should have
his body, as well as his emotions, under control at all
times.

"An unfortunate accident, obviously," he ground out.
"Where did you find her?"

"That's not important. Just put her safely away, if you
please."

"Certainly," he said between his teeth, resenting her
poise. How could she remain so cool, so unaffected,
when he needed the tablecloth to conceal the evidence
of his hunger? Desire represented weakness, a power she
could wield over him—the one situation he would
never allow.

Meghan walked past him and left the room before he
could think of a suitable retort.

A muscle ticked beneath the scar on his cheek. What
was it about Meghan that savaged his self-control, first
with anger, then with desire?

She was as dangerous as any enemy, for in a way he
couldn't define or logically explain away, she threatened
his pursuit of *fudoshin*, that plateau of serenity that every
samurai sought to separate his emotions from life's
upheavals.

Akira-san had attained that calm steadiness. Nothing
shook his friend's harmony, Jake thought enviously.

There was only one way to purge this fascination.

Confront it, just as he had every other danger in his life.

After his temper and his blood cooled, Jake started down the hallway toward the atrium.

CARL OVERHEARD MEGHAN'S name as a footman conveyed a summons to Jacob Talbert. Talbert's initial reaction—complete with tight lips and anger sparking from his eyes—told Carl everything he wanted to know.

His sour mood lifted as Talbert left the ballroom. Apparently he needn't worry about Talbert after all. Following that initial moment of concern before dinner, Carl had carefully watched Meghan whenever the captain was near, noted her reaction every time his name was mentioned.

Even a blind man could sense the antagonism between Carl's chosen bride and the rough-hewn captain. Talbert hadn't intruded on his territory . . . lucky for the man, considering the saber skills Carl had gained as a Union calvary officer during the Civil War. His proficiency with his fists went back long before that.

Meghan couldn't miss the contrast between his charm and polish and Talbert's vulgarity. Let her cross swords with the captain a few more times. Within the week Carl would ask Meghan to marry him again. Her acquiescence would be all the sweeter for the pursuit.

Buoyed by a renewed sense of victory, Carl celebrated by asking Miss Dunleavy to dance. He teased the brunette, brought a blush to her cheeks, and speculated on the merits of an affair with the delectable chit. Deciding it would be safer to wait, he put aside the idea for now. He couldn't afford to alienate Meghan until her fortune was securely in his control.

He was a man of patience, though it was growing harder and harder to wait for the rewards he deserved.

. . .

MEG CRINGED WHEN she spotted the glass atrium door standing ajar. *Please let the other iguana still be in here,* she prayed fervently. Hurrying forward, she cupped her hand around the elaborate brass lock and pulled the door open.

She jerked back with an exclamation of pain. Lifting her hand into the light, she stared, dumbfounded, at the long cut across her palm. Blood welled up from the scratch.

Meg quickly squatted down and tore a strip from one of her petticoats. Damn. The last thing she needed was to return to the party with drops of blood on her gown.

She glared up at the suspicious lock. Light from the wall scone reflected off the shiny brass . . . and something more.

A piece of metal jutted from the mechanism. She leaned closer, touching the raw, broken edge. She tested the latch and found it jammed. Had Talbert broken off the key in the lock? Highly unlikely, she mused, for he qualified as the least clumsy man she'd ever encountered. Besides, this remnant appeared too thin to be a—

Meg lurched to her feet. Someone else had forced the lock . . . someone without a key. If not Jacob Talbert, then who?

Meg entered the atrium and stalked toward the far end, attuned for sounds other than the soothing music of the fountain. She must hurry. Talbert would be here soon to return the first iguana. She didn't want to cross paths with the captain again so soon.

Something scrambled through the plants as she passed, creating a burst of noise where a moment before there had been only silence. Meg nearly jumped out of her skin. She pressed her fist to the base of her ribs, then laughed at her jittery reaction. At least now she knew the other reptile remained safely here. She needn't dread finding it climbing up some lady's dress or taking a swim in the champagne punch.

Boots crunched in the gravel, the sound of a much larger beast intruding on the peace of the garden.

The darkness melted away from Talbert as he neared the fountain. The lights reflected off the moving water, dancing across his face in constantly shifting patterns—carving the image of an ancient, stern god in granite.

"I'm returning the little jailbreaker, ma'am, as instructed." He bent over and released the reptile. It crawled into the thick foliage at a leisurely pace, no doubt too stuffed with her fruit too manage its usual speed.

"I found your iguana feasting in the middle of my fruit table, or rather Mrs. Harcourt did. The poor woman fainted dead away when it bit down on a strawberry."

"Sounds entertaining. I'm sorry I missed it." He strode toward her with tigerlike grace.

Meg backed away.

"I swear the iguana's escape wasn't my fault," Talbert said, following Meghan around the perimeter of the fountain. "I didn't let her out. If I had, don't you believe I would have taken full credit for it?"

"No doubt you'd throw such a triumph in my face."

"Exactly. I couldn't pass up an opportunity to infuriate you. Your eyes flash like blue fire when you're mad."

Startled by his words, Meg stopped. While she stared at him, questioning his sincerity, he caught her right wrist in a lightning-quick grab.

That damning tingle swept up her arm again. Shaken, Meg said hastily, "I discovered the lock jammed, which gives me reason to believe you weren't the culprit. After all, you have a key. I gave it to you myself. It doesn't make sense that you—"

He drew her under the lights.

"That you . . . would force your way—" Her breath caught as he turned her fist over, cradling it in the warm, sun-bronzed expanse of his hand. Barely managing to finish, she whispered, "—into the atrium." Good heavens, she was babbling! Worse, she couldn't form a coherent thought in her head. What the hell was wrong with her?

"Your faith in my integrity is gratifying," he muttered ironically.

"I still have plenty of other reasons to be furious with—What are you doing? Stop that!" He peeled back her fingers and removed the bloodstained piece of cloth. "What is this stupid fascination you have with my hands, anyway? First you practically drag me into the parlor before dinner, and now—"

"What did you do to your hand?" he interrupted, scowling.

"I cut it on the door, if you must know. There was a jagged piece of metal broken off in the lock."

He released her hand and shrugged out of his coat, turning to lay the garment over the back of a nearby bench. A small corner of her mind spotted an opportunity for escape—just a wee portion, mind you, as any good half-Scots lass would say. The vast majority of her jumbled thoughts focused on the impressive width of his shoulders, the way his vest stretched across a broad back, the play of muscles in his arms as he rolled up the sleeves. He returned, his gaze intent with purpose.

"My hand is all right."

"No, it's not." He grasped her wrist again.

"Be careful not to get blood on your vest!"

His mouth slanted up at one corner. Holding her hand over the fountain, he reached into the cascading water and dribbled the cool, clear liquid over her palm. "Does that feel better?"

She could only gape at his black hair as he bent forward to blow on her wet palm. The soothing chill changed abruptly to a sizzling heat that shot along her skin like flames across drought grass, setting her heart to pounding.

"I have some salve that will help, too," he offered, straightening. "Send a maid to fetch it from Akira."

Meg's stomach did a queer little flip. Thoroughly rattled, she snatched her hand free and muttered, "Must you be so agreeable?"

"Is it more difficult to dislike me this way?"

"No, disliking you comes naturally, regardless of your manners." Despite her surly answer, his smile broadened. Must the man be so contrary? Was he so thick-skulled he didn't recognize a rebuttal when she thrust one in his face?

"I can be very agreeable when I want to be, Meghan, though no doubt you find that hard to believe."

"If you're searching for some other means to coax the swords out of me, you're wasting your time. I intend to hold you to our original agreement."

Talbert's magnetic smile faded . . . thank goodness. Even at his most angry and ferocious, towering over her with all that undeniable strength, Jacob Talbert presented less of a threat than when he attempted to be charming.

With a softness that didn't conceal the underlying note of steel, he said, "If that's the best you can think of me when I'm trying to be nice, then I might as well be a cad."

Before she realized what he intended, he pulled her

hard against him. His left arm encircled her waist, crushing her against the solid wall of his body. Sliding up the nape of her neck, his right hand cupped the back of her head and expertly tilted it for his kiss.

His mouth came down across hers.

Chapter Eight

For whom has my heart, like the passionflower patterns of Michinoku, been thrown into disarray? All on account of you.

—ARIWARA NO NARIHIRA (NINTH CENTURY)

IGNORING HER INJURY, Meg speared her hands into his hair, fully expecting the kiss to crush her lips against her teeth. If a chilling response failed to deter him, she intended to yank his head back.

The silky thickness of his warm hair slid sinuously between her fingers. His surprising restraint held her captive with gentleness in a compelling, powerful way that force could never duplicate. Firm yet resilient lips explored every inch of her mouth, mapping out its shape with velvety thoroughness.

The tip of his tongue brushed her lower lip, testing, tasting. The essence of peppermint mixed with pure male spiraled through her senses.

Her own lips responded, molding to his in ever-changing patterns, learning new, intriguing textures.

What did she want from the enigmatic captain? Perhaps the new sense of daring she'd discovered tonight tempted her to dance on the edge of darkness. Some scrap of sanity whispered that she toyed with a dangerous passion, but restraint had fled with the first commanding touch of his lips.

Her thumbs traced the masculine outline of his face, from bold cheekbones to the corners of his square jaw. A groan rumbled from his chest, sounding like distant thunder. His tongue slid inside her lower lip, gliding hotly over the slick surface of her teeth.

A wild tingling began in her breasts and cascaded down through her body. It poured through her like a hot waterfall, fed by the leashed intensity of his hungry hands roving over her back, pulling her closer. But instead of filling her, the downpour only intensified the strange, aching emptiness growing in her woman's core . . . an emptiness that reminded her of the unfathomable shadows in Talbert's eyes.

Meg's limbs trembled, stealing the strength from her knees. Dazed and off balance, leaning into him seemed the prudent and natural thing to do.

Jake felt her shiver, and echoed with a tremor of his own. His blood surged when she entrusted him with her weight. Only shedding these encumbering clothes, lying skin to skin, and sliding into the core of her feminine mystery could bring them closer. His body tightened with fresh urgency.

Desire pulled him deeper down a dark tunnel. Something else stirred on the fringes of his awareness, something calling from beyond years of bleak denial. He shied away from naming it, concentrating instead on tilting her hips to press against his arousal.

A soft whimper escaped her throat. It was a sound of discovery, not fear, as if she was overwhelmed by new sensations. Bloody hell, he could understand the feeling.

Actually, maybe they should both be frightened.

What the hell was he doing? She was the wrong woman, the wrong culture, the worst possible time and place.

If you're searching for some other means to coax the swords out of me, you're wasting your time. I intend to hold you to our original agreement.

Not only did she endanger his honor, she questioned it.

Jake tore his mouth from the clinging softness of her lips. Grasping her arms, he set her back at a sane distance. She blinked, looking disoriented . . . as if she'd just awakened in a strange bed. The thought of her lying among his tangled sheets caused his manhood to tighten painfully.

The lingering moisture from their kiss formed a pearly sheen on her lips. She looked thoroughly kissed, bemused, a sheltered innocent with her first real taste of passion. In truth, Meghan was the least helpless, most willful woman he'd ever encountered. She could slice a man's ego like butter and spread it on her scones for tea.

Between ragged breaths, Jake gritted out, "Just so you'll know, the thought of taking the swords from you by any means other than our agreement hadn't even crossed my mind."

He pivoted, grinding his heel into the gravel. Snatching up his coat, he left before he lost control and pulled her back into his arms.

Stunned, still trembling, Meg watched him go, her thoughts churning with confusion.

JAKE TOOK THE stairs three at a time, the muscles in his jaw working in synchrony with the hard flex of his thighs.

Kissing Meghan ranked as one of the most idiotic things he'd ever done.

Although he intended to put this bodyguard situation behind him as soon as possible, now he couldn't walk away unscathed. He would carry the memory of her sweet, surprisingly passionate response with him forever.

But he had a more immediate problem. Between the iguana causing her distress and his taking liberties he should never have allowed, he owed Meghan.

He'd been raised to place immense value on the concept of *giri*, or indebtedness. The Japanese need to discharge debt approached obsession, from repayment for a gift to owing *giri* that lasted generations. A man who did not know giri, or how to clear his debts and keep his name untarnished, was a miserable wretch, scorned by others. Jake should know, since he already carried a weighty sense of something left undone in his life—his quest for the swords and the redemption of his honor.

He must show the full spirit of the samurai, to honor his teachers and not shame himself any further than he had already.

Jake knocked on the door to Akira's bedchamber. Granted admittance, he strode furiously into the room.

Akira kneeled on the burgundy Axminster carpet, sitting on his heels. Paper, paints, and brushes were spread out before him on the floor, lighted by an oil lamp he'd removed from the desk. In quiet moments Akira practiced *shodo*, the way of ink. The Japanese form of calligraphy was one of many arts that samurai warriors practiced in their pursuit of spiritual harmony.

"Unpolished gems do not glitter, Takeru-san," Akira-san said softly, his tone neutral. His steady hand applied strokes of black ink to the paper, shaping the graceful Japanese characters.

Jake flushed under the subtle criticism. Akira-san was right. If he expected to attain *fudoshin*, that pinnacle of spiritual peace, he couldn't allow frustration to touch him, much less enter a room like a snorting bull.

He'd come so close in the last few years. Now everything was crashing down around him. Whenever that
stubborn golden-haired minx was about, he was in the
grip of either anger or lust. Self-discipline was the key,
the mental training to polish away the rust of the body,
making a man like a bright, sharp sword.

Jake bowed stiffly. "My humble apologies for disturbing you, Akira-san. I'm looking for the large chest. The
butler told me they brought it to your room."

A jab of the brush pointed him toward the sumptuous
western bed. Jake stepped over the pallet on the floor,
formed by the counterpane and folded bed linens. The
obstacle didn't surprise him. Akira-san was accustomed
to a simple futon, and shunned the soft feather bed.

Sitting on one heel before the chest, Jake lifted the
heavy lid and sorted through the multicolored kimonos
that had been carefully folded and stacked, separated by
rice paper.

"Did you know today is her birthday?" Jake said irritably as he worked to the bottom of the first stack and
started on another, looking for one specific kimono he
had in mind.

"The servants say this, yes."

"Well, it seems those hypocritical guests value her more
as a hostess to provide their evening of entertainment."

Without looking up, Akira commented, "Why you
care, Takeru-san?"

"I don't, of course. It just emphasizes how much we
don't belong here. Aha! Here it is," he exclaimed with
satisfaction, carefully slipping the folded kimono out of
the stack.

"Ah, yes," Akira murmured, glancing his way. "The
color suits you."

Jake's head jerked up just in time to catch the twitch at

the corner of Akira's mouth. "Very funny. It's for Miss McLowry. A birthday gift."

"Because you not care. I see."

Jake nearly choked. "I merely . . . owe her. One of the iguanas escaped from the atrium and created a sensation with the guests. And then—," he hesitated, jaw clenched. "Suffice it to say that I managed to make her angry at me. I owe her *giri*."

Serious for a moment, Akira said, "To wear a debt, even for so trivial a thing as a glass of water when one thirsts, affects the honor. To owe an apology . . . for the pride to suffer when wrong . . . this is more costly than death to a samurai."

Jake bowed his head, acknowledging the teaching, then added the one thing Akira had left unsaid. "However unwilling I might be."

"Yes. You must repay," Akira-san agreed. He bent over his paper again. "The color of the kimono matches her eyes."

"Really? I hadn't noticed," Jake countered with a shrug. He spread the blue silk gown on the bed.

"I find box for you."

"Would you?" Relief washed through him. "I need to get back downstairs and check on Douglass. Could you ask one of the servants to see that it's brought down and put with the other gifts?"

"What do you want the card to say?"

"No card," Jake said firmly. "In this culture, a gift from a man to an unmarried woman is considered extremely forward. Besides, she'll know it's from me." His fingertips brushed over the embroidered cranes and water lilies. "Who else would give her a work of art from Japan?" he murmured.

"What about the box? How should it look?"

The question jarred Jake, making him realize that his

thoughts had drifted to soft skin and lips more sumptuous than a banquet. He jerked his hand back. "Just wrap the damned thing before I change my mind," he growled impatiently.

Akira chuckled as Jake left the room.

He rang for a servant to fetch a box and white paper and sighed as he set aside the black paint to mix his colored pigments. "Ah, Takeru-san, perhaps soon you admit the passion in you and stop this struggle to find the Japanese way. A tiger cannot attain *fudoshin* without giving up his fire, his spirit."

DOUGLASS CLAMPED HIS teeth around the cigar and grinned. He loved the camaraderie of a good poker game with his friends, but the competitive side of his nature thrilled to the challenge of beating these financial giants of San Francisco.

Darius Ogden Mills, the driving force behind the Bank of California, was visibly upset with Douglass's good fortune.

"Your luck is running high tonight, Douglass, and that's a fact," offered the more genial John Mackay.

"A man makes his own luck. That's the adage I live by." Movement in the corner of the room caught Douglass's attention. Jake Talbert had returned to dismiss Phillip and take his place. The Scotsman frowned. He'd practically chased Jake from the room earlier in the hope that the captain would remain in the ballroom, dance with Meghan, and otherwise prove unable to avoid her company.

Meggie's antagonistic attitude toward the captain intrigued Douglass profoundly. The lass had never reacted to a man with such fire before. Douglass stroked his sidewhiskers, only half his concentration on the table as

Mills dealt the next hand. Then there was the way Jake watched Meghan—as if he'd like to devour her . . . or shake her until her teeth rattled.

Aye, it smacked of possibilities.

Mackay followed Douglass's brooding gaze. "I'm curious about this Talbert fellow. Is he really your bodyguard?"

"Aye."

James Fair, the Comstock bonanza king known for his quarrelsome nature, challenged, "Then there must be danger about, something that has you worried, Douglass. How does that fit in with making your own luck, eh?"

"Nothing I canna handle. A bit of trouble from a client of the bank, 'tis all, someone who didna appreciate it when I called in his loan. You know how it is . . . a bad risk." Chuckles sounded around the table. Douglass smiled to himself, thinking of how well he'd profited from that deal and its intricate planning—even though his bold, darling daughter had conned him out of the fruits of his labors. A passion for those swords had driven him for months. The last thing he wanted Meghan to know, however, was the role he'd played in bringing about his current trouble.

"Well, I can see why you like having Captain Talbert around," stated Lloyd Tevis. "The man strikes me as very capable." The president of Wells Fargo, breeder of blooded horses, and one of the town's favorite hosts punctuated his observation with a crisp nod.

"Aye," Douglass agreed.

"Wonder if Talbert would be interested in checking over my security arrangements," Tevis muttered to no one in particular.

"Best watch your daughter around the man," warned Mills. "He could be a seducer of innocents, for all you know."

"No' to worry. Meggie does not even like him,"
Douglass murmured thoughtfully. He rolled his cigar
between thumb and forefinger, listening to the crackle
of tobacco leaves, recalling the instant respect he'd felt
upon meeting Jake Talbert. The cool confidence in
those gray eyes bespoke hard experience. Douglass
knew himself an excellent judge of character, and Jake
was clearly a man who could take care of his own.

Douglass wanted to see his daughter settled with a man
who truly deserved her. Lately, he'd begun to regret his
enthusiasm in pushing her and Carl Edwards together.

As the poker hand finished, with Tevis the winner,
the object of Douglass's uncharitable thoughts entered
the room.

"Good evening, gentlemen."

Mackay offered, "Care to join us, Carl?"

Douglass stubbed out his cigar in a crystal ashtray.

"Thank you, no. I've come to tell Douglass that
Meghan has started opening her gifts."

Mills and Fair coughed. Mackay found renewed interest in arranging his chips.

"You don't mind if we continue to play, do you, Douglass?" queried Lloyd Tevis. "I doubt we would add much
to the proceedings."

"Of course," said Douglass, rising. "Just save my seat.
I'll be back soon."

"Maybe not as soon as you think," Fair muttered, "considering that stack of boxes I saw."

Douglass and Carl left the card room, side by side.
Captain Talbert followed at a discreet distance.

"Enjoying the party, Carl?" Douglass asked.

"Absolutely, sir, particularly since it's in celebration of
Meghan's birthday."

The Scotsman grunted. He watched the colorful mix

of twirling couples on the ballroom floor as they passed by. The majority of guests continued to enjoy the music, fine food, and champagne.

Carl cleared his throat. "I intend to ask Meghan soon to be my wife. Perhaps, if you speak with her again—"

"Why do you think she'll respond differently this time?"

"She's given me reason to hope, sir," Carl said stiffly.

"Oh?" The Scotsman felt a twinge of disappointment. Was that true, or did Carl's arrogance see encouragement where there was none? Four years ago, Douglass had seen great promise in this man, newly arrived in town. Increasingly, however, his protégé revealed a pompous nature and a measure of intolerance.

Douglass also had difficulty respecting anyone he could manipulate.

"I've been meaning to discuss that with you, Carl. Since Meggie has been hesitant to accept your proposal before, I'm withdrawing my support."

"What!" Carl choked out, coming to an abrupt halt. He glanced back irritably at Talbert, who paused at a distance. Lowering his voice, Carl said feelingly, "Surely you don't mean that."

Douglass sighed. "You heard me right."

"But you've actively supposed the idea of our marriage before."

"I've changed my mind."

"Does this have to do with the loan to Chen Lee?" Carl demanded, his voice strained. "I know you were disappointed that his second shipment from China disappeared, but it seemed like a good risk at the time. I did everything you asked in arranging the loan."

Douglass had no intention of pursuing that topic, knowing he'd maneuvered Carl, for his own purposes, into approaching Chen Lee. "Nay. I told you I'd take care of Mister Chen, and I did." *I forced Chen into an untenable position, his cash reserves depleted, the loan due. To avoid arrest, he had to give up those bonny swords, which he'd repeatedly refused to sell outright. Aye, the swords were well worth months of planning, the expense of repaying the loan out of my own pocket, and the bribe paid to the ship captains to take Chen's money and sail the Atlantic for a while.*

"Then why?"

"Meggie would have accepted you by now if she wished. Perhaps I'll advise her against the marriage." Annoyed with Carl's persistence, Douglass simply walked away. A glance back showed his protégé still rooted to the same spot, his handsome looks spoiled by bitterness. The Scotsman snorted in disgust.

"You'll no' get far in business, Carl," Douglass grumbled to himself, "if you pout every time you dinna get your way."

He slipped into the drawing room where those guests interested in the gift opening had already collected. Meghan looked very bonny sitting on a small sofa. Tiffany, barely containing her excitement, sat next to her and handed over packages one by one. Almost thirty guests filled the room, some seated, others lining the walls and talking in muted tones.

Jake Talbert followed Douglass into the room, where he took up a position against the wall close to Meghan. He crossed his arms tightly over his chest, then fixed an impatient gaze on Meghan's profile.

Douglass suppressed a satisfied grin.

MEGHAN WAS DOWN to the last few gifts, with no sign, yet, of his own.

Jake maintained his vantage point next to the arm of the sofa. He wanted to see her reaction, up close, when she opened the box. Would her face reflect the same wistful admiration she showed when examining his vest? Would her expression soften, her mouth curve into a smile?

He shook himself mentally. The only thing of importance was that he repay *giri* and discharge his obligation to her.

A stack of opened gifts had grown on the table to her left, the pile of trash at her feet. Crystal vases and candy dishes, silver-plated candlesticks, fans, handkerchiefs, enameled trinket boxes—all lovely in an impersonal way, all expensive. Not one fit Meghan's taste, which had become familiar to him after only one day in her home.

Tiffany reached for the largest of only three remaining gifts on the table.

"Oh! What a pretty box!" she exclaimed, handing it to Meghan. "Who could it be from?" Practically bouncing on the sofa in her excitement, Tiffany clapped her hands and urged, "Hold it up so everyone can see."

Side conversations in the room ceased. In the resultant hush, Jake heard the creek of corset stays, the rustle of satin, the squeak of new shoe leather as men and women leaned forward slightly, disdainful of showing vulgar curiosity but unable to resist a peek.

Meghan held up the large box.

Jake suppressed a groan. Akira-san had not only succeeded in wrapping the gift, he'd adorned it with his own special flair.

The wrapping was white, without ribbon or trimming of any kind. An exquisite floral design painted across half of the box distinguished it from every other package. Several women sighed in admiration; men nodded in recognition of artistic talent.

"What kind of flowers are those?" someone asked eagerly.

Muttered responses of wild roses, poppies, morning glories, and other conjectures floated around the room.

Jake resisted the urge to correct their ignorance by blurting out "cherry blossoms." Despite their wordly attitude, these people were not well traveled, had never been to the Far East in spring to witness the glory of nature's breathtaking display.

Eagerly, Tiffany asked, "Who is it from?"

"I don't see a card," Meghan muttered, turning the box.

That started a new round of speculation. Meghan ignored them all and set the box on her lap. Jake straightened, focusing on her as if she were the only person in the room.

A slight frown fluttered gracefully across her brow, like a perched butterfly folding and opening its wings. She touched, then gently stroked the painting. His chest muscles contracted as he remembered her questing fingers against his vest. She stared at her fingertips, then rubbed them together.

Haste hadn't allowed the watercolors sufficient time to dry. Somehow, he could sense what she felt: the cool nubbiness of the dampened paper, the lingering moisture that only sensitive skin could detect.

"Open it, Meghan!" came a voice from the back of the crowd.

"Don't keep us in suspense."

She carefully removed the paper without tearing it, then laid it among the gifts rather than with the discarded wrappings. The gesture surprised and pleased Jake. Akira-san should be here to see the way she reverently preserved the old samurai's artistry.

Meghan lifted the lid of the box and froze.

Tiffany pressed a hand over her open mouth.

"How beautiful!" exclaimed Camilla Smythe-Jones, a red-haired woman in a green gown, who stood behind the sofa. She peered over Meghan's shoulder.

"The embroidery is exquisite," declared a silver-haired matron. "What are those designs?"

"It's Chinese," proclaimed Mrs. Harcourt with a disdainful sniff.

"No, it's from Japan," Meghan said, staring down at the folded garment. "The style of the gown is called a kimono, I believe."

Several people called out, "Let us see."

"No, I don't think—"

"Oh, please, let me!" Tiffany offered, overriding Meghan's weak protest with her enthusiasm. She lifted the kimono and shook it out gently, letting it settle across Meghan's lap like rippling water in a jewel-tone sea.

Miss Smythe-Jones gasped, then giggled. "Why, it's a dressing gown! How shockingly personal! Who would have done such a thing?" She leaned forward eagerly. The entire room seemed to shift along with her in pursuit of titillating curiosity. "Did you find a card?"

"There is none."

Jake instantly realized his gaff. He closed his eyes, letting frustration wash through him in waves as caustic as the gossipy whispers circulating throughout the room. Dammit, would he ever fully understand the customs of this country? Both Japanese men and women considered the kimono an everyday garment, worn in public. Here it was looked upon as scandalously personal.

Warily, he opened his eyes. Meghan sat with her lips compressed into a thin line. Slight color tinged her cheeks. If the others weren't present she'd no doubt be peeling off his skin with that sharp, clever tongue.

He'd rather she use it to explore his mouth with hot, intimate curiosity.

Damn, he hadn't meant to embarrass her. Things would only grow worse if people continued to speculate on the giver's identity.

Jake stared at Douglass, recognizing Meghan's father as the only possible solution. The Scotsman looked up; their gazes caught and held. Jake communicated a plea for intervention with a tilt of his head toward Meghan. Thankfully, Douglass seemed to catch on. His brows rose, then he abruptly straightened and stepped forward. His voice reverberated through the room like a bass drum.

"Meggie, lass. I see you've opened my special gift. I saved it for tonight, wanting it to be a surprise."

Jake had never heard a more timely intervention in his life. Let Douglass stave off her embarrassment for now. They could clear up the misconception later, once the gossipy guests had departed.

"This is from you, Father?" Doubt edged Meghan's voice.

"Aye," Douglas confirmed cheerfully. "Pretty thing, is it no'?" When he rubbed his knuckles against his chest, Meg's eyes narrowed. Jake received the unsettling impression that the Scotsman had just revealed something he shouldn't have.

"I bought it from Captain Talbert," Douglass added. "He allowed me the pick of his cargo, and a difficult choice it was."

Meg's brows lifted a notch. "And when did you have time—"

"You mean, there are more of these beautiful gowns?" interrupted one of the women excitedly, saving Jake the trouble of clamping a hand over Meghan's mouth and hauling her from the room. Didn't she know when to leave well enough alone?

"Are they all as pretty as this one, Captain Talbert?" another asked him.

The ladies began to cluster around him like hounds on the scent.

"What colors do you have?"

"Please tell me you have one in yellow? Blue is just not my color."

Meghan joined in, "Yes, Captain, do tell us more about your kimonos."

He glanced up sharply at Meghan's dry tone and patently false smile. She met his gaze for the first time . . . she knew. Despite her father's claim, she knew the gift was from Jake . . . and she thought he'd done this on purpose to embarrass her!

"Ladies, please, another time," he interrupted the eager women. "Miss McLowry hasn't finished opening her gifts."

"When may we see the kimonos?"

"Are they all for sale?"

"Why don't you come by the house tomorrow?" he said hastily. "Now, if we can return to the matter at hand? I, for one, want to see what other treasures Miss McLowry unwraps."

The situation diffused when Meghan folded the kimono and returned it to the box. She opened another of the remaining gifts, revealing a brass mantel clock. Similar clocks already adorned every mantel in this sprawling house. After all, Jake thought cynically, what did one buy a wealthy girl who had everything?

Finally, only a small box remained, no larger than his hand.

Tiffany handed it to Meghan, leaning close to whisper, "This wasn't my choice. Mama insisted."

Jake glanced about in surprise. Judging by the impassive faces, no one but himself had overheard Tiffany's comment.

Meghan peeled back the paper and opened the lid.

She froze, staring down into the box.

Mrs. Harcourt beamed. "I have noticed you never wear hummingbird jewelry, dearest. It's so very fashionable. Shocking neglect of your wardrobe by your father," she scolded, wagging her finger and chortling. "So I took it upon myself to resolve the matter."

A hot rage burst in Jake's chest. He'd heard of the practice of killing and stuffing hummingbirds as fashion accessories—earrings, brooches, hair adornments—but he'd never had the misfortune of seeing it up close. He thought it terrible that they destroy living creatures for the sake of vanity.

Meghan tentatively touched the tiny stuffed birds, once so free, so vibrantly alive.

Bile threatened to rise into his throat. How could she participate in this? It didn't seem like something Meghan would—He caught himself just in time. Other than her gentleness with the iguanas, a few brief displays of humor, and the intoxicating taste of her lips, what did he really know about her?

Yet, despite his anger, he noted that she didn't remove the hummingbirds from the box or hold them up to her ears.

Meghan extended warm thank-yous to all her guests. With the gift opening at a close, Douglass and the guests drifted from the room, returning to the dancing, though several women lingered a few extra moments to admire the kimono up close. They fingered the silk and vied over who should have first pick of his cargo tomorrow. The disagreement threatened to break into a full-fledged argument as the women left the drawing room.

Jake cared nothing for their petty bickering. One of the last to leave, he hesitated outside the door, allowing everyone to exit the room until Meghan was alone. Instinct urged him to wait. A muscle ticked in his cheek. This was insane. With a muffled curse, he turned to go.

A tiny, choked-off sound halted him in his tracks. He glanced back into the room.

Meghan stood at the rear door. In her right hand, she clutched the small box. She opened the door, looking back over her shoulder as if to ensure that no one followed.

Unshed tears caught the light, glittering like diamonds on her lashes.

Chapter Nine

Someone must be unstringing them wildly—white beads shower down without pause, my sleeve too narrow to catch them.
—Ariwara no Narihira (ninth century)

MEG FOUGHT BACK the tears. She couldn't return to the party with reddened eyes and tear-streaked cheeks, not without inviting another wave of sordid speculation. She would give in later to the clawing grief, the guilt—after the guests were gone.

Lifting her skirts with one hand, Meg clutched the small box to her chest and hurried through the garden to the greenhouse. Light from the garden torches illuminated her way.

That stupid, vain woman! Mrs. Harcourt must be incredibly obtuse, having failed to recognize that Meg never wore hummingbird jewelry because she abhorred the practice of killing and stuffing the tiny birds. Meg didn't think she could do it . . . could ever be civil to Mrs. Harcourt again, even if the woman was the bank vice-president's wife.

Reaching the greenhouse, she fumbled around the workbench just inside the door. After finding a hand trowel, she stepped outside and picked an open stop between two bushes.

The least she could do was give the poor creatures a decent burial.

Squatting down on her heels, Meg set the box aside with trembling hands and set to work.

This is what came of keeping her opinions locked inside, of saving her father embarrassment by avoiding controversy. She paused in her digging. But what would her opinion matter in society's headlong rush for personal adornment? The newspapers condemned the practice, yet the fashion frenzy continued without pause.

Maybe one person couldn't make a difference, but at least if she'd let her feelings be known, she wouldn't be ranked among the eager participants in hummingbird genocide.

Meg swallowed hard, battling a thick lump in her throat. She jabbed the trowel into the dirt. Why did everything have to go wrong tonight? First the tension at dinner, then the iguana, finally the gauntlet of opening gifts . . . and in the midst of it all, dear heaven, that stunning kiss. The feel of Talbert's seductive mouth had released something wild and primitive, as dangerous as the man himself . . . the wrong man, to make matters worse. She had betrayed Carl's honorable intentions by behaving like a wanton.

She turned out an inch of dry soil, then dug some more. The hole grew only slowly, which added to her frustration. Gripping the trowel like a dagger, Meg stabbed it into the ground repeatedly, escalating the force of each strike to match the mounting pressure in her chest.

Footsteps sounded on the path behind her.

Meg struggled to her feet.

Jacob Talbert materialized out of the night. A tingling sensation centered in her breasts as her body remembered being crushed against the unyielding hardness of his chest.

As she stared speechlessly, Talbert went past her into the greenhouse and reappeared with a long-handled spade.

He poised the spade at the edge of her paltry hole, then sank the metal deep into the earth with one kick from his booted foot. A slight flex of his shoulders turned out the dirt, exposing a hole of more than adequate depth.

Resting the point against the ground, he cupped one hand over the handle and leaned against the shovel.

Uncertainty beat around inside Meg like a swallow trying to escape a windowed room. How could a man look so gorgeous and appallingly male leaning on a shovel, for heaven's sake? The wretch flaunted an unfortunate knack for looking natural and confident in any surroundings. It was a curse . . . her curse. She shouldn't notice such things. He was driving her mad.

"There's something to be said for economy of effort, Miss McLowry. Bigger shovel, less digging."

She really hated it when he was right. Grudgingly, she murmured, "Thank you, Captain. I appreciate the help."

"You're welcome."

"I'll be fine now," she said through her teeth. "You may go. I'd rather be alone."

"I've no intention of leaving you here by yourself." He nodded toward the hole. "I recognize the box, and the contents."

Expecting more of his characteristic mockery, Meg lifted her chin and said defiantly, "I'm burying the hummingbirds."

"So I noticed. Relax, I'm not trying to stop you."

"As if you could," she insisted, planting her fists on her hips. "This is my property and I can do anything I please here."

"I never questioned that." He arched his brows and

added, "Why are you on the defensive? Because you're afraid I'll think you look ridiculous burying a pair of earrings?"

How dare he! "I could care less what you think of me, Captain, and those are more than a pair of—"

"I don't, you know," he interrupted softly.

His low, husky tone vibrated through her bones, melting the tension in her arms. Her hands slid limply off her hips. "You don't what?"

"I don't consider you ridiculous, Meghan. Actually, what you're doing strikes me as . . . very thoughtful."

His praise, although hesitant, took the sting out of her anger. He approved? She couldn't imagine anyone else who would understand her eccentric behavior.

"Oh," was all she could think to say.

He was the epitome of dark temptation, like sinfully rich truffle candy. And like too much chocolate, he made her nerves jittery, her muscles quiver—as if an excess of energy challenged the limited confines of her own skin. She imagined unbuttoning his vest, sliding her hands inside his shirt to explore the textures of smooth flesh and crisp black hair.

Appalled by the direction her thoughts were taking, Meg panicked. The need to keep that safe, sensible wall of antagonism between them urged her to say tartly, "I still haven't granted you permission to call me by my given name."

His mouth kicked up at one corner. "It's a requirement I demand of every woman . . . when I dig a hole for her, that is."

The roguish smile, the teasing comments . . . with any other man she would suspect flirtation. Not Talbert. He ladled out sarcasm as if he held the secret to a bottomless supply.

Turning her back on him, she sank down on her heels

and laid the tiny stuffed birds, in their makeshift coffin, in the bottom of the hole. Tears burned behind her eyes. If only she'd found the courage to be herself, to speak sooner, to defy convention—When the hummingbirds lay in their final, tragic resting place, she rose.

She felt as fragile as glass. One caustic word from Talbert, one mocking comment, and she would shatter.

Thankfully, he didn't seem to notice her vulnerability. Surely he wouldn't resist taking advantage of it. He filled the hole while she stood with arms wrapped tightly around her middle. Muffled sounds of gaiety from the house formed a depressing contrast to the thump of the spade as he tamped down the dirt.

He carried the tool back to its place inside the greenhouse. When he emerged, he headed toward the corner of the building.

Meg came instantly alert, blurting out, "Where are you going?" This was insane. A minute ago she'd been trying to chase him off; now she rejected the notion of his leaving.

"I'll be right back," he tossed over one shoulder. "Don't go anywhere." Then he disappeared around the greenhouse.

"No, I—" she stared to object, then clamped her lips together. What did she intend to say? *No, I don't want you to leave me here alone? The grounds beyond the garden are dark and creepy in a way I never noticed before? Do you think you might consider holding me for a minute?* Wouldn't he get a good laugh out of that.

He came back around the corner, carrying a large, flat rock at least twelve inches across.

"Here," he said, gently laying the stone over the freshly turned dirt. "I saw a pile of these earlier today while checking the grounds. This should keep the gardener from accidentally digging up the grave."

Meg stared at the smooth white rock. He intended it as a headstone. Without prompting, he'd thought of something she needed, even before she recognized the requirement herself. Not since her mother was alive had someone seen past Meg's mask of strength to the needy woman inside.

She had feared Talbert's caustic comments. . . .

His kindness proved her undoing.

Something fractured inside. Aching sobs tore upward from her chest, emerging in gasping breaths. No matter how tightly her wrapped arms clamped about her waist, she couldn't control her emotions.

Her tear-blurred vision filled with a white shirtfront and black lapels.

"Meghan, don't," he said gruffly.

"I couldn't bear—" she tried to explain, but her voice broke.

"It's all right," he smoothed in a rough velvet tone. "You did the right thing, burying them." He grasped her upper arms, stroking up and down with gentle friction, pausing again and again to massage taut muscles.

Her sobs quieted with surprising speed. The agony receded to a dull ache—except for the disappointment over the way his grip kept her at a distance at the same time he offered comfort.

"I should have s-said s-something back there, when . . . when I opened the box."

"Those people wouldn't have understood if you did. They don't want to think about what they're doing, or the injustice of something innocent paying the price for their vanity."

She nodded stiffly. "I should . . . do something to try to stop it."

"Another opportunity will come. The younger women

look up to you. I think they will listen. You heard Tiffany say that the gift wasn't her choice."

"Really?" She looked up with renewed hope, licking the taste of salty tears from her lips. His face remained a blur. "But what would I say?"

"Speak from the heart," he answered gruffly, his tone rougher than a moment before. "You know these people better than I do. You'll think of the right words."

He pressed something into her hand, then backed away. A handkerchief. His warm fingertips touched her cheek, a brief parting gesture before he turned to leave.

Drying the rest of her face, Meg lingered before heading back inside. The burning in her eyes faded; the heat in her cheeks cooled. Insects began to sing again, encouraged by her stillness.

The wait provided plenty of time to think. Talbert may have shown a new, surprising depth to his character, but only a lonely, foolish woman desperate for a bit of flattery would read more into his actions than a simple offer of comfort.

MEGHAN'S WRENCHING SOBS reverberated in his mind, tugging at something that should be kept buried.

Jake crossed his arms over his chest and leaned back against the wall. Douglass's unlit study offered a shadowed, welcome refuge from the waning sounds of the party. The merriment was drawing to a close. Flushed by liquor, sated with excellent food, pleasantly tired from the dancing, the satisfied guests were finally departing.

He tilted his head back and stared, unseeing, at the dark lines of the molded ceiling.

Damn those hypocrites for hurting Meghan. Damn them for making him even notice and, worse, care. A man with so little honor shouldn't be rushing to the rescue. Yet, he'd felt compelled to follow her into the garden.

He closed his eyes, remembering how he'd come dangerously close to pulling her into his arms and kissing the tears from her mouth, her cheeks, her eyes. Her unexpected compassion for the hummingbirds, her endearing uncertainty, those tears . . . his preconceived notions about Meghan had just taken a serious beating.

Jake banged his head back against the wall once, twice, three times. Which was worse, paying for his stupidity with the pain in his head or the ache in his loins?

What kind of warrior allowed lust to distort his sense of purpose? Eliminating the danger to Douglass fell within his range of experience . . . samurai were the consummate soldiers for hire. With his goal of sixteen years so close, Jake couldn't afford the distraction of a woman who wanted to chew his head off one minute and cling to his chest the next. A triumphant return to Japan with the swords would seal the restoration of his honor, enabling him to return to the family and village who had shunned him so long ago. Only Akira-san and Matsuda Takashi, Shinjiro's father, had forgiven him.

Pushing away from the wall with a grunt of disgust, Jake headed for the rear of the house and a final security check.

He avoided servants who bustled about cleaning up the mess. Once outside, his gaze sought out the guards he'd stationed at either corner of the white brick building. Peter and one of the footmen paced, their sense of loyalty keeping the two men alert and wary.

Despite the eight-foot wall surrounding the three-plus acres of Douglass's land, the unlit area beneath the fruit and nut trees gave him reason to be uneasy. The deep shadows would appeal to any assassin. A samurai bent on vengeance would approach boldly from the front, integrity and the daring display of courage more important than caution, but he wasn't dealing with noble warriors among the Chinese Tongs.

He inspected the perimeter of the property. Tomorrow he would gather the male servants and coat the top of the wall with tar and broken glass. He only wished there'd been time to take care of that precaution before the party.

Meghan wanted him for his expertise in security, nothing more. She'd get her bargain's worth, dammit.

As he came full circle, someone extinguished the torches in the garden. The back of the house plunged into darkness. He sighed, taking mental note to keep any approach from the rear illuminated.

Just then, a second-story window brightened.

Jake stopped short, rooted to the spot.

Meghan's room. The location was etched into his mind. Securing the house against intruders had carried certain privileges, including the right to enter the lady's bedchamber.

The heavy curtains stood wide open. Compared to the darkness outside, the interior shone like a beacon, the scene inside visible albeit hazy through the gauze window liner.

Meghan crossed the room, her arms burdened with a stack of boxes. She set the load on her bed, then removed the lid of the topmost box. Slowly, she lifted out its contents. The light shone softly on blue silk.

The kimono.

Jake caught his breath.

The maid came up behind her and began to unfasten the buttons at the back of her mistress's gown. Didn't Meghan realize how easily she could be seen? He cursed her carelessness even as he continued to stare.

His heart thudded harder when Meghan wriggled to

loosen the cling of the gown around her narrow waist, then dropped the garment into a pool on the floor. She discarded the petticoats next, then the corset. She stepped out of the pile, the grace of her long, tapered legs apparent despite the unflattering drawers. The maid gathered the discarded clothes and left the room.

Meghan's chemise, cut low to allow for the deep décolletage of her ball gown, hugged her torso and barely covered the crowns of her breasts.

Jake's mouth went dry.

She tilted her head and rubbed the kimono against her cheek.

"Put it on," Jake whispered through his teeth.

He'd given her the kimono to repay *giri*, to avoid the entanglement of a debt. Now he found himself imagining how she would look in it, the rich color bringing out the blue of her eyes. Her hair would flow loosely about her shoulders, as gold as the metallic thread running through the embroidered design. The graceful curves of her full breasts would sway gently beneath the silk, her nipples rubbing against the erotically soft material. The kimono sash would be his to leisurely unwind, until the front parted and he cupped those pale globes in his hands, using his thumbs to rub already sensitized tips into hard, straining buds, not stopping until she squirmed and moaned for him to take her into his mouth.

The night suddenly became hot, stifling. Jake tried to shake off the fuzzy boundaries of the fantasy. Hell, he was the one hardening and squirming.

Meg folded the kimono, closing the box and setting it aside. From her hard-lipped expression and air of finality, Jake knew for certain she intended to return the kimono . . . despite the obvious pleasure she found in the gown.

His eyes narrowed. Just let her try.

·   ·   ·

AFTER A RESTLESS night's sleep, Meg dressed in a simple day gown of blue muslin and hurried out to the greenhouse. She must seek out the gardener and explain the significance of the stone before he thought to move it.

The garden was deserted except for Talbert's Japanese companion, who sat on his heels by the hummingbirds' grave. What was he doing?

With a gasp, Meg lifted her skirts and broke into a run.

She stopped abruptly next to him, startled to find him painting the stone.

The exquisite painting displayed two hummingbirds in all their natural glory, gathering nectar from a cluster of flowers. Talbert must have told Komatsu Akira about the poor birds. Meg's chest tightened with a complex combination of emotions.

"It's beautiful," she said thickly. "May I watch?"

The man inclined his head in a gracious nod. With mounting eagerness, Meg sought out something from the greenhouse to act as a stool. The best she could find was a bucket. Overturning it on the path near his left shoulder, where she had a clear view, Meg sat down and arranged her skirts.

A moment of watching him work brought a revelation. "You painted the flowers on my box last night!" she exclaimed.

"My gift to you."

She looked up, startled that this stranger would even know of her birthday, much less think of giving her something, but his attention was focused on the delicate lines of a hummingbird wing. She was dying to know why, but it seemed crass and unappreciative of his generosity to quiz him about it.

"The flowers were lovely. I saved the paper. I plan to frame the painting so I can hang it in my room and continue to enjoy it. Thank you, Mister Komatsu."

A hint of a smile lifted the corner of his mouth. "You may call me Akira-san."

"Uh, thank you," she said awkwardly, surprised by his offer. "Please call me Meghan . . . if you'd like, that is."

"Meg-an-san," he corrected.

Meg smiled over the hard, syllabic way he was forced to pronounce her name with his Japanese accent. "You add 'san' to the names. What does that mean?"

"It is an honoring among friends."

Dozens of questions knocked around inside Meg's head. She wanted to know everything about his home culture, and the places he had visited in his travels. Most of all, she ached to probe him for insight into Jacob Talbert. The horror of where her curiosity might lead sealed her lips.

A hibiscus blossom took shape under his talented manipulation of the brush. The trumpet-shaped flower spread velvetly red petals, an open invitation to the hummingbird hovering in front of it.

Something struck her as wrong. Suddenly, she realized the source of her unease.

"You're using watercolors," she observed in dismay. She wanted the beautiful painting to last forever, but now it would wash away with the first rain. Didn't he realize his painstaking work would soon be lost?

"Yes." After rinsing the red from his brush, he dipped it into a thick deep green pigment and added, "But I use very little water today."

"Even if the paint is nice and thick, won't it be ruined by the rain?"

Lifting the wet end of his brush, he gestured toward

the sky. "Do you not trust the loving Father to protect them?"

"I believe hummingbirds are one of God's most beautiful and cherished creations, but I hope He will not inflict a drought on all of central California to shelter their grave."

Akira-san added highlights to the hummingbird's iridescent breast feathers. "No one ever stumbled lying snug in bed," he countered calmly.

"Excuse me?"

Akira focused exclusively on his work. His silence gave her time to mull over the odd poignancy of his statement.

"You understand now, Meg-an-san?"

Meg stared at his profile, a face that reflected supreme self-confidence as well as serenity. A shiver ran down her spine, a sudden sense of awareness. This man was no mere servant. There was much wisdom at work here, a patience born of world-weariness and painful experience. Who was he? What role had he played in Jacob Talbert's life?

Intrigued, Meg scooted her bucket a little closer. "I believe I understand your meaning. If one does not venture out, does not take risks, then there is little hope of accomplishing anything in life."

He nodded slowly. "When the paint dries, I protect with a coat of lacquer."

He'd planned to preserve his art all along. "Like the lacquer coating on katana scabbards?" she probed, her excitement returning. "I have one with flakes of gold suspended in the resin, and another with an inlaid wisteria vine fashioned of silver. They are beautiful."

"Not sca—sca—" he struggled with the foreign word, then gave up with a shrug. "Saya."

"Saya," she imitated. The strange word apparently

warmed up her recalcitrant tongue, because the next question rolled off with little or no discipline from her brain. "How long have you known Captain Talbert?"

"Twenty years, since before we leave Nihon."

Encouraged, she ventured a little further. "Is he also a man who takes risks, who meets life head-on?"

"First among blossoms the cherry, among men the warrior."

Another proverb, yet she felt Akira-san had very succinctly answered her question. Talbert was indeed a warrior. She'd sensed it from the first moment she saw him. That kind of skill could only have come from facing violence and conquering it.

"Do you miss your home?"

"Many times."

"Yet, you continue to travel with Talbert. Why?"

"I am sworn to him."

"Sworn? Talbert has held you bonded to some promise all this time? Why, that's barbaric!"

Akira-san chuckled. "You not understand the Japanese, Meg-an-san. To repay *giri*, what you call debt, is as important to us as food, as drink, as love."

"You owed Talbert some great debt?"

"Not I. My brother by marriage, Matsuda Takashi."

Meg nearly groaned. These tidbits were growing more fascinating by the moment. "If your brother-in-law owed Talbert a debt, then why are you the one repaying it?"

"I offer," he responded simply. "Takashi-san have large family, good business making katana, much importance in village. But Takashi-san insist that Takeru-san should not leave Nihon alone."

"Takeru-san?" She frowned. "Do you mean Captain Talbert?"

"It is the name given him by the Matsuda family. His birth name very difficult for Japanese tongue to speak."

"What does it mean?"

"Fierce man. Warrior."

She should have guessed. "Please continue with your story."

"Takashi-san intended to go with Takeru-san, to repay *giri*. He would have to leave his family. I have no one. So I offer to go in his place." Unexpectedly, he winked. "I share secret with you, Meg-an-san, that not even Takeru-san know. I want to see the world, so I happy to go with him. But I never say this to Takeru-san. I let him think I make big sacrifice."

Akira-san's humor was infectious. She smiled, deciding she really liked this man. Leaning forward slightly, she whispered, "I won't breathe a word of it to him, I swear. What did Captain Talbert do for your brother-in-law to earn such gratitude?"

His smile faded abruptly. Meg felt like kicking herself for obviously prying too deep. But it was sadness that drifted across his rugged features, not censure. "A special service he do for Takashi-san's second son. It is not my story to tell," he responded in a tone laced with regret. "When you know Takeru-san better, you ask him why he name his ship the *Shinjiro*."

She blushed, remembering the kiss in the atrium, the moments of intense emotion just hours before, in this same spot, when they buried the hummingbirds together. "I seriously doubt the captain and I will be getting to know each other that well."

"A big rock must be chipped away."

"Huh?"

"I am done," he said crisply, gathering together his materials and rising.

Meg jumped to her feet. "Thank you, Akira-san, for the painting. It's perfect."

He bowed. Then he was gone.

WISTFULLY, MEG STROKED the soft material of the kimono, then lifted it from the box for one last look at the exquisite embroidery. She folded the gown away and closed the lid, sealing the kimono from her sight and the niggling temptation to keep it.

Carrying the box under one arm, Meg resolutely left her bedchamber and started for the stairs.

No matter how beautiful, she simply couldn't accept the gift. Despite Douglass's cockeyed story about buying the kimono from Captain Talbert, she knew the thought had never crossed her father's mind to seek out something so unique, so artistic, so . . . perfect. She loved her father dearly, but Douglass considered himself a robust man's man. He found the mysterious world of women's garments extremely intimidating. Not to mention the fact that this gown was Japanese.

That left Talbert, acting alone.

The cool marble of the banister slid though Meg's hand as she started downstairs. Had Talbert really intended to embarrass her in front of her guests? Perhaps he hadn't anticipated the kimono being mistaken for a dressing gown. Then again, why else would he give her a gift? They'd known each other less than three days, and not under the best of circumstances.

After his kindness in helping her bury the hummingbirds, his offer of comfort, she'd hoped, foolishly, that his resentment had begun to fade. But just because she'd found him innocent of releasing the iguana didn't mean the warrior had ceased his assault on her peace of mind.

Seeking out the butler, she asked, "Robert, have you seen Captain Talbert this morning?"

"I believe you may find him in the ballroom, Miss Meghan."

Her brow creased. "What could he be doing in there?"

"I cannot be certain," Robert muttered, smoothing down his already immaculate neckcloth, "but it seems to be some sort of athletic pursuit." He looked somewhat put out, but then Robert didn't like anything occurring in his domain that defied explanation.

Neither did she. On the other hand, she also loved a good puzzle.

With mounting curiosity, Meg hurried to the ballroom. She paused outside the closed door. Muffled thumping noises, like the impact of feet on the hardwood floor, added to the intrigue.

Her hand inched toward the ornate brass knob. A twinge of guilt caused her fingers to tremble. She should knock, or otherwise announce her arrival, but then he would stop whatever he was doing and she would miss a key opportunity to delve into one of Talbert's many mysteries.

Besides, she reasoned, she'd already intruded on the man at his bath. What could be more brazen than that? It wasn't as if he cavorted naked in her ballroom.

No, just half-naked, she discovered upon easing the door open a crack.

He moved in the center of the open floor, stripped to the waist, wearing only a pair of loose-fitting pants as black as the hair flowing loosely down his shoulders. Even his feet were bare.

Meg bit her lip to prevent a gasp from escaping her throat.

Katana in hand, Talbert worked his body with a vigor and intensity unlike anything she'd ever seen, so intense that he didn't seem to notice that he had an audience. He'd evidently been at it a long time. His hair clung, shiny and wet, to his neck and shoulders. Sweat coated his torso, collecting in thin rivulets that failed to defy gravity . . . unlike the powerful, graceful movements of his body propelling every turn, every sweep of the katana with unnatural lightness.

In the dimly lit bathhouse, the sight of his broad chest and flat abdomen had been impressive as he'd relaxed insolently in the tub. But until now, Meg had never fully appreciated the difference between repose and action.

Dozens of distinct muscles flexed beneath his skin. Bright sunlight, unforgiving to most people, streamed through the eastern windows and highlighted every ridge, every hollow of his body with a warm glow. A number of thin white scars crossed his chest and upper arms at haphazard angles, adding to the picture of chiseled masculinity.

Talbert lunged low in a bold thrust with the sword. The katana hissed as it sliced through air. The flexing motion of his legs flashed a different color at his hip, below waist level. A tawny color, not quite ivory, as if . . . oh heavens—

Meg's eyes widened.

Pale skin, untouched by the sun like the rest of him.

Talbert's baggy pants were an odd style that tied just above each hip, leaving a gap on each side about the size of her hand. Even a half-blind grandmother could surmise he wore nothing underneath . . . nothing but the physique God had blessed him with. Meghan longed for a fan to cool her cheeks. She gnawed the inside of her mouth, attempting to banish a sudden, strange tingling in her lips.

Despite a lifetime of training in propriety, Meg couldn't tear her gaze away. That's what a decent young woman should do.

Then again, the type of demure woman Talbert admired would surely faint from excessive modesty, or possibly expire on the spot from the shock to delicate nerves.

Nobody had ever accused her of being overly delicate. It would serve him right if she took a closer look, a repayment for comparing her to demure Japanese women, as if she were some lower form of life. Besides, when would she have another such opportunity to indulge her love of beauty, to watch a living sculpture at work . . . to watch *him*?

She eased the door open a little more. Talbert seemed so wrapped up in his own universe that he didn't notice the slight movement.

He reminded her of a mountain stream—frothing white water in some areas, smooth and clear as crystal in others, violent, then calm, ever fluid, ever advancing in an infinite variety of patterns. At times the katana clearly acted as a weapon, wielded in powerful, slashing movements. At others he handled it more like an artist's tool, rolling the hilt across his hand, releasing for a split second to change his grip, then pivot and strike in yet another direction.

Mesmerized, Meg devoured the skill, power, and daring of his unique dance.

Talbert seemed to find no such satisfaction in his own performance. His rigid face and clenched jaw formed a stark contrast to his fluid body. Flinty gray eyes focused with daggerlike intensity on imaginary foes.

Meg shivered. This went beyond practice or exercise. There was violence here, retribution. Anger pulsed outward from him in tangible waves.

Who had caused such fury? The man who originally stole the five swords so many years ago? Herself, for demanding he play bodyguard, paying a very personal price for recovery of the blades?

He spun, swinging the sword with such speed the silver blade blurred before her eyes. Without warning he stopped, flipped the katana so that he gripped it point down, then dropped to one knee and stabbed the blade into the floor.

Wood cracked, the sound blasting through the room like a gunshot.

Meg jumped and pressed a hand to her chest. She stared as he wrapped both hands around the hilt and bent over the sword, his hunched shoulders glistening with sweat in the sunlight, his ribs expanding as his body hungered for great draughts of air.

An instant later he threw back his head. Black hair cascaded down his back like the pelt of a wild animal. Thick, rigid tendons carved the column of his neck.

A groan erupted from his throat, deep, wrenching, as if the sound carried shredded bits of his soul with it.

Meg spun away, pressing her back against the outside wall. Her heart thundered, pounding into her ears until her own blood sounded like crashing surf.

Shock mingled with a strange excitement. She felt buoyant, energized with a sense of discovery, of revelation.

She had thought Jacob Talbert cold, arrogant, not only resilient, but completely resistant to all the ugliness life dished out. So hardened and cynical that he no longer cared—about anything.

The stranger she'd just seen was a man ripped apart by strong emotions, who concealed his pain so well behind a mask of indifference that no one saw the shadows.

Akira knew. Now she understood the sadness in the old man's expression, the compassion in his tone when he spoke of his friend, Takeru-san.

She'd been the arrogant one, thinking she understood Jake Talbert. In truth, she didn't know him at all. That kind of sound could only come from a soul in torment.

What had happened to Jake to burden him with such agony?

Chapter Ten

Ice wedged fast in the crevice of the rock this morning begins to melt—under the moss the water will be feeling out a channel.
— SAIGYO (TWELFTH CENTURY)

MEG KNEW SHE should leave, pretend she'd never witnessed the astonishing scene in the ballroom. That was the socially correct thing to do, to spare both Jake and herself embarrassment.

She didn't turn away. She couldn't stop thinking about Jake, his pain, his loneliness. The wall of cynicism had collapsed, baring a need so strong it reached out, coiled around something deep inside her soul, and tugged in a compelling fashion she couldn't ignore.

Loneliness was something she understood only too well.

Meg wrapped her arms around the box, hugging it close to her chest. Her vow to return the kimono dangled like a carrot, tantalizing, providing the perfect excuse to enter the room.

Taking a deep, fortifying breath—which didn't control her trembling in the least—Meg pushed open the door.

Jake had risen and moved over to a chair draped with his clothing. He scrubbed his chest with a towel, as if nothing volcanic had just happened, as if he hadn't just attacked her floor in a fit of rage.

He saw her and froze, the towel pressed to his neck.

For an instant, surprise flickered across his rugged features and he forgot to conceal the dark stirrings in his eyes.

Then the mask of cynicism dropped back into place.

He was good at that.

She clutched the box tighter, hoping he wouldn't see the rapid rise and fall of her chest as she drew nearer. He smelled of masculinity and purifying sweat from a clean, strong body.

"I'm afraid I damaged your floor." Jake broke the tense silence. His voice held a disarming combination of defiance and sheepishness.

Meg bit back a smile. "Gracious, how did that happen?" she exclaimed with sham amazement. "You must have been a little overzealous in your . . . well, whatever it is you are doing. Did you put your foot through the board?"

"Not exactly," he muttered, a frown creasing his brow. "I'll pay for the repairs, of course."

"Oh, no hurry. The ballroom is only used for parties, and I don't plan to entertain again anytime soon."

His gaze dropped to the box in her arms. His lips compressed into a thin, hard line. "Were you looking for me?"

"Yes. I—"

He lifted his arms over his head and began toweling his wet hair. Meg's voice faltered, but her gaze filled the gap by voraciously taking in every detail.

Ridges of muscle stood out cleanly across his flat abdomen and rippled up his arms. His biceps flexed, bulging into corded knots of muscle that contrasted intriguingly with the paler skin of his inner arms—skin that appeared as soft as velvet. The lean, hard mounds of his chest stretched, moving sinuously over bone, tugging at the cords in his neck. Every part of him worked in powerful, perfect harmony.

Meg cleared her throat. "I . . . uh, I need to return the kimono to you," she finished in an unsteady whisper.

With a snap of his wrist, he draped the towel over one shoulder. "Why?"

"You and I both know my father did not buy this."

After only a brief hesitation, he said, "True. It's from me, for your birthday. Consider it repayment for distress caused by the iguanas."

"Regardless, I cannot keep it." She thrust the box toward him.

He ignored the box. "I always honor a debt."

"This is ridiculous. You don't owe me anything. It wasn't your fault the iguana escaped."

"I won't take the kimono back. It is a gift, freely given."

"But it's not proper. I hardly know you! You must take it back!" The words tumbled out as the tingling in Meg's knuckles spread up her outthrust arms. His broad chest offered a devastating distraction. So close. If she unfurled her clenched hands, her fingertips would just brush his crisp black hair.

Jake raised his brows in that I-dare-you fashion that always set her blood to boiling.

"How do you intend to force me?"

She suddenly longed to whack the box over his infuriating head. "I'll have a servant return it to your room."

He took a step forward, lowering his brows. "And I'll bring it back to your bedchamber, personally."

"You wouldn't dare!" She caught her breath, then rolled her eyes. "Oh, what am I saying. Of course you would. In your arrogant fashion, you'd dare anything." Lifting her chin, she countered, "Well, Captain, I can be just as stubborn as you. I'll simply return it as many times as it takes, until you tire of this game."

Without warning, Jake grasped her upper arms and jerked her toward him, trapping the box between them, yet not quite crushing it.

"I don't regard this as a game, Meghan. The kimono is yours. There's not a woman in this world who would look better in it. If you try to give it back, you will find it on your bed, any time of the day or night, whether the bed is empty or not."

In that low, husky tone, his words came across as a dark, seductive promise rather than a threat.

A sizzling tingle swept through Meg's body. Although Jake's dark side still frightened her, her discoveries this morning compelled her to explore the astonishing depth of his hidden emotions.

Meg's death-grip on the box slackened. The stupid thing was in the way. It started to slip from her fingers.

Several voices sounded in the hallway.

Jake released her abruptly. They broke apart, struggling for neutral expressions and a complete lack of guilt.

Robert backed through the open door of the ballroom, looking rather distraught—for good reason. He was outnumbered and overwhelmed by nine women, Tiffany among them, who were so busy bickering that they didn't listen to a word of protest as the butler tried to convince them to wait in the drawing room.

The arguments stopped abruptly, however, when the women caught sight of Jake.

"Meghan!" gasped Elizabeth Wiley. "What are you doing in here with a partially dressed man!"

"In case you hadn't noticed, Lizzie, you are *all* in here with a partially dressed man," Meg retorted dryly, daring them to disagree.

"We are here to see Captain Talbert's chest," said Camilla Smythe-Jones, not bothering to feign modesty. The redhead stepped forward. "I mean his sea chest, of course, containing his cargo of kimonos." Her full mouth curved in a seductive smile while her gaze roved every inch of sculpted muscle.

A deep red suffused Jake's face and chest, darkening the bronze of his skin.

Meg stared at him, stunned by a reaction that seemed so out of character. Jake Talbert . . . blushing?

Rather than feeling amusement, a sharp sting of annoyance shot through Meg. He didn't blush when she looked at his bare chest! Why not? Did she matter so little in his scheme of things? Or worse—a kernel of doubt thickened her throat and triggered a burning behind her eyes—having once kissed her, did he find her naive and unappealing?

The nine women stared in varying degrees of boldness. Fury gripped Meg, spreading through her middle like a writhing, fire-breathing dragon.

What the devil did they think they were looking at? She felt the most absurd urge to step in front of Jake, to conceal that superb physique from their covetous gazes. She ached to grab these women by their upper arms, dig angry fingers into their pampered flesh—most particularly Camilla's—and steer them out of the ballroom on a direct course for the front door.

Shock halted Meg's thoughts before they became bloodthirsty. Was this jealousy? This searing feeling of possessiveness?

An icy chill dipped into her belly. No, it couldn't be, she thought desperately. Jealousy implied that . . . oh, heavens, it was true. She was attracted to Jake Talbert! Terribly. It wasn't supposed to happen this way. She didn't even like him. Not really.

Jake pulled a loose-fitting linen shirt over his head.

A collective sigh shuddered through the group of women.

Meg ground her teeth. "Ladies, let's move to the drawing room. Captain Talbert can join us there with the kimonos in a few minutes."

Tucking the box once again under her arm, Meg herded the women toward the ballroom door like a flock of geese. Thankfully Jake hadn't turned sideways, where they could see the triangles of bare flesh at his hips.

"We apologize for the early hour, Meghan," offered Tiffany, "but apparently we are all competing for the best pick of the captain's collection of kimonos."

"Really, my dear, it's so simple," complained Camilla in a bored tone. "Whoever offers the highest dollar earns first pick."

"That will be for Captain Talbert to decide," Meg insisted.

Passing Robert, she handed him the box and asked that it be returned to her bedchamber. Although she hadn't abandoned her determination of returning the kimono to Jake, she couldn't bear the thought of one of these women wearing it instead.

Touching Tiffany's arm, Meg whispered, "When we reach the drawing room, I intend to speak to these women about discontinuing the practice of wearing humming-bird jewelry. It's so cruel. Will you support me?"

Tiffany's eyes widened with obvious pleasure. "Oh, yes, as long as you speak first. I never could find the courage to say anything."

"WHAT DO YOU mean, she is missing?" Chen Lee shouted.

Enraged, he swung a fist toward Yeung Lian—who was unfortunate enough to be standing within reach—knocking the tea tray from her delicate hands. She screamed as the tray and its contents tumbled in the air, then crashed to the floor just beyond the edge of the red carpet. Pottery shattered. Green tea spread quickly, seeping into the narrow cracks between the lacquered wood planks.

Lian stood frozen, trembling violently. Chen had never slapped her, too cautious of damaging her face, but she'd seen him strike the other women servants often enough to fear his temper. Although Lian regarded her beauty as a curse, having brought her to Chen's attention, she knew it also protected her for now and kept her from an early life in the brothels.

Chen scowled at the mess.

"Clean it up," he snapped, then spun away.

Lian almost wilted with relief. Chen's anger was directed toward the two Chinese men who stood, shame-faced, by the door.

Her gaze slid toward Sung Kwan. He stood in his place against the red curtains covering the walls. Perhaps Kwan's status as Chen's most trusted boo how doy, or bodyguard, had sheltered them from Chen's suspicions. Surely if Chen suspected their love, he would keep them separated with his characteristic ruthless efficiency.

He would never risk his pearl losing her prized virginity to a mere servant, Lian thought with a new bitterness that had grown since the handsome black-haired sea captain had come. The sympathy in the captain's eyes had triggered a growing awareness of herself as a prisoner.

Kwan took a step forward, his expression anxious, his dark eyes tortured as he watched her. But he wisely hesitated, realizing he could not reveal their relationship by showing concern for her distress.

Dear, beloved Kwan. They managed to speak only in brief, stolen moments, yet over the years, that had proven enough to make him the man of her heart. She desperately wanted him to be her first lover . . . her only lover . . . her husband. But her fate, her very body, was not her own.

Tears blurred Lian's vision as she knelt on the carpet,

using napkins to soak up the tea. She righted the tray and began collecting the broken pieces of pottery.

"Explain this to me," she overheard Chen hiss at the two men. "How did you lose Tsao Ping?"

Lian's breath caught high in her throat. These two men had taken Tsao Ping away just yesterday, when the girl turned fourteen. Lian's stomach clenched, remembering Ping's sobs and babbling protests as they dragged her from the house where she'd served as a drudge for three years. Only a brief flicker of distaste had disturbed Chen's impassive face—until he put a stop to the noise with a slap to Ping's face.

Shivering, Lian wondered whether she would shame herself like that, and lose face, when her day came.

Chen had promised her a wealthy patron, one man rather than a string of rutting beasts in a brothel. Yet she felt nauseous at the idea of anyone but Kwan sharing her bed.

"Last night. I looked, she was gone," one of the men whined in Cantonese.

"Where could she go? No one would dare give her shelter."

Amidst muttered excuses, Lian caught the name Mary Lambert.

Chen's chin jerked up a notch. "The mission woman," he snarled.

Ping had escaped? She found a place to go, to hide, where Chen's long reach could not touch her? Despite her fluttering heart, Lian retrieved pottery pieces as quietly as a mouse, tuning her ears to the low conversation. She prayed her master had forgotten her presence in the midst of his anger.

Hope shimmered through her again, a daring feeling she'd experienced for the first time when she'd thought, for a brief moment, that she'd seen an offer of help in the sea captain's intense face. He possessed the spirit and courage of a tiger, that one. But, at the same time, he had frightened her with his rugged hands and hard gray eyes.

Her courage had failed then. Maybe fate was offering her a second chance.

"Lian!" Chen shouted.

She dropped a piece of the broken teapot on the tray with a loud clatter.

"Why are you still here?" he ground out, displeased by her lingering presence in the room.

Did he guess that she'd overheard? She knew, as surely as she harbored ambivalent feelings about the terrifying yet alluring world of freedom beyond Chinatown, that Chen would keep her closely guarded if he knew of her interest in Ping's escape.

Fear clamped her throat in a clawlike grip. Mutely, she pointed to the tray.

Chen scowled. "Go now. Someone else will clean it up."

Hastily, she left the room, bowing stiffly as she backed through the curtain. A wild mixture of hope and dread gripped her body with a strange tension.

One glance at Kwan told her he'd overheard as well. She'd never seen such fiery intensity in his black eyes.

For her, Kwan would seek out this woman, Mary Lambert.

CHEN SMILED GRIMLY as Lian's terrified face disappeared behind the red curtain. Although he disliked frightening his perfect pearl, just like any other girl, Lian needed fear to keep her humble and submissive to his wishes.

He turned back to the two men. "This Lambert

woman, she is a thorn that must be plucked. The girls must not have a place to go." His lip curled. "I want this woman, her house, destroyed. You take care of this, at once."

The fools retreated out the door, apologizing profusely and making rash promises. Boredom settled in Chen's body like a lead weight. If they failed him this time, it would mean their death.

A servant poked his head through the still-open door and informed Chen of another visitor. Chen's slender brows arched upon hearing the man's name.

"Bring him to me."

The servant bowed away, returning a moment later with a tall, nattily dressed gentleman.

Carl Edwards bowed, his blond hair and fair skin out of place in this exotic eastern room. "Good afternoon, Chen Lee."

"I do not wish another loan from your bank, Mr. Edwards."

"I'm not here on bank business, Chen. This is a bit more . . . personal. There is something I wish to discuss, of mutual benefit to us both." His lips thinned in a cold, calculating smile that immediately caught Chen's interest.

It appeared there was a dark side to this American that he hadn't suspected in their previous dealings.

Reaching inside his coat, Edwards pulled out a sheet of folded paper. He spread it open, holding it up to display a roughly sketched diagram in black ink. "This is a map of the grounds of Douglass McLowry's home, as well as the portion of the interior that I'm familiar with. Are you interested, Chen Lee?"

"Should I be?" Chen responded serenely, ruthlessly concealing the excitement that had leapt to life in his chest. The diagram offered the advantage he'd craved. Until now, Chen had not dared send his boo how doy to attack McLowry in his home, a place of mystery in the heart of the white man's world, beyond the reach of Chen's power in Chinatown. Stealth and speed were essential for success, but impossible if the assassins must fumble through an unknown house of enormous size in search of their target. But with this . . . his men could be in and out of the mansion before the police arrived, leaving no clue to link Chen Lee to the crime.

Smugly, Edwards replied, "Yes, I believe you should, after the bit of detective work I've done at the bank." He folded the map and returned it to his pocket, as he smoothed the lapels of his black frock coat.

Chen's smile faded quickly. "Explain. I have little patience for riddles."

"I discovered that McLowry called in your loan quite early, using an obscure clause in the contract that even I overlooked. Then he repaid the loan himself, though he made the transaction difficult to trace, through a series of accounts. Why would he do that, I asked myself. Very curious, considering that, since then, there have been two attempts on his life. I believed he wanted something, Chen, and in the process of getting it he made a very powerful enemy. You, to be precise."

Chen clasped both hands behind his back to relieve the sudden tension gnawing at his shoulder blades. "You indulge in a great many assumptions, Mr. Edwards. What proof do you have?"

"I don't need proof. I have no interest in taking this matter to the police."

"Indeed. Then what do you hope to gain?"

"It's very simple, really. Douglass McLowry has proven himself a hindrance to something I desire. I want him out of the way. With my help, you can accomplish our mutual goal fast enough to suit my needs."

On his quest for vengeance—for what Douglass McLowry had taken from him, for the unforgivable affront to his honor—Chen had longed for a weakness to exploit. He would have killed McLowry on the spot the day he demanded the swords as payment for the loan, but the banker had been savvy enough to bring along a dozen burly police officers. Chen had deliberately lied to Jacob Talbert about the blades, pride demanding he not acknowledge the five swords now in McLowry's possession. They were symbols of Chen's success, spoils of war, and he would not stop until McLowry was dead and the swords returned to their rightful place.

"Well, are you interested?" Edwards prompted impatiently.

"Yes." Chen held out his hand. Edwards handed over the map, wisely demonstrating that he knew who was in charge.

At the first touch of the paper between his fingers, satisfaction flooded Chen, dispelling the dark edges of the boredom that so often haunted him. He smiled. "My servant will show you out, Mr. Edwards. You will soon hear of the results of our efforts. Such shocking news ought to travel quickly through San Francisco."

"DOUGLASS, DO YOU think you can manage without me for a while?" Jake asked as he eyed a curious sight through the window of the Bank Exchange saloon.

Meghan rode down Montgomery Street inside an enclosed landau, the type of carriage typically reserved for evening outings. One of the twins sat up front, handling the reins to the matched pair of bays. Just as they passed

Duncan Nicol's popular saloon, Meghan closed the window shade, as if she didn't wish to be seen or recognized.

"Aye, I'll try not to trip over anything dangerous," Meghan's father responded cheerfully.

Laughter rippled among the group of businessmen clustered at the long, polished bar. Douglass's exalted status as a bank president with a personal bodyguard had provided fuel for a great deal of good-natured ribbing—but then, the Scotsman had been the one to tell his cronies. Douglass thrived on the attention.

"I should be back in a few minutes."

Jake strode outside, glad to escape the stuffy confines of the popular bar, the monotony of the rich patrons in their black sack coats, and the immaculate cleanliness of walls, mirrors, and neatly arranged glasses. The Bank Exchange radiated an aura of near-sanctification. He felt uncomfortable here, preferring to gaze out at everyday people on the street rather than listen to financial gossip or share a glass of Nicol's potent Pisco Punch.

Wistfully, he thought of Abe Warner's Cobweb Palace, with its monkeys, parrots, brawls, and watered-down whiskey. No one there talked obsessively about the money they'd made that day, or how their shares in the Comstock mines had performed on the stock market.

He crossed the cobblestoned street, dodging other carriages while keeping an eye on Meghan's brown landau. The buildings cast long, cold shadows in the late afternoon sun. A crisp wind blew in from the sea as Jake followed Meghan on her mysterious errand.

A brisk pace kept him warm—but not as much as the simmering frustration still remaining from their confrontation this morning. Nor had he found an opportunity to pursue the argument to a satisfying conclusion, for as soon as the women finished going through his cargo like a swarm of locusts, Douglass had sauntered in to say he was ready to leave.

At least Meghan had left the room before she saw the additional kimono he'd held back, the best of the lot. He'd refused to part with it, no matter how much the women pleaded. For some reason, he couldn't let the white kimono go.

The landau quickly reached the edge of the financial district, where the buildings were older and more dilapidated. It halted in front of a small curio shop.

Peter—Jake recognized him from the way he moved— stepped down and open the landau door. Meghan climbed out gracefully, looking very fetching in a mauve walking dress trimmed in black braid. Reaching inside the carriage, Peter burdened his arms with two bulky bags and followed her into the shop.

Jake hesitated outside, watching through a window crammed with china, silver, clocks, and knickknacks of every kind—an estate auctioneer's dream. The proprietor, a round little man with thinning gray hair, greeted Meghan enthusiastically and kissed her gloved hand. She smiled, greeting him as if they were of long acquaintance. Peter set the bags on the counter. She reached into one and pulled out a small brass clock.

Jake's eyes narrowed.

It was one of the gifts she'd opened at the party. What was she up to?

He watched, incredulous, while she unpacked items from the night before. Every expensive gift she'd received covered the counter . . . everything except, of course, the hummingbird jewelry—and the blue kimono.

Meg and the proprietor dickered animatedly over price, finally coming to a total they could both agree on, as evidenced by the thick wad of folded bills the proprietor handed over with obvious reluctance.

Meghan drove a hard bargain.

Jake could testify to that from his own experience.

She stuffed the money into her reticule, then bid the proprietor good day with a broad smile. Peter stopped his exploration of the cluttered shop and accompanied his mistress to the door.

Jake ducked behind the corner of an adjacent building.

Instead of heading home, they continued in a direction that would take Meghan straight into Chinatown. Jake's curiosity quickly shifted to concern. Little fool. Why was she venturing into the dragon's lair?

Hailing a hansom cab, Jake ordered the driver to keep the landau in sight.

Did she plan to bribe people on the streets of Chinatown for information? Was she reckless enough to try to buy off the Tong leaders intent on hurting her father?

An icy wave of dread washed through him. She didn't understand the utter ruthlessness of men like Chen Lee. His hatchet men would kill her and Peter without a qualm, then take the money and dump their bodies in the bay.

Jake disliked the concern beating at him like a mallet. Every cross-street brought them closer to the town-within-a-town that isolated the Chinese from the often violent prejudice of people who termed them "Celestials."

Just as the familiar stench of fish and crowded humanity reached his nostrils, Meghan startled him yet again by turning down Sacramento Street.

Nothing, however, could have prepared him for the shock of seeing her stop at Mary Lambert's Mission Home for Chinese Girls.

Meghan and Peter climbed the steps to the porch of the three-story white house. Determined to discover what had brought her to this little-known place, Jake paid the cabbie, then concealed himself behind a sprawling oak tree.

A dozen Asian girls, ranging from small children to willowly teenagers, rushed out the door. They greeted the visitors excitedly. The younger ones hopped around, exclaiming in rapid-fire Cantonese, while the two oldest girls glanced shyly at the blushing German from under black lashes.

An attractive woman in her early forties joined them, her thick brown hair shot through with gray.

Mary Lambert. Jake easily recognized the Christian missionary. When she'd opened the house a year ago, he'd helped her paint, fix the storm gutters, and replace broken windowpanes. He'd offered more, but in lieu of money Mary asked him to bring bolts of fabric, thread, and other supplies she could use in teaching the girls how to sew. He honored her request, donating a portion of his last three shipments.

If only Mary had arrived in San Francisco a year earlier, the Chinese slave girl he'd tried to rescue would have had a place to go, a refuge.

Mary's commanding voice carried as she asked the girls to find Peter something to eat. They took him inside, their glossy heads clustering around him like black butterflies about a massive blond tree trunk.

The two women stood alone on the porch.

Meghan opened her reticule and eased out the wad of money, just enough for the housemother to see. Mary's trembling hand pressed to her mouth. She appeared close to tears.

Suddenly, the two women laughed and embraced. They went into the house, arm in arm, still laughing.

Jake braced one stiff arm against the tree and stared at the ground, stunned.

Bloody hell, Meghan had sold her birthday gifts to give money to the mission!

The Nob Hill society of San Francisco would suffer mass apoplexy if they knew their expensive trinkets were being used to feed, house, and teach girls that—until Mary Lambert intervened—had been destined for the whorehouses. Those same people turned a blind eye to the trafficking in human flesh going on right under their upturned noses. Girls were kidnapped or, more often, sold into slavery by their own impoverished families in China, as early as the tender age of six. Their owners used the younger children as household drudges until they were old enough to prostitute themselves.

Meghan defied convention, coming here. She risked her reputation and her precious social standing. She even gambled with her safety, for the girls were very valuable, and battles with the flesh-peddlers often grew heated, ugly, and potentially threatening.

A dark shape detached itself from the shadows on the east side of the house, then disappeared behind the building.

Jake came alert, scenting danger.

He moved silently, his tread light, his breathing measured. He passed the front parlor window. A quick glance inside showed Meghan at the piano, most of the girls clustered around her as she played. Beautiful sounds drifted outward, tempting him to forget his unfounded suspicions and pause, to listen. But he trusted his instincts and moved on.

Beneath the next window, he found a bundle of three sticks of dynamite.

Fury lanced through him.

He pulled out the fuses and stuffed them in his pocket, then concealed the dynamite in a thick bush. The bastards couldn't light the explosives without the fuses.

Another bundle rested on the kitchen windowsill, a dormant yet malevolent threat. Someone was strategically planting dynamite around the perimeter of the house, apparently to return, at any moment, and light the fuses in quick succession.

Jake could easily guess who was responsible.

The Tongs profited highly from the prostitution and sale of the girls. Mary Lambert must rate as a serious threat. She not only battled the owners in court, gaining custody of the girls and ultimately their freedom, she provided a haven for other victims in search of refuge.

She offered hope.

For that offense, the Tongs wanted her out of the way—permanently.

And Meghan had chosen the wrong bloody time to visit.

A cold rage gripped him. Easing around the corner, he spotted a Chinese man planting another bundle of dynamite under the back porch. Sneaking up behind, Jake clamped one hand over the man's mouth so he couldn't cry out. He hauled the wretch roughly to his feet, then knocked him unconscious with a sharp blow to the neck. Dammit, he'd like to beat the man to a pulp, but there might be more than one villain and he had no time.

Jake added the fuses to the growing tangle in his pocket. It felt like a swarm of snakes.

A quick look down the opposite side of the house revealed another man, planting more deadly dynamite. Jake hesitated, caught by a sudden idea. His lips curved in a grim imitation of a smile.

He removed one stick of dynamite from the last bundle, inserted a fuse, then searched the unconscious man's pockets for a flint. Luckily, the fuses they'd brought were extra long, supposedly so the culprits could be several blocks away before the explosions shattered the quiet of the neighborhood.

Jake lit the fuse.

The second man turned as he drew near, warned by the sound of the crackling fuse. Jake kicked him in the jaw before he could react, then hooked an arm around the villain's neck and jerked him tightly back against his chest.

Holding the dynamite up before the man's livid face, Jake growled in Cantonese, "Tell me who sent you."

The would-be bomber struggled and tried to blow out the flame. The fuse only burned faster.

He filled his lungs to yell for help. Jake choked off the scream by tightening his arm until the man gasped for air.

"I took care of your friend. There's no one to help you. Answer me, or I'll shove this dynamite down your pants. Even if you survive, you can say good-bye to your future generations." He waved the dynamite slowly in a figure eight. The Asian's head followed it as if a string tugged on his nose.

He babbled hysterically, begging Jake for mercy.

"I'm only interested in who sent you," Jake barked, finding no sympathy for the bastard who had every intention of blowing up Mary, the children, and Meghan. Cold anger slithered through him. "Talk!"

"Chen Lee!" the man cried as the fuse burned to within an inch.

Jake pinched out the flame.

The man sagged with relief. Jake shoved him away, then laid him out with a vicious blow. He didn't move after that.

Seething with rage, Jake gathered up all the dynamite and hid it in a bucket in the storage shed. He could dispose of it properly later. As he closed the lid, a tremor ripped through his body, stealing his breath. Dear God, what this amount of dynamite would have done to the house, its occupants . . .

A muscle ticked in his cheek while he seized some rope from the shed and tied up the two felons. Grabbing them both by the collar, he dragged them to the front, then a short distance down the street. He hailed a hansom cab, and when that one stopped, he hailed another.

"Hey, mate," the first driver protested. "I can handle your fare!"

"I have a special errand for you," insisted Jake. He pulled out two gold coins and pressed them into the cabbie's palm.

"Sure, whate'er you say," the man said agreeably, grinning.

"Go to the Rincon Hill address I'm going to give you and ask for Komatsu Akira. When he comes to the door, tell him Jake sent you, and to bring both his swords and mine. Then take him to this Chinatown address. Two more coins await your arrival. And hurry." Jake detailed the street and house numbers for both locations. "Understood?"

The cabbie spat on the ground. "You gonna fight them heathen Chinee? You shoulda asked me to do it for free, mate."

Jake stiffened. In a low voice, he said sarcastically, "My friend is Asian, *mate*. He's a Japanese warrior, not Chinese, so you'd better treat him with the proper respect. Otherwise, he just might cut off your head if you insult him."

Flinching, the cabbie reassured quickly, "Yeah, sure."

After he drove off, Jake shoved the two limp felons into the other hansom. He repeated the address of Chen Lee's residence. There he would await Akira-san's arrival, then pay an unannounced visit on the Tong leader.

·   ·   ·

JAKE DIDN'T APPLY the brass dragon knocker. He didn't wait for the doorman to answer a summons.

He simply kicked in the door.

The latch ripped through the frame with a thunderous crack. Splintered wood flew into the foyer as the door swung hard on its hinges and crashed into the adjacent wall.

Katana in hand, Jake stepped through the opening, prepared for the two boo how doy he'd seen on his first visit. They attacked from either side, wielding the favorite weapon of Tong soldiers-for-hire: short, deadly carpenters' hatchets.

Knowing he must quickly disable the opponent on his right, or risk getting hacked to death from behind, Jake slammed the katana's hilt into the man's wrist. Bone cracked. The boo how doy howled, dropping his hatchet and cursing. Jake finished him off with a paralyzing knee to the groin.

Jake pivoted sharply. His vision filled with the glitter of steel—on a downward stroke meant to cleave his skull.

He caught the curved edge of the hatchet on the katana blade just inches from his forehead. Metal ground against metal. A fist connected with his ribs. Pain shot through his chest, stinging like a thousand needles when he drew his next breath. Enraged that the man was able to sneak in a blow, Jake grabbed a handful of the Asian's tunic and slammed him against the wall.

The man's head shot forward, cracking against Jake's chin. Black spots danced before his eyes. His grip slackened. As the man attacked again, Jake jumped back and swung the katana. The lethally sharp edge sliced cleanly across his opponent's thigh. The boo how doy staggered back, his face registering shock, blood welling from the deep, disabling cut.

Spotting the little doorman cringing in a shadowed corner, Jake snapped, "Tell Chen I want to speak to him. Now!"

Despite violent trembling and wringing of his hands, the doorman nodded vigorously and dashed off.

Three more boo how doy materialized at the various entrances into the foyer, Sung Kwan among them. They hesitated, taking in the scene.

Jake drew a deep, cleansing breath. His body tingled with the pump of adrenaline-heated blood. He swung the katana to the side, his wrist jerking at the outer edge like the crack of a whip. The Asian's blood flicked from the blade and misted to the carpet in tiny droplets.

He resheathed the blade and shifted into an *iaijutsu* stance, a pose just as deadly as having the katana already drawn.

The eyes of all three boo how doy widened, whites flashing.

Kwan spoke for all of them, whispering in awe, "He is samurai."

As silent as a wraith, Chen Lee came into the foyer and stopped. He raised a hand to signal his men.

Jake never knew whether the signal meant to hold or attack, for just then Akira created a distraction by dragging the first of the conscious bombers through the door and dropping him in a tightly bound heap on the carpet.

Chen stiffened, his face rigid.

"Here are the mangy dogs you sent to Sacramento Street, Chen," snarled Jake. "I'll say this only once: If anything happens to Mary Lambert, her girls, or her house, I'll test the sharpness of my blade by slicing you into little chunks."

Jake's gray-eyed gaze locked with Chen's furious black. The powerful Tong leader was not accustomed to being thwarted.

Akira hauled in the other struggling bomber and dumped him next to the first. Then the old samurai stood at Jake's side and smiled, clearly anticipating the fight to come, the lives he would take. The three boo how doy did not move. Apprehension flickered across two of their faces. Kwan's expression was alert, alive with speculation rather than fear.

Chen Lee said nothing, his throat too constricted with blazing fury as he allowed the two intruders to back out his damaged door and escape.

Sourly, Chen thought, *Now that I see him handle a katana, I remember where I've seen Jacob Talbert before.*

Although nearly half a lifetime ago, Chen would never forget that rain-drenched, muddy battlefield on the island of Kyoshu. There he'd captured the greatest prizes ever taken in his raids across the sea on the coastal villages of Japan. The image of a tall white man, wielding a katana like a true samurai, would always stick in his mind—not only because of his own shock, but the chaos of his band of raiders nearly bolting in superstitious fear. But he had rallied them, emphasizing that they outnumbered the band of Japanese four to one.

He'd worn a helmet that day, so it wasn't surprising Talbert didn't recognize him now. Nor was he dismayed by his own lack of perception. Sixteen years had changed Talbert dramatically, hardening the young, reckless combatant into a truly dangerous warrior.

Chen cursed inwardly. He should have checked the bloodied, motionless form on the battlefield, felt for the beat of life in the white man's neck. Instead, he'd assumed the mud-caked youth to be as dead as the headless body of the Japanese samurai lying next to him—even as Chen took the five swords from their limp forms.

He had been wise to lie to Talbert at their first meeting. If he had admitted that the descriptions of the five swords matched the blades taken by Douglass McLowry, Talbert would have pursued their recovery with the same zeal he'd displayed in trying to defend his friends on the battlefield.

Chen glared at the two henchmen who should have efficiently disposed of Mary Lambert. Instead, they'd brought violence into his household and threats down upon his head. They cowered under his glare.

Well they should. He was glad Talbert had gagged them, for now he wouldn't have to listen to them beg.

Chen turned away in disgust, signaling Kwan to follow him. As he passed the remaining boo how doy, he ordered coldly, "Kill them."

Chapter Eleven

Are the vast heavens some keepsake of her I love? No, that is absurd. What then makes me stare skyward whenever I think of her?
—SAKAI NO HITOZANE (D. 931)

I

T WAS WELL PAST dark before Jake returned to the Rincon Hill mansion.

Robert opened the door.

"Where is Meghan?" Jake demanded immediately upon entering the foyer. He wasn't in the mood for pleasantries. Meghan had left Mary's house by the time he returned. Despite every effort to discipline his temper, ignorance of her whereabouts and concern for her safety had punched holes in his mood all evening.

Warning Mary of the danger from Chen Lee, arranging for the *Shinjiro*'s crew to watch the mission in shifts, and disposing safely of the dynamite had all prevented Jake from reaching the Bank Exchange before Douglass left. The banker had sauntered home, apparently rather drunk, without his celebrated bodyguard at his side.

Jake might find the flash of anger in Meghan's blue eyes invigorating, and enjoy provoking a fiery response, but right now just the expectation of her inevitable anger caused his muscles to tense and his hands to itch with the urge to hit something.

A samurai is always in control of his emotions.

Meghan wrecked havoc with his inner harmony. In all the years since he'd begun training as a samurai, he'd never felt so far from his goal of *fudoshin*. That would explain this growing restlessness, the frustration and emptiness gnawing at his soul, the compulsion to seek something he didn't have.

He must eliminate the threat to Douglass as soon as possible, take the swords, and return to Japan and the life he'd fought so hard to regain. There he could remain at peace, separated from the chaos of human passions and life's upheavals.

"*Miss McLowry*," Robert stressed with freezing dignity, "is in the music room."

Jake turned in that direction.

"Begging your pardon, sir," the butler interjected hastily, "but Miss McLowry does not wish to be disturbed."

"She'll want to see me, I'll wager, if for no other reason than to ring a peal over my head."

Drawing himself to his full height, Robert countered, "It is the lady's custom, supported by her *rigid* instructions, not to receive anyone when she is in the music room."

Glowering, Jake retorted, "Well, I saved her life once today, and I bloody well intend to make sure my efforts haven't gone to waste."

Robert gave a sniff of patent disbelief. Jake tried to ignore it, but the man's lack of faith irritated him nonetheless.

Jake spun on his heel and stalked off, his mind burning with the cynical idea that he should have brought back a stick of dynamite as a souvenir—to prove that he'd spent his afternoon in worthwhile endeavors rather than capricious pursuits. At least Mary Lambert had taken his word seriously, especially after showing her a bucket full of nearly averted tragedy.

Anger clung to him like the stinging tentacles of a jellyfish as he neared the music room.

Then he heard the piano.

Meghan had left the door ajar. The same rich sounds he'd heard from the mission's parlor slipped through the opening, claiming their freedom.

Jake hesitated just outside the door. The beautiful notes filled his mind and worked their way into the flow of his blood. He leaned back against the wall, listening. Fury and frustration receded like the quiet withdrawal of the tide.

Chopin.

How did he know that?

Stunned, heart suddenly pounding, Jake reached for the elusive memory. Since the age of ten, the only piano music he'd heard had been raucous tinklings in a crowded saloon. Nothing cultured . . . nothing like this. So why could he recognize the composer?

With a jolt of insight, he realized the memory tugged at him from early childhood. His mother had played Chopin. This piece had been one of her favorites.

Jake closed his eyes, concentrating so hard his clenched teeth began to ache. Although he could see the black thickness of his mother's hair, smell the rose scent of her toilet water, he couldn't picture her face. She had played this piece with graceful precision, true to Chopin's original design . . . .

Meghan, on the other hand, made it her own.

The energy in Meghan's music dominated his senses, shutting out the past. At times the chords whispered mournfully beneath her gentle touch; at others, they welled to a powerful crescendo, susceptible to her every mood as she poured her heart into the song.

Joy, struggle, determination, loneliness . . . oceans of

loneliness . . . all these, and more, resonated from her music. He discovered new evidence of the elemental woman beneath the satin-and-lace facade, a woman who felt things deeply, passionately.

The realization proved devastating.

The passion sank into him like silver talons. He drew it in with each breath, felt it brush across his skin like the silken caress of her lips. His blood turned to molten lava, hardening his manhood in a rush. Visions of lifting her from the piano bench and making wild, sweet love to her on the carpet consumed his mind in the same way images of fresh water would torment a man lost in a desert.

Jake shoved away from the wall and staggered down the hall, burning. A cool draft from a nearby window drew him like a magnet. Blindly, he leaned his forehead against the chilled glass, allowing it to draw the heat from his body. The music stopped, thankfully releasing its spell.

He wasn't sure how long he stood there, but finally the fire in his loins became a manageable ache rather than a clawing hunger. The rising moon topped the roof of the house, its gray light penetrating his eyelids with a soft glow.

Looking up, Jake exhaled a long sigh. The lush gardens of the atrium came into focus through the glass.

Suddenly, the significance of the cold window struck him. The temperature outside was dropping.

MEG HELD THE last chord of the sonata a long time, loath to let the music end. Her fingers pressed hard against the piano keys, until the skin beneath her fingernails whitened and the reverberating crash of the notes faded into grudging silence.

Now what? Meg thought a little desperately. She'd poured her emotions into the music for almost two hours, until her arms trembled with exhaustion.

She stared at her rigid fingers, the same hands that had brought pleasure to so many through her music. Was this the only measure of her significance? A pretty tune on the piano and a reputation as an exemplary hostess?

Where was the substance in her life?

No one ever stumbled lying snug in bed. Akira-san's words came back to her. Crossing her arms over the base of the music stand, Meg dropped her forehead onto her wrists.

Meg saw no difference between her own existence and that of a porcelain doll in a showcase—something lovely and fragile, kept safely tucked away until someone needed her or wanted to play. Even though she'd forced her eyes open the night of the party, and now recognized the gilded cage, the most daunting question remained: Was the perception of fragility justified? Did her father shelter her because he perceived a need for protection that she did not?

How would she ever know . . . if she didn't test her boundaries, offer something of herself other than money?

Mary Lambert didn't just talk about the need to stop the Chinese slave trade, she unselfishly dedicated her life to offering the girls shelter and an opportunity for a new beginning. Although she expressed gratifying appreciation for the gifts Meg brought, money certainly didn't help Mary with the training of so many girls, or give her strength to face the owners in court and fight for custody, or endure the seething animosity of the Tongs.

In Meg's opinion, Mary qualified as a heroine. A quiet, unassuming heroine whose light shone all the brighter because she gave the glory to God.

It was unpleasantly humbling to be surrounded by heroes.

Her mind's eye filled with an image of broad shoulders, long black hair, and steely gray eyes.

Meg's head jerked up. Why should she think of Jacob Talbert in the same context as Mary? He was arrogant, stubborn, and—so far—hadn't done a damn thing to prove himself as a bodyguard!

With a groan, Meg acknowledged that she craved an affirmation, proof that her confidence in Jake stemmed from something more than a growing obsession with the man. And even though her top priority was her father's safety, she also wished Jake would finish the job and leave, go away, remove her reason for constantly dwelling on the wrong man's kisses—and wondering irritably why he hadn't tried to kiss her again!

HESITATING OUTSIDE THE door to the atrium, Jake watched and listened for any approach. The last thing he needed was the household staff—or, heaven forbid, Akira-san—to catch him on his present errand.

Never mind that he took his responsibilities seriously. The teasing loomed as potentially merciless.

He opened the atrium door, now repaired, and slipped inside. With eyes already accustomed to the dark, he searched for the scaly companions who'd shared his ship cabin for several weeks. The two iguanas shouldn't be difficult to find. Like little military generals, they always sought the high ground.

While in his cabin, they'd lounged atop his bookcase, or the upper edges of the window shutters. The rice paper on the shutters was forever scarred with claw marks.

As expected, he discovered them stretched out, tails

dangling, on two different limbs of the tallest tree. He reached for the lizards slowly. Numbed by the cold, they didn't have the wherewithal to leap away with their usual speed. Disentangling their claws from the bark proved a more difficult matter.

Finally, feeling like a seamstress picking the stitches from a ruined seam, he lifted the iguanas down. They moved sluggishly as he draped them across his folded arms, rolling their eyes slowly to look up at him. At least hypothermia hadn't set in.

Relief spread through him, making him feel completely foolish. Damn, he was a sucker for a pair of reptiles.

If Akira-san got wind of what he was doing, he'd never hear the end of it. But then, Akira-san was not the one who'd spent hours earning their trust so they wouldn't tear up his cabin, nor found it endlessly fascinating to discover their favorite foods or laugh at their frequently amusing antics. The iguanas had definitely entertained him on the voyage up from Mexico.

Reaching his bedchamber, Jake checked the room for any possible means of reptilian escape. Finding everything secure, he set the iguanas in a chair and covered them with a blanket . . . though he knew, from experience, that they would end up somewhere else before dawn.

JAKE CAME AWAKE in a heartbeat.

Darkness still enveloped the room in a charcoal mist, relieved only by the weak moonlight through the window. It was not yet dawn. He stretched out with his senses, seeking the unknown that had mysteriously jarred him from sleep.

Only the sounds of a city that never quite slept drifted in from a distance. All seemed normal.

Maybe it was nothing. The day's events had put him on edge.

Regardless, he couldn't exactly leap out of bed.

Tucking his chin, Jake stared into a pair of gold-black eyes not six inches from his nose.

He shook his head ruefully. The first time the yellow-striped female had crawled onto his chest during the night, he'd reacted as if some practical joker had lit a row of Chinese firecrackers beneath his bed. He'd thought the incident a fluke, but when both lizards persisted in seeking out his warmth every night, he'd grown so accustomed he barely noticed when they joined him. There was something oddly comforting in their trust.

He reached behind his head. Sure enough, the female with olive-green stripes lay snug under his pillow.

Sometimes he wondered whether they sought companionship as much as warmth, strange as it may seem. On more than one occasion, as he'd worked on the ship's log and manifests, they'd scrambled right across his desk, scattering papers everywhere. Their behavior was so much like a cat demanding attention that he'd been shocked by their display of intelligence.

Suddenly, the nape of his neck tingled.

The iguanas also tensed, confirming his instinctive sense that danger lurked nearby.

Jake scooped the lizard off his chest and slid out of the bed in one smooth motion. Cold air pricked his bare skin. He tucked the female between the covers, where his lingering body warmth should keep her comfortable.

He pulled a black silk shirt over his head, then yanked on a pair of like-colored hakama and tightened the strings over his hips. Standing at the window, he wound the sash about his waist while he scanned the back garden.

A shadow detached from a tree and slunk toward the house.

Another wraith garbed in black followed, then a third.

Jake grabbed his katana and thrust it through the sash as he raced for the door. He ran soundlessly down the second-floor hallway. The alternating textures of soft carpet runner and cold hardwood floor under his bare feet shot lightning messages to his brain. Adrenaline charged him fully awake.

He must reach the ground floor before the intruders broke into the house. Otherwise, they could split up to carry out their sinister agenda, making it impossible to hunt down all of them in time . . . before someone died.

Speed was critical, any shortcut welcome.

Halfway down the curving front staircase, he grabbed the banister and vaulted over the side. His feet and legs flexed when he hit the marble ground floor, absorbing the impact, muffling all but an indistinct thump of sound. He froze in a half-crouch, fingertips resting lightly on the cold stone, toes curling to grip the smooth surface.

He briefly debated waking the staff, then decided against it. The servants were no match for experienced, ruthless hatchet men. If there was a fight, more lives would be forfeit.

Creatures of the shadows must be stalked—with the same silent, deadly efficiency they sought to employ.

He would deal with them alone.

Seeking direction, Jake listened for the chink of cut glass, the whisper of curtains swaying in a sudden breeze, the soft scrunch of feet on carpet.

Nothing. The men hadn't yet entered the house. If he could anticipate their point of entry—

The French doors were the most vulnerable, of course, but which ones? There were six sets of the damn things on the ground floor alone. Since Douglass was the most likely target, the Scotsman's study was as good a place as any to start.

In the same instant his fingers touched the study door, Jake heard the gritty scrape of glass being cut. He eased silently into the room just as three men stole through the French doors.

Jake held back, sizing up the enemy, using his black garb to blend into the darkness. Oblivious to his presence, they paused and whispered harshly at each other in Cantonese. Paper crackled as one held up a crumpled sheet to the moonlight.

With deliberate lack of finesse, Jake drew his katana. The distinctive hiss of metal sliced across the room.

The intruders jumped and yanked out their weapons. They froze, their gazes searching the shadows, still unsure of the source of the threat.

Anticipation sang through Jake's blood. Here were flesh-and-blood opponents, not the phantom, taunting enemies of his nightmares. Smiling grimly, he purposefully turned the katana until moonlight rippled along the length of the polished steel, revealing his location.

The three assassins reacted instantly, attacking.

Jake deflected their initial blows, striking back with his sword or a well-aimed kick. The katana responded instantly to his every thought, infusing him with an invigorating sense of strength and invulnerability.

Only one other thing had made him feel this alive, this on fire, in recent years—his unexpected, undisciplined lust for Meghan McLowry.

The nearest man lunged forward. Jake countered with his sword, capturing the lower edge of the hatchet blade against the katana. With a violent, twisting motion of his wrists, he broke the man's grip. The hatchet wrenched free and sailed into the shadowed recesses of the room.

Jake whipped the katana over his right shoulder, coiling his body's energy for a single horizontal strike at neck level.

At the last second, he remembered that this was not a Kyoshu battlefield, nor the violent streets of a port town—where the rule was kill or be killed. If he stained this room in crimson, leaving decapitated bodies lying at his feet, Meghan would surely regard him as a bloodthirsty savage. The intriguing fire in her eyes would turn to horror; her melting warmth would change to cold revulsion.

Defying years of training, he stepped forward into the swing instead, using his clenched fists on the katana's hilt to smash into the assassin's jaw. The man dropped like a stone.

Pivoting toward the next man, Jake slashed the katana toward his vulnerable belly, using a reach just short of the target. The ploy gained the desired results. The second assassin doubled over to avoid the steel tip, failing to wield his own weapon. He thrust out his chin in open invitation.

Jake caught the man on the chin with a powerful kick. The assassin's body jerked upright, then arced backward, his feet leaving the floor.

In the darkened room, only a faint whooshing sound warned Jake of the speeding threat.

He jerked his head to the left a heartbeat before the whirling hatched buzzed by his right ear like the low drone of swarming, angry wasps. The hatchet embedded in the door frame with a sickening thunk. It could just as easily have been the sound of his forehead splitting, if the third man's throw found its mark. It was a sound Jake would never forget.

A tremor of rage shuddered through him from head to toe, multiplied by the shock of a close brush with

40.671   0.001

death. Jake sheathed the katana, allowing himself the pleasure of feeling his knuckles connect with the bastard's body. After several sharp jabs, Jake smashed his fist into the man's mouth. The fellow crashed onto his back, still conscious.

Jake pinned the boo how doy to the carpet with one knee pressing roughly into the center of the man's chest. "Why are you here?" he snarled, knowing he shouldn't assume these men were after Douglass. After his own confrontation with Chen Lee this afternoon, it was possible that they were here to eliminate one Jacob Talbert. It wouldn't be the first time he'd become the target of a vendetta.

A malicious grin spread across the assassin's narrow face. Blood shone slick on his teeth. A low chuckle slipped from a throat that Jake suddenly ached to crush with his bare hands.

The low laugh crawled across Jake's skin like something slimy and decaying. The man's vengeful satisfaction could mean one thing.

There were more assassins, dammit. Another group of hatchet men must have entered the house separately, enjoying free run of the place while he dealt with these three.

Cold dread poured down Jake's spine.

He slammed the heel of his palm into the ridge between the man's eyes, knocking him unconscious.

Jake sprinted out the study door. He took the stairs three at a time. Within seconds, he reached Douglass's bedchamber.

He opened the door without hesitation—and discovered two boo how doy poised at the Scotsman's bedside. The nearest stood with hatchet raised, ready to hack Meghan's sleeping father to death.

Fury shot through Jake's mind like a hot red mist. The assassins were too far away. Even his fastest *iaijutsu* move would not be sufficient to reach them with the katana.

But he was far from helpless. He yanked out the *kogai*, a slender dagger tucked in a special pocket in the side of the katana's saya. Grabbing the steel tip between his thumb and forefinger, Jake threw the kogai with ruthless accuracy. The blade found its mark, completely piercing the biceps of the arm wielding the hatchet.

The man cried out, dropping the weapon. The companion cursed and caught the wounded man as he staggered back, gripping his skewered arm.

Douglass jerked awake with a gruff shout. He whispered hoarsely, "Who's there?" Then, more forcefully, he growled, "Where are you, you yellow bastards? I'll shoot you!"

As Douglass fumbled beneath the pillows, the two boo how doy bolted for the window. Jake launched himself in pursuit.

Just then a revolver appeared in the Scotsman's unsteady hand, waving indiscriminately at anything that moved in the dark room. Jake froze. He much preferred not getting shot, particularly by the man he was supposed to be protecting.

The intruders disappeared the same way they'd come in.

With an irritable sigh, Jake snapped, "Douglass, put the damn gun away!"

There was a moment of silence, broken only by Douglass's ragged breathing. "Jacob, is that you?"

"Yes." Jake moved to the far side of the bed.

"Why are you in my room, lad?" Meghan's father exclaimed. "Dinna you know I could have shot you?" He clambered out of bed, nearly tripping over the hem of his baggy white nightshirt, and turned up the nearest gas sconce. Light swelled, reclaiming a portion of the room from the sinister darkness.

Jake bent over to pick up the fallen hatchet. "You'd like to know that I'm earning my keep as bodyguard, wouldn't you?"

Douglass's eyes widened at the sight of the weapon, with its obvious link to the Tongs. The open window also stood in mute testament of a narrow escape from disaster. His mouth opened, then closed, then opened again before any sound emerged.

"Did you just save my life?"

"Something like that," Jake growled. "I'll send some servants to board up that window, after I take care of a few problems downstairs."

Moving with surprising speed for a man of his bulk, Douglass intercepted Jake before he could reach the door, grabbing his forearm. The digging pressure of his fingers betrayed the fear he otherwise tried to conceal.

"You dinna plan to tell Meghan about this?"

Taken aback, Jake exclaimed, "Not tell her?" His eyes narrowed. "Why not?"

"So she will not worry herself sick, of course."

"That must be the weakest excuse I've ever heard," Jake countered, thinking of how the old man had chosen to seek his entertainment at the card table last night rather than help his daughter with the burdens of hosting a large party. "What are you really getting at, Douglass?"

Ignoring the question, the Scotsman urged, "Promise me. Swear to me that you'll protect my Meggie."

"Of course I will. You know that."

"No, you dinna know my full meaning," the older man hissed, his voice vibrating as he shook Jake's arm for emphasis. "Meggie is to be your first priority, no' me. I want you to watch over her. I'm an old man, most of my life gone. If you must choose her safety over mine, then protect my lassie."

"You think she's in danger?"

Douglass's hands slid limply from Jake's arm. His shoulders slumped, his gaze growing distant and unfocused as he stared at the window. "I just dinna realize it would be like this. They were so very fine, everything I'd heard and more. I just had to have them. . . ." The strained whisper drifted away into silence.

"What have you gotten involved in, Douglass? What is going on here?"

The Scotsman snapped to attention, straightening, instantly reverting to his persona of confident banker. "Nothing is going on! I'm just a victim of some Chinese madman, a Celestial with a misguided vendetta."

The untruth in the words tickled unpleasantly across Jake's skin like a crawling spider. His temper slipped, the anchor pulling free of its moorings.

Jake raised the hatchet and threw it. It spun between the mahogany posts of the huge master bed, slicing through the air to embed deep in the wall over the headboard.

Douglass winced. His face took on a pasty hue as he stared at the hatchet. The implication was clear—without Jake's interference, that blade would be embedded in his skull instead.

"Don't lie to me, McLowry! Or to yourself, dammit." Jake raked a hand through his loose hair. "I can't fight phantoms. I can't go to the source if you don't tell me the truth."

At least Meghan's father had the grace to look sheepish. He rubbed the knuckles of his right hand against his chest.

"Do you swear to protect her?" Douglass persisted.

"I promise," Jake answered gruffly, his throat suddenly thick with an intensity he didn't understand. He'd never meant an oath more in his life.

The Scotsman sighed. "Very well, lad." He sank weakly onto the edge of the bed. "I'm a collector of swords. 'Tis my one great passion, besides my work. Six months ago, I heard tell of five magnificent blades, owned by a Chinese businessman named Chen Lee. Chen had kept them a secret, very likely for years, until one of his servants tried to steal them. He recovered the swords, but word leaked out. I offered to buy them, increasing my offer several times, but he would not accept."

So Chen lied to me, Jake thought with simmering fury. *He was in possession of the Matsuda blades.*

"I hired a man to investigate Chen, watch him, search out any weakness," Douglass continued. "Soon after, my man brought word that a large shipment of Chen's goods had sunk off the coast. Chen had tied up most of his assets in purchasing that shipment, and its loss left him hurting, his business faltering without sufficient cash to invest in another cargo. The opportunity was there, staring me in the face. I sent Carl Edwards to offer him a loan. Then—" Douglass faltered, reddening. His hand clenched in the white linen of his nightshirt.

"Go on," Jake prompted impatiently.

"Well, lad, in a weeeee bit of a manipulative fashion, I paid the captains of the new ships to take Chen's payment and sail in the opposite direction. Then I waited three months, until those ships should have sailed to China and back."

"And knowing full well Chen didn't have enough cash on hand, you called in the loan, demanding the swords as collateral."

"Uh . . . aye." The Scotsman lurched to his feet, his voice shaking as he cried, "The swords, you know, they were all I wanted. I had to have them, lad!"

Although the banker's motives had been entirely selfish, Douglass had done Jake a tremendous favor, for otherwise Jake might never have learned the hiding place of the heirloom blades. But in Chen's eyes, the act ranked as a great offense. No wonder the Tong leader avidly sought the banker's death.

"Do you have any idea what you're dealing with?" Jake snapped.

Dragging his hands down over his face, Douglass moaned, "I'm beginning to see. Maybe if I gave back the swords—"

Starting to pace, Jake countered bluntly, "It's too late for that. You've insulted Chen, made him lose face. That's an unforgivable offense and he won't stop until you're dead."

"What can I do?" the Scotsman whispered, stricken.

Despite his fury, Jake felt a ripple of sympathy for the man. His covetous nature had blinded him to the consequences, like a greedy child. "I'll deal with Chen Lee myself."

"You will?"

Jake didn't elaborate that he had his own reasons for pursuing the Tong leader. Besides the threat Chen Lee posed to Mary Lambert and her girls . . . beyond the fact that he was a ruthless bastard who profited from the forced prostitution of young girls . . . it was possible, however remotely, that those swords had been in Chen's possession all of the sixteen years since their disappearance.

"I will, for a price."

"Aye," Douglass agreed readily, his tone buoyant with renewed hope. "And what would that be?"

"The swords. I want all five of them: the burgundy wisteria pair, the golden chrysanthemum pair, and the ceremonial tanto blade." One way or another, the Matsuda family heirlooms would end up in his hands, even if he had to hedge his bet by bargaining with both the daughter and the father.

The Scotsman gasped. "You've seen them?"

"I've not only seen them, here, in this house," Jake said roughly, "I grew up with them in Japan. My adoptive father gave the wisteria daisho to me on my thirteenth birthday. His only son was a toddler when I arrived in Japan, too young to train, and I begged him to teach me in the meantime."

"You were a samurai?" Douglass whispered.

At the banker's use of the past tense, something clenched inside Jake like a fist around his heart. Perhaps Douglass was right . . . perhaps he'd lost the privilege of considering himself samurai long ago.

"But I gave the swords to Meggie for her birthday. They're no longer mine to give."

So that's why Meghan felt she had the right to bargain with them. "Isn't your daughter's safety more important?"

"Aye, of course, but she would never forgive me." Sighing, Douglass added morosely, "You dinna know what it's like to have the lass mad at you. It fair rips up a body. And when you've done something to hurt her, and that look comes across her pretty face—" He shuddered.

Jake's mouth twisted. Oh, yes, he knew. "Don't worry, I'll deal with Meghan."

Douglass brightened considerably. "There's a grand idea. 'Tis that very thing I've been hoping for."

JAKE PAUSED AT the door to Meghan's bedchamber on his way downstairs, listening, reaching out with his other senses as well. He wouldn't be satisfied until he assured himself of her safety.

Silence. No sense of danger pricked at him.

Jake slipped into her room just to be sure—the impropriety of entering a woman's bedchamber be damned.

After the violence in Douglass's room, he came upon the most peaceful sight imaginable.

Meghan lay on her back in the bed. Her head turned slightly to the left, her full lips parted softly, her unbound hair spread over the pillow like a bronzed cloud. Even in the darkened room, the curls captured stray moonbeams, glittering like antique gold. The fingers of her left hand, which rested near her cheek, curled like an unfurling flower. White lace from her night rail peeked out from beneath the coverlet.

The air whooshed from Jake's lungs. There was something incredibly erotic about the contrast between her demure gown and wildfire hair.

He crossed to the bed . . . to verify Meghan was all right, of course, at her father's request. She slept so soundly, he had to lean close to make sure she was truly breathing. He held the back of his right hand close to her mouth. The brush of her breath warmed his skin.

As if controlled by some force beyond his own will, his index finger curled outward. The knuckle lightly traced the lush curve of her lower lip. Meghan sighed. Her small tongue moistened her lips where his touch had tickled the delicate skin.

The thickened ridge of Jake's manhood flexed against his hakama. The sound of his own breathing filled the bedchamber like the ceaseless, rhythmic pull of receding surf across a rocky beach.

With an internal groan, he wrenched himself away.

AFTER LEAVING MEGHAN'S bedchamber, Jake returned to the study, only to find that the three boo how doy had regained consciousness and fled. It hadn't been essential to keep them captive, for now he knew who'd sent them, but it galled him to know he'd have to fight them again.

How long had Chen Lee possessed the swords? Could he be the one? Jake had never allowed himself to hope that one day he would confront the leader of the Chinese raiders responsible for Shinjiro-san's death. The murderous thief had worn a helmet, his face obscured. Items as valuable as the heirloom swords could also change hands, multiple times, bartered for money or power. But now, the odd sense of recognition Jake had felt upon first encountering Chen took on a new significance, whispering of possibilities, of justice long denied.

Vengeance was the lifeblood of the samurai. If only he could be sure of the truth!

Frustrated fury swept through Jake, resurrecting the old horror of watching his Japanese comrades fall one by one against overwhelming odds. He could still feel the gritty slide of his katana blade between the plates of an opponent's armor, still remember looking up to see an exhausted Shinjiro paired off against the helmeted leader of the raiders.

No matter how furiously Jake had fought, how many Chinese died on his blade, more kept coming. He'd looked on, powerless to reach his adoptive cousin in time, as Shinjiro took a blow to his sword arm. Shinjiro's katana had dropped to the ground as he braced himself courageously for a killing strike from the victor. Instead, the Chinese leader had turned and walked away, as if knowing the greatest insult to a samurai was to wound him and leave him helpless rather than finish him off honorably in battle.

Mud had sucked at Jake's sandals as he struggled to his friend's side. The muscles of Shinjiro's right forearm had been severed. He couldn't grip the hilt of his katana, couldn't fight. He weakened rapidly, bleeding from several wounds—none of them fatal, if treated soon.

Jake's rain-soaked hair had clung in long strands around his neck. Each had felt like an icy finger of death as Shinjiro-san looked up, his gaze shadowed by a knowledge that should never have darkened the eyes of a twenty-year-old warrior.

A samurai never allowed himself to be taken prisoner.

Jake wrenched his thoughts back to the present. His heart raced. He shuddered, and several drops of sweat between his shoulder blades shook free to slither down his spine.

A white object on the study carpet caught his attention. Abruptly Jake remembered the paper the boo how doy had been examining. They must have dropped it during the fight.

He snatched up the paper.

His gaze swept over the ink drawing. It revealed the layout of the McLowry mansion, each floor of the three-story house roughly sketched out. Although parts of the map were incomplete, Douglass's bedchamber was clearly outlined in heavy black.

Jake's mouth compressed into a hard, grim line.

Someone had provided a crude map of the mansion . . . someone familiar with the layout but not intimate with every detail. Which hardly narrowed down the field of suspects, he thought caustically. Considering the frequency with which the McLowrys entertained, and the number and variety of guests that navigated the hallowed halls of the wealthy, it wouldn't surprise him to learn that half the Nob Hill society of San Francisco knew their way around the mansion.

Anyone attending Meghan's party could have drawn that map.

Chapter Twelve

If I'd known you were coming, love, I'd have spread gems in my weed-covered garden.

—Anonymous

"YOU ASKED TO see me, Meghan?" Jake asked stiffly as he strode into the library the next morning.

He expected to find her barricaded behind the massive mahogany reading table, safely ensconced in her queenly role of Nob Hill socialite. Instead, she stood near the gray marble fireplace, her slender hands touching the objets d'art on the mantel.

She glanced at him when he came through the door, then turned toward the gold and silver chess set on an adjacent table. Her air of uncertainty gave him pause. Her riding habit of forest green velvet hugged her sleek torso, narrowing to a small waist. An army of pins restrained her hair in a tight chignon. A jaunty little hat, crowned with a pheasant's tail feather, rested in one of the two high-backed chairs facing the chess table.

"I heard that you left my father alone at the Bank Exchange saloon yesterday, Captain. Nor did you return in time to escort him home."

Her accusation hit him like a full broadside. "I had urgent business at Mary Lambert's mission."

A blush climbed up her cheeks. "You followed me?"

"Why should I follow you? Mary and I are old acquaintances."

"What business did you have there?"

"Saving the mission house from being blown up," Jake tossed back, not at all accustomed to being called to task for his decisions.

"That's not possible! I was there. Mary would have told me."

Jake stiffened, gut-punched by her disbelief. "Why don't you ask her?"

Meghan tilted her chin at a defiant angle. "I'll do exactly that at the first opportunity, Captain Talbert."

Dammit. Jake seethed in rigid silence, unsure which left him feeling more annoyed—her lack of faith or her cool, aloof attitude.

She picked up one of the bishops from the chess table, balancing the weighty piece of gold in the graceful curve of her right hand. "Regardless, the situation with my father has not been resolved. I'd like to know when you're going to do something about it."

"Going to—" Jake echoed incredulously, thinking of how he'd risked his life to save Douglass just that morning.

"Exactly. I expect results if I'm to turn the swords over to you."

His eyes narrowed ominously. She hadn't believed him about the mission . . . he had no intention of groveling to justify himself now. Besides, he had sworn to Douglass that he would keep the attack a secret.

"Don't you think you're being a bit impatient, Miss McLowry? It takes time to ferret out a killer."

She looked down at the bishop, turning it over and over in her hands. Hesitantly, she said, "Yes, well, I'm . . . I'm certain it does. But I was just thinking how you've complained, repeatedly, about having to stay here. The only way you can leave sooner—after honoring our bargain, of course—is to take some type of action."

"Action. What do you suggest, Miss McLowry?"

The delicate skin under her eyes flinched at his blatantly sarcastic tone, but she glared back at him and countered, "Anything, Captain! Something that disrupts the status quo, uncovers the truth, elicits a response."

He quickly crossed the distance between them and grasped her upper arms. She blinked up at him, stunned into immobility by his abrupt change in tactics.

"Right now, there's only one response I want to elicit," he said huskily, his voice deepened by the shaft of desire that tore through him.

His mouth descended in a savage kiss even as he swept her unresisting body into an embrace. The gold bishop hit the carpet between them with a solid thud.

The kiss was partially meant to punish, but she didn't flinch. Her lips slid across his in changing patterns, meeting his demand with equal fervor. Jake shuddered. She felt so good . . . too good. Desire tightened its grip, making him want more, everything, from the taste of her soft, secret places to the snug inner caress of her body when he plunged inside.

His hand found its way to her left breast. A tremor rippled through his muscles, almost masking the jolt that shook her body as his fingers measured the soft fullness. He massaged the resilient flesh through thin velvet, his thumb teasing the small peak into a straining bud. She arched against him, almost making him forget that this was wrong—too much, too soon. Suddenly, she stiffened.

Meghan tore her mouth away with a little cry. He let her go instantly, rather shocked himself by the uncontrolled nature of his response. He'd groped at her like an adolescent.

With an expression of confusion and dismay on her flushed face, Meghan turned and fled.

Jake followed, his throat too tight with frustrated passion to call her name. He cursed his lack of self-control with every step. He hadn't meant to frighten her, or so callously forget her innocence. What the hell was wrong with him?

He slammed out the rear of the house just in time to see her disappear into the stables. A minute later, she came bursting through the doors astride a bay mare. Jake shouted. Phillip, running through the stable door, shouted as well. She ignored them both and dug her heels into the mare's sides.

Swear to me that you'll protect my Meggie.

"I'll go after her," Jake told Phillip briskly. "You watch over Douglass while I'm gone. Don't let him out of your sight."

Phillip nodded gravely. "Yes, Peter and I watch."

Jake eyed the lanky stable boy, who shifted restlessly from one foot to the other while awaiting instructions. "Which horse is the fastest?"

"Dat'd be Miss Meghan's mare, suh, and she's done gone."

"The second fastest, then."

The youth pointed toward a gray roan in one of the stalls. The gelding stuck his head over the door and snorted.

"I'll saddle him; you bridle," Jake ordered briskly. "I want to be out of here in two minutes."

JAKE FORCED HIS temper to cool, abandoning his original goal to catch up with Meghan, throw her across his saddle, and drag her back home. Not only did his curiosity escalate as he realized she was heading out of town, he didn't trust himself to resist the temptation of her curvaceous derriere across his lap.

No more than he'd resisted the lure of her breast. Despite the disastrous results, Jake couldn't regret the exquisite feel of her. She'd filled his hand to perfection.

The rolling hills beyond the sprawling city enabled him to follow Meghan while staying out of sight. A warm wind whipped in from the ocean, tearing across the tall grass, concealing any sound of his pursuit. At first he expected her to turn back, loath to stay out on such a blustery day, but she doggedly pushed her bay mare ahead at an easy canter.

Where was she going with such determination?

They rode for over an hour. Just as Jake lost all patience with the cat-and-mouse game, he crested a hill and pulled up in amazement.

A forest of redwoods spread out before him in primeval majesty. Meghan and the mare, no bigger than toys in comparison, disappeared between the massive trunks.

Jake spurred his horse forward. He could quickly lose her in that dense forest.

Deep beneath the shadows, he found the bay mare tied to a fallen log. Meghan's hat, with its jaunty pheasant's feather, hung from the saddle horn.

Tying the gelding next to the mare, Jake continued on foot. He caught glimpses of Meghan through the trees. The long ride had whipped her hair free of its chignon. Tangled strands of gold cascaded down her back, swaying gently against a body that moved with supple grace— an unspoiled woodland nymph very much at home in this fantasy world.

When she stopped at a huge redwood, Jake slipped behind a smaller tree. She reached out to the redwood with both hands, then paused, looking over her shoulder. Her brows drew together in a tight frown as she scanned the surrounding forest.

Intrigued, Jake watched her closely. He hadn't made a sound. Yet, now that he was close enough, she'd apparently sensed something wasn't quite right.

Meghan turned and stood quietly at the base of the massive tree. Her fingers fidgeted with the cameo at her throat. Her gaze restlessly searched the shadows. To Jake's surprise, she pulled a Colt revolver from a deep pocket in her skirt, then stepped away from the tree and started back the way she'd come.

But instead of retracing her steps exactly, she traversed a wide circle around the path.

Jake smiled. Smart girl, he thought proudly, watching her circle around to investigate the threat. She stepped daintily, yet with confidence, like a doe picking its way silently through the undergrowth. When she was almost upon him, Jake stepped out and grasped her wrist, startling a choked gasp from her throat.

With a trace of humor, he said, "You caught me, Meghan. I surrender."

The frightened look on her face vanished instantly.

"What are you doing here?" Meghan demanded, her mercurial expression seething with anger and accusation.

He expected no less. Finding him here was guaranteed to trigger her volatile temper. Jake removed the gun from her hand and braced for the storm.

"You're supposed to be guarding my father!"

"I'm honoring your father's wish that I see to your safety before I attend to his."

"No . . . he didn't. You're making that up," she accused, but doubt laced her tone.

"Douglass specifically requested that I keep an eye on you."

"He . . . oh, damn," she floundered in frustration, apparently accepting that the order was characteristic of her father. The wind caught her hair and swept thick strands into her face. She swiped them back impatiently. "That's not how it's supposed to work! Regardless of what he says, I hired you to watch my father. I'm not the one needing—"

Suddenly, a deep rumbling groan undercut her tirade. It was unlike any sound Jake had ever heard, seeming near, yet far away at the same time. He looked sharply around but couldn't pinpoint its origin. Nothing seemed out of place.

"Don't ignore me, Captain!"

"Did you hear that?" he demanded, then added with a taunting grin, "or were you too busy using that sharp tongue to lash at me like a cat-o'-nine-tails?"

She flushed. "I heard . . . something. But the forest often makes strange sounds. I'm sure it was just the wind."

When the sound didn't repeat itself, Jake relaxed enough to respond to her challenge. "First of all, let me emphasize that you did not hire me, madam. You bloody well coerced—"

"That's your choice of terminology!" Meg spun around and stalked away several paces, then turned to face him, arms crossed tightly. "I never phrased it that way."

"Of course, you didn't. It's not exactly flattering to admit that's the only way you could gain my cooperation."

Her chin tilted at a haughty angle. "Nevertheless, we have a bargain—"

The groan rumbled again, this time louder, yet still a disembodied tremor that seemed to come from every direction.

The ground beneath his boots shuddered. The feathery pattern of sunlight on the forest floor unexpectedly moved, as if the sun sped up its sojourn across the sky.

Realization dawned suddenly, sinking into his body

like sharp, icy claws. His gaze wrenched to the left, to the towering redwood where he'd discovered Meghan.

The huge, ancient tree started to tilt. Dirt sprayed up on the far side of the redwood's base as its roots ripped free of the earth.

"Meghan!" he bellowed in warning.

She stared at the falling giant, motionless with shock. Directly in the path of destruction.

Jake dropped the gun and surged forward. With a last desperate burst of energy he dove at Meghan, grasping her about the waist and hurtling them both into a bed of ferns.

The massive trunk crashed to earth less than ten feet away. The lower tree limbs cracked explosively, rivaling the sound of cannon fire.

The shock of impact slammed against them with enough force to drive the air from Jake's lungs. He gasped, then choked on the cloud of dust and dry, decaying vegetation thrown into the air. The deafening roar continued reverberating throughout the forest, bouncing off distant trees and echoing back like repeated claps of thunder. The whole world seemed to shake, as if mother nature herself had been torn asunder.

Jake dragged a coughing Meghan farther back from the worst of the gritty cloud. He dropped to one knee as she sat up.

"Dammit," he rasped as he brushed loose brown needles from her hair. Her face and clothes were covered with a thin film of red-brown dust.

The thunder of the giant's demise faded. The ground tremors stilled, but the shaking in Jake's gut continued without mercy.

They'd come so close to oblivion. The image of Meghan lying dead, crushed beyond recognition beneath that massive trunk, pounded ruthlessly at his brain.

Wrapping his right arm tightly around the base of his ribs, Jake braced hard against his upper thigh, pressing against the internal trembling. He fixed his gaze on Meghan's pale, drawn face and touched her hair with his left hand, seeking tangible reassurance that she was alive, whole. Finally, the shaking began to recede.

"Are you all right?" he asked roughly.

Meghan stared past him at the fallen tree. A sad little whimper escaped from her mouth.

He speared his fingers into her hair and captured her cheeks between his palms, forcing her to look him in the eye. "Meghan! Answer me! Are you hurt?"

She shook her head. Relief was piercingly sweet, surprising him by its intensity.

He bit back the urge to shout at her about common sense and self-preservation. Later, he would deliver a rousing lecture on the idiocy of standing frozen in the path of certain death. After that, he would pull her into his arms and kiss her senseless.

Actually, maybe he could just skip the lecture part—

"Dammit," he muttered harshly, digging in his pocket for his handkerchief. He began to wipe the dust from her face, then acknowledged that it was a lost cause without any water to dampen the linen. Jamming it back into his trousers, he swore again.

What the hell was wrong with him? The woman made a mockery of his self-control. Jake lurched to his feet, stepping back abruptly. He spun away, staring toward the tree's summit—that part of the redwood that had so recently tickled the underside of the clouds. He felt a piercing regret for the loss of one of nature's greatest achievements. Why did the best things in life have to die—this tree, his father, Shinjiro-san, his honor as a samurai?

Scowling fiercely, Jake turned back, just in time to see

Meghan scale the jutting branches like a nimble youth and settle down on top of the tree.

The birds broke into song again. The dust had nearly settled. Everything was returning to normal—except for the oddity of a highbrow San Francisco socialite sitting quietly atop a fallen tree.

His impression of her as a woodland nymph came back strong. Rather than an ethereal creature cavorting in the sunbeams, however, Meghan now appeared even more beautiful, earthy, a natural woman with leaves in her hair.

"What are you doing up there?" he demanded.

"Sitting."

At least she was talking, even if her actions didn't make a lick of sense. "I surmised that much myself. Come down."

"I prefer to stay."

"Why?"

"If you really must know, I'm grieving."

He looked up and down the length of the fallen giant, incredulous. "It's only a tree, Meghan."

She squeezed her eyes shut. Two tears escaped from beneath her eyelids and slid down her cheeks. Jake swore beneath his breath and thumped the heel of his palm against his forehead. That had obviously been the wrong thing to say.

"There are rotting logs scattered throughout the forest," he added. "Apparently every redwood topples with extreme age. It's the natural course of things."

"Not this one." Wrapping her arms about her bent legs, she hugged her knees to her chest. "Not my tree. I wasn't ready to say good-bye yet."

Her voice was so soft he had to strain to hear. He wished she would look at him, although he wasn't certain what a full view of her tear-filled eyes would do to him. "This is ridiculous, Meghan. Come down from there."

"No."

Jake drew a deep breath of the scented forest air and bid himself be patient. With admirable calm, he asked, "Can you at least tell me how long you intend to stay up there?"

"Forever."

So much for patience. "That's a very illogical thing to say."

"I'm entitled to be as ridiculous as I want," she retorted peevishly. "If you don't like it, you can just leave."

"You know I can't do that."

Her throat muscles worked. "Of course. You're obligated to stay, to watch over me, according to my father's orders." Meghan rested her chin on her knees and sighed, the picture of utter dejection.

He grasped a limb and started to climb. The coarse, ropy bark, now horizontal, provided hand and footholds between sparsely placed limbs. The distinctive, almost sweet scent of redwood still dominated the mustiness of churned-up dirt and decaying vegetation.

Meghan gasped. "What are you doing?"

"Since you won't come down, I'm coming up to get you."

"Don't you dare," she hissed.

"You should know by now that I dare anything," he goaded deliberately, gaining confidence from the resurgence of her arrogant tone, which he much preferred to the sadness of grief.

"But I don't want you up here!"

"Then you'll have to figure out a way to get rid of me."

To his astonishment, Meghan did exactly that. She planted one foot flat against his chest and shoved. The rough feel of bark gave way to empty air. The rapid descent was hardly just reward for his efforts. Managing to keep his feet beneath him, Jake landed upright, staggering back only a step. The impact jarred him from his heels to the base of his skull.

"You would land on your feet like a damn cat," he heard her grumble.

The strength in her slender legs amazed him. With a muttered curse, Jake began climbing again.

He tried to concentrate on the temptation of wringing her stubborn neck. Instead, he found himself wondering what it would be like to feel the strength of those legs wrapped around his waist—sleek, naked legs, with nothing between their bodies but heat and the slick dew of her woman's core.

He attained the top the second time without incident, having chosen to climb up behind her this time, out of striking range. Although the breadth of the trunk inspired awe, it was not as arresting as the sight of sunlight slanting through the new hole in the overhead canopy, bathing her back in a warm glow and setting her hair afire.

"You're wasting your time. I won't come down until I'm ready," she swore, hunching her shoulders and tightening her hold on her legs—as if that could stop him from hauling her off.

He couldn't stand it, seeing her so dejected. It tangled up some kind of knot beneath his breastbone, which made no sense, but then neither did the conflicting urges to touch her, to growl like a grumpy bear, to smooth the tears from her face. He didn't know which was worse: the uncertainty of how to help her or the resentment that she'd somehow gotten under his skin.

"Then I'll stay up here with you," he said irritably.

She kept her gaze fixed on the opposite end of the tree. "Why would you do that?"

"Because it's lonely down there."

She sniffed at his sarcasm. "Suit yourself. There's plenty of room."

Despite the approximate three-hundred-foot length of the downed giant, Jake folded up his coat and dropped it on the bark directly behind her. Some long-forgotten instinct within him began to whisper that, however temperamental, the woman needed a hug . . . and a strong chest to lean on, warm arms to embrace her.

He sat down, his chest only inches from her back. Stretching out his long legs, he fenced her in on either side.

She sat bolt upright. "You're too close!"

"Actually, I'm not close enough." Sliding his arms quickly around her waist before she could scoot away, he pulled her back against his chest. He interlaced his fingers, locking his hold against her sudden attempts to pry his hands loose.

"Let me go!" she said breathlessly.

The words lacked their usual caustic force.

"You need somebody to hold you, Meghan," he said gruffly.

She stiffened. "Just anybody?"

"Someone strong, capable of protecting you."

"Then maybe you should take me home after all," she said tartly. "Carl can perform that duty."

Pushing aside her hair with his cheek, he pressed his lips to the bony ridge behind her ear and whispered hoarsely, "No, no one else. It must be me."

A shudder rippled through her.

"You need me to hold you," he insisted.

"No, I don't."

"Yes, you do. Admit it."

"You are so arrogant."

"It's part of my charm."

She grunted. "You know, sometimes I fantasize about feeding you to the sharks, one piece at a time."

With the graceful undersides of her breasts brushing his wrists, he could think of better things to fantasize about. "Don't change the subject. Say it's all right for me to hold you."

"You seem determined to do whatever you want, regardless."

"I'll let you go, if you insist."

"Well . . . all right. Just for a few minutes."

Jake expected her to sound coldly resigned, as if consigning herself to the hangman's noose. Instead, her tone held a hint of longing.

"This place must hold a special meaning for you," he said.

"I come here to get away from everything, to think."

He looked around with new understanding. "The redwoods are an excellent choice of refuge."

She turned her head slightly, just enough that he could see the curve of her cheek. "That is how I think of this place. How did you know?"

"I have a special place of my own. Whenever I'm in Japan there is a church I like to visit. It's a beautiful place built by the Jesuits in the village where I grew up. Even though the missionaries themselves were banned from Japan by the *shogun* decades before, the villagers maintained their faith and cared for the church as a place for individuals to pray and meditate. I like to sit and contemplate the stained-glass images and watch the dust dance in the colored beams of light."

"Do you pray there?"

"I used to," he said thickly. He couldn't tell her that he'd stopped praying sixteen years ago, when he ceased to be worthy, when the western Christian beliefs of his early childhood came into direct, violent conflict with his samurai upbringing.

The sweet scent of her hair wrapped in and around his senses like a velvet ribbon. The gentle rise and fall of her ribs as she breathed fed his imagination with images of more potent, erotic rhythms.

"This redwood was my favorite," Meghan murmured, wrenching his thoughts back from their downward spiral. "I felt linked to it somehow. I suppose you think that's strange."

He thought of the katana, and how the blade was believed to contain the soul of the samurai. "No, I don't think it strange at all."

She twisted around to look up at him . . . and he was lost. Her eyes were like windows into her spirit—sad, glistening with unshed tears.

Even the deafening crash of another redwood wouldn't stop him from claiming a kiss.

Chapter Thirteen

*Wind that tossed the pines subsides in the grass of the foothill plain,
rain races the clouds of the rising storm.*
—KYOGOKU TAMEKANE (1254–1332)

MEG WATCHED THE descent of his hard, sensual mouth, gazed into the dark, passionate intensity of his glittering eyes . . . and lost her nerve.

Oddly enough, she trusted Jake. It was her own mercurial changes of mood that defied reason. She no longer knew what she wanted, except for one thing: She craved Jake's kiss with an irrational eagerness, ready to sacrifice her self-respect, her identity, her soul.

"We'd better go," Meg squeaked nervously, pulling back.

Jake released her, but not before she saw the alluring fire die in his eyes. Without a word, he helped her climb down from the tree. She felt as if she'd just taken a fragile, irreplaceable moment of trust, and destroyed it.

After retrieving Meg's gun, they made their way back to the horses.

"Oh, no!" Meg cried as they neared the fallen log. She rushed forward to touch the raw end of a broken limb, the only evidence remaining of where her skittish mare had been tied.

"The crash of the redwood must have panicked her. Don't worry, she'll head straight home," Jake said, coming up from behind. The gelding nickered a greeting, sounding relieved that it hadn't been completely deserted. Jake tucked the revolver into one of the saddlebags.

"I know, but how am I going to get home?" Meg asked.

"Well, you could walk." Jake rolled up the sleeves of his shirt, his face impassive. "Or you could double up with me."

Ride double? That close to him, for over an hour? Her mouth went dry. "On that horse, with you?" she rasped.

"That's the general idea."

Meg lifted her chin. "I have a better idea. You let me take the gelding, and *you* walk back to Rincon Hill."

"And deprive myself of your company?"

Quicksilver eyes darkened to a smoky gray as he came closer. Meg's heart leapt as his fingertips gently traced over her right cheekbone and down her jaw.

"I'd rather hold you in my arms all the way back to town," Jake murmured, his voice dropping to a low, husky tone that rippled across her skin and left goosebumps in its wake. "I can't stop thinking about how sweet you taste, Meg. Your lips fit perfectly against mine."

Thrilling, frightening sensations washed through her body. "Back . . . back at the mansion . . . you took liberties you shouldn't have."

"I don't deny it. And perhaps I should be wallowing in self-condemnation, except for one overriding fact—" His fingers came to rest beneath her chin. His thumb brushed lightly back and forth in the hollow beneath her lower lip. "You responded to me, Meghan, if just for a moment."

The pressure of his fingers urged her head to tilt, giving access to her open mouth. His lips sought hers with unnerving accuracy. Muscular arms came about her in a fierce embrace, one encircling her back, the other capturing her head in the cradle of his hand.

Meg's traitorous body curved into his with the languid ease of a sunning cat, ignoring the remote corner of her brain that warned of danger.

The nubby texture of Jake's tongue explored the recesses of her mouth, a gentle invasion, an unmistakeable possession. Meg imitated his sliding penetration, answering with explorations of her own. When her tongue slid into the slick well between his teeth and lower lip, a powerful shudder rippled through his body.

With a shock, she realized he was vulnerable to her as well. She grew bolder, exercising her newfound power by catching his roving tongue between her lips and sucking lightly.

Jake groaned. Large hands cupped her buttocks, kneading her resilient flesh, pulling her tighter against his grinding hips.

Her own body responded, vibrating with desire, matching him breath for hard breath. She was beyond thinking about the proprieties. She only wanted to get closer, to flow over and through him in ways she didn't understand. Even though her hips strained against his, she couldn't get close enough.

A great emptiness burned in her woman's core, like a fire with black flames, devouring light rather than creating it. The gnawing hunger made her want to weep with frustration. Overwhelmed by strange new sensations, Meg whimpered.

Jake broke the kiss.

He released her backside and pulled her into an embrace, one hand pressing her face into the curve of his left shoulder. In that way, he simply held her for several minutes. His heart pounded beneath her cheek; his chest rose and fell rapidly.

He smelled of redwoods, forest secrets, and the slightly spicy scent that was uniquely his own.

Before she was ready, he grasped her by the shoulders and set her back—stiffly, as if separating their bodies caused him the same wrenching pain that suddenly stole her breath.

"Unless we stop now," he said gruffly, "this is going to go way too far."

Meg stared, unblinking, into his harshly drawn face.

A flush slowly climbed up her cheeks. She nodded mutely, appalled by her lack of modesty. She'd succumbed to the magic of his kiss, forgetting her self-respect, her future, and her intention of marrying Carl Edwards. This was insane. Soon Jacob Talbert would be gone from her carefully planned life. An arrogant warrior with a wanderlust, whose heart belonged to the Orient, would only bring her pain.

Jake spun away and untied the gelding. "Come on, let's get cleaned up. I saw a small stream near here."

They walked to the stream, Jake leading the gelding. Squatting, he dipped his handkerchief in the clear water, then wrung it out.

"Your face is dirty," he said, his voice still an octave lower than normal. He handed her the damp linen as she knelt beside him.

Dismayed by his scowl, she whispered. "Are you mad at me?"

His deeply ironic chuckle contrasted with the peaceful sound of the stream. "No, Meg, I'm mad at myself. I take pride in my self-control. Around you, however, it seems to crumble into dust." He scooped up a handful of water and flung it, creating an arc of shimmering droplets.

Meg scrubbed her face, hiding a sudden, very feminine smile. She caused this hardened warrior to lose control?

When the thrill of satisfaction faded enough for her to school her expression, she lowered the handkerchief.

"Is that better?"

"Yes and no," he said with a lopsided grin. "I thought you made a rather adorable urchin."

Meg dropped her gaze, suddenly shy. The impact of his boyish grin burst inside her like a flock of birds taking flight.

He washed his own face, then rose.

"Hold still," he said, helping her stand. "I want to see if I can get rid of the worst of this debris."

His broad hands swept down her back and brushed the dirt from her skirt, his movements brisk, seemingly impersonal. Nevertheless, Meg's breath froze in her throat.

What would it be like to return the favor, to sweep her hands over those broad shoulders, across the carved shape of his back, down over chiseled buttocks and thickly muscled legs—

Jake stole the opportunity by stepping back to brush off his own clothes. Meg swallowed her disappointment. He finished quickly, then washed his hands and led the way to the waiting horse.

"Kick your right leg over," Jake said gruffly.

He grasped her waist and swung her effortlessly into the saddle. Dazed by his strength, she wondered how it would feel to slide her fingers through his black hair.

"Are you all right?"

"Uh-huh," she confirmed in a vague, distracted tone. Despite his dark, rugged looks and the aura of danger he wore like a mantle, Jake Talbert really was incredibly attractive.

He grasped the saddle horn and mounted the gelding without further comment. Meg's heart rate quickened as he settled behind her, slowly, almost gingerly, as if he were in some kind of pain.

"I should be asking you the same question, Jake. Is something wrong?"

"I'm fine, dammit."

His thick, muscular forearms wrapped around her waist. Lean, powerful thighs pressed intimately against her hips. Although nearly engulfed by his large frame, Meg had never felt more secure in her life.

Jake urged the gray into a relaxed canter as they cleared the forest. With each surge forward of the horse's rhythmic gait, Meg's shoulders bumped lightly against Jake's chest. When the gelding gathered its hindquarters for each push, the sway forward caused the underside of her breasts to brush his forearm.

He swore softly under his breath.

After that he remained silent. Meg didn't mind the lack of conversation. She needed nothing to make her more aware of Jake Talbert at her back.

The horse's hooves thrummed against the dry ground. Gulls rode the wind overhead, their raucous cries complementing the rugged, windswept landscape. An occasional small animal ducked out of their path with a burst of sound, scurrying through the tall grass.

The ride stretched into an odd, breathless sort of torture—if torture could be considered something pleasant—in which Meg's body hummed with life and a growing tension. After nearly an hour, Jake slowed the gelding to a walk.

"The horse needs rest," he said.

Meg nodded. Her hair caught on the stubble of his beard, tugging gently.

Jake's chest vibrated with a low, throaty growl. Without warning, he pushed her hair aside with his chin and buried his face against her neck. His cheek rasped against the delicate skin beneath her ear. A shiver swept down Meg's neck and dipped into her body, causing her belly to tighten. Her breath came low and fast.

"It's . . . it's hot. Must be the sun," she muttered thickly. Her fingers pushed free the buttons at the neck of her green velvet habit.

He rumbled his approval deep in his chest. The vibration spread to her back, branching outward like questing fingers, inspiring her to undo a few more buttons . . . just down to the top of her chemise, no more.

Transferring the reins to the hand about her waist, Jake used the other to pull back her collar, baring most of her shoulder. His lips pressed against the juncture of her neck, searing her skin like a velvet brand. Meg shuddered, her whole body reacting to the exquisite pleasure.

She leaned her head to the left, resting it against his shoulder, opening herself to his lavish attention. His lips kissed and nibbled their way up her neck, each touch punctuated by a wild tingle. When his tongue probed the back of her ear, she bit down on her lip to keep from crying out. Then he closed his teeth gently on the slope of her shoulder. Her body jerked.

"Are you still hot?" His voice resembled the deep purr of a very large cat.

"Yes, too hot," she whispered.

Before Meg realized what he was doing, Jake lifted the green velvet away from her chest and blew a strong blast down her front. The cool air slipped beneath her chemise like a caress, penetrating the thin cotton of her riding corset. Her breasts tightened, their tips tingling wildly.

His hand released her collar and drifted slowly downward. When it reached her waist, Meg realized he'd unfastened the remaining buttons.

She lifted her head just as his hand slid inside, under

her chemise. His sculpted, sun-bronzed fingers curved around her left breast and lifted it free of the corset.

The contrast of his dark skin against her white flesh represented all the many ways his masculinity complemented her softness. Fascinated, frozen by the riot of sensations gripping her body with unbearable excitement, Meg allowed him to touch her in that intimate way . . . no, wanted him to touch her.

"Let me, sweetheart."

She relaxed her head back against his shoulder, amazed and warmed by the raw need in his voice. Long fingers began to stroke her breast, stopping just short of the tip each time, until her nipple hardened into a tight, sensitive bud. She arched her back, straining into his hand.

He pinched her nipple delicately. An invisible cord between her breast and belly stretched taut. Meg gasped at the piercing sweetness that jolted through her woman's core. She pressed her head into his shoulder and arched her back.

"Such fire."

The deep tenor of his voice rippled across her sensitized skin. He rolled her nipple gently between his fingers. The strange black emptiness tugged at her belly again. She was on fire with wanting.

He released her breast. Meg nearly cried out in protest.

Without warning, his fingers slipped into the V of her divided skirt. His palm curved around her mound, pressing hard, branding her with possessive heat.

"What . . . what are you doing?" she managed breathlessly.

"Do you have any idea how passionate you are? I'm just helping you discover it." His cheek rubbed against her hair as his hand flexed, sending flickers of lightning throughout her body. "My gift to you. I'll stop whenever you say."

His words soothed her; the slow massage of his hand mesmerized her into a strange lassitude. *Yes, discovery, that's what this is all about,* she thought languidly. Testing her boundaries, taking some risks. He'd given his word—she could ask him to stop when she wished.

She didn't count on his unbuttoning her skirt, or slipping his hand inside her drawers. She tried to protest, but the erotic feel of his rough hand against her belly strangled the words into an inarticulate mumble. His middle finger slid between the folds of her feminity with shocking intimacy. For one heartbeat she tensed with fear . . . the next she melted with pure pleasure.

His finger stroked in circles, sending tendrils of fire down her legs. Of their own volition, her hips started to move, rocking against his hand in a rhythm that matched the commanding strokes of his finger.

"Don't move, Meg."

"I can't help it," she gasped.

"You're perfect, so passionate, but you're making the horse nervous. I can't control the beast if you keep rocking your hips like that . . . the one we're astride, or the one between my legs."

She obediently froze. The inability to move, to answer the instinctive urgings of her body, only magnified the wild feeling coursing through her like a stampede. The world narrowed down to the exquisite pleasure of his forbidden touch, the slide of his finger in a slick moisture produced, amazingly enough, by her own body. A new scent teased her senses, as untamed as the wilderness around them. Something spiraled tighter and tighter inside her, holding her poised mercilessly in its grip, trembling on the edge of expectancy.

A whimper escaped her throat as the tension became almost unbearable in its fire, like a voracious hunger.

"Beautiful. You're so beautiful, Meg. Reach for it, sweetheart. I'm here to catch you."

The beautiful timbre of his voice vibrated to her core, then tipped her over the edge of the precipice. Meg convulsed, her entire existence blinded by white lightning.

As her body tingled in the powerful aftermath, Meg watched dreamily as Jake's hand retreated, refastening the buttons of her skirt. Slowly the world regained texture and sound. Her drawers felt wet, clinging. A gust of wind brushed over her bare breast and chilled the dampness between her legs.

Reality doused her like a bucket of ice water.

She sat up, flushing with hot embarrassment as she shifted her corset back into placed and buttoned her shirtwaist.

Tears stung the backs of Meg's eyes. That had been the most incredible experience of her life, but in succumbing to his caress she'd just exposed herself as utterly wanton. Did Jake think her a loose woman, a . . . a trollop?

He leaned forward. She stiffened. With his cheek brushing her hair, Jake murmured, "You are a beautiful and passionate woman, Meg. Thank you for sharing that with me."

Then he urged the gelding into a canter.

Tears rolled over and spilled down Meg's cheeks, quickly dried by the wind. She relaxed, just a little, reassured by his understanding. She wanted to curl back into the protective shell of his body, but her emotions were so confused that she didn't dare add to her vulnerability.

The last of the ride proved a grueling form of sensual torture. A new awareness of Jake's sensual power sang through her blood.

Silence reigned the whole way.

When they reached the edge of the Nob Hill district, Jake reined the gelding to a stop and dismounted. He rested one hand on Meg's knee.

"You'll be all right from here," he said roughly.

"Where are you going?"

"Look at us, Meg," he said in evident frustration. "Dirty, disheveled . . . it looks like we've just taken a tum—" He jerked his hand away from her knee. "How will it look if we ride up on this horse together? Dammit, think what it will do to your reputation."

She nodded mutely, suddenly frightened more by his anger and withdrawal than any danger to her reputation.

"I'll be there soon. Go straight back to the house. No detours." He slapped the gelding on the rump.

Meg glanced back at his rigid form. He looked so isolated that she ached for him . . . and felt a stab of loneliness in her own heart.

Despite knowing that she'd been a reckless, wanton fool to let him caress her so intimately, her body refused to forget the magical sensations. What if it were to happen again? She wanted to feel his heartbeat beneath her cheek and touch him in return . . . everywhere.

No! Meg shook her head, shaking the reckless fantasies from her wayward mind. Jake Talbert didn't love her. Without love, such passion was shallow, destructive.

The sad admission sliced through her like a dagger.

JAKE STRIPPED OFF his shirt and boots, then dove off the deck of the *Shinjiro*.

His hands cut through the surface of the choppy bay. The cold water closed around him, enveloping him in silence. He stroked beneath the waves, letting the sea draw the scalding heat from his body.

Finally, he broke the surface, a good distance from the ship. He closed his eyes and shivered, not from the cold but from the memory of Meg's incredibly passionate response. Cradling her trusting body in his arms had been like holding liquid fire in his hands. The pulse of her hips had driven him mad with desire. If he'd allowed himself to lift her down from that damn horse, he would have shattered her innocence and shown her the meaning of that erotic, primeval rhythm.

A wave slapped Jake in the ear, wrenching his eyes open. The salty smell of the water reminded him of the scent of aroused woman and his own sweat—the sweat of denial.

He couldn't spend all his time in the bloody ocean. Avoiding Meg offered the only bearable solution.

And how was he supposed to do that while making sure she was safe from Chen Lee?

The term *bodyguard* took on a new and significant meaning.

Jake swore as he swam back to the ship. After he returned to the house and relieved Phillip from guarding Douglass, he would have both the father and daughter to watch over.

"ROBERT," MEG CALLED out as she hurried down the front staircase two days later. She lifted the hem of her ivory dinner gown to avoid tripping.

"Yes, Miss Meghan?"

"I thought I heard Mary Lambert's voice. Has she come to visit?" Meg asked eagerly, pausing on the bottom step. Her right hand gripped the banister. She'd invited her new friend on several occasions, but this was the first time the missionary had come to the Rincon Hill mansion. Meg refused to examine her excess enthusiasm for a visitor, someone to offer a brief respite from haunting memories of a fiery, intimate touch and her own wanton response.

If she felt relieved that Jake had kept a respectable distance since that day at the redwoods, then why was she so lonely and miserable?

Robert replied, "Yes, Miss Lambert had arrived, but—"

"Why didn't you tell me right away?" Meg interrupted, glancing around. "Where is she? The blue drawing room?"

"Actually, I showed her to the library—"

Meg's brows shot up at the odd choice of rooms. "Miss Lambert is a friend, an honored guest even though she dresses plainly. From now on, you may show her to one of the drawing rooms." Her soft slippers made no sound as she stepped down and started toward the east wing and the library.

"Miss Meghan!"

Meg spun around, startled by the butler's distressed, somewhat urgent tone.

Robert ran a finger under his starched collar. "I showed Miss Lambert to the library because the lady specifically asked to see Captain Talbert . . . privately."

"Oh. I see." Disappointment curled inside Meg like a shriveling flower. Mary must need help of some kind, but the missionary and Jake chose not to involve her. Meg felt excluded, hurt.

"I'm sorry, Miss Meghan. Perhaps I can announce—"

"Thank you, no. I can manage from here, Robert," Meg said, determined to stop by the library. At least Meg could grab the opportunity for a visit before Mary returned home. Although too late for tea, perhaps the missionary would accept an invitation for supper. Meg would just wait outside the room until they were finished.

The library door stood ajar.

"You've offered me aid on several occasions, Jacob," Meghan overheard Mary say.

"Yes, ma'am, and you've consistently refused each time."

Their serious tones gave Meg pause, holding her captive in the hallway. If her friend was in trouble, Meg needed to know.

She inched closer to the opening. A large mirror on the far wall reflected most of the library. Jake leaned one arm against the mantel. The thick cords of his neck showed through the open collar of his white shirt.

"Well," Mary replied, taking a deep breath and releasing it in a rush, "pride evidently goeth before the fall." She sank down onto one of the wing-back chairs at the chess table.

Jake's brows snapped together. "What do you mean?"

"I now have a situation I cannot handle on my own." Smoothing the folds of her brown gingham dress, Mary explained, "Yesterday a young Chinese man named Sung Kwan came to me. He sought help to free the women he loves, one Yeung Lian, from a future of slavery and prostitution."

Jake's chin jerked up. The intensity of his reaction went through Meg like a jolt of lightning, arcing across the space between them—almost as if she was inside his skin, feeling what he felt. Her heart began to race.

Mary missed his response as she focused on the reticule in her lap. "I met the girl yesterday, briefly, in secret. She was very frightened, wary, and though I convinced her of my sincerity, she couldn't bring herself to sever all ties on the spur of the moment. We arranged a second meeting for this morning, when she could finally take refuge in my care, but . . ." The missionary's words choked off, swallowed by an awkward silence. Twin teardrops fell from her bowed head to her hands.

"Lian didn't show up," Jake finished for her in a flat, angry tone.

Mary nodded and looked up.

Unease rippled through Meg at the sight of Mary's pale, taut skin and the gray circles shadowing her eyes.

"Sung Kwan cannot find Lian anywhere. He is frantic. He suggested I come to you, that you are the only one with the necessary skills to help," Mary emphasized, the strength of conviction returning to her voice. "Kwan fears that Lian's master discovered her intent to escape and, in his fury, has imprisoned her. You know what will happen as well as I, Jacob. If we do not get Lian out of there, tonight, she will disappear forever, shipped off to another city, sold to some depraved beast, or buried alive in the most filthy brothel her master can find."

Jake raked a hand through his hair. "If it's not too late already."

"It's not. I must believe that or be unable to live with myself." Mary rose from her seat and moved to stand before him. "I know you believe in the loving Father as we do, that it is His wish that we save these poor, abused children," she pleaded earnestly. "These girls are so helpless. For the love of God, please help me rescue Yeung Lian. She is the most incredibly beautiful girl, like a fragile flower, with an intelligence in her eyes and an air of culture I've rarely witnessed."

"I know," Jake said through his teeth.

Mary gasped. "You've seen her?"

"Yes."

Something squeezed tight around Meg's heart. She'd almost forgotten Jake's reputation for preferring raven-haired Asian women . . . and this Yeung Lian was exquisitely beautiful.

"Then you will help me?" urged Mary.

"You do realize what you ask?"

"Chen Lee is the leader of the Hung Shun Tong, the most powerful in San Francisco. I'm asking you to confront the dragon in its lair." The missionary fingered the cross at her throat, then said resolutely, "God will watch over you, Jacob Talbert. This is a divine errand if I ever saw one."

Jake pivoted sharply on his heel and began pacing. His long strides took him quickly to the wall of books at the far end of the room. "Don't believe that God has any interest in protecting my scurrilous hide, ma'am. I've disappointed Him mightily."

"So have we all," Mary countered with a gentle smile.

He stopped abruptly. His eyes gleamed like pewter from a harshly etched face. "Have we all killed, Mary?" Jake snarled.

"War brings many evils that we cannot avoid."

"You speak of America's recent War Between the States. I was sailing the Pacific at the time."

Mary blinked, taken aback. "Then you must have been defending your own life, or the life of someone dear."

"Oh, he was someone dear, all right, but I helped him from this life rather than managing to save him." Jake's renewed pacing radiated energy, like a wild animal prowling its cage.

Mary's mouth tightened in a thin, bloodless line, providing the reaction Jake apparently sought with his blunt, almost hostile admissions. He seemed to crave Mary's condemnation.

"Are you speaking of murder, Jacob?" the missionary whispered hoarsely.

Jake made a rude sound in his throat. "No, ma'am. Worse. I helped a dear friend commit suicide." He slammed the heel of his palm into the wheeled ladder against the bookcase, causing it to roll several feet, rumbling across the parquet floor. "Is that not the greater sin in God's eyes? You shouldn't trust me, or treat me as if I'm some warrior sent from heaven for a holy cause. I don't deserve your respect."

In the hallway, Meg clenched her hands together and pressed them against her mouth. Is this why Jake tormented himself, drove his body to the point of exhaustion, and had cried out in agony when he stabbed the point of his sword into the ballroom floor?

Mary stood in silent reflection for only a moment longer, then went to him and laid a hand on his rigid arm. "I know your goodness, Jacob. I believe you must have had a sound reason for what you did. God might already have forgiven you, but you won't accept it because you refuse to forgive yourself."

His eyes closed. Muscles rippled along the rigid line of his jaw.

Meg shuddered in her hiding place, shaken by the sudden, intense ache to touch him. His pain was so tangible it hit her in agonizing waves, despite her shock at what he'd just admitted. She wanted to be where the missionary stood, soothing away his self-hatred.

"Thank you," said Mary, breaking the silence.

Jake's eyes flew open. A bitter laugh erupted from his chest. "For what?"

"For agreeing to save Yeung Lian. I can see in your face that you've already resolved to help me."

He sighed. "You should have been a politician, Mary."

She lifted her chin. "Well, I certainly would have made a better one than those fools currently in office who ignore all my pleas for stricter laws."

He took her hand and lightly kissed her knuckles. "Don't worry, I'll get her out."

"Kwan awaits your instructions at the mission. He will help you get into Chen Lee's house."

"Then he'll have to flee the city afterward. Chen Lee will guess that Kwan aided in Lian's escape. His death will be as unpleasant as Chen can make it."

Mary blanched. "Oh, my."

Meg turned away, the intensity of Jake's promise vibrating through her mind. Her step lightened as her feet broke into a run. Excitement built to a crescendo.

This was it! A rescue mission! It offered the perfect opportunity to prove she was capable of taking risks, to offer more of herself than just money. There must be some essential part she could play in saving this girl.

Just one problem . . . Jake would never let her go with him.

She needed an ally.

Chapter Fourteen

This night of no moon, there is no way to meet him. I rise in long-ing—my breast pounds, a leaping flame, my heart is consumed by fire.
                              —ONO NO KOMACHI (NINTH CENTURY)

THIS WAS INSANE. She barely knew Akira-san, so why did she feel confident he would help her? With her heart attempting to climb its way up her throat, Meg knocked on the door to his bedchamber.

"Ah, Meg-an-san," Akira-san said upon opening the door. He wore a brown kimono crossed over a white undershirt. The baggy brown pants brushed across the top of a pair of odd white socks with a slit between the toes.

"May I come in?"

He bowed, then stepped back so she could enter. At any other time, she would be fascinated by the way he'd rearranged the room, and the paints and brushes laid out on the floor—but right now the situation was too urgent.

"I overheard something I shouldn't have, something I'm about to tell you. I hope you won't think ill of me for it," she said in a rush.

A smile narrowed his eyes to dark slits. "Go on, Meg-an-san."

"Mary Lambert has asked Jake to rescue a Chinese

girl named Yeung Lian from the house of Chen Lee. Tonight. He'll want you to help him, won't he?"

"If not, he knows I will be very mad," Akira responded, his expression suddenly grim.

Before she lost her nerve, Meg blurted out, "I want to help save this girl, but I know Jake won't allow me to go with you."

"Yes, much danger."

Meg flinched at the idea of Jake risking injury. It made her even more determined to be there. "There must be something I can do. I'm tired of remaining safe while everyone else takes risks and does something heroic."

Akira-san hooked his thumbs in the sash at his waist. "Through adversity, one builds strength."

"Exactly!" She exhaled a gusty sigh of relief. "I knew you would understand. How can I help?" She took a step closer and lowered her voice. "Do you know of a way to sneak me along?"

After a long, thoughtful pause that began to undermine her wild hopes, he said, "Can you drive a buggy?"

"Yes. I know how to drive a carriage," Meg said eagerly, the possibility of a valid, useful role dawning.

"Most Chinese here are too poor to own horses. Yeung Lian not know how to ride, very sure. She must escape in a buggy."

"My landau is enclosed, with curtains. It will be perfect."

"Good," he answered briskly. Crossing his arms, Akira walked around her, intent on inspection. Meg stiffened, afraid she wouldn't meet with his approval.

He touched her hair. "Like gold fire," he murmured.

"Thank you . . . I think. Is that good? I—I know that Japanese women have black hair, without all these horrid curls."

Out of the corner of her eye she saw Akira-san smile.

"For some men, yes, fire is a good thing. But you need to cover hair so you become one with the night, and so Takeru-san not see your face."

"I can do that."

Akira-san's head turned towards the door. "He comes."

Meg caught her lower lip between her teeth. She hadn't heard a thing, but she believed the old man. "Where can I hide?" she whispered. "It will spoil everything if Jake catches me here. There will be awkward questions—"

"Here." Akira lifted the lid of a huge sea chest. "With the kimonos gone, you find room."

Meg stepped in. Perhaps he was right . . . if she didn't have to contend with all the petticoats and padding dictated by fashion. Warily, she said, "Are you sure? Parts of me might squeeze through the cracks."

He chuckled. "You fit."

She glanced down, noticing a package in the bottom. Nearly translucent wrapping hinted at white silk and rich embroidery. "There's one kimono left. I thought Jake sold them all—besides the blue one I have yet to return to him, that is."

"He saved this one. Very special."

Meg knelt down and curled her body over. Akira helped her tuck in the folds of her gown. Then he closed the lid with a gentle click.

Darkness enveloped Meg. When a tingle of awareness swept down her spine, she instinctively knew that Jake had entered the room.

She tried to listen to their plans, but the chest muffled the rapid-fire conversation. Sooner than expected, the lid lifted.

"He is gone."

Meg stood, blinking at the abrupt change in light.

"Quickly," Akira-san murmured, thrusting a black shirt and baggy trousers into her hands. "I convince

Takeru-san that I find a boy to drive the buggy. Now you must change into these."

MEG CLIMBED DOWN from the driver's seat of the landau. The silk and cotton of Akira's borrowed clothing brushed against her skin. This freedom of movement was a great deal more fun and daring than descending gingerly from a carriage on lowered steps, wearing enough garments to choke an elephant.

Her soft slippers touched the dirty floor of the alley behind the waterfront warehouse. She'd chosen the slippers to maintain the same quiet stealth that Jake and Akira employed by wrapping the metal harness, horses' hooves, and landau wheels in thick strips of cloth. Very likely outnumbered, the men needed the advantage of surprise.

Now that the landau had stopped, only the lazy slap of waves against the adjacent sea wall disturbed the quiet. Not much activity disturbed this lonely corner of the waterfront at two o'clock in the morning . . . if one didn't count Jake and Sung Kwan sneaking in through the front of the warehouse.

She glanced at Akira as he dismounted and tied his horse to the back of the landau. His stern expression reflected his concern at this last-minute change in plans. They'd rendezvoused with Sung Kwan, only to learn he'd discovered that Lian had been moved to the waterfront, apparently to ship her off to parts unknown later this morning. Chen Lee ironically regarded Lian's plans to escape as a grave insult, and intended to make her pay for the betrayal.

This rescue attempt would be their only chance.

Akira stood motionless, arms crossed over his chest, feet braced shoulder width apart, while he vigilantly watched the building's only back door. Two swords thrust through the sash at his waist.

Meg tied off the reins and moved to the heads of the matched pair of grays. The pungent odors of sweaty horses, stagnant brine water, and wet wood stung her nostrils. Her hand brushed the revolver weighing down the pocket of her black cloak, her own bit of insurance to lessen the over-riding feeling that she was out of her depth here.

Stroking the horses' velvety noses, she murmured soft, soothing words to keep them calm. The gray on the right nickered a greeting, a low, throaty sound that was little more than a resonating vibration in the darkness. Resting her forehead against the gelding's forelock, Meg groaned inwardly.

"Shush, now. I'm trying not to think about it," she whispered. This was the same gelding she and Jake had . . . shared on their ride home from the redwoods.

As if resentful of her efforts to shove them aside for the past two days, the memories engulfed her without mercy.

Her breasts tingled at the memory of Jake's gentle, masterful caresses. Just the thought of his hand between her legs sent lightning dancing through her body.

The strange, foreign clothes she now wore left her body so . . . accessible. With a simple release of the tie, Jake could open the front of the shirt and cup her breasts in his hands. The daring slits up the sides of the hakama trousers left her most private woman's parts vulnerable, even though the shirt concealed the openings. She imagined Jake sliding his hot hands inside, stroking that tender place again until a silent scream of aching need rushed through her blood.

The same slick dew that had dampened her drawers that day misted between her legs again. The musky scent of her own arousal carried on the cool, damp sea air.

This was madness! She couldn't want Jake Talbert and all the complicated, dark depths he carried with him like a shadow. He would never fit into the world she had built for her father and herself. Allowing herself a heady taste of the unknown, the forbidden world of passion, was proving bittersweet indeed.

Akira hissed a word of warning, shattering her thoughts.

Meg tensed as his hand went to the hilt of his katana.

Then she heard it, too. Shouts erupted inside the warehouse. Suddenly, the sound of gunfire punctuated the night.

An icy chill swept downward from Meg's throat, freezing her blood. "Jake," she forced out in a choked whisper.

Meg didn't realize she was running for the rear entrance until a sharp, commanding voice brought her to a stop.

"No!" Akira-san snapped. "Trust Takeru-san. We stay here."

"But—"

Just then, the back door crashed open.

JAKE SLIPPED THROUGH the front door of the warehouse, leaving two unconscious guards slumped on the ground outside. He followed closely behind Sung Kwan, wondering—not for the first time—whether this entire rescue mission was an elaborately orchestrated trap.

Chen Lee had every reason to want him dead. Mary Lambert and Kwan could both be ignorant pawns in a deceptive game of life and death . . . or Kwan could be willingly leading Jake into an ambush in exchange for Lian's freedom.

Then again, everything could be exactly as Mary had described it. There was only one way to find out. Whether or not Kwan deserved to be trusted was about to be put to the test.

Jake touched the hilt of his black katana. In the likely case the boo how doy didn't stick to honorable hand-to-hand combat, Jake had also thrust a Colt pistol into the back of his sash. Energy danced along his nerve endings.

They crept silently between two rows of stacked wooden packing crates. Jake kept Kwan in sight at all times. A light shone from a small office at the far end of the building, casting even deeper shadows into the darkness. The office seemed the most likely place for Chen's lackeys to be holding Yeung Lian.

A cat meowed. The sound bounced off high rafters and cut through the quiet like a knife. Kwan froze.

Why was Kwan so nervous? Concern for Lian, fear of the fight ahead—or guilt because a trap was about to be sprung?

Jake nudged him in the back. Kwan nodded and moved forward again. The cover of crates ended short of the office. They paused at the edge of the open gulf between shelter and success.

Kwan peered around the edge of the last crate. He jerked back, signaling Jake to be quiet. A knife appeared in his hand.

Jake gripped the hilt of his katana, ready to counter the first sign of betrayal. In a swift, aggressive move, Kwan reached around the crate and hauled back a struggling boo how doy, one hand clamped over the man's mouth. Without hesitation, he cut the guard's throat.

Jake arched one brow as Kwan let the dead body slide from his grasp. The younger man's face registered no emotion other than cold determination. His gaze shifted immediately back to the office, intent on a single goal.

Kwan had just passed a critical test, but Jake still had no intention of trusting him completely.

Together, they sized up the situation. Two boo how doy stood watch on either side of the office door. Another pair, barely visible in the shadows beyond the office, guarded the warehouse's rear entrance. Two silhouettes moved inside the room, outlined against the curtained windows.

Six soldiers-for-hire, not counting the three they'd already dealt with. Obviously, Chen Lee had anticipated a rescue attempt.

The two nearest guards began to fidget, murmuring to one another. One called out. Seeing an opportunity, Jake whispered urgently into Kwan's ear, "They're looking for the one you killed. Step out there and take his place. Act sick. Try to get them to come over."

Kwan grinned with feral satisfaction, understanding immediately. He rose and stumbled forward, staying out of the light. Even Jake found his moan believable as he complained of stomach cramps.

As Jake had hoped, the two guards came forward to assist their comrade. He tensed, ready to pick them off without alerting the others. But just as they neared Kwan, one glanced down and saw the blood.

All hell broke loose as they shouted a warning and raced back to the office. The two inside wrenched open the door, guns in hand. Shots erupted in the night. Kwan dove behind the crate.

"Dammit," Jake hissed in frustration as he pulled out his own pistol and returned fire.

A woman cried out, only to be cut off mid-scream.

"Lian," Kwan ground out, surging forward.

Jake grabbed the back of his shirt and yanked him back.

"You're no good to her dead, you idiot." A bullet slammed into the wood behind his head, emphasizing the danger. Large splinters rained down.

"They take her!" Kwan hissed.

Two boo how doy ran for the rear entrance, one with a human-sized cylinder wrapped in white canvas thrown over his shoulder. The guards at the exit joined them. Gunfire continued from the office, pinning Jake and Kwan down while the others escaped.

Gripping Kwan's shoulder, Jake warned, "We'll go after them, once we've eliminated the risk of being shot in the back." He slipped the dead guard's gun into Kwan's hand. "Do you know how to use this?"

The younger man nodded, albeit hesitantly.

"Just don't shoot me, dammit. You go in from this direction. I'll work my way around to attack through the side door of the office."

Racing behind stacks of crates, Jake prepared to attack. He and Kwan were putting their plan into action, but would they be too late to save Lian?

FOUR MEN BURST through the rear door of the warehouse, one carrying a large white bundle draped over his shoulder.

Meg lurched back in surprise, then ducked behind the landau. Her heart thundered, racing in mingled fear and excitement. With a battle cry in Japanese, Akira wielded his sword and jumped forward to intercept them.

The man burdened by the bundle raised a gun. Meg gasped as he pulled the trigger. The unmistakable click of an empty chamber jarred through her body with piercing relief.

The man swore and threw the useless gun to the ground.

The other three attacked Akira with hatchets raised. The fourth man stood back to watch, his angular face and evil, slitted eyes focused on the fight.

Meg yanked her gun from the cloak. Her mind frantically sought a way to help, but the close-quarter fighting put Akira directly in the line of fire.

Akira countered their blows, slashing with his katana. Metal clashed against metal with discordant clangs that pricked at Meg's nerves like the sting of angry wasps. Akira fought with impressive skill, but how long could he survive outnumbered three to one?

Meg's thumb curled over the cold hammer of the gun. Gritting her teeth, she pulled it back, cocking the pistol. In the same instant, Meg realized that the crack of gunfire from inside the warehouse had stopped.

A hot lump thickened in her throat. Did that ominous silence mean Jake was injured, even now bleeding out his life on the warehouse floor?

One of the hatchet men unexpectedly stepped back. The opening left a clear shot.

Meg grasped the opportunity. With grim determination, she squeezed the trigger. Knowing Akira's life depended on accuracy lent a rock-steadiness to her hand.

The gun kicked as it fired, knocking Meg back a step. Yellow fire streaked through the darkness. The bullet struck the assassin in the shoulder, sending him spinning into a wall. The loud report echoed between the two buildings.

The man with the bundle turned, discovering her hiding place.

Meg pointed the gun at him. She stepped out from behind the landau, the hooded cloak still concealing her face and hair.

"Don't move," she said hoarsely.

The bundle suddenly shifted, lifting its head. A low, distinctly feminine moan emerged from beneath the wrapped canvas.

"Lian," Meg whispered, stricken. How horribly ironic. While Jake and Sung Kwan endangered their lives inside, the prize was being taken from the building.

She mustn't let this man escape. Yet how could she fire without risking hitting Yeung Lian? The girl hung over the man's shoulder, shielding him as effectively as a breastplate. Under normal circumstances, Meg took her expert aim for granted—when faced with inanimate bottles and cans as targets. But in this case a young woman's life hung in the balance.

Meg lowered the gun, knowing she didn't dare shoot.

The man turned and ran, struggling under the weight of his kidnapped victim.

Meg raced after him, her cloak flowing out behind her, the gun still gripped in her hand. Under no circumstances must she let this bastard get away with Lian, not after all they'd risked to rescue her.

She didn't have a prayer of matching his wiry strength or fighting skills. Instead, she did the only thing she could think of: She grabbed the trailing end of his waist-length pigtail and threw her weight against it.

"Aiyeee!" he screamed as his head wrenched to the side.

They both stumbled and fell. The ground rushed up to meet Meg's shoulder, slamming into her. Something heavy landed across her ribs, knocking her flat on her back. Dazed, Meg lifted her head. She stared at the cylinder of canvas stretched across her middle. Lian had tumbled on top of her from the falling man's back.

The assassin lurched to his feet.

Meg leveled the barrel of her gun at his chest.

His foot flashed in an arc, striking her hand. The gun—her only source of protection—flew into the darkness. It clattered to the ground several feet away. Trapped under Lian, Meg had no hope of recovering it.

The man stood over her with a superior grin, reveling in her helplessness.

Meg rammed her heel into his groin.

He doubled over, howling.

Frantically, Meg shoved at Lian. Unless she squirmed free, she would be at this man's mercy. He wouldn't stay disabled long. But the girl's weight, magnified by her completely limp state, rivaled that of a dead horse. A sob of frustration broke from Meg's throat. She'd only succeeded in pushing Lian as far as her hips when the man straightened, swearing in his native language.

His right hand jerked up next to his ear. Moonlight rippled across the blade of a hatchet.

Meg's body went rigid, braced for the blow that would rob her of life. Powerless to prevent it, she watched the man's body coil with energy, the hatchet start its descent—

A roar sounded to her left, just before something slammed into the assassin with the force of a freight train.

Bodies crashed into a stack of empty packing crates. Wood cracked and splintered. The sickening thuds of fists slamming into flesh filled her ears.

Meg twisted her head around, but she could barely distinguish the two struggling shapes in the darkness. On the opposite side, she caught sight of a familiar figure rushing to Akira's aid. Sung Kwan! Please God, she prayed, let that mean her own avenging angel was black-haired, arrogant, and so sinfully handsome that he must have fallen from grace long ago.

She shoved at Lian with renewed strength, moving the girl just enough this time that Meg could wriggle out from under.

The hiss of a sword leaving its scabbard whispered

through the night. A man grunted. The sounds of combat behind Meg ceased.

Meg jumped to her feet, just as Sung Kwan dropped to his knees beside Lian. Only one opponent remained for Akira to deal with.

Sword in hand, Jake stared down at the huddled body of a boo how doy. He swung his katana outward, jerking it with a flick of his wrist before resheathing the blade. The lines of his stiff, angry face appeared carved in granite.

"Jake, thank heavens you're alive!"

The strange, tight knot in Meg's chest began to unravel as she ran to him. Now Jake would hold her and offer reassurances that he'd come through the battle in the warehouse unscathed.

Jake grasped Meg's shoulders and shook her.

"What the hell are you doing here?" he exploded.

"Why shouldn't I help?" she snapped back. Tears burned behind her eyes. Stupid man! Didn't he know how grateful she was to find him alive, unharmed? For one brief, happy moment, she'd forgotten that her disguise's original intent had been to conceal her identity from him. Now she had to deal with the full force of his anger.

"You could have been—" Jake spun away. "Dammit, Meg!" he growled.

Stung by his rejection, she looked away—just in time to see Akira deal a death blow to his opponent.

The old warrior braced his feet, knees flexed, and swung his katana with blinding speed. The boo how doy's head separated cleanly from his body and dropped with a sickening thud.

Blood sprayed, a black fountain in the darkness, as the lifeless body crumpled to the ground. Akira calmly flicked his katana with the same technique she'd just seen Jake use.

Shock washed over Meg and her knees wobbled. A dark mist closed in, crowding her vision.

She recalled the silk painting of a fierce samurai warrior severing his enemy's neck with a katana. Sweet mercy, why hadn't she made the connection before? But the painting had been rendered nearly three hundred years ago. Why should she think an ancient warrior caste still existed in modern-day Japan? But they did, she thought a little hysterically . . . two samurai were alive and well, taking heads in San Francisco.

"Is she all right?"

Jake's deep voice broke through Meg's veil of shock. She drew a long, shaky breath.

Jake stood over Yeung Lian. Kwan was still on his knees beside the Chinese girl, his face twisted in concern as he peeled away the canvas.

Lian's pale face caught the dim light like a pearl, shining in oval perfection. Her eyes fluttered open. She looked at Kwan, dazed for a moment. When he helped her to rise, Lian recovered from her ordeal sufficiently to fling herself against her beloved's chest.

Kwan swept her into his arms. He grinned at Jake. "Yes, she is fine."

Pride swept through Meg, as well as relief—pride in Jake that he was the kind of man to risk himself to help these two people, and relief that Lian was alive and well.

Akira sauntered up. "Did Meg-an-san tell you she shoot one of the boo how doy who attack me?"

"It was you who allowed her to come?" Jake retorted with a fierce scowl. "You shouldn't have encouraged her recklessness."

"Then I would be dead," Akira-san said with inescapable logic.

Jake's lips compressed into a thin line.

Meg interjected, "Do we take Lian and Kwan to the mission now?" She wanted to get out of this place as soon as possible. She feared she would be ill all over her slippers if she looked at that headless body once more.

"No. Too dangerous," Jake answered. "Chen will search for them. I won't put Mary and the mission girls at risk."

"Where, then?"

"Another of my ships came into port this morning. The *Venture*. Even on the off chance that Chen thinks to look for them there, a ship surrounded by water is easier to defend than a house. They can hide there for the next few days, while the cargo is unloaded and new shipments are taken on. After that, the *Venture* sails north up the coast, then on to China. Kwan and Lian may choose where they want to go."

"Do we take them now?"

"Not 'we,' Meg. You're coming with me to the *Shin-jiro* while Akira-san takes our guests to the other ship. I have some things I need to get from my cabin, and I don't intend to let you out of my sight."

"All right," Meg agreed.

His eyes narrowed. And why shouldn't he regard her easy capitulation with suspicion? Her rebellious nature had countered his wishes at almost every turn thus far. Meg couldn't explain the reaction either, other than that she was secretly pleased he chose to stay with her rather than Yeung Lian.

Lian's exquisitely beautiful face had triggered a strange disquiet within Meg, a sense of urgency. The Chinese girl embodied Jake's ideal woman—raven-haired, fragile, a gentle daughter of the East. Was he, even now, drawing unfavorable comparisons with Meg's tangled blond curls and the lack of modesty demonstrated by wearing men's clothes?

With a firm grip on her upper arm, Jake steered Meg into the landau. Then he leaped onto the driver's seat and took the reins. Akira climbed into the carriage, followed by Kwan with Lian still cradled in his arms.

The landau lurched into motion. Meg stared out the window, her gaze avoiding the occupants as she struggled to reconcile this violent image of Akira with another impression of a gentle man painting an epitaph for hummingbirds.

Two rowboats awaited them at the pier. Meg climbed into the one Jake indicated. Akira and his companions took the other boat.

As they pushed off, Akira said cheerfully, "I do not have your temper, Takeru-san, but I also wish a bottle of sake. Bring another for me."

Jake swore under his breath, then bent his strength to the oars with a vengeance.

MEG GAZED ABOUT the captain's cabin of the *Shinjiro* as Jake shuffled through papers on his desk. Hints of Japan were everywhere, reminders that Jake Talbert's heart belonged to the Orient.

He would be sailing away soon, swallowed by distance, wanderlust, and a love for foreign, violent places that she couldn't understand. Surely that was a good thing. It wore on her soul to deal with the constant emotional upheavals from a hot-tempered, overtly passionate man . . . one who was so thick-skulled that, even when they were alone, made no attempt to kiss her again.

His efforts to ignore her made for a degrading end to a perfectly awful day.

Jake finished collecting the papers and a change of clothes. He opened the cabinet and took out two squat bottles made of light brown pottery.

Meg cleared her throat. "Is that the sake Akira-san mentioned?"

"Yes," he growled without looking up.

"You can at least stop being a grumpy bear long enough to tell me what it is," Meg countered irritably.

He raised his head. Black brows arched sardonically. "Rice wine."

Wine made of rice? It must be pretty mild, Meg thought with disappointment. After tonight's violence, she could do with something a lot stronger. Dealing with Jake's anger hadn't allowed her jangled nerves to calm down one bit, either.

"Do you have any brandy?"

"No."

She sighed. "Then I'll try some of your sake, please."

He gave her an odd look. His stern expression softened slightly. Unless she was mistaken, a hint of amusement entered his gray eyes.

"Whatever you say, Meg-an-san," he said dryly, imitating Akira with uncanny accuracy. Reaching inside the cabinet again, Jake took out two matching pottery cups. Actually, they were more bowls than cups, without handles. He poured a measure of sake into one and handed it to her.

"I recommend you sip it slowly, Meghan."

Taking the little bowl, she defiantly tipped it and downed the clear liquid in one swallow.

Fire burned down her gullet. Her eyes widened until she thought they might pop out of her head. When her chest recovered from the shock enough to breath, Meg started to cough.

"I warned you."

She wished she had enough strength to punch him.

The coughing continued unabated. With a muttered expletive, Jake set the bowl aside and gathered her into a light embrace. He patted her back and rubbed her arms. As the spasms quieted, his thumbs gently wiped away the tears that had squeezed from her eyes.

Confused, Meg gazed into his unreadable face. One moment Jake Talbert acted the snarling beast; the next, he offered comfort and a tender touch.

More than anything, she wanted to understand this enigmatic man. The need to fathom what had created those shadows in his eyes gnawed at her heart.

Recalling Akira's hints about Jake's past, Meg asked softly, "Why did you name this ship *Shinjiro*?"

Jake's body went rigid. "Why do you ask?" he countered coldly, turning away.

"Akira mentioned that you named the ship after someone you knew."

He moved to the windows at the rear of the cabin. Silently, he gazed out over the bay, as upright, dignified and lonely as a lighthouse standing sentinel over coastal shoals.

His chest expanded on a deep sigh. "Matsuda Shinjiro was the nephew of the Japanese man who adopted me into his family. Shinjiro-san and I were the same age, inseparable, trained together as samurai as we grew up. He was like a brother to me in every way."

"What happened to him?"

"He died." Jake propped one foot on the window seat, then leaned on his upraised knee. He continued to stare fixedly out the window, maintaining a stubborn silence.

No, that couldn't be all! She refused to come this far, only to have Jake shut up as tight as a clam. Daringly, she prodded, "I overheard you tell Mary Lambert that you helped a dear friend commit suicide. Was Shinjiro the one?"

His head turned slowly, his angry gaze cutting into

her like shards of a broken silver mirror. "You want to hear the whole sordid story?"

"Yes."

"I suppose you might as well know," he hissed, breaking away from the window to descend on her with swift, predatory grace. He grasped Meg's upper arms and yanked her close to his chest. "Just so you'll understand what type of man you've foolishly chosen to put your faith in."

Chapter Fifteen

Whipped by a fierce wind and dashed like the ocean waves against the rocks—I alone am broken to bits, and now am lost in longing.
—MINAMOTO NO SHIGEYUKI (D. 1000)

NEITHER HIS WORDS nor his angry grip on her arms caused Meg as much inner agony as Jake's obvious self-hatred.

His voice emerged harsh, grating, as if it took all his willpower to force the dark secret past his lips.

"There were twelve of us that day, all young, brash samurai anxious to prove ourselves . . . which was not easy during the relative peace of the ruling shogunate. When we came across a Chinese raiding party sacking a village, it seemed the perfect opportunity. I cautioned that we were outnumbered. The others scoffed at the idea that Chinese raiders could best samuari warriors. Shinjiro, who led our group, ordered the attack.

"But more Chinese waited over the crest of the hill. Once we realized the mistake, it was too late. Although every samurai fought valiantly, we were trapped in a losing battle." Jake paused, swallowing hard. The cords of his neck stood out. "A samurai's code of honor is very strict. To be held for ransom or executed by an enemy is an insult beyond bearing."

His gaze locked on the window, looking far beyond

the present and San Francisco Bay, his eyes dark pools of pain and regret. Meg felt him tremble. The vibration traveled through her arms and lodged in her heart.

"What happened?" she urged softly.

"Shinjiro was wounded, badly, no longer able to fight. He begged me to act as his second, his *kaishaku*, in committing *seppuku*, an ancient samurai tradition of ritualistic suicide." Jake faced her, eyes glaring like silver daggers. Then he snarled, "Shinjiro knelt in the mud, sliced deep into his abdomen with a knife, then awaited the killing blow. As his kaishaku, it was my duty to cut off his head with a katana."

Meg stared at him, frozen in shock, stunned as much by his hostile tone as his words.

His grip on her arms suddenly slackened, as if he expected her to wrench free in disgust. The light went out of his eyes, grim anticipation diminishing their characteristic gray fire. His challenging attitude cultivated condemnation.

Rather than the horror he sought to invoke with that blunt, harsh declaration, Meg felt tears of sympathy push into her eyes. She ached to cry for his loss, to substitute for the cleansing grief he apparently would not allow himself.

No wonder he was so hard, so strong, with a will chiseled in granite. The self-inflicted torment of his guilt acted like the repeated blows of a sculptor's mallet.

"How very selfish of Shinjiro," she countered angrily.

It was Jake's turn to look shocked. "What?"

"To burden you with such a task, then leave you to suffer the consequences alone. You must have suffered terribly."

He shuddered. "It ripped out my soul to do it."

Meg cupped his cheek in one hand. Her thumb

brushed over the corner of his mouth. "Nevertheless, you honored Shinjiro's wish. You said I should question my faith in you. On the contrary, I think such loyalty deserves my absolute faith."

Without warning, Jake captured her face between heated palms. A groan rumbled from his chest just before he claimed her mouth in a fiery, possessive kiss.

Meg clung to him, realizing that she'd almost lost him—not just tonight at the warehouse, but during the course of the battle sixteen years ago.

Her hands eagerly explored the muscular planes of his back. Sensitive fingers dipped into the hollow of his spine, tracing it down to his waist. He shivered, a reaction Meg found all the more tantalizing because he couldn't seem to control it. An answering tremor rippled through her body.

Her thumbs brushed the stiff cotton ties over his hips.

Excitement jolted through Meg. Jake wore the same strange, naughty hakama trousers that she wore, with the open sides where the front flap tied to the back. What if—? Could she be so bold?

She wanted so very badly to touch him everywhere.

Her hands slid inside the openings on either side. The sensuous length of his black silk shirt smoothed against her palms. Her fingers curved around his taut buttocks.

Jake's mouth froze, still clinging to her lips. Every muscle in his body tensed in anticipation of what she would do next. Meg smiled, knowing she had his complete attention.

Her hands squeezed, reveling in the feel of his tight, resilient flesh. Her nails scraped lightly over his buttocks.

A primitive sound of pure hunger rumbled from Jake's throat. His tongue plunged into her mouth, stroking with sleek, hot intensity. A sweet, aching tingle swept through Meg, softening her bones like warm wax. She leaned into him, molding her body to his hard length. Shivering, she tightened her hold on his buttocks, suddenly anxious for the ridge of his manhood to press harder against her belly.

He broke the kiss, breathing hard. "Too much . . . I can't—" he gasped. Gripping her forearms, he tugged her hands free.

Meg's growing elation dipped sharply. Had she done something wrong?

She looked up, fearful of finding disgust and rejection in his face. His expression was harshly etched, true, but not with anger. Sexual hunger radiated outward from him in waves. Need tugged at Meg—seductive, compelling—until she couldn't tell where his desire stopped and hers began.

Jake wanted her . . . not Lian, not some fragile flower of the Orient with ebony hair and doe eyes.

Meg's confidence blossomed with the discovery of her feminine power. Bewitched by the newfound knowledge, her lips curved in a slow, sensuous smile.

His gaze dropped to her mouth. "Meg," he whispered huskily.

The world tilted as Jake swept her into his arms. In the next instant, he settled her onto the low mattress. He came down gently alongside her. His arousal pressed against her hip, a tangible reminder of his masculine strength even as his lips caressed her mouth with tender restraint.

Jake coaxed her to sit up. He untied the shirt. Although embarrassment warmed her face, Meg's hands eagerly helped to strip away the unwanted garments. Cool air caressed her skin, but it was the glittering intensity in his gaze that caused her nipples to tighten.

His head dipped as he laid her down again. Meg's

heart pounded erratically as his tongue touched the peak of one breast, circling and flicking the pebbled tip. Exquisite sensations shot through her. Then he drew the taut peak into the warm, enticing recess of his mouth, continuing to tease her nipple with his tongue while he sucked lightly.

Meg caught her breath in a ragged gasp. Aching to touch him in return, she threaded her fingers through the silken length of his hair.

His mouth left an erotic trail of moisture and heat as he shifted to the other breast. Threads of fire danced between Meg's breasts and her woman's core, bursting into a shower of sparks that tingled down her legs.

"If you want this to stop, Meghan, you'd better say so now," he said huskily.

"But don't you want to—?"

His chuckle emerged low and throaty as he pressed his forehead to hers. "So much so that I fear the intensity of my own dark urges. You'd be wise to push me away, Meg."

"No, I . . . I want you too much. Don't stop," she murmured.

Jake closed his eyes. A shudder rippled through his powerful frame.

Then he was up with a swiftness that made Meg gasp, untying the strings of her hakama. With one quick, impatient jerk, he yanked off the trousers. Then she lay naked before his gaze, suddenly uncertain, shrinking before the possibility that he might not find her looks pleasing.

The warm, callused texture of his palms closed around her calves. "You're so beautiful," he said thickly.

Tears of happiness pricked behind Meg's eyes. He thought her beautiful. His hands slid slowly, seductively up her legs.

"I promise to be gentle, Meg," he murmured in a rich, velvety voice that shivered across her skin.

He reached the juncture of her thighs, his thumbs brushing back and forth over delicate white skin. Although his fingers barely touched the feminine triangle of dark blond hair, the silken center of her desire tingled wildly in anticipation. Meg wriggled her hips, seeking, urging his fingers to dip deeper.

The warmth of his hands suddenly retreated.

Meg lifted her head to protest. But the objection died as Jake settled his hard length alongside, so that their bodies touched from shoulder to foot. There was only one problem—

"Your shirt. Take it off," Meg insisted hoarsely. "I want to feel your skin against mine."

He yanked the shirt off over his head. Gold glinted amidst his black chest hairs. The cross . . . the one he'd mentioned as a gift from his mother. He still wore it. Then he flipped the heavy pendant onto his back as his mouth lowered to her breasts again. Simultaneously, he slipped his finger over the tight, sensitive knot between her legs.

Meg forgot everything else but his erotic touch. Her back arched like a drawn bow.

Jake groaned. "I can't believe the passion in you. You're already wet."

His dark voice filled her mind with heated images— fantasies that came instantly to life when his finger began to move, sliding through her slick heat. Wildfire raced through Meg's body. A moan slipped from her throat. His finger stroked deeper, inspiring her hips to rock like before.

"Yes, just like that," he said throatily.

Meg's chest rose and fell rapidly, keeping pace with

her racing heart. Rolling waves of sensation built into an exquisite expectation, a building pressure, like a boiling pot about to blow off its lid. Just as Meg neared the point of explosion, she realized something vital was missing.

Her fingers dug into Jake's wrist, pulling the drugging power of his hand away.

"Don't you dare," she gasped. "I don't want to go there alone again."

Lifting his head, Jake stared down at her. His glittering gaze searched her face with touching uncertainty. Then his mouth slanted in a roguish, endearing grin. "There's nothing I wanted to hear more than that."

After one more deep, probing kiss, he moved to kneel between her legs. He impatiently untied the strings of his hakama. The impressive size of him sent a sizzling tingle of apprehension and excitement down Meg's spine. He lowered himself into the nest of her legs, his large frame engulfing her, but Meg felt only treasured and protected.

Jake pressed into her slowly, a gradual filling. Meg felt her body's sheath clutching at him. The incredible feeling was like nothing she could have imagined.

Then he pressed against the barrier of her maidenhead, and discomfort intruded. Meg tensed.

"I wish I could spare you this," he whispered, then thrust deep into her body.

A sharp pang shot through her belly. Meg gasped and dug her nails into his shoulders.

Jake tolerated the attack. He lay perfectly still, kissing her forehead and eyes. The pain faded. Then he shifted, just a slight adjustment of his weight, but the feel of his thick shaft moving inside her made Meg abruptly forget about any discomfort.

She wrapped her legs around his waist.

Jake started to move, slowly at first, sliding deep enough to touch her heart, then retreating until Meg could feel the head of his shaft tugging at the opening to her body. Each time, tiny muscles clenched around him, responding to her fear that he would slip free. Each time, he rewarded her instinctive efforts to hold him captive with a kiss and another plunging stroke.

Meg met his thrusts eagerly, her hips pulsing with a purpose this time, intensified by the fervor of Jake's passion wrapping around their straining bodies like a veil.

She clutched at him, kneading the sweat-slicked muscles of his shoulders, almost frantic with the tension building within. The last of her control shattered, until she moved with him like a wild thing, tiny moans slipping from her lips in synchrony with the thump of his hips against her buttocks.

Then suddenly she reached that pinnacle, plunging over the top in a glorious blaze.

"Jake!" she burst out, sobbing his name.

With a growl, Jake abruptly pulled free of her sheath. His body stiffened. An animallike groan rumbled deep in his chest as Meg felt pulses ripple along the heavy, hot length of his shaft where it rested against her hip. He rolled her away from a strange, sticky warmth, then gathered her into an embrace with his face buried in the curve of her neck.

Meg snuggled against him, drifting in the pleasurable aftermath. The warm, rhythmic brush of his breath caressed her shoulders and breasts. The steady stroke of his hands over her hair made her feel like purring with contentment.

His strength surrounded her, freeing her of any regret for the daring recklessness of what she'd just done. She was reminded again of a living work of art . . . his chiseled beauty never more apparent than when he'd risen over her, his face taut with desire.

Starting at his waist, Meg ran her right hand slowly up his side, feeling the thick muscles that fanned out from his back. A low sound rumbled from his chest, vibrating through his ribs and into her palm. Jake's fingers slid deeper into her hair, brushing her scalp. He kissed the top of her head. Meg smiled. He was an intriguing study in contrasts, this man with a legacy of violence, this warrior who could hold her with such tenderness.

The realization of how little she really knew about Jake began to prick holes in Meg's euphoria. Her fingertips moved to his back, tracing smooth ridges until she encountered the uneven texture of an old scar. The evidence of violence tempted her with a link to the mystery of his past.

"The battle you told me about . . . how did you survive it?" she asked softly.

He pulled back slowly. Meg regretted the gradual unraveling of her warm cocoon, but she felt a compelling need to know.

"A panicked horse slammed into me, knocking me unconscious. The raiders thought me dead and left me there, lying in the mud. But they didn't hesitate to rob my body, or anyone else, as I discovered later, when I awoke to find all my comrades dead."

"Then the raiders were the ones who stole the swords?"

"Yes."

"And you've been searching for them all this time?"

"For sixteen years," he said flatly.

Without warning, he stood, unfolding his long body with sleek, tigerlike grace. Something in the region of Meg's heart tightened at the sheer beauty of him.

But as he yanked ups his hakama, the anger in his movements penetrated her elation.

Too late, she realized her mistake. By mentioning the swords, she'd rubbed salt in his wound. Worse, she'd bluntly reminded him of their bargain—that he must earn the swords by protecting her father.

No wonder he'd exhibited such sensitivity about the weapons from the beginning. The five swords were more than heirlooms Jake hoped to return to their rightful owners—they were his means of redemption.

MEG STOOD FROZEN in the door of the mansion's display room. Plagued by nervous uncertainty, her fingers curled tightly into the folds of her lavender day gown while she watched Akira's back. The old warrior examined a display of rapiers in a lighted case, his hands clasped behind his slate gray kimono.

"Beauty is silent, yet it speaks to us," he said, without turning around.

Meg didn't think he spoke of the rapiers. Nor did the abrupt acknowledgment of her presence startle her. It seemed only natural that he had sensed her quiet approach.

"I . . . I wish to speak with you," she said hesitantly, entering the room.

He turned and bowed.

"As you suggested, I asked Jake about his friend, Shinjiro. Last night—or, rather, early this morning."

"Did he share the story?"

Meg toyed with the wide swath of white lace falling from the neckline of her gown. "Well . . . in a way. He was harsh, blunt, challenging. I believe he wanted to shock me, drive me away in disgust. I don't think he told me quite the whole story, either."

Akira sighed. "Were you chased away, Meg-an-san?"

She blushed, remembering what came after. "Not exactly."

"Good," he responded with an upward curve to his mouth. "Takeru-san build a bridge over the ocean in his heart. He not yet understand that it is too late, the distance too far."

"He is determined to torment himself with the memory, isn't he? He cannot forgive himself for the role he played in Shinjiro's death."

"It is good you see this, Meg-an-san."

"I need to better understand the life of a samurai, Akira-san, and the meaning of this . . . this thing you call seppuku."

"May I see the swords?"

"Certainly," Meg answered readily. She opened the low, wide drawer where the five Japanese blades were stored. How ironic that she'd insisted Jake earn their return. Now she was tempted to just give them to him, to tell him to take the blades and their violent history of blood and vengeance, and seek the forgiveness he craved.

Until her father was free from further threats, however, she refused to do anything that jeopardized Douglass's safety.

Akira helped her arrange the swords on the center table. He ran his fingertips along the silver wisteria design inlaid in the two burgundy sayas.

"This daisho was Takeru-san's," he explained, referring to the matching pair of long and short swords. "It was a sign of much respect that Matsuda Hiroshi give the blades to him. They were meant for a second son, passed down many generations. Hiroshi-san have three daughters, but only one son—little boy at the time."

He drew the katana from its saya. Meg took an involuntary step backward, her heart pounding with memories of spurting blood and a headless body.

Akira lowered his chin and gave her a searching look. "Ah, I see. It trouble you that I take a man's head this morning."

She nodded. The shock of seeing a man decapitated clung to her like hot tar, but she couldn't forget the way Akira had also painted beautiful flowers for two dead hummingbirds, showing such tenderness and compassion.

"A samurai fights for good against evil, Meg-an-san. Was this boo how doy not evil?"

"Yes, but it seems so . . . cruel."

"To sever a head is the most merciful way to take a life. Quick. Painless. No agony in death."

Gnawing on her lower lip, Meg saw his point with new clarity, though it still seemed so barbaric. But, then, who was she to judge the incongruity of an entire class of people who practiced the art of war as fervently as they sought after art, beauty, and nature? To a samurai, decapitating an enemy or committing ritualistic suicide apparently fit into the natural course of things. How was that different from European knights of old hacking each other to death with broadswords? Meg shivered, relieved that she was a woman living in an enlightened age.

Akira resheathed the katana and returned it to the table.

Meg took a deep breath, bracing herself for the grisly details. Pointing to the smallest blade, she asked, "Is this the one Shinjiro used to . . . to cut open his abdomen?"

"Yes. It is a tanto, or short sword."

She'd always suspected it was a ceremonial blade of some sort. Gold, colored enamels, and small jewels decorated the hilt, creating an expert piece of craftsmanship. How could a thing of such beauty also be an instrument of self-inflicted agony and death?

"Tell me how it was used," she said fiercely, determined to know everything.

Grasping the hilt with both hands, Akira pointed it toward his abdomen, just above the waistline of his hakama. "A samurai remove his kimono, push the tanto in here, then over to here," he explained, drawing the point across from left to right. Completing the gruesome demonstration, he twisted the blade and drew it up toward his solar plexus.

Despite her horror at such an act, Meg couldn't begin to fathom the courage it took for a man to actually thrust a dagger into his own body.

"And this one," she persisted, lifting the wisteria katana from the table. "Did Jake use his sword to finish the job?"

"No." Akira set it back in place, lifting the sword with the golden-brown saya instead. "Takersu-san show honor by using Shinjiro's own katana. That is the way of seppuku."

The inevitable question burst out with a sob, "But why would a young, healthy man choose death? Shinjiro had his whole life ahead of him."

"Honor is life and breath to a samurai. Without honor, a samurai is shunned by his people, unworthy. He and his future generations suffer shame. Without honor, a samurai has no soul. Seppuku is the way to restore honor and clean his name."

"What about Jake? If he hadn't been knocked unconscious on that battlefield, if the Chinese hadn't thought him dead and left him there, would they have taken him prisoner?"

"No, they not take Takeru-san."

His simple answer told Meg more than she wanted to know. Cold waves of horror swept through her.

"You mean Jake was also supposed to commit seppuku that day?" she forced out in a hoarse croak. "That if a horse hadn't slammed into him, he would have cut open his belly and . . . and . . ."

"He knew seppuku his duty."

Meg gripped the edge of the table. This morning she'd given Jake the gift of her body, shared the ultimate, glorious intimacy with a man who, other than through a bizarre twist of fate, would have suffered a ghastly death sixteen years before.

Another terrifying possibility arose. What about Jake's self-disgust, his ridiculous male obsession with honor? What if he felt it was never too late to carry out his duty? What if, after fulfilling his obligation to return the heirloom swords, his goal was to commit seppuku and finish what a merciful God had interrupted?

Seeking some reassurance, she whispered, "What about you, Akira-san? You said you chose to leave Japan, to see the world. You've been away for sixteen years. Could you bring yourself to commit seppuku now, for the sake of duty?"

Akira unsheathed Shinjiro's katana and held it up to the light. His gaze followed the reflection shimmering along the polished steel. "I accept the ways of the West I like. I ignore what I do not like. Nihon not change. I change. I am no longer worthy of my country. But I have no . . . no . . . how you say?"

"Regrets?"

"Yes," he agreed, nodding. He resheathed the blade. "No, Meg-an-san, I enjoy my life too much to end it."

"And Jake? Do you think he would—?"

"Here you are, Meghan," interjected a loud male voice.

Meg spun around, startled and annoyed by the interruption. Carl's cheerful greeting grated on her nerves.

"Hello, Carl. How nice of you to visit," she answered with forced serenity.

He grinned. "I couldn't stay away. It seems like forever since your party."

Smiling wanly, Meg returned the swords to their drawer, using the activity to school her breathing into a semblance of calm.

Carl stepped closer and looked over her shoulder.

"Exquisite," he murmured, then added in an offhand tone, "Your father must have acquired these swords just recently. Odd that he doesn't have such beautiful pieces on display in his collection. They look quite Oriental. Are they?"

"Yes, they're Oriental," Meg replied, closing the drawer quickly. She wasn't sure why she experienced this sudden urge to conceal the swords from Carl. Turning to him, Meg said, "Did you wish to speak with me?"

"Of course, darling. Why else would I come?" He looked down his nose at Akira, saying stiffly, "Privately, however."

She blushed at Carl's rude, dismissive manner. His demeanor suddenly brought to mind past, more subtle, signs of bigotry. The realization stunned Meg. Had she noticed before and just chosen to ignore his attitude?

"All right. We can go to the blue drawing room."

As she led the way from the room, Akira muttered, "Take care, Meg-an-san. Hidden and silent worms destroy the wood."

Another proverb. This time Meg felt too weary and heartsore to decipher its meaning.

HIS TIMING COULDN'T be worse.

Meg left Carl poised on one knee while she poured

the tea. Thank goodness Robert was so efficient at providing the necessary social amenities. The tea service offered a much needed distraction . . . a moment to gather her fractured thoughts.

She had convinced herself she wanted Carl to propose again, and that this time she would accept. So why did his profession of devotion leave her feeling so cold?

What the hell was wrong with her? Of course, Meg thought with cutting sarcasm, it could have something to do with having betrayed him by sleeping with another man. But even that knowledge failed to give rise to the expected guilt. If offered the choice, she would succumb to that intoxicating passion with Jake again.

She handed Carl a cup of tea, wishing he would get off his knee and return to his seat.

"I'm very flattered, Carl."

A scowl marred his forehead as he set the cup back on the adjacent tray with a rattle of china. Tea sloshed over the edges, pooling on the saucer. "You always say that, Meghan."

"Well, it's true. I am flattered when you propose marriage. You are handsome, witty, charming, and sought after by every marriageable girl in San Francisco."

Without warning, he leaned forward, arms outstretched, as if intending to embrace her and hold her prisoner until she provided the answer he sought.

Meg thrust a service plate in his face, cutting off his advance. "Cake?"

Carl lurched to his feet, snapping, "I don't want every marriageable girl. I only want you."

She winced at the hurt and anger in his face. Did she really mean that much to him?

All she had to do was say yes. One little word separated her from a sparkling future at the pinnacle of San

Francisco society . . . a handsome, popular husband at her side, beautiful children with hair like sunshine.

Carl recovered his composure and smiled at her, then fervently captured her hand. "Meghan, I think you're tired today, simply not yourself."

The smile was his most charming, but it never reached his eyes. No maelstrom churned in their green depths, no excess of passion or dark secrets, no complexities of a soul in torment.

Jake had shared his body, his pain—every touch, every caress filled with tender giving and aching need.

The image of a little girl with golden hair remained, but suddenly Meg also envisioned two boys with hair as black as midnight, so headstrong and independent they drove their mother mad. A protective warmth flowed through her body, centering in some deep, hidden core.

"You know I love you, darling. We could have such a glorious future together," Carl insisted in a coaxing tone. "Make me the happiest man in the world."

She must be insane, allowing her emotions, her fantasies, to be consumed by a wandering rogue who would leave San Francisco at the first opportunity. Nor had Jake Talbert professed deep feelings of any kind. Up until a few days ago, they couldn't stand one another! She could very well be turning down a path of only pain and heartache.

"I'm sorry. Carl. I-I don't know what I want right now," Meg whispered, stricken by the confusing nature of her feelings. Why did her unruly heart insist on becoming attached where it damn well didn't belong?

Carl dropped her hand as if she'd burned him. He spun away in a frustrated rage, storming to the door, where he turned and paused dramatically.

"I won't give you up, Meghan," he said through clenched teeth. "I won't."

"WHY HAVEN'T YOU done anything yet?" Carl Edwards raged as he paced across the red carpet.

Chen Lee's grimace belied his serene pose. He smoothed one hand over the fierce gold dragon embroidered on his dark green tunic, trying to control his growing disgust for this haughty white man. "I sent my boo how doy the night of our last meeting. They disappointed me with their clumsiness. The next time they know not to fail."

"Well, make it very soon, Chen. Some very carefully laid plans are starting to fall apart around me. I simply won't tolerate it," Carl snapped, his frustration tangible, his lack of self-discipline consuming Chen with distaste. "Once Douglass McLowry is dead, Meg will turn to me in her grief. It is the perfect opportunity, and I refuse to miss it. And while you're at it, kill that interfering son of a bitch, Jacob Talbert. I don't like him."

Chen stiffened at the name. "Ah, yes, I will kill Jacob Talbert. But not for you, Mister Edwards. The pleasure will be for me alone."

"Well, whatever the damn reason, just get rid of him."

Coldly, Chen stated, "I do not like your tone, Mr. Edwards. Do not forget who I am."

Edwards paled at the warning, then swallowed hard. He seemed to have difficulty finding his voice.

Smiling with satisfaction, Chen clasped his hands behind his back and walked slowly around the rigid man. "I could as easily choose to get rid of *you*."

Clearing his throat, Edwards lifted his chin with lingering bravado. "I've done nothing to anger you. Don't forget, I helped you by providing that map of the McLowry mansion."

"You annoy me. That is enough," Chen replied with mounting boredom. "As a bargaining tool, that map was useful only once. What else could you possibly have to offer me?"

"I believe I've found something else of interest."

"Indeed? I find this difficult to believe," murmured Chen, stopping in front of his unwelcome visitor.

The cold, calculating gleam flickered to life in Edwards's eyes once again. "Why would McLowry go to the trouble and expense of repaying your loan, I've asked myself, unless you had something he coveted? The man has very few passions beyond his work, his collection of weapons chief among them. Then I saw some items at the mansion today that I believe have satisfied my curiosity." He paused dramatically, a confident smile curving his mouth.

Chen clamped down on the visceral urge to thrust a dagger into Carl Edwards's throat, to forever transform that arrogant expression into a mask of shock and death. Pompous little worm.

A shallow bow conveyed Chen's disrespect, though he doubted Edwards was discerning enough to catch the message. Blandly, he responded, "By all means, continue, Mr. Edwards."

The white man's smile widened. "I saw a set of Oriental swords, evidently quite valuable. They were hidden away, which is quite strange, since Douglass McLowry is typically eager to put any new acquisitions on immediate display. Why would McLowry choose to conceal them . . . unless he had come into possession of the swords through dishonest means, and feared retaliation? For obvious reasons, that made me think of you."

"Describe these swords."

Edwards did so, then offered slyly, "I know where the swords are kept, Chen. Your men won't have to waste precious time and effort tearing apart the house to find them."

Although his patience had been pushed to the limit, Chen was always willing to pretend a little tolerance . . . as long as he found a way to use Edwards in pursuit of a much-desired goal.

Chapter Sixteen

Like those lovely seaweeds, yielding, you slept with me, deeply as deep-sea fleece I think of you. But the nights we slept together were not many . . . I came away, parting with you as trailing vines do.
—Kakinomoto no Hitomaro (c. 700)

LEANING OVER THE keyboard, Meg rested her left arm across the base of the music stand, her forehead propped on her wrist. She stared down at the ivory keys. Her right hand picked out a slow, lilting waltz on the piano.

With a dejected sigh, she wondered what had become of the woman she knew: the banker's daughter, safely established in her world, comfortable in her social routine. Who was this sensual creature, this stranger whose mind kept reliving every detail of their lovemaking?

The break in her relationship with Carl added yet another complication to her present dilemma. Now she didn't have plans of marriage to arm her against Jake's assault on her senses—and she needed all the help she could get to keep from becoming emotionally involved with a man who was sure to break her heart.

Meg sat up, placing both hands on the keyboard, and began to play in earnest. In mid-sonata, a tingle of desire swept through her—fresh, real, not some trick of her heated imagination. Without looking around, she knew Jake had entered the room.

Her hands froze on the keyboard. Butterflies fluttered in her chest as she felt suddenly, unaccountably shy. She'd shared the ultimate intimacy with this man just this morning.

His earlier words, when they'd first met, came back to haunt her. *I admire a woman who practices extreme modesty.* What did he think of her now?

Jake came up from behind. Warm hands settled on her shoulders, massaging gently. "May I listen?"

Meg closed her eyes, awash in relief that he didn't regard her with disgust.

"What would you like to hear?"

"Anything." His hands slid into her hair, pulling out pins until the mass of curls tumbled down her back.

Her trembling hands would fumble all over the keyboard if he kept up this tender assault. "No preferences?"

Bending low, he murmured in her ear, "Only to make love to you again." Lifting her hair, he set the back of her neck afire with a kiss.

"Play for me, Meg." The warmth of his hands slid away. Then he sat on the floor next to her and leaned back against the leg of the piano.

Meg burned in the aftermath of his touch. Her eyes widened in offended disbelief. He seduced her, then left her wanting?

With a sigh, Jake tilted his head back and closed his eyes. Long black lashes curved against the gray shadows beneath his eyes. Suddenly, Meg recognized his weariness. Her heart softened. He'd been through so much last night in rescuing Lian.

She longed to stroke his brow, soothe away the creases of exhaustion that bracketed his down-turned mouth. Instead, she chose one of her favorite pieces of music to play, pouring her heart into it for him. When she finished, Jake spoke unexpectedly.

"Don't you dare play like that for anyone else, Meghan McLowry," he said, his voice vibrating with intensity. "I must be a selfish bastard, because I don't want another man to share in those things I hear—the heartache, the joy, the loneliness, and most of all, the passion."

Meg stared down at him in amazement. In all the years she'd played, among all the compliments showered upon her, not once had anyone recognized the passion in her music.

Jake looked up at her.

For once his eyes were unshuttered, a clear pathway to his soul. As she gazed into their passionate, needy depths, Meg's heart gave a lurch.

She feared getting emotionally involved with this man? Mercy, who was she trying to fool?

She was in love with Jake Talbert.

He rose, coming to his feet with fluid grace. Without warning, he swept Meg up into his arms, sat on the piano bench, and settled her onto his lap.

Meg twined her arms about his neck, searching for a way to counteract his strange, melancholy mood.

"My mother used to play the piano," he said quietly.

"Really? In Japan?"

"No, my real mother, Sophia. We lived in Portsmouth, England. I don't remember her face, but I can recall her black hair, how she smelled of flowers, and the way she would lapse into Italian whenever she lost her temper." A wistful smile curved his lips. "She and my father, Michael Talbert, loved each other dearly, but theirs was a stormy relationship. The last time they saw one another they fought . . . about me. Father, knowing my love for the sea, insisted it was time I sail with him. Mother disagreed." He wove a strand of Meg's hair between his fingers. "Perhaps she had a premonition of disaster."

Unable to bear the sadness in his eyes, Meg stroked his cheek, brushing her thumb along the thin scar. His gaze shifted back, focusing on her face.

"You were only ten," she said softly. "Surely you don't hold yourself responsible?"

"No. But it always saddens me, knowing how they parted in anger."

"Once you left Japan, did you try to find your mother?"

"Twice, when my travels took me to England. But she'd remarried, and some critical church records were destroyed in a fire. I was unable to trace her."

He tried to speak nonchalantly, but Meg sensed the pain and disappointment threading beneath the surface.

A thrill of excitement curled through her. Success in searching for his family had eluded Jake because he didn't have the benefit of an army of lawyers at his side. The power of the Comstock National Bank extended to New York, then on to London. Tomorrow, Meg resolved, she would visit her father's lawyers at the bank and put their resources to good use.

Smiling gently, Meg traced the sensuous, carved lines of his mouth with one finger.

"Kiss me, Jake."

JAKE SLID HIS fingers into the warm hair at Meg's nape. Everything about her was so incredibly soft. As his thumb stroked the hollow beneath her ear, a wave of tenderness swept over him like the first ray of sunshine after a particularly dark and violent storm.

He was accustomed to dealing gently with delicate women. But he'd never before experienced this overwhelming urge to cherish a woman for her strength as well as her fragility, to make love to all the complexities of her spirit as he buried himself in her body. It amazed and humbled him that Meg could still look at him with such warmth after learning of his violent history.

Teasing her lips with his tongue, Jake savored the pure scent of woman. Meg opened her mouth on a sigh, inviting him into paradise. He laid her back on one arm and kissed her like there was no tomorrow.

His other hand roved lightly over her breast and side, then squeezed a tapered thigh through a thick padding of petticoats. Damn, this wasn't offering the freedom he wanted to touch her. Stifling a groan, Jake sat her up straight on his lap. She stared at him, looking as dazed and soft as a small kitten, her lips red and swollen from his kisses . . . and he wanted nothing more than to bury himself in her hot body.

Swallowing hard, Jake murmured, "Humor me on something."

"What?" she whispered.

"Straddle me. Lift your left leg over so you wrap around my hips."

A blush colored her cheeks a rosy hue. "All right."

As she levered upward, half standing to maneuver her leg over, Jake smoothed her dress out behind her. She settled slowly onto his lap, legs spread and skirts bunched around her hips. At the sight of the pearly white skin of her bare thighs, Jake thought he might burst through the front of his trousers.

"That's perfect," he said unsteadily.

"You don't seem very comfortable."

"Believe me, there's no place I'd rather be right now." *Except inside you.*

"What now?"

"I can already think of one improvement." Reaching around her, he worked free the dress buttons and corset ties down her back. Her shuddering breath caressed his ear, causing his hands to tremble and his progress to slow as he reached the end.

"Why do women wear these infernal contraptions, anyway?"

She chuckled. "Don't you want to see me cinched into a fashionably trim waist?"

"You have a trim waist, dammit. You don't need to fake it." To demonstrate his point, Jake freed the last corset tie and easily spanned her waist with his hands.

Unexpectedly, he imagined her slender body swollen with child . . . his child. A fierce protectiveness gripped him, leaving him shaken. He'd carefully laid out his future, planning his triumphant return to Japan in minute detail, so why did he feel bereft that Meg wouldn't be there to share it with him?

Meg rolled her shoulders, dropping her bodice forward and baring her breasts.

Every rational thought tumbled out of his head.

He cupped her full, high breasts in his hands. "More beautiful than a sunrise," he murmured.

Jake tossed the corset aside and slipped her arms free of her sleeves. Then he bent to taste her fresh, dewy skin. He rubbed his lips back and forth across one nipple, marveling at the way it tightened at his touch. He touched it with his tongue.

Meg's shuddering gasp inspired him to take her full into his mouth. Her answering moan, as she gripped his shoulders, sent a hot twinge of need through his loins.

The scent of her misting desire wafted upward, driving him mad. His body demanded that he plunge into her tight heat, but the urge to cherish took priority, encouraging him to tease and taste her delectable body until she melted in his hands.

Meg arched back against his arm, offering him the full

bounty of her breasts. He gloried in the uninhibited gesture, knowing he was the one who'd introduced her to this passion.

She tilted her head back, her hair rippling like molten gold. The slender column of her graceful neck was smoother than ivory. He'd sailed the world, trading in every kind of exotic merchandise, but he'd never encountered a treasure as rare as this unique woman.

He sucked harder at her breast, savoring the sweet taste of her nipple. Meg's breath came in short, quick pants. Her nails dug into his shoulders.

"Jake, please."

"Did you want something?" His free hand slid up her thigh. His thumb brushed over the wet cotton of her drawers.

She shuddered. "I want you, inside me."

"Not just yet. Damn, these things are in the way."

"I'll . . . have to stand up to take off the drawers."

Her voice held the same mournful tone he felt at the abhorrent idea of separating the firm heat of her backside from his thighs for even a moment. "Don't you dare move. I've got a better idea."

Reaching down, he hooked his fingers in the slit of the drawers and ripped them open.

Meg's eyes widened. Wryly, she muttered, "If I didn't know better, I'd say you were an impatient man."

"Dire situations call for quick solutions."

"Is this . . . a dire . . . situation?" she whispered hoarsely, her voice breaking as his thumb penetrated the moist nest of hair between her legs.

Jake tensed, every muscle in his body tightening with leashed desire as he watched the play of pleasure across her face. "Very dire," he rasped. "Life or death, in fact."

"Oh?" she said dreamily.

"Yes. I want you so bad, sweetheart, I'll die if I can't bury myself inside you."

She smiled, one of those teasing glimpses of feminine mystery that quickened his blood. Her hands moved between them. Just as he wondered what she was doing, her fingers began to unbutton his trousers.

Jake couldn't move. Every muscle froze in anticipation. Each hard draw of his breath echoed in the room, until his engorged staff sprang free and he stopped breathing altogether. When she wrapped her hand around him, Jake thought he actually might die on the spot . . . of pleasure.

"Meg," he whispered roughly, overcome by sensations that he didn't understand. His mind filled with frantic images of a hard, quick possession, branding her as his own . . . yet he also wanted to leisurely, tenderly bring her to a shattering climax.

His thumb stroked her passion. Her hand squeezed tighter.

Unable to stand any more of the sweet torment, Jake lifted Meg and embedded his shaft deep within her body. He groaned as her silken heat slowly descended and closed around him.

"Now, rock against me," he said throatily, reaching back to guide her calves over the edge of the piano bench.

She flexed her legs and rocked her hips forward, burying him to the hilt. He felt the tip of his shaft touch her womb.

Jake growled with enthusiasm. Reaching a shaking hand down to where they joined, he caressed the center of her desire. She moaned and rocked harder and faster as his free hand guided her hips.

Jake's mind blanked out to everything but the sensation of Meg's tight sheath, the sight of her gently bouncing breasts, the pleasure that intensified just as he thought it couldn't get any better. His jaw clenched. Sweat broke out on his chest and back.

A guttural groan reverberated through the room as Jake lost the battle for control, shuddering in the most powerful climax he'd ever experienced. His fingers grasped Meg's hips. She joined him with a sweet cry, convulsing around his pulsing manhood. The darkness within him cracked at the edges, letting in glimpses of sunshine.

Meg collapsed against his chest, clinging to him. Jake stroked her back, breathing hard, gradually coming back to earth from a very high plateau.

"What's that rippling sensation?" she whispered into the peaceful silence.

Smiling, he rubbed her lower back in lazy circles. "That's your body pulsing, rather like aftershocks."

She nuzzled her nose into the curve of his neck. "Now it makes sense. I thought an earthquake just ripped through this room. I'm surprised the house didn't shake down around us."

Jake chuckled, a rich, relaxed sound . . . not surprising, considering he felt more satisfied than ever before in his life. This was more than sexual repletion. A warm sense of contentment permeated his lax muscles and settled into his bones. He could sit and hold Meg like this all night.

After a while, she fell asleep in his arms. He rubbed his cheek against her hair. Maybe, just maybe, since she bestowed it willingly, he did deserve her trust. Meg didn't seem to regard him as a failure, a man without honor.

He finally glanced at the clock. They'd been in here almost two hours. Someone was bound to come looking for them soon. If a servant walked in on them like this—

"Meghan, wake up," he whispered.

She mumbled a protest. It took all his strength of will to ease her kitten-soft warmth away from his chest. She blinked at him, slow sweeps of tawny lashes.

"Time to get up, muddlehead," he teased, using his voice to break the spell that held them both enthralled. "We can't stay here, like this."

She nodded. They separated reluctantly. Standing up, Jake helped Meg reassemble her clothes and hair. Then he gathered her into his arms at the door, resting his forehead against hers.

"More than anything, Meghan, I want to lift you in my arms, carry you upstairs, and make love to you again in your bed."

She sighed. "The servants would see."

"That's the only thing preventing me from carrying you off and ravishing you."

The corners of her mouth tilted upward. "Maybe you can come to my room later . . . after everyone's asleep."

Jake couldn't find his voice as his imagination dwelled lustily on the possibilities. He let a kiss answer for him, claiming her lips in a way that demonstrated his enthusiasm for the idea.

MEG STOOD AT her bedroom window, watching the stars. Her arms hugged her cotton night rail. Although she'd turned down the lamp, the soft glow cast her shadow into the night, where it was quickly swallowed by the darkness.

She was a wanton fool to wait for a man who hadn't declared any feelings for her other than desire. Although her body tingled wildly in anticipation, disappointment and heartbreak hovered like a specter in the back of her mind. The sea, his business, his passion for the Orient—unless Jake loved her, all these would lure him away in the end.

Her love alone could not hold him.

A slight movement, little more than a shift in the shadows beneath the trees, caught Meg's attention. Her gaze dropped, searching. It was probably an owl. The nocturnal predators commonly hunted the orchard, welcomed by the groundskeeper as a control for mice. Meg watched the same spot, apprehension trickling down her spine for no apparent reason. The shadows remained motionless, the night quiet. After a few minutes, she laughed at her foolishness.

Apparently waiting up until one o'clock in the morning for a lover's tryst made her nervous. It wasn't exactly something she was accustomed to.

A light tap sounded on the door. Meg gasped, nearly jumping out of her skin. She opened the door. Jake slipped in, stealthy in his bare feet, then closed the door behind him. The sight of his bare, bronzed chest, visible through the open front of his dark blue shirt, caused her mouth to go dry. After a quick, playful kiss, he grinned and held up an uncorked bottle of wine and two glasses.

Meg smiled. Joy trickled through her like a stream of effervescing bubbles.

She followed Jake to a small table near the window. He set down the wine and glasses, then swept her into his arms. His mouth slanted across hers.

He slowly gathered up her night rail from behind, bunching the material into his large hands while his mouth devoured hers with hot, probing kisses. Meg wondered what he would think when he reached the hem and found her buttocks as bare as the day she was born.

But just before reaching the hem, Jake froze. His head lifted, listening, as alert as a tiger scenting prey.

"What is it?" Meg whispered.

"I don't know," he muttered, a frown creasing his brow. "Probably nothing."

She glanced toward the window. "Perhaps you heard the owl I saw earlier, hunting amidst the trees."

Jake's response startled her. He abruptly set her back at arm's length.

"You saw something?" he asked tersely. "How long ago?"

"I don't know . . . ten minutes? I—it was while I was waiting for you. A shadow, nothing more."

"Dammit," Jake hissed, wrenching away.

Cold dread settled heavily in Jake's gut.

It had been a mistake to keep the earlier attack by the Tong a secret from Meg. He never should have listened to Douglass's plea. She should have been warned to be suspicious of every shadow.

Jake's hand went to his waist. Bloody hell, he wasn't even armed. He'd let his desire for Meg blind him to the dangers of the night and Chen Lee's continued obsession with vengeance.

He had to get his katana and gun.

"What's wrong?"

His teeth clenched as she touched his arm lightly. If his instincts proved correct, and assassins were making another attempt, he didn't deserve her tender concern. He'd shirked his responsibilities for the mind-shattering pleasure of her kiss.

"Perhaps nothing. I need to go see, however. Stay here. Lock your door."

"But—"

"Just do it."

On his way to his own room, Jake opened the door to

Akira's bedchamber and hissed a warning, knowing the samurai slept lightly and would awake, instantly alert to danger. Then Jake retrieved his weapons, thrusting the pistol into the waistband of his trousers. Without the time to tie a sash, he carried the katana, gripping it so tightly he half expected the black wooden saya to crack in his fist.

Jake was almost to Douglass's room when a scream tore down the hallway from Meg's bedchamber.

Douglass thrust his head out his door. "What the devil is going on?" he demanded.

Scowling fiercely, Jake jabbed a finger at the Scotsman. "Call Phillip and Peter, *now*, and tell them to stay with you. And stay in your room, dammit!"

"What about Meggie?"

"I'll take care of her!" Jake shouted over his shoulder as he sprinted barefoot back down the hall.

He overheard Douglass shout, "Where is my gun? I'll be damned if they'll get what they came for!" Meg's father stomped back into his room.

A rage unlike any he'd ever known shook Jake when he heard the sounds of a struggle from Meg's room. She'd locked the door, as instructed, so he kicked it in.

One of two boo how doy held Meg about the waist, wrestling her back toward the open window. She struggled and cursed. Jake apprised the situation in an instant. There was only one reason Chen Lee would send his men after Meg: bait. If the attack on Douglass failed yet again, Chen wanted insurance that the banker would come to him.

With a feral roar, Jake attacked the second man, killing him on the first blow with the katana. The other released Meg, but his attempt to flee proved useless.

Holding the bloodied sword so it wouldn't touch her, Jake caught Meg into a crushing embrace and buried her face against his chest. The aftermath of fear for her safety rippled through him like a volcanic tremor.

Akira appeared at the door, armed and ready.

Jake thrust Meghan into Akira's arms. "Protect her," he said through gritted teeth. Having dealt with one danger, he hastened to counter the next.

The servants milled about, speculating on the source of the chaos. Peter and Phillip stood outside Douglass's room, blinking in confusion.

"Where is Douglass?" Jake demanded.

Peter's mouth sagged open. "He is not with you?"

"Didn't he call you to guard him?"

The brothers glanced at each other, then shook their heads.

Douglass's words came back to Jake like a clap of thunder. *I'll be damned if they'll get what they came for.*

Bloody hell, the old man wouldn't be that stupid!

A gunshot sounded downstairs. Jake spun on his heel. *No, please—not that.*

Another gunshot echoed through the house. Swearing, Jake descended the curving staircase at record speed. The servants watched him race by in stunned, frightened silence.

He burst into the sword display room. The sight of the bloodied form on the floor slammed into Jake like a mule kick to the chest. A red mist of wrath colored his vision. His body moved with the swift expertise of years of training as he wielded the katana and dispatched the two boo how doy with ruthless efficiency.

"Robert!" Jake bellowed before falling to his knees beside Douglass. One of the assassins had turned the Scotman's own gun on him during the struggle.

Wrenching off his shirt, Jake pressed it to the bloodied hole in Douglass's chest. Claws of despair sank into his throat. He'd witnessed enough death to recognize a mortal wound.

"Dammit, Douglass," he whispered hoarsely, "why didn't you stay where I told you!"

"B-bastards. I couldn't let them have . . . have the swords," Douglass replied haltingly, his body wracked with pain. He waved a limp hand toward the open drawer. The Matsuda blades lay scattered on the carpet, but all five were there.

"The swords aren't worth your life, dammit. I could have gone after them, even if it took another sixteen years."

Robert arrived, stopping in the doorway. Color drained from his face at the sight of Douglass.

Jake looked up. "Find Meghan," he croaked. "And hurry."

The butler nodded grimly and left.

"Jacob, lift me off the floor," said Douglass. "I-I dinna want . . . to die flat . . . flat on my back."

Nodding numbly, Jake grasped Douglass carefully beneath the shoulders and eased the Scotsman up onto his lap, propped against his angled thighs. Douglass groaned.

Jake's jaw clenched. "Better?"

"Aye, lad. Thank you."

Thank you? Something ripped apart inside Jake at the appalling irony of those words. He'd failed to safeguard the very man he'd been brought here to protect. Meghan's father. Jake turned over his free hand and stared, horrified, at the blood smeared across his palm.

There was blood everywhere. Red. Damning.

Dear God, old man, why didn't you listen to me? Why didn't Shinjiro listen to me when I warned him we were outnumbered?

Once again he'd failed, and the life of someone dear was forfeit.

" 'Tis odd, lad. I never thought d-dying would be . . . like this. I'm sh-shaking like a leaf."

"It's not you, Douglass," Jake said through gritted teeth. "It's me."

Tremors radiated outward from a huge, throbbing knot beneath his breastbone. Jake clenched his free hand into a fist, but it wouldn't stop. The shaking spread like wildfire, until it held his entire body in a ruthless grip. He felt his control unraveling at the edges.

"Meggie will no' blame you."

Of course she will. He pressed the shirt padding tighter. "Don't try to talk. Save your strength."

"And waste my last minutes? Nay, I think no'." Douglass stiffened in pain, then whimpered, "I want to see Meggie."

A spasm gripped the muscles of Jake's throat. He swallowed hard. "She'll be here any minute now," he rasped. *And, dear God, I'm not ready to face her. Not now. Not ever.*

"I'll t-tell her, lad," offered the Scotsman. "I'll t-tell Meggie . . . 'tis no' your fault. She should not think that. 'Tis m-mine for . . . for taking the blades . . . from Chen Lee, a greedy thing to do." He took a shuddering breath, then added, "Remember your promise. T-take care of my Meggie."

Jake didn't have the heart to destroy the dying man's hopes. He wanted nothing more than to take care of Meghan, to cherish her. Instead, she would hate him, vehemently. He couldn't have failed her more miserably than this.

Running footsteps sounded in the hallway—one set recognizable as Akira's the other light, feminine, achingly familiar. Jake felt, rather than saw, Meg freeze in the doorway. He couldn't bring himself to look at her face.

Then her scream ripped through him like the blade of a knife.

Jake shook his head, dazed, suddenly disoriented. He looked down at his bare chest, wondering if the pain had come from plunging the tanto into his abdomen. The sounds of a waning battle surrounded him. The death cries of defeat from fellow samurai chilled Jake as much as the mud soaking through the knees of his hakama. His hands convulsively gripped the hilt of the tanto, still sticky with Shinjiro's blood, as he held the sharp point to his own abdomen. Another samurai waited over him, katana poised over his neck, ready to fulfill the honorable role of kaishaku.

The wrenching conflict inside him overshadowed everything, even the fresh, raw grief of Shinjiro's death. Samurai duty and honor demanded he thrust the blade into his belly. But his western Christian beliefs from early childhood, his own mother's teachings, howled in his mind. . . . Suicide is wrong . . . an offense to God . . . a sin.

Meg dropped down next to Douglass, sobbing, jarring Jake in much the same manner as the horse that had slammed into him long ago. The panicked animal had knocked him unconscious, interrupting the attempted seppuku. He would never know if he would have followed through with taking his own life. Which side would have prevailed? His samurai upbringing, or his European origins and the western abhorrence of suicide?

Clasping her father's hand, Meg talked in low murmurs punctuated by sobs. Akira stood nearby in respectful silence. Robert gathered up the gawking servants and hustled them away from the door.

As if from a great distance, Jake realized he was still staring at his bare chest. In morbid fascination, he used his stained fingers to paint a line of blood across his abdomen. His gaze drifted to the tanto blade on the carpet. He'd kept Chen Lee from regaining the swords, thus keeping his vow to the Matsuda family . . . but at what price?

Douglass's raspy voice penetrated the haze.

"Meggie, lass, there's no' a thing can be done."

"No, Da. Don't say that. You can't die," she said raggedly. "You're so full of life! How can you die?"

"My own folly brought me to this, lass."

"What . . . do you mean?"

"The swords, Meggie," he gasped, pushing out the words with difficulty. "I–I tricked Chen Lee. Took them . . . from him." His voice faded to a strained whisper. "Wanted them . . . so beautiful."

She stroked his arm, his cheek. "It's all right. It doesn't matter. You just need to get well." Her voice shook.

Douglass tried to touch her cheek, but he couldn't find the strength to lift his arm. Meg caught up his bloody hand and pressed it to her face, nuzzling her cheek into his palm while tears streamed down in glittering paths.

"My . . . lovely lass. Be happy . . . Meggie."

His voice faded; his body sagged. Meg struggled to keep his limp, heavy hand pressed to her cheek. "Don't leave me all alone, Da. Please. You're all I have." She began to sob in earnest—great, racking sobs that sounded capable of tearing her delicate body apart.

Douglass didn't answer.

Jake knew the moment the life force slipped away from the man in his lap, even as Meg moaned, "No . . . no. Da?"

Jake couldn't move. His brain seemed incapable of the simplest function. He knew only one thing—Douglass was dead. It was all over.

Everything was over.

Meg looked up with a haggard, tear-streaked face. Jake eased Douglass onto the carpet, sensing the momentum building within her.

"You bastard! This is all your fault. You were supposed to protect him!"

He squeezed his eyes closed.

"You promised, Jake!"

Grief, confusion, accusation . . . all flowed from her voice. The agony of her words threatened to crush his heart. He couldn't breathe.

"Talk to me, damn you!" she shouted. A small fist struck his shoulder. "Why won't you tell me why this happened? Why?" Suddenly, a barrage of blows rained down on his head, neck, and shoulders . . . though not nearly as painful as the harrowing sound of her sobs.

Still, he didn't move, welcoming the punishment, wishing she could inflict more damage.

"Meg-an-san!" Akira cried out. "Stop! You must not."

The hysterical attack ceased as abruptly as it had begun.

"Get out, Jacob Talbert! Get out of my house!" Meghan screeched. "I never want to see you again!"

Sounds of a struggle punctuated her screams of fury as Akira, muttering calming words that fell on deaf ears, pulled her out of the room.

Jake slumped over, curling around the agony in his chest, bracing his elbows against his knees. He speared his hands through his loose hair. Stiff fingers, still sticky with Douglass's blood, clenched slowly into fists.

The tanto lay within reach on the carpet, its image branded on his vision, his mind. He reached out blindly.

His fingers curled around the jeweled hilt—

But in one last taunting failure, he couldn't find the courage to use it.

Chapter Seventeen

All through the night black as leopard-flower seeds, through the day till the red-rayed sun sets, I grieve, but there's no sign, I brood, but I don't know what to do.

—LADY OTOMO NO SAKANOUE (EIGHTH CENTURY)

SLATE GRAY CLOUDS scurried before a gusting wind, dimming the morning sunlight to a gloomy hue. The rain had held off, sparing the large group of mourners gathered around Douglass McLowry's grave.

Jake stood at a distance, partially concealed behind the corner of a marble mausoleum. He had no right to stand among them. It was his fault Meg had suffered this loss.

He had positioned himself where he could see her face, though the sight of that pale oval framed by the black hood of her cloak caused him a feeling of immeasurable loss. Four days of shock, grief and exhaustion showed in her wan expression. She looked so fragile, as if the wind could pick her up and carry her away like a puff of dandelion seeds. The fire had gone out of her eyes.

He couldn't bear to see her like this, but since he was the cause of her misfortune, no matter how he wracked his brain he couldn't see how to help her.

Bloody hell, he wanted to gather Meg into his arms and comfort her, shelter her from a world whose cruelties he understood only too well. But he'd stayed away since that fateful morning, not wanting to further provoke her grief.

After the police arrived, he and Akira had packed their belongings and returned to the *Shinjiro*. Reluctantly, he'd agreed when Akira insisted they take the Matsuda blades for safekeeping—particularly when Robert pleaded that the motivation for Chen Lee's attacks be removed from the house posthaste. As far as Jake was concerned, however, it was a temporary arrangement. He couldn't take the blades back to Japan. He hadn't earned that privilege.

Only the iguanas remained at the mansion. Jake disliked the idea of removing them from the garden's healthy setting. At least the telegram he'd sent to Daniel, telling the naturalist where the lizards could be found, would soon see to their safe delivery.

The preacher finished booming the words of the funeral service against the blustery wind. The pallbearers stepped forward to grasp the ropes beneath the coffin and remove the supporting boards. The crowd began to drift away. Meghan stepped forward to lay a white rose on her father's coffin.

As she straightened, her knees gave way.

Jake surged forward instinctively to help. He came to a grinding halt when an elegant blond gentleman grasped her elbow.

Meghan clung to Carl's arm for support. She looked up at him with gratitude.

Staggering back, Jake leaned against the mausoleum. That slimy bastard, Edwards, was taking advantage of Meghan's vulnerability.

In that moment Jake realized what all the pain and soul-searching in recent days had been trying to tell him.

He loved Meghan . . . more than his quest for the swords or his desire to return to Japan.

But instead of being able to explore and nurture the miracle of that love, everything had crumbled around him.

I never want to see you again!

He winced as her angry words echoed in that black emptiness that had so recently been filled with a dawning joy. The idea of facing her hatred terrified him more than any threat from an armed enemy ever had. Nevertheless, he had to talk to her, make one more attempt to set things right.

"DID I HEAR someone downstairs?" Meg asked as Carl returned to the sitting room adjoining her bedchamber.

She sat a little higher on the sofa, her breath coming shallow and fast. Ever since she'd spotted Jake at the cemetery this morning, her body had trembled with tension. Why did she expect him to come? Surely he wouldn't dare set foot in this house again!

"Just more mourners, darling," Carl murmured soothingly. "Business acquaintances of your father, paying their respects."

Meg started to rise, protesting, "I should greet them."

Carl squatted down in front of her and grasped her hand. "Certainly not. You've been through enough in the past four days. You should rest. Besides, they're already gone."

Cautiously, she asked, "Has anyone else come to visit?"

"No one of significance. Why?" Carl's thumb rubbed back and forth across her knuckles. A frown flickered across his brow. "Were you expecting someone in particular?"

"No, I just wondered—" she said haltingly, unable to bring herself to mention Jake's name aloud.

"You don't need anyone else, now that you have me to watch over you. Just remember that." Carl patted her hand.

Meg compressed her lips, suppressing a sudden sting of annoyance. She would *not* allow herself to snap at Carl. A pillar of strength in recent days, he'd taken charge of draping the house in black, dealing with visitors, and making funeral arrangements. It was uncanny, really, how he'd appeared just when she needed him that nightmarish morning.

"I am concerned, however," Carl said as he stood, "the way you've bottled up all this anger at Jacob Talbert. He may have failed you miserably, Meghan, but it can't be healthy for you to keep those feelings locked inside."

Meg looked away. More than anger at Jake Talbert crushed her heart. It was fury, a sense of betrayal, disillusionment, and something she couldn't define . . . all rolled into one.

"So, I have the perfect solution to help you purge this anger." Carl grasped her elbow, coaxing her up from the sofa.

"What is it?" One minute Carl told her to rest, the next he was guiding her across the room to her secretary. The pressure on her elbow urged her to sit at the small desk.

"You should write a letter to him," Carl explained. "Talbert should know how you feel, not escape the consequences of his actions in the same way he shirked his duties."

Meg stared at him, frowning. The idea held a certain appeal, but for some reason hearing Carl berate Jake Talbert made her flinch. "I'm not certain—"

"You won't know until you try," he insisted.

Meghan's personal maid, Suzanne, appeared at the open door to the sitting room, carrying a small tray with a single glass upon it.

"Mr. Edwards, sir," the maid said, curtseying. "Here's the lemonade you mixed for Miss Meghan."

"Set it down over there," Carl said sternly, pointing at a small table next to the sofa. "That will be all."

Meg glanced up, catching a concerned look cast her way. Suzanne's gaze filled with sympathetic sorrow . . . and something more as it shifted to Carl. A glimmer of defiance? Fear?

"You may go," Carl stressed, irritated by the delay.

The maid caught her lip between her teeth, then quickly departed. Carl closed the door after her and went to the tray.

A sense of responsibility resurrected itself. Meg's emotions had been so ravaged over the past few days that she'd grown numb in self-defense, withdrawing into a dark and sheltered cocoon devoid of feeling.

But it seemed possible, however remotely, that Carl was terrorizing her staff. This was still her home. Tomorrow she would start recovering from this suffocating grief and begin to rebuild her life . . . though she had no idea where to go from here.

Taking charge of her household was a place to start.

For today, however, she needed Carl's strength to lean on. He'd been so kind, so patient. As he'd suggested, this letter could be part of a necessary healing.

The glass of lemonade appeared in front of her.

Meg took it automatically, downed a large swallow, then wrinkled her nose in distaste. "This tastes odd, Carl. Sweet, in a strange sort of way. Perhaps the lemons weren't fresh."

"I'm sure they were fine," Carl reassured. "Exhaustion can do strange things to the body. Drink some more, Meghan."

"But I don't—"

Carl pressed one finger to the bottom of the glass and

pushed with gentle insistence. "You need to keep up your strength, darling."

Meg took another swallow—to humor him, to keep the glass from engulfing her nose.

"Excellent," he murmured, setting it aside. Then he moved away, giving her a small measure of privacy.

After releasing her breath in a long, shuddering sigh, Meg began to write. Once she started, she couldn't stop. Bottled-up emotions surfaced with a vengeance, holding her thundering heart in a brutal grip. Her anger gained momentum, finding voice in the scratch of the quill. Her existence centered on the sheet of paper and the maelstrom within her soul.

In a last flood of caustic bitterness, she insisted Jake take the swords back to Japan, to return them to the Matsuda family—as her gift, since he hadn't earned them honorably.

Finally, her body stiff with tension, Meg stopped. Dazed, she stared down at a page full of angular black writing. There was just enough room to scrawl her signature at the bottom.

Carl hovered over her shoulder. "I believe you forgot to sign your name. Let me help you." Curling his cool hand around her own, he dipped the end of the quill into the silver inkwell.

"That's too much ink, Carl," she protested.

He released her hand. "It's fine. Sign your name, Meghan."

Meg froze, the quill poised above the paper. She couldn't stop staring at the ragged scrawl of her own handwriting. The words on the page vibrated with anger. Had she really written such bitter accusations? Now that she'd purged her feelings, she felt lighter. Suddenly, every line of the letter seemed overly harsh, cutting, meant to strike . . . to wound.

A drop of ink fell onto the paper like a black tear. The droplet splattered, eerily resembling a bullet hole. The memory of her father's death loomed, bright red blood everywhere—staining Douglass's shirt, her hands, Jake's bare chest. Grief clutched at Meg, but this time her mind focused on Jake's tormented expression as he tenderly held her dying father.

"Sign your name, Meghan," Carl coaxed in a low voice. "There's no need to hesitate. This is the right thing to do."

Her brain felt strangely fuzzy. Unsettled by conflicting images, Meg allowed Carl's hand to steady her own. Her name appeared across the bottom of the page.

He took the sheet, blew on it to dry the ink, then folded it neatly into thirds.

She licked her lips, tasting that unpleasant, sweet taste again. Feeling as if she weighed ten times more than normal, Meg's sluggish gaze focused on the glass in dawning suspicion.

"Carl, was there something in that lemonade?"

"Nothing, darling. Don't worry your pretty head about it."

Irritation flashed through her. Suddenly, Meg felt certain he was patronizing her. She tried to stand.

Nothing happened. Her legs felt lethargic, detached, as if they belonged to someone else. She gasped, fear curling through her.

"You're lying, Carl. What was in the lemonade? Tell me!"

"There's no cause to upset yourself, Meghan. It contained just a bit of laudanum, that's all."

"Laudanum!" she choked out, appalled. "I've never had cause to take laudanum in my life. It comes from the poppy, just like that vile opium smoked in the China-town hells—that curse that steals men from their families and turns them into disgusting, worthless addicts." She clutched the front of her gown, fighting the panic rising up her throat. "Why did you do this?"

"The doctor recommended it. He felt you were not getting enough sleep. Really, Meghan," Carl reasoned, sounding somewhat impatient, "laudanum is an accepted remedy for grief and other female maladies. One dose will not turn you into an addict."

In truth, she'd managed very little sleep in the past four days. Regardless, there was nothing she could do now to stop the effect of the laudanum.

But what if it only exaggerated her nightmares? What if she became trapped there, unable to escape the echoing sounds of her own hysterical screams, the haunting memory of Jake's tortured face when she'd struck him and hurled those hateful words at him?

"Here, let me help you to your bed." Carl grasped her elbow again and helped her to rise.

With the other hand, he tucked the folded letter into his inside coat pocket.

"No!" Meg burst out with a vehemence that surprised them both. "I've decided not to send the letter. I must tear it up."

"Talbert really should know how you feel."

"Please, give it to me," she pleaded, feeling her control slipping away. Her hand trembled visibly. More than anything, she just wanted to lie down, but she couldn't . . . not until she was certain Jake's eyes would never see that scathing letter.

"Very well," Carl said stiffly. He reached inside his coat and pulled out a folded sheet. "You'd best sit down before you fall down, Meghan."

After regaining her seat at the desk, Meg focused all her concentration—and it took a lot, for such a simple task—on tearing the folded letter into little pieces.

"Feel better now?"

"Yes, thank you," she responded unsteadily. "I'd like to . . . lie down now."

The next thing she knew, she was lying on her bed in the adjoining room. Carl hovered over her, as blond and handsome as an angel.

But there was nothing angelic about his expression. His green eyes burned possessively; his face was taut with desire.

"Meghan, I've wanted you for so long," he murmured huskily. "Soon you'll be mine."

She felt a hand at her waist. It slid up her ribs and closed over one breast.

"Don't," she rasped. "Please stop."

"I won't hurt you, darling. You won't even remember this."

She felt like a toy, something on exhibition for his desire. She hated this dreadful lethargy, the helplessness! Clumsily, she pushed his hand away from her breast. The effort took all the energy she had left. But he didn't stop there, didn't cease taking advantage of her drugged state. His hand curved around her ankle and slid up her stockinged calf.

"Don't," she whispered through a throat that seemed coated with grit. She tried to lift her head and couldn't.

The hand slid hotly up her leg, above her stocking, until his fingers probed at the tender skin of her inner thigh.

"No . . . no," Meg moaned. This felt wrong, dirty. It wasn't beautiful as it had been with Jake. "I don't want this. I don't love you, Carl."

His hand clenched on her thigh, digging in painfully. "You'll come to love me in time, Meghan. This is right between us. Don't fear me; I just want to touch you. But

I promise I won't compromise you. I want you to come to our marriage bed a virgin."

"I'm not a virgin," she sobbed, willing to admit anything to stop the vile heat of his groping hand. "I gave myself to Jake."

His hand jerked away. "What did you say?"

"I love him. I'll love him always," she repeated, realizing the truth of those words as a piercing sense of loss cut through her chest. "I'm sorry. As long as I love him, I'll have no room in my heart for you, Carl."

"How can you love a man who has deserted you, failed you?" he snarled. "Has Jake Talbert been here in the last few days to help you? No! I have!" He loomed like an avenging giant, his expression twisted with wrath. "You'll feel differently once you've had me between your legs. And since you're no longer a virgin, there's no point in waiting until the vows are spoken!"

His mouth came down on hers, hard, punishing. The pressure ground Meg's lips against her clenched teeth, but she refused to open her mouth to him. His hand groped beneath her skirts again.

Wrenching sobs of fury and shame worked their way up her throat.

Without warning, Carl's head jerked up.

Meg wondered wildly why she'd been spared. Then she heard it, too—a knock at her bedroom door. She tried to call out for help, but her drugged voice only emerged as a hoarse croak.

Then Meg mercifully lost consciousness.

"I–I've COME TO s-sit with Miss Meghan," Suzanne said shakily, quailing before Carl's fierce scowl.

"I think not," he countered coldly, blocking the doorway. "Be about your business."

Stepping up behind the maid, Robert interjected firmly, "If something concerns Miss Meghan, it is our business." The butler's expression, stiff with disapproval, hardened further when he glanced over Carl's shoulder at the bed. His brown eyes flashed with uncharacteristic anger.

"You have no right to gainsay me, man!" Carl exploded.

"And what right do you have to order me about, sir? I have no recollection of Mr. McLowry granting you that power."

"My right comes from the fact that Miss McLowry and I are to be married."

"There has been no formal announcement."

"You are risking your position, you imbecile. The announcement will become fact very soon now, after a decent period of mourning is observed, and then I'll see that you are immediately sacked!"

The butler glared back, unperturbed. "A risk I am willing to take. In the absence of her father, I am taking charge of Miss Meghan's welfare. I think it best you leave."

"You think you can remove me from this house, old man?"

"I would not soil my hands trying," Robert retorted. "It is a simple matter to call two footmen."

Carl's short fingernails dug into the door frame. A servant was treating him with disdain. A servant! Not since the miserable poverty of his youth in Philadelphia had anyone dared treat him so shabbily!

How ironic that the prestigious snobs of San Francisco had accepted his story of a comfortable birth, a noble West Point education, and an illustrious, heroic career in the military. If one left out the heroic part, at least the military career was genuine. The fools hadn't an inkling of his crude beginnings growing up neglected on the streets of Philadelphia, fighting for survival, scrounging for bare sustenance, and caring for his lush of a mother. Crazy dreams had often lead him to the rich part of town, where he gazed hungrily through windows at sparkling crystal and shiny silver . . . and his fingers proved as nimble as those of any thief.

No more sneaking through alleyways. He'd made inroads into the affluent, pampered world of San Francisco society.

But now, Carl saw his fixed, secure future wavering before his eyes. Marrying Meghan was the key. It was essential that he be here every day, supporting her. She was quickly learning to depend on him. He dismissed the idea she loved Talbert, since he would see to it that her feelings suffered a particularly quick, brutal death.

By tomorrow, Talbert would shun Meghan and set sail for some distant port. Carl had what he needed to make that happen.

As for not being a virgin—she would pay for that betrayal every day for as long as he chose, in subtle ways that society couldn't see. Regardless, he had to have her. Since the first day he'd met Meghan McLowry, he'd known she was the perfect trophy to complement his good looks, the key to the position and wealth he deserved.

Squaring his shoulders, Carl growled, "I'll be back tomorrow, Robert. Then we'll see what Miss Meghan has to say."

"Shall I show you out?"

"I'll show myself out, you pompous son of a bitch!" Carl yelled, his temper succumbing to the butler's superior airs.

He shoved his way past Robert and stalked down the hallway.

Carl paused at the top of the stairs, cooling his anger by pulling the folded letter from inside his coat pocket.

He opened the paper, his smile widening with malice as he read Meghan's bitter message to Talbert. The anger and hurt in her words surpassed even his highest expectations. He couldn't have asked for better if he'd dictated the letter himself.

Having anticipated that she might wish to tear it up, brilliant foresight had inspired him to stash another sheet of paper in his pocket. It has been a simple enough matter to hand her the wrong one . . . and a good thing, since the laudanum hadn't taken effect as quickly as he'd hoped.

Women! he snorted with disgust. Always wanting to use words to solve a problem. Carl perceived a much more expedient solution. Now that he knew Meghan fancied herself in love with Jacob Talbert, he would doubly enjoy destroying what little remained of their relationship.

Meg's last instructions for Talbert to take the swords to Japan caused a shiver of disquiet to pass through Carl. Then he forced a shrug. No matter. Chen Lee had twice failed to retrieve the blades, so their disappearance was the Celestial's problem. McLowry was dead. As far as Carl was concerned, the achievement of that goal had automatically severed his uneasy alliance with Chen.

A commotion sounded at the bottom of the stairs. A deep, familiar voice argued with the footman at the front door.

How convenient, Carl thought with anticipation as he descended the stairs. He ran his fingertips over the creases in the paper. Now he needn't trouble himself by going down to the waterfront to look for the bastard.

Jake Talbert had come in search of Meghan.

• • •

"I BLOODY WELL know that she's at home, Wilkins. Don't try to tell me otherwise. Inform Miss Meghan that I'm here to see her," Jake demanded as he shoved the door open and stepped through.

Jake seethed over the footman's attempt to deny him entrance.

"It won't do any good, Captain. Miss Meghan left strict instructions that she doesn't wish to receive you. Now or—" At Jake's fierce expression, the footman shrank back and finished weakly, "—ever."

"I have to talk to her."

"I'm sorry, sir," the footman returned mournfully. He clung to the knob, as if unsure whether to close the portal or not. "Truly, I wish I could help, but it could mean my position—"

"Well, well . . . what have we here?" interrupted a smarmy, self-satisfied voice.

"Edwards," Jake acknowledged, stiffening with distaste.

"I believe I can take care of this, Wilkins," Carl said, stepping forward. "The message should be clear enough, Talbert. Your presence upsets and offends Miss McLowry. She wishes to have nothing more to do with you. I suggest you leave this house and never return."

Jake saw Robert descending the curved staircase. He brushed past Carl and met the butler in the center of the foyer.

"Is this true?" Jake demanded. "Has she refused to see me?"

"I am afraid so, Captain Talbert," Robert confirmed, his expression glum.

Lowering his voice, Jake insisted hoarsely, "I must talk to her, Robert."

A look of chagrin crossed the butler's normally stoic

face. "I am sorry, sir, but Miss Meghan left adamant instructions that you not be admitted to the house."

"I have to make her understand," Jake said between clenched teeth. "I had to make a choice . . . either save Meghan or protect her father."

"I understand, though my opinion will do little to solve your dilemma, Captain. But if it helps at all, know that you have my eternal gratitude. Although I profoundly regret the loss of Mr. McLowry, I am ever so glad you saved our Meghan."

Jake stared, stunned by Robert's support and the sincerity in a face typically stiff with disapproval. He'd expected condemnation from the McLowry staff as well.

"I tried to talk to her, sir, but she will not listen," Robert added sadly. "She is too stricken by grief."

"This is ridiculous," Carl interrupted. He shoved a paper under Jake's nose. "Read this, Talbert. It should answer all your questions."

Jake glared at the folded sheet. "What is it?"

The corners of Carl's mouth curved upward. "A letter from Meghan. She penned it not fifteen minutes ago."

"Open it, Robert. Tell me whether it's truly Meghan's handwriting."

Carl's face reddened. "You doubt my word?"

"Absolutely." Ignoring Carl's sputtering anger, Jake solemnly focused on Robert. "Well? Is it?"

Robert scanned the paper. His face paled. "A bit . . . ragged, but yes, it is characteristic of her handwriting." He handed over the letter with obvious reluctance.

The bottom caved out of Jake's existence as he read the outpourings of Meghan's broken heart. He hadn't realized, until this moment, how much he depended on her forgiveness . . . or how little he could count on absolution for the unforgivable.

He kept his face impassive while tucking the letter into his coat. "Thank you, Robert."

Then Jake clenched one hand into a fist and smashed Carl's smug smile against his teeth.

Jake turned away, finding no satisfaction in Carl's howl, or in his string of foul curses. Nothing in this world could make him feel better—not even watching Robert hustle Carl out the door with a smile of satisfaction.

"Captain, please," called out Robert, stopping Jake just as he started to leave. "Miss Meghan's letter requested that you return the swords to their original owners."

"I don't deserve them, Robert."

"Nevertheless, as I said the other morning, I'd like you to take them as far away as possible. As long as they remain in San Francisco, those swords are a danger to everyone in this household, Miss Meghan most of all."

Jake nodded grimly.

"Thank you," Robert replied with a sharp exhale of relief. "The staff knows, sir, that Mr. McLowry brought this trouble down upon his own head by coveting those swords. We wanted to tell you, Captain, that we appreciate the efforts you put forth to save him."

I didn't do enough. I let my guard down, with no thought in my head beyond bedding your mistress.

"If you ever need anything when you are in San Francisco, please do not hesitate to let us know," finished the butler.

Wilkins nodded, adding his vote of confidence.

Jake appreciated their support, but he wasn't sure he'd ever return to San Francisco. There was too much pain here. Life without Meghan stretched before him, incredibly bleak.

He stepped outside the mansion for the last time. Something in his chest was trying to explode. His vision of the street blurred.

Relying on habit and instinct, he somehow found his way back to the *Shinjiro*. The members of his crew, wary of the expression on his face, melted out of Jake's path as he headed straight for his cabin. Rage and frustration burned a caustic path through his body as he stripped to the waist and grabbed his black katana.

The dummy erected on the quarterdeck—built of a thick post and extended wooden "arms" to simulate an opponent—paid the price for his anger. An hour later, Jake paused, sweat streaming from his body.

An awareness of being watched prickled down his spine. Jake glanced over his shoulder. "How long have you been standing there?"

"Long enough," Akira said.

Jake ground out, "She hates me, Akira-san. She refuses to see me."

A strong hand gripped his shoulder in sympathy.

Pain washed through Jake. He had to find a way to pull himself out of this mire. All he had left were his original goals, but would they prove enough? Even returning the blades to the Matsuda family was a hollow and meaningless victory without Meg.

"What do you wish to do now, Takeru-san?"

"Forget about her, of course. What the hell else can I do? She hates me!" Jake slammed his katana into its saya and headed for the stairs. "We set sail for Japan at dawn!"

Chapter Eighteen

I've grown so wretched, I'd break this sad body off from its roots, drift away like a floating weed if the current were to beckon.
—ONO NO KOMACHI (NINTH CENTURY)

MEG GAZED OUT her moonlit window from the sitting-room sofa. With a sigh that emanated from the depths of her soul, she picked up a large pillow and pressed it to her ribs.

Eight hours of her day had disappeared in a laudanum-induced sleep. Now it neared midnight, and no matter how much water she drank, her mouth still tasted as if it were stuffed with cotton.

Her father was gone from her life forever, buried this morning. Carl had violated her person this afternoon—despite what he'd assumed, she did remember. Things might have gone worse if Suzanne and Robert hadn't interrupted, demonstrating how glaringly she'd misjudged Carl.

Dear God, she'd misjudged a lot of things . . . most of all in the way she'd hurled hateful words at Jake. Grief-stricken hysteria explained her raging tirade, but nothing could excuse her behavior.

Carl had been right about one thing. Writing that letter had allowed a cleansing, a release of pent-up feelings. Now all she could think about was Jake.

Meg curled around the pillow, using her arms and legs to hug it with a ferocity bordering on desperation. She might never be able to hug Jake again, or feel his strong arms around her, or revel in the passion of lying beneath his powerful body. Her cruel words might have driven him away forever.

I think such fierce loyalty deserves my absolute faith.

She'd actually said those words to him, just before they'd made love the first time. Uttering them with sincerity, she'd believed she possessed the courage to live by them. Then, in a moment of shock and hysteria, when it had been too painful to acknowledge that inviting Jake to her bedchamber had prevented him from saving Douglass, she'd betrayed that faith.

The dagger in her heart twisted deeper. Tears burned behind her eyes.

Meg glanced at the bare surface of her secretary. The torn remnants of the letter were gone. At least she'd been able to destroy that outpouring of anger before the laudanum took full effect. Her worry and guilt would have blossomed into full panic by now if she thought Jake had read that horrid, bitter letter.

No, he couldn't have. She distinctly remembered the paper ripping between her hands.

A timid knock sounded on the door.

"Come in," Meg responded.

Suzanne entered with a tray piled high with covered dishes.

"I brought you some food, Miss Meghan. Even though it's so late, we figured you should have somethin' in your stomach before you go to sleep," she explained, setting the tray down.

"Suzanne, what happened to the shredded bits of paper on my secretary?"

The maid's slender brown brows shot up. "Why, ma'am, I took the paper down to the garbage."

"Thank you." Still fidgeting internally, Meg reasoned that Suzanne would probably think her eccentric if she asked to see the destroyed letter. It wasn't necessary to examine the shredded pieces. The very notion was silly.

"Won't you try to eat, Miss Meghan?"

Meg eyed the dishes listlessly. "I'll try."

"You'll be needin' to keep up your strength, you know. We all think so."

"Tell the staff I appreciate their concern," Meg said, truly touched.

"Will there be anythin' else, ma'am?"

"No, thank you."

The maid turned to leave.

"Suzanne," Meg called out, impulsively stopping her at the door. "Has Captain Talbert come by?"

"Why, yes, ma'am. He stopped by this afternoon."

Meg clutched the pillow convulsively. "Why wasn't I told?"

"You were asleep, from that lemonade Mister Edwards gave you. But don't you worry none, Miss Meghan, 'cause we done our duty. Mr. Robert gave your message to the captain."

"What message?" Meg whispered hoarsely, dreading the answer.

"Why, that he wasn't to be allowed in this house. Not one foot inside. And don't you worry about that awful Mr. Edwards, neither," Suzanne finished with a sniff. "Mr. Robert made sure that man—the nerve of him, taking advantage of you like that—left at the same time."

"Thank you, Suzanne," Meg said wearily. By following instructions stemming from her hostile, childish anger, her staff had thrown Jake out of the house, emphasizing that she never wanted to see him again.

How could Jake ever forgive her?

The maid left the room, but not before casting an encouraging look at the food that Meg had lost all interest in eating.

The silence of the night wrapped around Meg, leaving too much time for thought and bitter regrets. *The swords, Meggie. I tricked Chen Lee. Took them from him.*

From the very beginning, there had been nothing random, nothing mysterious about the attacks from Chen Lee's men. Her father had triggered a bloody trail of vengeance, coveting the swords without regard to the consequences, then keeping the reason a secret from her. And although Douglass had paid the ultimate price, others were left behind to pay for his mistake as well.

But that didn't alter the fact that she'd loved her father dearly, or lessen the agony of missing him. The wrenching pain of that moment, when Douglass had died in her arms, had proven unbearable. She'd looked for someone solid, strong . . . someone able to shoulder her crushing grief and the self-blame that came with knowing *she* had played a part in her father's death.

And Jake Talbert was the strongest man she'd ever known.

By striking out, she'd wounded the man she loved.

She must see Jake in the morning, sacrifice her pride to beg his forgiveness. She'd maneuvered him into an impossible situation as the only capable barrier between Douglass and Chen Lee—a relentless force that would stop at nothing until the swords were recovered. Jake deserved to know that she trusted no one more, that after coming out from under the tarnish of hysteria and grief, her underlying faith in him shone brilliantly again.

Curling around the pillow, Meg shivered with the

knowledge of something more crucial, more personal. She must also hazard the possibility of Jake's rejection by taking the greatest risk of all: by opening her heart. Even if he couldn't return her feelings, she wouldn't let him leave without revealing how much she loved him.

JAKE LEANED ON the *Shinjiro*'s railing. His interlaced fingers hung listlessly over the side as he stared, unblinking, at the city across the bay. A glow radiated from behind the San Francisco hills, streaking across the cloudless sky to herald the arrival of dawn. The golden fire taunted him with the memory of Meghan's hair, until he ached to reach out and touch it.

Whether he longed for the immeasurable distance of the sky or the treasure of Meghan's heart, both were equally unattainable.

Her final rejection couldn't have been more clear.

A favorable wind tugged at the *Shinjiro*'s tightly furled sails, as if coaxing the white canvas to spread and yield the ship to the alluring power of the Pacific. The *Shinjiro*'s capable first mate, Henry Jennings, shouted orders to the crew. The sounds of a ship preparing to get under way drifted around Jake, muffled by the even greater chaos of his thoughts and a growing restlessness that coiled like a spring beneath his breastbone.

He had everything he needed for a triumphant return to Japan: The swords were safely stowed; his honor would be restored upon their return.

But it no longer held any meaning for him.

He felt empty, as if distant cries of anguish echoed around inside a vacant, cavernous shell. Japan would not be able to fill the emptiness. Only Meghan could fill the void he felt.

Jake's gaze strayed back to Rincon Hill. Suddenly, he

realized his sixteen-year quest had been supplanted by another goal.

He must see Meghan. He couldn't give up until he earned her forgiveness.

"You needn't worry, Akira-san," he said without turning. "I've decided to stay in San Francisco."

"For how long?" Akira responded. His light tread moved soundlessly across the deck. Jake tracked his approach by the flutter of his hakama in the rising wind.

"I don't know. Weeks . . . hours. It all depends on Meghan and whether or not she can bear the sight of me." Jake laughed cynically, a bitter, unsteady sound. "This may be the shortest shore excursion on record."

"Have faith, Takeru-san."

"I don't want the return of the swords delayed, however. Would you see that they are returned to the Matsuda family?"

Akira bowed deeply. "I would be honored to carry the blades back to Nihon, Takeru-san."

Staring into Akira's intelligent brown eyes, Jake felt a heaviness settle on his heart. He was going to miss this man, dreadfully. They'd traveled together for sixteen years. Komatsu Akira was irreplaceable, a unique combination of witty friend and wise teacher.

Jake grasped the older man's shoulders. "It may be a long time before I see you again, Akira-san. I wish you Godspeed."

"Three, maybe four months is not so long. The *Shinjiro* bring me back by then."

Taken aback, Jake faltered, "But . . . I thought . . . why would you return to America? This is your opportunity to stay in Nihon. That was our goal, what we've sought for years. Home, Akira-san," he emphasized, giving the samurai a little shake.

Akira-san smiled gently. "Your goal, Takeru-san, not mine. I leave Nihon to protect you, to repay *giri*, to search for the swords . . . this is true. But for many years now, I not intend to go back."

Jake released him and leaned back against the rail, gripping the weather-smoothed wood behind him. Nothing Akira could have said would have stunned him more.

Akira stood quietly, watching him in that calm, immovable *fudoshin* manner. As Jake recovered from shock, the unflappable composure he'd always admired began to grate on his nerves. His eyes narrowed.

Crossing his arms over his chest, Jake muttered sourly, "You've no intention of returning to Japan?"

"To visit family, this I would like, but to stay . . . no."

"How long ago did you decide this?"

Akira-san pursed his lips in a thoughtful expression. "Ten, maybe twelve years."

Jake threw back his head and groaned. "And you didn't see fit to mention this to me? Why the hell not?"

"Because each man find his own destiny, Takeru-san. I must not interfere in yours. You must make your own way."

Jake found himself at a loss for words. Akira-san's reasons fit not only the character of the man, but the samurai culture and beliefs as well. Hell, he should have realized this long ago, but he'd been too caught up in his own obsession of returning to Japan to notice that his friend did not share in his goal.

"Can you tell me why?"

Akira moved to the rail, casting his thoughtful gaze out over the deep blue water. "I am much spoiled by my freedom. I like this country, too, very much. I have no wish to go back to the strict code of life in Nihon. And do not forget, Takeru-san, the old way of the samurai no longer exists in Nihon," Akira continued, his tone changing from light to resentful. His voice suddenly shook with deep emotion . . . anger, disgust. "For two years, since Meiji become emperor, the samurai have been destroyed as a class. We are no longer given the right to wear swords in public. We must become merchant, craftsman, to support our families. Many samurai have become poor. It is a disgrace. You have helped many in Kyoshu prosper, by buying the silk, weapons, pottery, jewelry, and kimonos they make. Our people have not suffered as much as others, because of your help."

He looked at Jake, brown eyes burning with passion. "But I cannot live that way, Takeru-san. I am samurai," Akira emphasized, striking his own chest with a fist. "I choose not to sacrifice my dignity to Meiji's new laws. I must keep the old samurai ways in my heart."

Jake had never seen Akira-san react so strongly to anything. Although Jake had known of the changes brought about by the Meiji restoration, he'd shrugged most of them off as inevitable, knowing he would have to tolerate the lifestyle to meet his goal.

But now he saw how many of the Japanese ways were no longer right for him. He couldn't restrict his passionate nature to the strictures of a calm, well-ordered society, any more than he could force his six-foot-two inch frame into clothes made for a Japanese man.

Perhaps he'd known, in some hidden recess of his mind, that he no longer belonged there, but it had taken his love for Meghan to give him an alternative, a place to belong . . . in the unlikely event that she would have him.

With a renewal of his teasing tone, Akira said, "You not worry, Takeru-san, I see the swords home. In this I take much joy. I want to see the tears sparkle in Matsuda Takashi's eyes when I put Shinjiro's blades in his hands, to share a father's joy. When I give the wisteria daisho to Matsuda Hiroshi, I wish to tell him what a fool he was to send you away. From me he will hear of his adopted son's courage, how you take the blame for Shinjiro's mistake so that the Matsuda honor not be stained."

A cold wave washed through Jake. Incredulous, he whispered, "You knew Shinjiro ordered the attack on the Chinese raiders? But how? I told everyone that I was the one. No one knew the truth." *Until Meghan,* he corrected inwardly.

"Takashi-san always guess this is true. He knew his second son was—how you say—hothead? My sister's son was a good man, but Shinjiro seek war, not *fudoshin.* This other burden you have carried is part of the *giri* that Takashi-san and I owe you."

"There was no sense in my casting the blame on Shinjiro for the deaths of those samurai," Jake countered roughly. "All shared eagerly in attacking the raiders. Since I was already dishonored for failing to commit seppuku, there was no reason not to take on the additional shame."

"You protect Shinjiro's name."

"I owed him that much."

They lapsed into a few moments of companionable silence, watching a flock of gulls dip and turn in a display of aerial acrobatics.

Finally, Jake purged a painful admission from his heart. "I've also come to realize that, even if the horse hadn't knocked me unconscious that day, I still would not have cut myself with the tanto."

Akira sighed. "Sometimes I thought this might be, but I was not certain."

"I'm sorry," Jake murmured, ashamed to admit his failure.

"Why? It is best this way. You trusted your heart and

did not deny your western soul," Akira insisted. "And I am very glad you did not die that day, my friend. Who else would take me on this great adventure, make me an old man with much money?"

"Well, if you want to live in style," Jake countered wryly, "then stock a valuable cargo for your return to San Francisco."

Akira grinned. "Ah, not to worry. I will." Pushing away from the rail, he urged, "Come, Takeru-san. It is time you find your destiny. Perhaps you be lucky, like having a rice dumpling fly into your mouth."

Jake laughed. "I will miss your proverbs, though I must be crazy to admit it."

After reaching the captain's cabin, Akira assisted in packing Jake's belongings. Several changes of clothes and the black katana went into the bag. Actually, the samurai was a bit too helpful, insisting on packing the white kimono as well—the last one, which Jake had set aside for Meghan.

Jake wished he could share Akira's optimism. It seemed far more likely that Meghan would emasculate him. In fact, she could cut out his heart with just a glitter of unshed sorrow in her eyes—then crush any hope of forgiveness once and for all.

Back on deck, Jake dropped his duffel bag into a row-boat, then ordered the small craft lowered over the side. With no qualms, Jake put Henry Jennings in charge of the *Shinjiro*.

The first mate puffed out his chest, obviously proud to assume the new responsibility. "You can trust me, Captain. We'll take good care of the ship. Yes, sir!"

Jake gripped the man's shoulder, saying, "I know you will, Henry. You could make this voyage with your eyes closed." Looking around at the gathered crew, he shouted, "I swear, I've never had the pleasure of sailing with a more scruffy bunch of bilge rats." The men laughed, lightening the pensive mood brought on by Jake's abrupt departure. "I'll rejoin you again soon, mates. Bring her back in record time."

As the crew threw good wishes and teasing comments back at him, Jake climbed down a rope ladder and settled into the rowboat.

Leaning over the railing, Akira called out, "Remember, my friend, a good wife is the family treasure."

Jake fumbled one of the oars. Dammit, he hadn't said a thing to Akira about asking Meghan to marry him! The idea had only just taken root in his mind.

Swearing, he fished the oar out of the water before it floated out of reach.

JAKE PAUSED IN rowing for shore to watch the *Shinjiro*'s sails unfurl. The wind caught the white canvas, pushing the ship out to sea in all her glory.

This was the first time she had sailed without him. How he longed to be on that ship.

He raked splayed fingers through his hair. This was madness! He'd survived years of harsh discipline as a samurai, unflinchingly faced opponents armed with razor-sharp katanas—but here he was now, dreading a confrontation with a golden-haired minx who held his heart in her hands.

What if Meghan's hatred hadn't waned?

As his battered self-confidence wavered, Jake glanced at the *Venture*, anchored nearby. His second ship was due to depart later today, taking Sung Kwan and Yeung Lian up the coast to start a new life in Portland.

If Meg still refused to forgive him, he possessed the

means to escape San Francisco and its painful memories. He needn't be trapped here, tearing himself apart by craving something he couldn't have.

Jake rowed to the *Venture.*

The crew welcomed him aboard. Jake instructed Captain Hembley to delay their departure and not to sail until hearing from him. After promising Kwan and Lian that he would bid them good-bye soon, Jake endured whoops and catcalls from the crew as Lian bestowed a butterfly kiss of gratitude on his cheek. Then he returned to the rowboat to finish the trip ashore.

He'd obsessively clung to the dream of returning to Japan because, frankly, he hadn't known where else he fit in. For sixteen years he'd wandered the world, a man without a country, without a home.

Now he knew where he belonged.

Duffel bag in hand, Jake plunged into the bustling crowd of workmen on the pier, with an enigmatic mixture of dread and liberation. He lengthened his stride with growing eagerness.

Without warning, four men stepped in front of him, cutting across his path down a narrow, deserted back street. Three more closed in from behind.

Jake's defensive instincts snapped into full alert, particularly because these ruffians were not Chinese. He recognized their type: rough sailors of various nationalities, tossed off their ships as troublemakers, waterfront trash who would do anything for a bit of gold—murder included. Chen Lee would never lower himself to hire them.

So, if Chen the Dragon hadn't sent these thugs, who had?

There was no time to wonder or free his katana from the duffel. As the men attacked, Jake fought fiercely with every skill he possessed. But no matter how much damage he inflicted with his hands and feet, they kept coming like a pack of wolves, fists pummeling with agonizing precision.

A cudgel struck Jake behind one ear, shooting sparks of red-hot pain into his skull.

Then blackness engulfed him.

LEANING OUT THE window, Meg gripped the landau's door as she stared incredulously out over the bay. Two fingernails broke to the quick against the lacquered wood, but she was unaware of the pain. Despite the warmth of the morning sun, she shivered violently.

The *Shinjiro* was gone.

Dear God, she was too late!

Meg fell back against the tan leather cushions. Her harsh words had driven away the man she loved.

After what seemed like an eternity of stabbing pain and sliding tears, Meg wiped her cheeks. She lifted a trembling chin. There was only one thing to do. She must wait until Jake came back.

If it took until her dying day, she would apologize for the horrible things she'd said, even if Jake never returned her love.

But how to know when the *Shinjiro* arrived in port?

"Phillip, drive to Abe Warner's Cobweb Palace," she ordered.

Although Phillip's groan was audible from outside the carriage, he obeyed. When they arrived, Meg spoke to the two barkeeps, giving them her direction and a modest sum, with the promise of more money if they let her know when the *Shinjiro* returned.

Meg nurtured a tiny flicker of optimism as she climbed back into the landau.

"Drive on to Miss Lambert's mission, Phillip."

When they arrived, the sight of two armed men startled Meg. They stood on either side of the mission, rifles cradled in their arms.

"Wait for me here," she ordered Phillip as he handed her down from the landau. Meg climbed the steps to the mission porch, eyeing the guards with curiosity.

When Mary greeted her at the door, Meg whispered, "What is going on, Mary?"

The missionary sighed. "I so wish their presence wasn't necessary. I hate to put anyone to such inconvenience. Jacob insisted, however. The men don't need to be here on my account, truly, but the girls' safety must not be compromised."

"But who are they?"

"Sailors from Jacob's ship, the *Venture*. Men have been guarding the place in shifts, ever since that deplorable incident with the dynamite. Starting tomorrow, Jake has arranged for off-duty police officers to watch over the mission at his expense."

Meg closed her eyes briefly as a spasm of longing and regret hit . . . at the sound of Jake's name, at the further evidence of his goodness and the faith he deserved.

Once the two women stepped inside, Mary enveloped Meg's still form in a hug. "My dear girl, how are you doing?"

It was the only sincerely affectionate hug—other than Mrs. Crocker's—that Meg had received since her father's death. Her Nob Hill acquaintances apparently weren't given to unseemly displays of emotion.

"Come, Meghan. Some coffee will perk you up."

Meg dashed salty drops from her cheeks and nodded.

Once they were seated in the parlor, the missionary sent the two oldest Chinese girls to the kitchen for coffee.

"You look very tired, Meghan."

"I'm doing well enough. I saw you at the funeral. You didn't need to stand so far back."

"I thought it best. All the mourners were wealthy, the top rungs of San Francisco society. I didn't want to create uncomfortable speculation in my drab clothes," the other woman said, smiling wryly as she arranged a fringed paisley shawl around the shoulders of her gray muslin dress.

"It meant more to me that you were there than anyone else."

"Jacob was there," Mary pointed out, watching her carefully.

"I know," Meg forced out.

"He watched you all through the service, Meghan, reacting to every tear you shed, every movement you made, as if he were being tortured. I've never seen a man look more incredibly miserable, especially when Carl Edwards took your arm. I tried to speak to Jake, but he deliberately walked away before I could draw near."

Meg couldn't seem to breathe.

"It seems abundantly clear that Jake is in love with you."

Her heart began to race. "Is it possible?"

"I believe I can say so with confidence, yes," Mary stressed, smiling. "Do you love him, Meghan?"

"Oh, yes," Meg answered emphatically, scooting forward to the edge of her seat. She clutched the folds of her dress in her fists.

"Then what is the problem, Meghan? What has caused this rift that has you both suffering so much?"

"I drove him away, Mary! I said the cruelest things when my father died, blaming him."

"You were in shock, dear, torn apart by grief."

"That doesn't excuse what I said."

"Well, it's not too late to fix it."

"But it is! Jake's gone. The *Shinjiro* sailed this morning."

"Oh, dear." Mary sank back against the sofa, clearly stunned. She fingered the cross at her neck. "He'll be back. Don't you worry."

"He'll have convinced himself that he hates me by then," Meg moaned, voicing her greatest fear. "Or he'll have forgotten my existence."

Mary snorted. "You are pretty unforgettable, Meghan. And rest assured that a man clings to hatred to defend his more tender emotions, to armor himself from heartache. If Jake comes back with that much anger, it only proves that a powerful love lurks beneath the surface. You shall just have to peel away his thick, stubborn hide until you uncover it."

Meg dropped her head into her hands. "I wouldn't know how to do that."

"Just be yourself. It will happen."

"But what if he doesn't come back?" Meg whispered hoarsely.

"Why, he'd better! He owes me another shipment of material and sewing supplies for the girls," Mary exclaimed in a cheerful tone.

"Will you tell me when he returns?"

Mary smiled. "I feel confident you will know before I do."

Squaring her shoulders, Meg said, "Actually, I didn't come to burden you with my troubles, Mary. I wanted to let you know that I've reached a decision. Although I've yet to know the extent of my father's fortune, I want to put it to good use. I even plan to sell the mansion and move into a more modest home."

"But what of your social life?"

"I no longer have the heart for it. The round of entertainments seems so . . . shallow to me now. The house holds too many painful memories." Taking a deep breath, Meg plunged on, "I want to use my money to benefit others. I thought of starting a school for Chinese girls. We could hire a teacher to assist you. And I want to help you more, personally, teaching the girls to sew and cook. I could even teach them to play the piano. Do you think they would like to learn?"

"I'm sure they would like that above all things, but are you—?"

"Yes, I'm certain. My life's been too changed . . . I'm too changed . . . to go back to the way things were."

The coffee service arrived. Meghan cut the pound cake and handed a slice to each of the teenage girls while Mary poured the coffee. The girls ran off giggling.

Handing Meg her cup, Mary said with renewed eagerness, "Now, let's put our heads together and think of ways to keep you busy until Jacob returns to town. The nerve of that bullheaded man, anyway, bolting before the two of you had a chance to work things out." Mary harrumphed and sipped her coffee.

Meg dipped her head to hide a soft smile, feeling better already. The missionary's conviction gave Meg new confidence.

If only she didn't have to wait so long until she could see Jake again.

Chapter Nineteen

Loving you, my heart may shatter into a thousand pieces, but not one piece will be lost. —LADY IZUMI (TENTH CENTURY)

JAKE FORCED HIS eyes open.

A stained gray ceiling gradually came into focus. The throbbing in his skull reminded him that he should be dead.

"Things would have been much simpler if you'd left San Francisco, Talbert," came a smug voice from somewhere near his feet. "But you know, I'm rather glad you didn't. I do believe I'm going to enjoy this."

Despite the pain and the lingering dizziness, Jake shot up out of the narrow bed, anxious to wrap his fingers around Carl's arrogant throat.

Cold metal cut into Jake's wrists, bringing him up short. His arms jerked back with wrenching force.

"Tsk, we mustn't be impetuous," Carl reprimanded, laughing. He stood at the foot of the bed. His fashionable brown frock coat, tan trousers, and silk hat contrasted with the dingy surroundings of rumpled cots and peeling wallpaper.

Jake settled back on his elbows and glared at the shackles binding his wrists and bare ankles. Nearly choking on his rage, he growled, "Is this the only way you can best me, Edwards? By shackling me to a bed?"

Carl's smile dropped away. "It's true, I don't have your experience in vulgar waterfront brawls, but you're looking at a man who was an officer in the Union cavalry. If we were to face off with sabers, you're damn right I could defeat you."

"You're welcome to try," Jake countered with quiet menace. A sword fight was the one contest Edwards was guaranteed to lose.

"Unfortunately, that's not why I brought you here. I must deny myself the pleasure of killing you, for it would defeat a higher purpose."

"I'm surprised you're capable of having one."

Reddening, Carl retorted with malicious relish, "It would have suited my purpose if you'd sailed away, Talbert. If you had, the men I hired to watch you would have had no reason to bring you here. Your own actions forced a change in my plans."

"So why didn't you just kill me?"

"If you die, you will always live in Meghan's mind as some foolish, girlish ideal . . . a martyr, of sorts. My goal is to humble you, Talbert, to turn you into a pathetic shadow of a man. Once she sees what you've become, she will turn from you in disgust and go on with her life—in a nutshell: me."

Meghan. Just the sound of her name caused a gaping hole to open in Jake's heart. "Why are you so concerned about Meghan's opinion of me?"

"I will not tolerate my soon-to-be wife thinking of another man."

Wife. No, it couldn't be! Then he remembered the way Meghan had clung to Carl at the funeral. His own failure had driven her straight into Carl's arms.

Hoarsely, Jake counteracted the pain by taunting, "I'm too much competition for you, is that it?"

Carl snorted. "A silly infatuation, nothing more. You've

already hurt her terribly. Once she sees what you've become, she will quickly leave those naive feelings behind."

There were those words again: *what you've become.* Apprehension traced Jake's spine like skeletal fingers. The man was obsessed, perhaps not quite sane, and capable of any atrocity to get his way.

Eagerly, Carl continued, "Actually, Meghan gave me the idea herself when I used some laudanum to help her sleep. She was quite appalled. She condemned the elixir as a poppy derivative, like 'that Chinatown curse that steals men from their families and turns them into disgusting, worthless addicts.' " He grinned. "Those were her very words. Then inspiration struck me . . . turn you into an opium addict, Talbert, and the sight of you will sicken her. Any feelings she has for you will die."

A chill swept through Jake. He'd seen opium eaters all over the world, obsessed men and women, vacant expressions in their soulless eyes, who cared about nothing but their next pipe. That's what permeated this hellish place—the smell of despairing humanity.

"Two weeks should do the trick," Carl added with relish. "Then I shall tell her I've been searching for you . . . for the sake of her peace of mind, of course. I shall bring her here, show her how you chose to deal with the guilt over her father's death, how you escape from reality and wallow in self-pity." He took a step forward, smiling. "Truly, Talbert, I look forward to her reaction."

Jake didn't need to ask whether the shackles would be gone by then, substituted by a drug-induced lethargy. Hatred swept through him, so hot that sweat instantly sprang forth from his chest and upper lip. He yanked against the chains, to no avail.

A petite man, wearing the traditional blue tunic and pants of the Chinese, sauntered into the room. He bowed, causing his long pigtail to sway over one shoulder. The low gaslights reflected off his shaved forehead.

Jake's gaze riveted on the long, slender bamboo pipe in the man's hand. An accompanying tray held a burning candle, a slender wooden stick, and a small bowl containing ominous, dark brown lumps of raw opium.

"You can't force me to smoke that pipe," Jake snarled.

"Can't I?" Carl countered softly. "I've already proven what hired muscle can accomplish."

Four of the waterfront rats who'd attacked Jake came in behind the Chinaman. Their bodies were bulky and strong, their eyes hardened, ruthless, and glittering with greed.

Carl snapped, "Hold him down."

They grabbed Jake's legs and arms. Ignoring the agony of the shackles cutting into his wrists and bare ankles, Jake bucked and fought. One thought arose foremost in his mind, driving him into a frenzy of furious energy: If he let this happen, if he didn't find a way to get free, then he wouldn't be able to get to Meghan and tell her that he loved her. Edwards would have no obstacle in taking advantage of her grief-stricken vulnerability.

"Son of a bitch!" Carl roared as Jake's head cracked against one brigand's nose, triggering a howl and a flow of blood. "Can't the four of you control a man chained to a bed? I need him still."

The thugs changed tactics. One flung himself across Jake's legs, pressing him down. Another clutched a handful of Jake's hair, holding his head in a vicious grip, while the third pinned his arms. The fourth forced Jake's jaw open with clawlike fingers while the grim-faced Chinaman thrust the pipe between his teeth. The Asian touched the lighted taper to the raw opium.

Someone pinched his nose. Jake struggled, but the effort only made his body crave air that much sooner.

To breathe at all, he had to draw the pungent smoke into his lungs. Again, and yet again, they forced that damnable, accursed cloud down his throat.

A foreign lethargy flowed through Jake's body, stealing the strength from his muscles. He loathed the sensation, rebelled against it, for it violated everything he was as a samurai, as a man. He recognized pure evil in all the seductive power of its false promises . . . the snake in the Garden of Eden.

Nevertheless, he began to feel pleasure, as if he lay on soft, wet sand, floating gently while the warm sea washed over his skin and caressingly tugged him toward deeper water. Joy awaited him there in the sea's satiny depths, not death.

Strangely mesmerized, Jake's gaze followed the taper as it moved sluggishly through space and time to touch the bowl of the pipe. Another lump of opium flared briefly.

He felt his will to fight fall into that tiny flame, tumbling headlong into an endless eternity. And he let it go. No matter how much he struggled, he couldn't fight off the effects of the drug as it devoured his identity.

His failure offered one more thing to despise about himself.

Jake twisted on his side and retched on the floor.

MEG SAT ON the low stone wall encircling the atrium fountain. She nervously smoothed the front of her charcoal gray gown, then set the bowl of lettuce and sliced fruit in the middle of her lap.

This morning, she resolved, her patience was going to pay off.

A scrambling sound rattled through the garden's undergrowth. The iguanas ambled into the light, heading in her direction with their peculiar swaying walk. For each of the three days since Jake had sailed away, she'd coaxed the iguanas closer, learning their favorite foods, earning their trust.

With only slight hesitation, the lizards leaped onto the fountain wall, one on either side. Meg's heart rate quickened. It was working! Approaching from their respective sides, each iguana planted its front feet on her leg and gingerly stretched up to pick a strawberry from the bowl.

Their claws snagged the fabric of her gown. As they chomped down on the fruit, red juice dripped onto the delicate material, causing irreparable damage.

Meg didn't care.

Other than the blue kimono she wore next to her skin each night, the iguanas were all she had left of Jake. They offered an opportunity to feel close to him.

Robert entered the atrium. He shuddered delicately, keeping his distance. "Mr. Daniel Marsh is at the door, Miss Meghan. He has come for these creatures."

Meg caught her breath. *No, it was too soon!*

With a slight tremor in her voice, she said, "Show him in here, Robert."

A tall man entered the atrium a few minutes later. Meg warily studied the naturalist, noting his immaculate black frock coat, gray trousers, snowy linen, and brown hair. The impression of a lean, handsome face was partially obscured by a pair of gold wire-rimmed spectacles perched on an aquiline nose.

Meg forced a smile. "Mr. Marsh, I hope you'll excuse me if I don't rise. My movements are rather restricted at the moment."

"Certainly, ma'am. I—" Daniel began, then faltered.

"Is something wrong?"

"Yes . . . no . . . it's just, I've never seen a woman willing to handle reptiles before. Quite astonishing, actually." His strong tenor voice held a trace of a British accent.

With her thumb, Meg stroked the bony plate between the olive-striped female's eyes. "I've become quite fond of them," she said softly.

"I can see that." After a moment's hesitation, he cleared his throat. "Captain Jacob Talbert telegraphed me that I could find the iguanas here."

"He left them here, knowing this garden was the most healthy place for them."

Daniel came forward, his face alight with interest. "My word, they are bloody fine specimens."

"Don't call them that!"

He reared back, startled, his brown eyes blinking rapidly behind the spectacles. "Call them what? Specimens?"

"Exactly," Meg snapped, appalled by the sudden spurt of anger but unable to control it. Tears welled in her eyes. "It sounds like you intend to cut them up in some laboratory experiment. I won't permit it!"

Daniel smiled gently. "You needn't worry, Miss McLowry. That is the last thing I wish to do. I intend to breed these beauties, and study the iguana's reproductive patterns and other habits. I can see they like strawberries," he added, looking at the messy remains on her dress.

"Strawberries are their favorite," she agreed morosely. She gently rubbed the yellow-striped female beneath its chin. "You must be sure to feed them strawberries and other succulent fruits, but not as many as I've been feeding them. They're getting fat, the greedy things. And be sure to pet them—" Her voice broke as emotion closed off her throat.

"Uh, certainly," muttered Daniel, filling the awkward

silence. "I intend to give them lots of attention. You make me envious of the trust they place in you."

Tears welled over and spilled down Meg's cheeks. Horrified, Meg swiped the drops away. She'd never cried in front of a stranger before.

"Miss McLowry, please. I, uh . . . oh, damn it all."

"I'm sorry, Mr. Marsh," Meg murmured, taking pity on his awkwardness. "I'm normally not such a watering pot."

"I noticed the house is draped for mourning. Your butler mentioned that your father was killed a week ago. You have my deepest sympathies."

"Thank you, sir."

He gripped the corner of his spectacles and shifted them higher on his nose. "I shall be remaining in San Francisco a couple of days . . . friends to visit, supplies to buy, that sort of thing, you know. Why don't I leave the iguanas here during that time? I couldn't provide them better quarters than these."

His generosity warmed Meg. She smiled shakily. "Thank you. They'll be ready to leave in two days' time. Forgive me for acting so . . . oddly."

"Not at all. It's nice to see that they're thriving in your care." He bowed and adjusted his spectacles again. As he turned away, he muttered, "Where did that butler go with my hat?"

When he was gone, Meg lifted the full iguanas down and watched them saunter back to their favorite hiding places. In two days they would be gone, severing one of the last ties she had with Jake.

Listlessly, Meg made her way to the front of the house, prepared to go upstairs and change out of the stained gown. A loud knock sounded on the front door just as she crossed the foyer. Wilkins appeared promptly to answer it.

"See here," the footman exclaimed. "Deliverymen take their goods to the rear entrance."

An argument ensued, capturing Meghan's attention. She was heading for the door when Wilkins came flying backward, landing hard on his backside. The man who had managed to knock down the large footman stepped through the door.

"Sung Kwan!" Meg cried. "I thought you left San Francisco. You shouldn't be here. This is too dangerous! What if Chen Lee should see you?" As the footman rose, she murmured in chagrin, "I'm so sorry, Wilkins. I know this man. It's all right."

Wilkins groaned and nodded.

"Cap'n Talbert here?" Kwan asked.

Meg stared at him as if he'd gone mad. "No. Why would you think that?"

"He not return," Kwan said urgently. "We must find him."

"Jake is gone, Kwan. He left on the *Shinjiro*."

"No, no. He coming to see you, missy, three day now."

Meg's heart slammed against her ribs. "He's still in San Francisco? Where?" she rasped.

"Don't know. Cap'n Hembley say must wait, Cap'n Talbert come back when ready." The Asian man shook his head emphatically. "No good."

"He's missing?" Her eyes widened in horrified comprehension. "Chen Lee?"

"Not Chen. I ask in Chinatown."

Through Kwan's broken English, Meg discovered that he'd grown worried about Jake's continued absence from the *Venture* and started the search for him this morning. She had been the logical place to begin.

"We'll search every place in town if necessary," Meg said fiercely when Kwan finished.

Turning, she discovered the butler coming into the

foyer in response to the unusual noise. Meg said briskly, "Robert, send Phillip and Peter to the stables right away. We'll be going out in the landau. And tell them to come armed."

After calling for a cloak to cover her stained gown, Meg rushed to the stables. Kwan followed closely.

Her heart raced with a sense of urgency. Jake hadn't left San Francisco.

He'd been coming to see her, then mysteriously disappeared.

And she'd wasted three days feeling sorry for herself while he was very likely in danger, or—

No! She wouldn't think about that possibility. Dear God, she prayed fervently, please let us find him . . . safe.

AFTER THAT FIRST time, Jake didn't suffer the humiliating urge to empty the contents of his stomach.

But there were worse things than retching on the floor.

The stench of stale opium and his own unwashed body combined to fill Jake with disgust. His face itched from the stubble of a growing beard, but he'd long since given up trying to scratch it. For a man accustomed to the fastidious cleanliness of the Japanese, the filth felt like a hoard of spiders crawling across his skin. The assault of his senses added to the slow, grueling torture of being chained to the bed like a savage.

He couldn't track the passage of time in the windowless room, especially when he was in a mindless stupor most of the time. Jake glanced down at his open shirt, every button long since torn away. His ribs stood out boldly against bruised flesh. If he measured time by his loss of weight, he'd apparently been here several days. Carl's thugs fed him when it suited them, and then only a thin gruel to keep him alive. They took him to use the facilities only when he was too drugged to struggle.

Jake rolled his head, scanning the dingy back room of the opium den. Every rip in the faded wallpaper was as familiar as the scars on his own body. Time was running out, working against him to make Carl's predictions come true. How could Meghan not turn from him with loathing when she saw him in this filthy, wretched condition?

God help him, he was beginning to welcome the sweet, mind-numbing cloud of opium, to hide from the helplessness and the despair that came from repeated failures to fight those who held him prisoner.

He lifted one hand, staring at the fresh scabs and the angry circle of red around his wrist. Even slicked with blood, his large hands had refused to slip through the shackles. His attempts to kick the bed frame to splinters, hopefully to free his ankles, had failed. The cuts on his ankles and wrists were badly infected. Soon gangrene would set in, and it would be too late to save his hands and feet. Then he would become less than half a man . . . in more ways than he was already.

Air hissed between Jake's teeth as he struggled up. The chains provided just enough slack to sit on the bed.

No matter how much Carl's henchmen pinned him down, no matter how often they hit him to quiet his struggles, Jake would not give the bastards the satisfaction of hearing him cry out. At least his samurai training had taught him how to separate himself from the pain. If only it could help shield him from the mental agony of being kept from Meghan, the caustic jealousy of picturing Carl charming her while he beat down his rival to a pathetic shadow of the man Jake had once been.

Jake clamped his eyes shut, trying to block out the images of the passion in Meghan's blue eyes, her golden hair, the soft skin that tempted him to stroke her end-lessly. Two tears squeezed from the corners of his eyelids. He shook his head furiously, flinging the sign of weakness into his matted hair.

A commotion arose in the next room, where the guards whiled away the hours between opium doses. At first Jake took no notice, since they were in the habit of belittling one another and starting fights. But when it escalated to crashes and yelps of pain, Jake lifted his head.

The adjoining door opened.

Meghan appeared in the opening like a vision from heaven.

Her expression registered shock and horror. Jake turned his face away, unable to bear the inevitable disgust that would come into her eyes. Meghan's rejection would succeed in breaking him, when all Carl's efforts had failed.

Rage at his helplessness ate through him like acid. He did the only thing he could think of: He tried to drive Meghan away before she turned from him in loathing.

"Go away, Meghan!" Jake croaked in a voice roughened by opium smoke. "Bloody hell, woman, I don't want you to see me like this!"

She came forward, despite his hostile outburst, and dropped to her knees beside the bed. When she touched his arm, he turned to look at her. He couldn't help himself. She resembled an angel, clean and pure—a shocking contrast to his filth and the sin of his failures. He didn't deserve her touch.

"I think you're the most glorious sight I've ever seen," Meg said in a throaty whisper. "Kwan and I have been searching Chinatown for you all day. Now you're safe, and that's all that matters." Although tears sparkled in her eyes, she finished on a teasing note, "I didn't realize you were so concerned about appearances, Jake Talbert."

She'd searched for him. . . . Carl hadn't brought her here. Hope surged, then just as quickly sank. Then she didn't know about the opium.

Sung Kwan appeared behind Meghan. Jake lashed out at him next. "What the hell are you doing here, dammit! I told you to stay on the *Venture*."

Kwan grinned as if he'd said something funny. "We find you. This is good. Now I repay you for saving Lian."

"We need to find the key to these shackles, Kwan. Hurry," Meghan urged. "See what you can find on those guards."

Kwan's jaw clenched as he took in Jake's battered condition. "They will tell me." He left the room.

Meghan lifted Jake's right hand. The shackle slid down to expose his mutilated wrist.

"Oh, Jake. Why did you fight the shackles so much?"

His skin drank in the magic of her gentle hands. Nor could he stop wanting her, he discovered, as his lower body tightened.

"What was I supposed to do?" he grunted. "Just lie still and let it happen?"

"Let what happen?"

He couldn't live a lie. Jake ground out the nasty truth. "They forced me to take opium."

"Oh, God. For three days?"

Shame curled through him, hot and writhing. "I should have been able to stop them."

"While chained to a bed?" she said incredulously. "Are you crazy? I saw the size of those monsters out there."

"Didn't you hear me?" he growled, trying to make her understand. "I smoked the opium!"

Meg jumped to her feet and plunked her fists on her

hips. "Do you think I care about that? You are the strongest man I know, Jake Talbert, and the bravest, but you're still just a man . . . and an incredibly obtuse one at times. Tell me, how could you have stopped them?"

Jake stared. Her challenging tone demanded that he believe in himself as much as she apparently did. There was no condemnation in her eyes, no disgust.

Love for Meghan surged through him, the all-consuming nature of it almost frightening.

Kwan reappeared, jingling a small ring of keys. He bent over the bed and tested the keys on the leg shackles until he found the right one.

When the last shackle sprang free, Jake climbed shakily to his feet. Peter and Phillip entered the room, but he refused their help.

"My bag," Jake insisted, his gaze seeking out the duffel Carl's thugs had negligently thrown into a corner. Phillip retrieved it for him.

Jake limped out of the building, barefoot and battered, his bruised ribs protesting as he straightened to his full height. But at least he walked out under his own power.

He paused on the street, drinking in the fresh sea air, the brilliant late afternoon sunshine, and the feeling of liberation.

"Kwan, my thanks. I know what you risked by coming back to Chinatown to look for me."

Sung Kwan bowed.

"I'll write you a note to take to Hembley, instructing him to sail immediately. I want you and Lian taken to safety."

"Who did this to you, Jake?" Meg asked. "Was it Chen Lee?"

"No, it wasn't Chen Lee," he responded vaguely.

"Then who? I want to know who did this!"

"Later, Meghan. I'm too tired to talk about it just now," Jake muttered, stalling for time. How would she react when she found out Carl was responsible?

Her face softened with solicitous concern. "Come on, I'm taking you home."

Home. The word struck a chord of satisfaction deep inside Jake. Although he cringed with the knowledge of how he must smell, he allowed her to support one arm across her shoulders.

Gazing down in wonder at her blond head, Jake realized Meghan hadn't once condemned him for her father's death. He must still be hallucinating from the drug, because her forgiveness and willing acceptance of his condition seemed too damn good to be true.

CARL EDWARDS TOSSED back the expensive whiskey as if it were rotgut, then poured himself another glass.

He paced from the cold iron fireplace to the far wall of his sitting room, seething with frustrated fury.

Years of planning and effort were crumbling to dust around him. Meghan had refused to see him for the past three days, ever since the incident with the lemonade. He couldn't fathom why, except that he hadn't allowed her sufficient time for mourning before revealing the passionate side of his devotion. He had only his own impatience to blame . . . and just when everything had been going so well, damn it all.

Without marriage to one of the most wealthy women in San Francisco on the horizon, Carl could no longer hold off his creditors. He'd even lost his ace in the hole: Someone had broken Talbert out of the opium den four hours ago.

Although the loss of the opportunity to humble and

break Jacob Talbert infuriated Carl, right now he had more immediate concerns.

With trembling fingers, Carl raised the note still clenched in his left hand. Once again, he read the chilling, thinly veiled threat.

I am still waiting for you to fulfill your part of the bargain. You have yet to tell me where I may find the swords.

There was no signature.

The note didn't need one.

Talbert had killed all of Chen Lee's boo how doy the night of Douglass's death. No one had been left to report back to the Tong leader that Jake Talbert took away his precious swords. Apparently, Chen Lee was also unaware that the swords were gone, shipped off to parts unknown on the *Shinjiro*.

Swallowing hard, Carl crushed the note and tossed it into the fireplace. *I could as easily choose to get rid of you.* He certainly had no intention of telling the murderous Celestial that the swords were out of reach.

Time to cut his losses and run, Carl resolved. Tonight— before somebody found his body in a back alley, his skull laid open by a hatchet.

Brisby—Carl's valet, butler, spy and all-around henchman since the war—appeared in the open doorway.

"Well, Brisby, what did you find out?"

"Miss McLowry has given her staff the night off," said the thin-faced little man. "Something about them having worked extra hard throughout her papa's lying-in and funeral."

A slow smile spread across Carl's face. Brisby had many uses, including the ability to ferret out all sorts of intriguing information. "Excellent. Her timing couldn't be more ideal."

"Yes, sir."

"I was considering New Orleans, Brisby," he mused. "What do you think?"

"Lots of possibilities there for a man with your skill at gambling, sir."

"Exactly."

"And a large number of wealthy widows and impressionable young debutantes."

"I do believe New Orleans sounds like the ideal place for a new start. See that everything is packed."

"It already is, squeezed tight and efficient into just four bags. We'll be able to travel fast."

"You're a man of many talents, Brisby. Remind me to increase your wages." Carl held the tumbler up to the light. He turned the glass in his hand, watching the whiskey glow with amber fire. "We'll wait until almost midnight, then pay a visit to the McLowry mansion on our way out of town. After all the time and energy I've invested in that cold bitch, Meghan McLowry owes me a stake for a new start."

Chapter Twenty

Before we've had our fill, must the moon so quickly hide itself? If only the rim of the hill would flee and refuse it shelter!
—Ariwara no Narihira (ninth century)

Jake settled into the brass tub placed in his bedroom, sinking deeper into the hot water. In the Japanese fashion, he'd washed most of the grime away before stepping into the portable tub. But there had been many places he couldn't reach because of his bandaged wrists and ankles, not to mention the limitations on his flexibility caused by bruised ribs. He rested his arms along the rim of the tub and propped his calves on the far end in an effort to keep the bandages dry.

His teeth suddenly chattered, not from cold, but from the last of the opium poison working its way out of his system. He'd endured the worst of the shakes and the nausea during the interminable afternoon and evening, though neither had been unbearable.

Doctor Radcliffe had assured him the worst was over. The lingering weakness and the constant dry mouth might take several more days, he warned. Jake had waited in dread for an opium craving to hit. It never came. Apparently three days wasn't long enough to develop an addiction . . . or maybe his aversion to the drug helped protect him. The true dependence on opium was for those who willingly sought the drug for its blissful escape.

Unfortunately, it would take a lot longer to wash away the abhorrent memories and the smell that had imprinted itself inside his head.

The door opened and closed quietly, and he caught sight of Meghan.

She wore the blue kimono. The significance of the gesture wasn't lost on him, but he didn't dare speculate for fear that he would latch on to wistful fantasies. She looked exquisite in the garment, just as he'd imagined she would.

Kneeling next to the tub, Meg set aside shaving implements and a stack of towels.

The scent of honeysuckle wafted over Jake, pushing away the memory of less pleasant odors. He breathed deeply, letting her delicately applied perfume soak into his senses and absorb into his blood.

When he glanced down and discovered bare feet peeking out from under the kimono, desire sank sweet talons into his loins. If she was naked under there, he was too weak to take full advantage of the seductive offer . . . although his swelling manhood didn't seem aware of the limitations of the rest of his battered body.

"Meghan," he said thickly as his gaze devoured the soft curves beneath the silk. "You shouldn't be here. The servants."

She smiled. "I gave them the night off, including Robert. The two footmen who carried your bathwater just left. We have the house to ourselves."

Dipping her hand into the water, she stroked one palm down the inside of his thigh.

Meg's eyes sparkled mischievously. "Is the water warm enough?"

"Getting warmer as we speak," he croaked.

"Good, because I'm here to help you bathe. Dr. Radcliffe says you shouldn't get those bandages wet." She pushed up the voluminous sleeves of the kimono, securing them at her shoulders with pins. "And I'm going to shave you, too. I prefer to see your face."

Capturing her wrist, Jake brought her hand up between them and kissed her knuckles. "I must know, Meghan. Did you mean what you said in that letter?"

She looked startled. "Letter?" Her fingers twitched against his chin.

"The one you wrote the day of your father's funeral. In it, you said I didn't deserve forgiveness for failing to prevent his death."

"But—" She swallowed hard. "I tore that letter up. I insisted on it. I never meant for you to—" Her voice failed.

Jake released her and looked away, a great heaviness settling inside. So she had penned the letter. He'd been hoping against hope that it was some kind of forgery.

Meg's hand tenderly cupped his cheek and turned him back to face her. Her mouth curved in a sad, wistful smile. Her eyes resembled warm pools of shimmering blue. "That letter was a childish outpouring of anger and grief, but it enabled me to clear my mind and pull back from those destructive, blinding feelings. I understood, then, that I did forgive you, without reservation. I also realized a great deal of fear was buried in that letter."

"Fear?" he echoed. "Of Chen Lee? Of living alone without your father?"

"No, of losing you." Her thumb stroked his cheek, rasping against the stiff bristles of a three-day beard. "Father was dead, no one could change that, but his death also meant that I no longer had a hold over you. I feared that you would walk out of my life . . . that I would never see you again."

Jake searched her face, his voice stolen by a sudden tightness in his chest.

Meg added softly, "I was a fool to condemn you in the first place. No one could have done a better job of protecting my father, no one."

"I should have been better prepared," Jake insisted.

"You weren't . . . because of me."

His dark brows snapped together. "What do you mean?"

"In asking you to come to my room that night, I took you away from the very role I'd asked you to perform. I only thought of myself, of how much I wanted you."

"That's ridiculous," Jake growled. "You have no reason to feel guilty."

"Don't you see, Jake? However inadvertently, we each played a role. We didn't make the wrong choices, because there were no right ones to be found. You did so much, more than any normal man could have done. None of this tragedy would have been necessary if Father hadn't succumbed to his desire to own those swords." She stopped suddenly, then hung her head.

Jake lifted her chin on the crook of his finger. "I'm so sorry, Meghan."

"I'm all right. Don't worry. It's just that I miss him." She picked up the shaving mug and began to brush foam across Jake's cheeks. "One good thing has come of all this. If Father hadn't been in danger from the Tong, I never would have met you. Perhaps it was fate." Her gaze connected with his, her eyes glowing with a deep emotion he didn't dare define . . . but it made his pulse race all the same.

"Meg, I—"

"Hold still while I shave you."

Jake subsided into silence as she scraped the stiff black bristles from his face. A declaration of love was too important to make with his body trapped in a tub and his face covered with streaks of foam.

After using a small towel to wipe his cheeks, she began washing his hair. Jake closed his eyes, luxuriating in the sensual massage of her fingers across his scalp. The bucket by the tub served to pour clean, warm water through his long hair.

"Time to get out, lazybones," Meg teased softly.

Jake rose slowly, taking care not to reinjure his ribs. He watched her face, wondering how she would react when she saw what the floating soap had concealed.

Meg's eyes widened at the sight of his full, heavy arousal.

"I can't help but react this way when you touch me," he said huskily. "You aren't going to stop now, are you?"

A faint blush colored her cheeks. "And leave you dripping water all over the carpet? I think not," she countered, scooping up a towel. "I just thought you'd be too weak from your ordeal to . . . well, you know. Obviously a stupid assumption."

Jake grinned.

Although he could probably manage to dry himself, Jake made no attempt to do so. He'd be a fool to pass up the opportunity for Meg to towel him off. As she dried his hair, back, and chest, he became aware of every pulse of blood through his lower body.

Then she knelt on the carpet in front of him.

"Brace your legs a little apart," she instructed innocently.

"Good idea," he said thickly. "Before I fall down."

She glanced up sharply. "Are you getting tired?"

"Hell, no. Actually, I'm experiencing an amazing renewal of my energy at the moment. But your touch does destroy my equilibrium, sweetheart."

With a shy smile, she started at his feet and worked her way up. By the time she reached his hips, Jake was coming unraveled at the edges. Pain and weakness were forgotten. He shuddered as she worked the towel around his loins.

Then her hand closed around him.

Jake jerked, a husky groan rumbling from his chest. He pulled her to her feet and tossed aside the towel.

Meg took his hand and backed up, leading him to the bed. With impatient fingers, he unwound her sash and pushed the kimono off her shoulders. The embroidered silk robe pooled on the floor around her feet.

The sight of Meg's nude body sent hot desire spiraling out of control.

He cradled her graceful breasts in his hands. When he rubbed her nipples, she wrapped her arms around his neck and swayed towards him. His hands slid around her body, tracing over velvety soft skin until they cupped her buttocks. He pulled her hard against his arousal.

Then he eased her onto the bed and came down beside her.

"I want to touch you some more," she whispered.

"Only if you let me touch you at the same time."

"Oh, yes." Meg sighed.

"Turn around the opposite way, like this." He helped her reverse her position, until her head was near his hips and the dark gold nest of her feminine curls was within reach of his mouth.

"Hmmm, I like this." Her fingers slid into his groin hairs, venturing forth in an erotic voyage of discovery, then sliding down over his scrotum to cup him gently.

Jake thought he would burst into flames. But that was nothing compared to the sensations that shook him when she kissed his engorged flesh. He moaned as her tongue traced his length.

He thought he would die if he didn't taste her in turn. Jake dipped his head into the V of her legs.

"Jake!" Meg yelped, shocked by the intimacy.

"You smell like heaven," he said raggedly. "Just relax and enjoy it, Meghan."

With a sigh, she opened her thighs wider. He reveled in her trust. Then he forgot everything else as her hand curled around him.

Jake went wild, the urge to cherish and seduce and possess surging through him with every beat of his heart. Meg gasped and shuddered with each stroke of his tongue. Just when he thought the tempest in his body couldn't grow any stronger, Meg took him into her mouth.

He growled his approval. His hips flexed, need howling through him as he intensified his assault on the sensitive nubbin of flesh between her legs. Meg writhed, sucking on his throbbing staff between frantic efforts to gasp his name. Jake had never experienced anything so incredibly erotic, but he knew it was his love for her that took their shared passion to new heights.

Just when he knew he could stand it no more, he swung Meg around and urged her up. Her hair spread about her shoulders in a wild tangle as she straddled his hips. Her shining blue eyes held his gaze in an unbreakable bond as he plunged into her tight heat.

Meg flung her head back, moaning. Jake grasped her hips, rocking her hard against him, wanting to hold back until he heard that soft, triumphant cry erupt from her lips. But he was already too far gone. After less than a dozen strokes, the world around him shattered in a glorious explosion.

Although held in the grip of sweet ecstasy, Jake felt the chill of disappointment . . . until he felt Meg shudder with her own climax. He slid a thumb into her nest of hair, heightening her pleasure. She cried out and rocked some more, nearly destroying his control, until she begged him to stop.

"I can't take any more," she said breathlessly, melting onto his chest with a care that demonstrated her concern for his bruised ribs.

Jake smiled with pure wolfish satisfaction as he stroked her back. Meg was his woman, his one true mate. Now he only had to convince her that they belonged together.

Then she whispered words that stunned him.

"I love you, Jake."

Jake thought there could be no greater ecstasy than the pinnacle of their lovemaking. He discovered he couldn't have been more wrong. He hugged her tightly.

More than anything, he wanted to say that he returned her love, but he felt there was one more thing he must do. The quest for the swords and vengeance had consumed his existence for sixteen years. Unlike his Japanese family, Meghan didn't require the restoration of his honor to forgive him. With unconditional love, she accepted even his flaws and failures. Only a man who had lived the strict code of the samurai could fully appreciate such a precious gift. He wanted to do something in turn . . . a final gesture to demonstrate that he was leaving his old way of life, and the violence, behind.

After cherishing the feel of her a while longer, Jake disentangled himself and rolled out of bed.

"Where are you going?" she murmured sleepily.

"There's something I want to give you," he explained as he donned a pair of clean black trousers and shrugged into a blue cotton shirt. "Will you meet me in the library in a few minutes?"

Meg sat up and slipped the kimono back on. With a secretive little smile, she said, "I'd rather meet in the atrium. There's something I've been wanting to show you, too."

· · ·

WHEN JAKE STRODE into the garden a few minutes later, he carried a long, slender object in one hand.

Meg's smile faded at the first glimpse of his solemn expression. She wanted to show him how the iguanas now accepted her, but his errand was apparently much more serious. She set the bowl of fruit and vegetables on the low wall of the fountain with trembling hands.

Stopping before her, Jake held the black katana horizontally and bowed over it with his head and shoulders. Then he extended it toward her like an offer of surrender.

"I want you to add this to your father's collection."

"Jake," she whispered, dismayed by the depth of his sacrifice. "This is not just a sword . . . it's part of who you are."

"Not anymore. There's too much violence and bloodshed associated with it," he said grimly.

He already knew that she forgave him. The unnecessary offer of atonement ignited her temper. Meg ground out, "Have you so quickly forgotten how I watched you perform your kata? You're a work of art, Jake Talbert, all fluid movement and powerful skill. Don't you dare deny me the pleasure of watching you work with your katana again!"

He hesitated. "You're serious, aren't you?"

"Damn right I am. Do you really think I could love you for less than the sum total of who you are?"

Slowly, Jake sat down next to her on the edge of the fountain. He leaned the katana against the stone ledge and drew her into his arms. Everything about the warm, tender passion of his kiss said that he loved her. If he didn't say the words tonight, Meg thought, she might succumb to frustration and shove him into the fountain . . . bandages or no bandages.

Jake lifted his head. The churning emotions in the dark centers of his eyes caused Meg's pulse to thunder in her ears. He gathered up her right hand and pressed it to the center of his chest. She could feel his heart beating against her knuckles.

"Meghan, I—" he began.

Unexpectedly, footsteps crunched on the white gravel, an ominous sound that shattered the expectancy of the moment.

"Well, isn't this cozy," Carl said snidely, his face twisted into a sneer. "The two lovers, together again." The fountain lights glinted off the barrel of Carl's gun.

Meg gasped. Rising with Jake, she kept her fingers tucked into the reassuring warmth of his large hand. Although Meg tried to resist, Jake insisted on pulling her behind him, providing a shield with the battered body that she longed to protect.

She gained strength from his steely calm and the alert readiness she could feel coiling beneath the surface.

Meg noted that Carl was dressed in elegant evening attire, including a pearl gray coat, slate gray trousers, and immaculate white linen. Trust her father's protégé to dress to the nines, she thought ironically, even when breaking into someone's house.

A small man with a thin, hard face came up behind Carl. The wiry man reminded her of a terrier that would take pleasure in catching a rat and shaking it to death in his jaws.

Carl spared his henchman a quick glance. "Did you find what we came for, Brisby?"

The rat-terrier man grinned. "Plenty of silver to choose from. You were right about that chess set in the library, too. It's worth a damn fortune."

Mouth open in astonishment, Meg exclaimed, "That's what this is about? Robbery?"

"I'm nothing if not practical, my dear. I've wasted years pursuing you. You owe me, Meghan."

"Then just take the damn stuff and go!"

"Not so fast." Carl looked them up and down with disdain. "I didn't expect the bonus of finding your lover here, though I should have considered that possibility." Focusing on Jake, he snarled, "I detest loose ends. You deserve to die, Talbert, for all the damnable inconvenience you've caused me. This time, you won't have someone to rush to your rescue."

A shiver of understanding swept down Meg's back. "You were the one who chained Jake, who forced him to take opium?"

"I didn't lower myself to perform the actual task, of course, but it was my idea. It would have worked, too, if he hadn't escaped. In a few more days, Talbert would have been so pathetic you would have turned from him in disgust."

With heartfelt conviction, Meg countered, "You're wrong, Carl. I was the one who freed him from that hellish place. I felt nothing but concern for him, and fear, and a tremendous anger at whoever had done such a despicable thing."

"What a silly little romantic you are," Carl retorted acidly. "Perhaps our parting is for the best, after all. I can see I would have soon grown tired of you, Meghan."

"You wouldn't have had the chance. I would never have married you, Carl."

"So, you prefer to be a sea captain's slut instead!"

Meg lifted her chin. "There is nothing shameful about my relationship with Jake, not when I love him so much. On the other hand, I would have been a slut if I'd lain with you!"

Warning pressure from Jake's fingers cooled Meg's

temper abruptly. With dismay, she noted Carl's reddened face and the way he'd raised the gun.

Calmly, Jake said, "I don't think you'll pull that trigger, Edwards. You're not the murdering kind. You prefer to have men like Chen Lee do your dirty work for you."

"I'm surprised you're that discerning, Talbert. It's true, I exist on a different stratum now. I left the dirty work behind me long ago, along with the vulgarity of the war."

"But you did provide Chen with a map of the mansion," Jake persisted.

Carl shrugged. "I merely offered some advantages to assist Chen along the path of his obsessive goal. It suited my purpose."

"Which was to kill Douglass."

"A circumstance that benefited us both. McLowry was in the way of something I wanted."

Meg almost retched on the spot. Carl had helped Chen Lee, contributing to her father's death! How could she have been so naive, so blind to the ruthlessness behind Carl's veneer of charm?

"Yet, after all your trouble, you didn't get Meghan," Jake pointed out with lethal softness.

"For which I blame you," Carl snapped. "But you needn't worry about my aversion to dirtying my hands, Talbert. In this case, I intend to have Brisby shoot you."

Jake didn't even flinch. "You claim you can best me at swords, Edwards. Have you changed your mind?"

Carl's eyes flooded with arrogance. "You wouldn't be so lucky."

"Then why deny yourself the one-on-one glory of a sword fight?" Jake's voice emerged in a low tone that coaxed and taunted at the same time. "You were a cavalry officer. You remember the satisfaction of defeating an enemy with your blade, don't you? There's no substitute for it."

Carl's eyes gleamed. "A valid point, Talbert. This is one pleasure I want to carry with me for the rest of my life." Stripping off his coat, he ordered, "Brisby, bring my saber."

Meg's breath lodged in her throat. What was Jake doing, provoking a fight in his weakened condition? Then again, what other chance did they have to come out of this alive? The gun certainly offered none.

Brisby scanned Jake with an assessing eye. "Maybe this ain't such a good idea, sir. Let's just kill them, grab the goods and get out of here."

Without taking his gaze from Jake, Carl snapped, "Don't interfere, dammit. Just do as I ask."

Brisby's lips pursed. Then he shrugged, and Meg could sense his greedy little mind churning over the fact that Carl was not a necessary ingredient in stealing the gold and silver. Perhaps Brisby even hoped that Jake would win the fight and eliminate the need to split the money. And whether or not Carl survived, Brisby intended to kill them and steal the valuables.

The additional threat sent dread coursing through her bloodstream as Brisby left the atrium.

Jake turned to face Meg, gripping her shoulders. He must have recognized the fear in her expression, for he said quietly, "It'll be all right, Meghan."

"But you're hurt! That gives Carl an unfair advantage," she hissed, taking advantage of Carl's inattention as he fastidiously rolled up his sleeves.

"Perhaps, but not as much as he thinks. I'll play up the weakness until he lowers his guard. Trust me."

"I do, but what will prevent Brisby from shooting you afterwards?"

Jake's mouth thinned. "The moment I strike the killing blow, grab Brisby's gun hand. Try to deflect his aim just long enough for me to get to you."

She nodded stiffly.

Brisby returned with the cavalry saber.

Carl handed him the gun. "Use this if anything goes wrong. And watch Meghan. I don't trust her."

Brisby waved the gun. "Get over here, missy."

As Meg reluctantly eased away from Jake, she spotted the neglected bowl of fruit on the fountain wall. A jolt of excitement shafted through her. The iguanas! Considering the shock or revulsion their unexpected appearance typically engendered, they could provide a much-needed distraction. If only the iguanas' hunger would overcome their fear of strangers!

Meg scooped up the bowl and crossed to Brisby. As she reached his side, she faked a stumble and spilled the bowl's contents over his boots.

"Clumsy bitch," he snapped.

"I can't help it," she retorted, setting the empty bowl aside. "You make me nervous."

With a snort, he took one step to the left. A strawberry crushed under his boot. The unique scent of the fruit teased Meg's nostrils and spread throughout the atrium. She tensed with hope. Would that be enough to draw the iguanas out of hiding?

The two combatants drew their swords.

Steel blades clashed, the discordant sounds ringing off the glass walls and adding to the already edgy state of Meg's nerves. She watched the fight intently, simultaneously tracking Brisby's slightest twitch.

Where were those iguanas when she needed them?

Plants rustled behind her, but the sound didn't fit the normal movements of the lizards. The hairs on her nape prickled.

Brisby suddenly jerked, stiffening. His lips moved, but no sound emerged. Instead, a thin line of blood slipped from the corner of his mouth. As he sagged forward, Meg saw the dagger embedded deep in his back.

Brisby's arm jerked convulsively as he fell, flipping the gun into the thick greenery.

Meg lunged for the revolver, knowing it was her only chance.

Someone grabbed her hair from behind, bringing her to a wrenching stop. She screamed.

"Meghan!" Jake shouted. His expression reflected the same rage and fear she felt at this new, more dangerous threat.

The fight stopped abruptly as Carl whirled around.

"Chen!" Carl burst out. A hunted look crossed his face.

The Tong leader released Meg's hair and thrust her toward the boo how doy who had killed Brisby. Another hatchet man came up on her right.

Chen Lee gingerly stepped over the spilled fruit and moved into the circle of light around the fountain. "Where are my swords, Mr. Edwards?" he said in a tone that managed to convey a wealth of implied threat.

Jake arched a brow. "Didn't you tell him, Edwards?"

Carl's mouth opened, then closed with a click of his teeth.

Scowling, Chen bit out, "Tell me what?"

"The five Matsuda blades are on the *Shinjiro,* several days out to sea," offered Jake when Carl still couldn't find his voice. "They're going back to Japan where they belong."

Chen Lee's mouth twitched at the corners. "You neglected to mention this, Mr. Edwards." He moved forward with sinuous grace, like a snake slithering towards its prey.

Meg saw the glint of steel hidden in the folds of his

baggy trousers. She choked back the shout of warning that rose in her throat, fearful that if she interfered it might go badly for Jake. Allowing the two predators to destroy one another could be Jake's only chance at survival . . . and a small measure of justice for her murdered father.

"Perhaps you can find a way to make up for their loss," Chen offered.

"Yes, yes, of course I can!" Carl agreed heartily, laughing with relief. "You can take anything from this house that suits you. There's even a room full of weapons to choose from."

Chen's mild tone lulled Carl into a false sense of security. Carl brought his sword up too late in an attempt to deflect the blow. Chen Lee's blade slipped past and stabbed deeply into Carl's chest.

Meg pressed a fist to her mouth as Carl's stunned expression registered awareness of his own mortality.

"The only thing you can give me of interest is your life," Chen snarled. "Even that will not repay my loss."

He stepped back, jerking out the blood-smeared blade.

Bile rose in Meg's throat. She looked away as Carl slowly crumpled to the ground. Over and over, she told herself that Carl intended to kill Jake; thus, he deserved to die.

"So now it's just you and me, Chen."

Jake's voice wrenched her attention back to the remaining danger. He stood with the katana balanced tightly in his right hand. His black hair flowed loosely around broad shoulders; his gray eyes glittered with the promise of retribution. Meg's heart swelled with love for this man . . . this wounded warrior who could gently caress her with the same hands that wielded a deadly sword.

"You're the one, aren't you," Jake continued with cold

certainty. "The one who stole those swords from the Kyoshu battlefield."

"Ah, you see why I treasure them. They were a prize from a great victory."

"But you didn't win them honorably, Chen," Jake growled. He raised the katana. "You were a bloody thief back then, and you're still no better than a thief."

Chen's face hardened just before he attacked. The clash of swords once again echoed through the atrium, but this time Meg could see a difference. Chen Lee's skill exceeded Carl's.

Lines bracketed Jake's mouth. Cords stood out in his neck. His movements slowed gradually as pain, exhaustion, and the lingering weakness from his ordeal overwhelmed him.

And with the two boo how doy watching her, there wasn't a thing Meg could do to help him.

Chen gradually backed Jake against the fountain, forcing him to step over the low wall into the pool. Chen followed relentlessly until they were both knee-deep in water.

Fear gripped Meg as Jake struggled to defend himself. She was so intent on the fight, she didn't notice when the iguanas finally came out of hiding. The large, spiny lizards brushed against the legs of the first boo how doy as they eagerly gobbled up strawberries.

The assassin screeched, cursing in Cantonese as he leaped back in astonishment.

Chen Lee glanced over his shoulder. Although only a momentary distraction, it was enough. Jake gathered his strength and swung the katana at neck level.

Chen's headless body collapsed into the fountain.

Water splashed in glittering sheets as Jake lunged for his saya at the fountain's edge. Meg scrambled for the gun at the same time, the second boo how doy hard on her heels. Suddenly, the man crashed to the ground beside her, a hatchet clenched in his hand, a skewerlike dagger imbedded in his throat. He made a hideous gurgling noise, then lay still.

Frantically, Meg reached for the gun in the undergrowth. Her hand closed around cold steel.

She swung around—just in time to see Jake clutch his ribs, ashen-faced, and sink to his knees in the bloody water. The boo how doy who'd been spooked by the iguanas moved in for the kill, taking advantage of the fact that Jake's strength was evidently spent.

Meg jerked up the gun and fired. The last Tong assassin clutched his wounded arm and ran from the atrium.

Meg rushed to the fountain and helped Jake climb from the macabre red pool. He sat on the edge, breathing heavily.

"Send for the police," he hissed between clenched teeth.

"And the doctor!" Meg cried out in concern.

Jake grinned crookedly. Hooking a hand around the back of her neck, he pulled her down for a quick, fierce kiss. "There's nothing wrong with me that time and lots of love from you won't heal."

Meg smiled, warmed by his kiss and the passion in his eyes.

He was safe. Their enemies were finally dead.

"I think I can manage that."

"Do you think you can manage to keep him in bed this time?" Dr. Radcliffe asked in exasperation.

Jake gave Meg a wolfish grin, evidently adding more significance to the suggestion than the old man had intended. She glared at him behind the doctor's back as the man packed his instruments away.

"I've wrapped his ribs. How did he manage to get the dressing on his ankles wet?" He glared at Jake over the rim of his spectacles. "Had an urge for a midnight swim, eh?"

"It's a long story, Doctor," Meg said, cringing at the memory of what the police had just finished cleaning up downstairs.

Radcliffe grunted and closed his bag with a snap. "Just see he gets plenty of bed rest. You may have to force him. Doesn't seem like the type to stay still for long, if you ask me."

There was no mistaking the gleam of desire in Jake's eyes. Meg hid a smile. "I'll see what I can do."

Dr. Radcliffe left the room.

Jake let out a gusty sigh of relief. His gaze followed her about the room as she tidied up. "Are you all right?"

She drew a deep, steadying breath. "Yes. Still rather jittery, though."

"There'll be no more bogeymen coming out of the night."

"I know. It's just hard to believe we're finally free of Chen Lee's hatred and Carl's selfish manipulation."

"I've got something that might take your mind off it," he said softly. "In my duffel bag, there's a white garment. Pull it out."

She did as instructed.

"Now, spread it out on the bed," he added, his voice low and intense. He watched her closely.

Meg gasped in amazement as the gown settled like a white cloud across his legs, covering most of the bed. "It's the white kimono." Her hands smoothed over the texture of flowing water woven into the fabric. Embroidered symbols of flying cranes, gnarly pine trees, and tiny rainbows decorated the garment with flashes of color. "How beautiful!" she exclaimed.

"The designs symbolize happiness and long life." He

hesitated. "It's more than an everyday kimono, Meghan. This one is very special. It's a Japanese bridal robe."

Her hand stilled. She looked up, meeting his gaze.

"I've been saving this for you. It took me a while to understand why I hung onto it, to know what my heart realized even back then. . . . I love you, Meghan." He caught up her hand. "Will you marry me?"

Meg lifted the robe with trembling hands, joy surging through her like crashing waves. She carefully laid the beautiful garment over the back of a chair. The charged, expectant atmosphere in the room made her skin tingle.

Crawling onto the bed, she curled against Jake's side, then smiled up at him. "Yes, I'll marry you, Jake Talbert."

She didn't realize he'd been holding his breath until he let it out in a rush. He bent to give her a fiery, possessive kiss.

When he leaned back against the pillows, wincing at the pain in his ribs, Meg gave him a stern look. "You're supposed to rest."

"I will, I swear," he said seriously, then added with a roguish grin, "this time. Stay close to me, though, or I might do myself an injury reaching for you."

Chapter Twenty One

I thought there could be no more love left anywhere. Whence then is come this love, that has caught me now and holds me in its grasp?
—Princess Hirokawa (Eighth century)

Four months later

THE PETITE JAPANESE woman backed away, bowing out of the main parlor of the Talbert's new home. Meg winced. This servile attitude from Akira's wife was driving her crazy, especially when the woman should consider herself an equal.

Akira entered the room, looking very dignified in a black kimono. He'd surprised everyone by returning home with a new bride—a woman near his own age, newly widowed. Even more startling had been the discovery that he'd loved Mariko from afar for years, even though she'd been married to another.

"I really need to teach Mariko-san how to assert herself more," Meg stated, smiling over the knowledge that Akira was a romantic beneath that stoic exterior. "After all, she lives in America now."

The samurai frowned.

Meg laughed. "Come now, Akira-san, don't be a hypocrite. If you enjoy the freedoms of this country, you should allow your wife the same privileges. How would you say . . . don't try to catch water in a wicker basket?"

Surprise flickered across Akira's face. "That is a Japanese proverb."

"Yes, I know. Jake started spouting them while you were gone, he missed you so much. It means—"

"It means if I try to keep Mariko-san in the old ways, she find out how woman live in America and change anyway. Perhaps because you show her, Meg-an-san?" He bowed ironically.

"Of course. Anyway, thank goodness you're back to reclaim your title as master of the proverbs. Jake is dangerous in the role. Just last night we were at a party with the board members for my new School for Chinese Girls— admittedly, not the most scintillating company. To alleviate his boredom, my charming husband leaned close and whispered in my ear, 'The naked man never mislays his wallet.' Everyone heard my crack of laughter from across the room. I was so mortified we had to leave soon after."

Smiling to herself, Meg didn't add that the mental image his playful comment conjured had ignited flames of desire that could only be satisfied by hustling him home and into bed.

Robert cleared his throat from the doorway, breaking into her thoughts. Although Meg hadn't needed a large staff after selling the Rincon Hill mansion, she had kept on Robert, Wilkins, Suzanne, and two other maids. Phillip and Peter had chosen to seek their fortune in the booming mining town of Virginia City.

"Yes, Robert. What is it?"

"A messenger delivered this letter from your solicitors, Miss Meghan."

Her lawyers? The only unresolved business she had with the lawyers was—

Meg shot out of her chair, her heart pounding. Less than a week after Chen Lee's death, she had called on the lawyers to fulfill a promise she'd made to herself earlier, to ask them to bring all their resources to bear in locating Jake's mother.

"Thank you, Robert," she said, eagerly accepting the slender package from his hand.

Meg broke the seal. Inside was another sealed envelope and a message on the law office's letterhead. The second envelope, originating from England, was addressed to Jake. Meg's hand trembled as she read the lawyers' letter. The first paragraph offered all she'd hoped to see: *In regard to your request to determine the whereabouts of one Mrs. Michael Talbert, lately of Portsmouth, England. We have located the lady, now Lady Sophia Abernathy of Wiltshire, widowed. A letter from Lady Abernathy is enclosed.*

Five minutes later, Meg opened the door to Jake's study. He bent over his desk, working out the final numbers from the sale of the lucrative cargo Akira had brought back from Japan.

Her gaze roved hungrily over the broad shoulders beneath his white shirt, the black waves of his hair, the flecks of gray at his temples. Wonder spread through her like a glittering rainbow.

Meg smoothed her rose-colored gown nervously. She'd kept the search a secret from Jake, reluctant to subject him to further disappointment if the lawyers' efforts proved futile.

"Are you going to just stand there all day?" Jake teased without looking up. "I'd rather you come sit in my lap, wife, and distract me with something much more interesting than these manifests." Then he raised his head, his gray eyes alight with that volcanic passion that always sent a shiver of need down her spine.

"I brought you something," she whispered. "A letter."

His brows drew together. "Your voice sounds strange. Is something wrong, Meghan?"

"No, everything is perfect." Feeling as if she'd imbibed a great deal of champagne, Meg moved to his side and pressed the sealed envelope into his hand.

He glanced at the graceful writing that formed his name and address, then looked up, bemused. "Do you know who it's from?"

"Open it."

Jake broke the seal, withdrawing two sheets of folded paper. As his eyes began to scan the pages, he sat bolt upright in his chair.

After a moment, he said hoarsely, "It's from my mother." He looked up sharply. "How?"

"I asked my lawyers to search for her. They have contacts with other solicitors in England."

He looked down again, his gaze devouring the words. "It says she waited for eight years before giving up hope. She believed my father and me both dead. Then she remarried, a baronet. He passed away three years ago, but . . . damnation, I have two half-sisters in their teens. She wants to come visit us, here, and bring the girls." Jake looked up, utterly stunned. "She actually seems to harbor some doubt whether or not I want to see her."

Smiling gently, Meg slid a sheet of paper across the desk and placed the quill in his hands. "Twenty-six years is a long time for both of you. You'd best hurry and write a response. They're welcome to stay as long as they like."

Meg retreated quietly into the hallway and shut the door, offering him privacy to digest the news and write the letter.

Tears of happiness rolled down her cheeks. For so many years, her beloved had been a man without a family, without a home. Suddenly, the mother he'd feared dead was restored to him, and he discovered two sisters he hadn't known existed.

Poor man, that wasn't going to be the last of his startling news today.

Meg pressed a hand to her belly with a secretive smile. Tonight, when they were alone together, lying in each other's arms after a bout of passionate lovemaking, she would tell him that his family was about to grow in new and wondrous ways.

JAKE CAUGHT MEG on the upstairs landing an hour later and pulled her into a rib-crushing hug.

Although startled by the intensity of his reaction, Meg slid naturally into his embrace, wrapping her arms around his chest. The warmth of his love and gratitude surrounded her. She stroked his back and massaged the taut ridges between his shoulder blades.

Turning her head toward his ear, she whispered, "You're welcome, husband."

"God, I love you so much." His voice vibrated with passion.

"So you've been telling me for months now, but I'll never grow tired of hearing it."

He swept her into his arms and carried her straight to their bed. Her eyes widened as he moved to lock the door.

Long, impatient strides carried him back to the bed as he ripped off his shirt. Buttons bounced on the carpet. The bed sagged as he rested one knee next to her hip, his fists braced against the mattress on either side of her shoulders. His eyes burned like molten silver.

Meg's lips curved in a sensuous smile. "Is this why you locked the door?"

"Damn right it is."

"It's the middle of the afternoon, Jake."

"We could be in the middle of the most public park in San Francisco and I wouldn't notice," he growled. "I want you too much. I can't wait."

She touched his lower lip. "I love you."

"You're more than my wife, Meghan . . . even more than the woman I love. You're the other half of my soul."

Meg smiled and opened her arms, welcoming him home.

ABOUT THE AUTHOR

Kristen Kyle has always been a die-hard romantic. Although roses and dinner by candlelight are nice, what really ignites her imagination are stories packed with action, conflict, a head-strong heroine, a dark and dangerous hero, and most of all, passion and love. Her goal is to provide the reader with a page-turner of a story. Kristen shares her home in a suburb of Dallas, Texas, with her two sons, both to-die-for heroes in the making.

Visit Kristen's web page at www.kristenkyle.com for the latest news, contest information, writing tips, and more, or send e-mail via kristen@kristenkyle.com

Teresa Medeiros

Breath of Magic
___56334-3 $5.99/$7.99 in Canada

Fairest of Them All
___56333-5 $5.99/$7.50 in Canada

Thief of Hearts
___56332-7 $5.99/$7.99 in Canada

A Whisper of Roses
___29408-3 $5.99/$7.99

Once an Angel
___29409-1 $5.99/$7.99

Heather and Velvet
___29407-5 $5.99/$7.50

Shadows and Lace
___57623-2 $5.99/$7.99

Touch of Enchantment
___57500-7 $5.99/$7.99

Nobody's Darling
___57501-5 $5.99/$7.99

Charming the Prince
___57502-3 $5.99/$8.99
